VELOCITY

ALSO BY ALAN JACOBSON

False Accusations
The Hunted
The 7th Victim
Crush

VELOCITY

A KAREN VAIL NOVEL

ALAN JACOBSON

Vanguard Press
A Member of the Perseus Books Group

Repl 2/15/11

Copyright © 2010 by Alan Jacobson

Published by Vanguard Press
A Member of the Perseus Books Group

Designed by Jeff Williams
Set in 14 point New Caledonia

Cataloging-in-Publication data for this book is available from the Library of Congress.
ISBN: 978-1-59315-621-3

Vanguard Press books are available at special discounts for bulk purchases in the U.S. by
corporations, institutions, and other organizations. For more information, please contact
the Special Markets Department at the Perseus Books Group, 2300 Chestnut Street,
Suite 200, Philadelphia, PA 19103, or call (800) 810-4145, ext. 5000, or e-mail
special.markets@perseusbooks.com.

10 9 8 7 6 5 4 3 2 1

For Jeff

As a toddler he called me "Onion"
As a teen it was "Herm"

But I'll always call him

my brother,
my best friend.

This one's for you.

The only way to make a man trustworthy is to trust him.
—HENRY STIMSON (1867–1950)

You may be deceived if you trust too much, but you will live in torment if you do not trust enough.
—FRANK CRANE

It is better to suffer wrong than to do it, and happier to be sometimes cheated than not to trust.
—SAMUEL JOHNSON (1709–1784)

PART 1

NOXIOUS FUMES

Old Tannery District
99 S. Coombs Street
Napa, California

He was not going to kill her immediately. No—if there was one thing he had learned, it was to savor the moment, to be deliberate and purposeful. Like a predator in the wild, he would waste no energy. He needed to be careful, efficient, and resourceful. And above all, he needed to be patient.

That's what he was now: a hunter who satisfied his hunger by feeding on others.

He sat alone in the dark parking lot, drumming his fingers on the dashboard, shifting positions in the seat. Talk radio hosts babbled on in the background, but he remained focused on his task. Watching. Waiting.

That's why he chose the Lonely Echo bar. Located in downtown Napa, the old Tannery District sat tucked away in an area devoid of scenic mountain views, posh wineries, or pampering bed-and-breakfasts. That meant no tourists. And *that* meant city planners had little incentive to expend valuable resources attempting to polish a hidden, unsightly flaw on the nation's crown jewel.

Drugs, alcohol, sex, and prostitution were in abundant supply—and in strong demand. While the valley's profit-driving centers blossomed over the past two decades, the district had become an overlooked pimple slowly filling with pus.

Ideal for his needs.

His eyes prowled the parking lot, watching people enter and leave the bar. With only a single light by the building's front door and one overhanging the quiet side street, he would be able to operate with relative impunity to roaming eyes—or mobile phone video cameras. With such scarce illumination, neither was much of a threat.

But it didn't matter: during the hours he'd sat in his minivan, no one had approached to ask him who he was. No one had even given him a glance, let alone a second look. A few women had left the bar, but they walked in pairs, making his approach extremely difficult, if not impossible.

The long wait had given him a chance to reflect on what had brought him to this moment: since childhood, strange, misplaced feelings had stirred him, but he hadn't known how to channel or utilize them. As he got older, although those urges persisted, the fear of making a mistake— shackling him with a very, very long prison sentence—held him back.

But given the right direction and tutelage, those needs took on substance, purpose, and direction. He was no longer fearful of failing. The only question was, could he *do it*? Could he kill?

The body that now lay in the shed in his yard was proof that he could do it, and do it well.

But killing a *woman*. He grinned at the thought. He was a virgin again, about to do it with a member of the opposite sex for the first time. Just like when he was a teen, his nerves were on edge, the fluttering in his stomach constant. Yet this was different. He was not going to chicken out like that time all those years ago. He was ready now. His first kill, waiting for him back home, provided all the proof he needed.

THE BARTENDER PLANTED two large hands on the nicked wood counter. "I'm not going to say it again. You've had enough, miss. It's time you went home."

"I told you my name before," she said, running the words together. "Don't you remember?" She scooped up the photo of her son and waved it at him. "My son. Remember me telling you? About him? You were all interested before. When you wanted a nice tip. Now, you're all like, get out of my fucking place." When the bartender failed to react, she wagged a finger at him. "You're not a very nice man, Kevinnnn." She drew out the last letter as if she were a scratched CD stuck on a note.

Kevin shook his head, tossed down his wet rag, then turned away.

A natural redhead whose hair sprouted from her scalp like weeds, the woman pushed back from the bar and wobbled as she sought enough balance to turn and walk out. She scrunched her face into a scowl directed at Kevin, then slid off the stool.

The woman swayed and groped for the steadying assistance of chair backs as she steered herself sloppily toward, and through, the front door. The painful brightness of a spotlight mounted along the eave blasted her eyes. She waved a hand to shoo away the glare.

THE MAN WATCHED the bar's battered wood door swing open, revealing a disheveled redhead. The light over the front entrance struck her in the face and she swatted it with a hand to fend it off, as if it was a swarm of flies. In that brief instant, she looked pretty hot. At least at this distance.

Her gait stuttered, stopped, then restarted and stuttered again. Drunk, not oriented to her surroundings.

He could not have ordered up a more perfect dish if he had spent hours searching for the recipe.

A CHILL SWIRLED AROUND the woman's bare legs. She swung her head around the parking lot, trying to recall where she had left her car. *To the right? Yeah, the right.* She stumbled off in the direction of a red sedan, concentrating on putting one foot squarely in front of the other.

Ahead, a man was approaching, headed toward the bar. "He's mean," she said to him. "Kevin is. He'll take your money, then kick you out." *That's what he did to me. Kicked me out.*

As she passed him, something clamped against her mouth—grabbed her from behind—squeezed and—

Can't breathe. Gasp— Scream!—can't.
Heavy. So—tired. Go to sleep. Sleep.
Sleep . . .

THE REDHEAD'S MUFFLED SCREAM did nothing but fill her lungs with a dose of anesthesia. Seconds later, she slumped against the man's body. He moved beside her, then twisted his neck to look over his shoulder, canvassing the parking lot to make sure no one had been watching.

The bar door flew open and a bearded man in jeans and flannel shirt ambled out. He stopped, put a cigarette and lighter to his mouth, then cupped it. As he puffed hard, the smoke exploding away from his face in a dense cloud, his eyes found the man. "Everything okay?" he asked, squinting into the darkness.

The man covertly crumpled the rag into the palm of his hand, out of sight. "All good. Little too much juice, is all."

"I saw," the witness said in a graveled voice. "Bartender sent her on her way. Need some help?"

"Nah, I got it. Just glad I found her. Been looking for two hours. But—good boyfriend, that's what I do, you know? One in the goddamn morning. Unfucking believable. Not sure it's worth it, if you know what I mean." He shook his head, turned away, and walked a few more steps, ready to drop and run should the witness persist in his questioning—or pull out a cell phone.

Since no one knew which car was his, if he needed to bolt he had time to circle back later and pick it up. Or he would leave it. It was untraceable to him, that much he'd planned in advance. If it was safer to abandon it, that's what he would do. He was prepared for that. He was fairly sure he'd thought of everything there was to think of.

The flannel-shirted witness glanced back twice as he walked toward his pickup, then unlocked it and ducked inside. The dome light flickered on, then extinguished as the door slammed shut. His brake lights brightened, and a puff of gray exhaust burst from the tailpipe.

He shifted the woman's unconscious weight and wrapped her arm around his neck. He walked slowly, waiting for the man's truck to move out of the lot. Then, with a flick of his free hand, he slid open the minivan door. After another quick look over his shoulder—all was quiet—he tossed her inside like a sack of garbage.

AS HE DROVE AWAY, careful to maintain the speed limit, he swung his head around to look at his quarry. The woman was splayed on the floor directly behind him. He couldn't see her face, but her torso and legs were visible.

And then she moaned.

"What the fuck? I gave you enough to keep you down for at least twenty minutes."

Perhaps he had been too conservative in figuring the dosage. He took care not to use too high a concentration, as excessive parts per million could result in death—and he didn't want to kill her.

At least not that way. His first time with a woman, it had to be special.

He bit down and squirmed his ass deeper into the seat, then gently nudged the speedometer needle beyond 45. Any Highway Patrol officer would give him some leeway over the limit. It was taking a little risk, but hell, wasn't this all one giant gamble on timing, luck, planning, and execution?

Really—how can you kill a person and not incur some degree of risk?

He rather liked it. His heart was thumping, the blood pulsing through his temples—and a look into the rearview revealed pupils that were wider than he'd ever seen them. What a fucking rush. All those wasted years. He had much time to recapture.

He checked all his mirrors. No law enforcement, as best he could see in the dark. Fast glance down at the woman. Her legs moved—she was waking.

Heart raced faster. Hands sweaty.

But really—what could she do to him? Scream? No one would hear her in this deathtrap. Scratch him? Big whoop.

He hit a pothole, then checked on her again—and in the passing flicker of a streetlight, saw a flat metal object poking out of her purse. What the—

He yanked the minivan over to the curb and twisted his body in the seat to get a better look. It was.

A badge.

He fisted a hand and brought it to his mouth. What to do? Is this good or bad? Well, both. He felt a swell of excitement in his chest and forced a deep breath to calm himself. Could this be better than sex? Sex . . . why have to choose? This really could be like his first time with a woman. But not just a woman. Some kind of cop.

He pulled away from the curb and had to keep his foot from slamming the accelerator to the floor. Slow—don't blow it now.

A moment later, his headlights hit the street sign ahead. He flicked his signal and slowed. Almost there. He grinned into the darkness. No one could see him, but in this case, it didn't matter. It would be another one of his little secrets.

HE LEFT THE WOMAN in an abandoned house at the edge of town. He thought about bringing her back to his place, where the other body was laid out in the shed. But he nixed that idea. One corpse was enough to deal with. It would soon start to smell, and he didn't want a neighbor calling the cops on him. If they found one of their own in his house, they might kill him right there. Forget about a long prison term. He'd be executed. It was an accident, they'd claim. Resisting arrest. They did that kind of stuff, didn't they? He wasn't sure, but he couldn't take the chance.

He needed to get to a coffee shop to sit and think all this through. Now that he was deeply committed, the reality of how far he'd gone began to sink in. And although he thought he had prepared properly, he was concerned he had rushed into it, letting the swell of anticipation cloud his planning. Certainly he hadn't figured on killing a law enforcement officer. But how could he have known?

As he drove the minivan back to where he had parked his car, he wondered if he could use this vehicle again. There was no blood, and he could simply vacuum it out or take it to a car wash for an interior detailing. If they did a good job, there'd be no personally identifiable substance of the redhead left inside. And then he wouldn't have to search again for an untraceable minivan. Still—what if someone had seen it in the Lonely Echo's parking lot and that guy in the pickup was questioned by police? He could give them a decent description of him. No. Better to dump the vehicle and start from scratch.

But as he pulled alongside his car and shoved the shift into park, he realized he had made a mistake. No one would find the woman's body for days, if not longer. He slammed a palm against the steering wheel. What fun is that?

Can't go back—that would definitely be too high a risk.

Turn the page, move on.

He thought again of the evening, of what went right, and what he could've done better. He didn't get caught, so, overall, he'd done a pretty damn good job. But something else he had learned this past week was that perfection was rarely there in the beginning. But it would come, eventually.

He would keep seeking until he found it. The next one he would do differently.

2

Smeared blood enveloped the hands and face of FBI profiler Karen Vail. It wasn't her blood—it came from a colleague who had just died. But blood did not differ among serial killer, philanthropist, husband, vagrant, soldier, or prostitute. Young or old. American or foreign. Blood was blood. And when it got on your skin, it all felt the same.

No, that's not true. Some blood did feel different; the blood coating Vail's fingers did not have the usual slippery, wet consistency that she had felt many times—too many times—in the past. No, tonight it felt like pain. Guilt and heartache.

But as the van carrying Karen Vail rocked and lurched, she realized the pain and guilt and heartache were not coming from the blood on her skin, but from the injury that festered in her soul. Her best friend and lover, Detective Roberto "Robby" Hernandez, had vanished. No note, no secretly hidden message. No indication last time they had spoken that anything was wrong.

In fact, just the opposite. They'd had passionate sex only hours earlier.

And now he was missing.

John Wayne Mayfield, the serial killer who might have had something to do with Robby's disappearance, was likely deceased, and a police sergeant who could have provided answers was growing cold in the morgue. But this man, Detective Ray Lugo, who had ties to the killer—ties Vail had yet to explore—did not mean anything to her.

His had just been blood, like anyone else's.

Now pain and guilt. And heartache.

"TURN THE VAN AROUND!"

Vail shouted at the driver, but he couldn't hear her. She was locked in the back of a state Department of Corrections transport truck, a thick metal cage surrounding her. Symbolic in some sense of what she felt.

Beside her, Napa County Detective Lieutenant Redmond Brix and Investigator Roxxann Dixon, stunned by the loss of their colleague, had watched Ray Lugo's body being off-loaded at the morgue. They were now headed back to the Hall of Justice to clean up and retrieve their vehicles. But Vail had other ideas.

"Get us back to the Sheriff's Department," she said to Brix.

Shoulders slumped and defeat painted on his face like makeup, Brix rolled his eyes toward Vail. "Why?"

"We don't have time to wash. We've gotta do something. We have to figure out what happened to Robby. The first forty-eight hours are crucial—"

"Karen," Dixon said, a hand on her arm, "we need to take a breath. We need to sort ourselves out, figure out what everything means, where we go from here."

Vail grabbed her head with both hands and leaned her elbows on her knees. "I can't lose him, Roxx, I can't—I have to find out what happened. What if Mayfield—"

"You can't think like that. If Mayfield killed Robby, don't you think he would've said something? Wouldn't a narcissistic killer do that? Rub it in your face?"

"I don't—I don't know. I can't think." Vail took a deep breath. Coughed—she'd inhaled smoke from a fire a few days ago and it hadn't fully cleared her lungs yet—and then leaned back. "He kind of did just that, Roxx. When we interviewed him. He was gloating that we hadn't really figured things out. We'd caught him, but that wasn't everything. That's what he was saying. That he was smarter than us. Superior to us—" She stopped, then turned to Dixon. "*Superior.* Superior Mobile Bottling."

"We've been down that road," Brix said. "César Guevara was a dead end."

Guevara, an executive of a mobile corking, labeling, and bottling one-stop shop for wineries that lacked their own in-house production facilities, had been their serial murder suspect until the task force failed to turn up anything compelling linking Guevara to the victims. When John Mayfield emerged as the Crush Killer, Superior Mobile Bottling—and César Guevara—fell off their radar. Vail shook her head. *That was only a few hours ago. So much has happened in such a short period of time.*

"I don't think anything's off the table now," Vail said. "We missed something. I've had that feeling all along. Something wasn't right, I just couldn't figure it out." She dropped her head back against the metal cage. Tears streamed from her eyes, streaking down the dried blood on her cheeks.

Dixon put an arm around her and pulled her close. Vail felt immediate guilt: Dixon had just suffered her own loss—Eddie Agbayani, her estranged boyfriend, someone she loved—had been John Mayfield's final victim. But at the moment, Vail could not summon the energy, the outward empathy, to grieve for her friend. She had only enough strength to keep herself together, to keep her wits about her before she fell apart and lost it.

"We'll figure this out, Karen," Brix said. "We may've caught Mayfield, but we're far from solving this case." He pulled his phone. "I'm getting everyone back to the Sheriff's Department. We'll hash this out."

As Brix sent off his text message, the Department of Corrections van pulled in front of the sally port roll-up door in the jail's parking lot. "Hold it," Brix said. Vail had used her shirt to keep pressure on Lugo's neck wound. Brix quickly unbuttoned his uniform top and helped Vail into it.

They got out, then climbed into their cars, frigid air sneaking into the vehicle like an unwanted passenger. Vail was silent for most of the short drive, lost in a fugue of disbelief and depression.

Finally, staring straight out the windshield, she said, "I'm sorry. About Eddie."

Dixon nodded but did not speak.

Vail turned to face her and saw tears shining on her cheek. The past week had been an emotional and trying time.

But what lay ahead for Karen Vail would be like nothing she had ever experienced.

3

After parking their car in the Napa County Sheriff's Department lot, Vail and Dixon headed up the two flights of stairs. In the restroom, they cleaned themselves up as best they could, replacing their soiled tops with Sheriff's Department T-shirts. Vail's nylon fanny pack was beyond cleaning, so she dumped it in the trash.

"I've got a paddle holster you can use," Dixon said, then led her down the hall and pulled one from a bin on a shelf in the detectives' off-duty office, which adjoined the major crimes task force conference room.

They pushed through the side door and saw Brix seated at the long table with Detective Burt Gordon and ATF Special Agent Austin Mann. Vail and Dixon took chairs. Vail settled beside Mann—an awkward choice. Because of his prosthetic left forearm, and the manner in which the Crush Killer collapsed his victims' windpipes, Vail had considered the highly regarded Mann a suspect. She came to regret the accusation. At present, that was the least of her concerns. *Robby. I have to find Robby.*

For a long minute, no one spoke—it was as if they were taking a moment of silence for their fallen comrades.

Vacant stares and bowed heads.

Brix cleared his throat. "This has been a tough week. For all of us. But if we're going to be effective in what we need to accomplish, we've gotta pull ourselves together and put our personal feelings aside." He pushed his chair back and walked over to the white board. Found a clear space and uncapped a marker.

Vail leaned closer to Mann. In a low voice, she said, "I'm sorry."

"Our deal is settled," he said. "We're good."

"Okay," Brix said. "We've got a lot of unanswered questions. Let's set them out, then start digging. As we answer them, we'll cross them off the list. And hopefully, when all our questions are answered, Detective Robby Hernandez will be safe, and in our custody." He looked around the room.

Vail pushed herself up straight in her chair. "The biggest question involves Ray."

Brix wrote "Ray Lugo" on the board. "What did he know? What was he involved in? What were his ties to John Mayfield?"

To Vail, Dixon said, "You sensed some strange body language when he and Guevara saw each other."

"I did. But everything we thought, all our conversations with witnesses, have to be reexamined in a new light." She turned to the others. "When we visited Superior Mobile Bottling, it seemed like César Guevara kept looking at Ray, like he was angry at him. Was he angry because he thought Ray was responsible for bringing us there?"

Dixon pointed at the board. "We need to follow up with Guevara. Find out what his relationship with Ray really was."

Brix made the note. "And that disc." He turned to Mann and Gordon. "In the ambulance, Ray said he had some kind of disc. He died before he could tell us what was on it or where it was."

"He also told us," Vail said, "that his wife and son had been kidnapped. By John Mayfield. That's why Ray shot him in the interview room. Revenge?" She shrugged. "Don't know. Maybe he just wanted to make sure Mayfield could never come after them again."

Brix held up a hand. "Before you ask, no, when they were kidnapped, Ray didn't know who was behind it, and no, he never said anything to us about it. Apparently Mayfield said he'd know if Ray told us. And he'd kill his family. Ray was also apparently forced into doing things for Mayfield."

"Jesus Christ," Gordon said. "What the hell does that mean?"

They sat in silence for a moment. Finally Mann cleared his throat. "We've also got Mayfield's comment, 'There's more to this than you know.' Maybe he was referring to Ray's involvement."

Brix's phone rang. He reached into his pocket and fished it out. "Brix." He listened a moment, then his eyes flicked across the face of each task force member. "And when will we know?" He nodded, thanked the caller, then snapped his phone shut.

"What's up, boss?" Dixon asked.

Brix shook his head, freeing him from his fugue. "Mayfield. He's still alive."

Vail rose so quickly from her chair that it flew back into the wall. "Let's go—"

Brix's hand went up faster than a crossing guard stopping traffic. "He just got out of surgery. They removed a .40-caliber round lodged near his brain."

Mann asked, "Is he gonna live?"

"They're going to keep me updated," Brix said. "Soon as I hear something, I'll let you know. When he wakes up, if he wakes up, whoever's closest when that call comes through, get your ass over there as fast as possible and find out what you can from him."

"He's not going to be motivated to help us," Vail said.

Brix capped his marker. "Any suggestions on how to approach him?"

Vail pulled her chair beneath her and sat heavily. "What I should've done from the start. My focus should've been to connect with him on a level he's never experienced before, to knock him off his pedestal. Throw him a curve. I should've related to him intimately, deferring to his superior abilities with a subtle sexual undertone. When I did finally get him talking, that's what I was doing."

"I may be able to do that," Dixon said. "But no offense—" she tossed a glance at the other task force members—"I can't see any of these guys connecting with him on a subtle sexual level."

That brought some chuckles and broke the tension for a fleeting moment.

"No," Vail said. "You guys would have to connect with him from a distance, in a less intimate manner. More professional. Be awed by his superiority. Tell him how great he is, dwell on how he outsmarted us by eluding capture for so long. Relate to him clinically, marvel at how efficiently he handled his homicides, how you've never dealt with a killer as clever as he is. It's similar to what I'd do, but where I'd admire up close and personal, you're admiring from afar. Done well, it can be very effective."

The men were all wearing frowns and expressions of distaste. Vail couldn't blame them. But this was the most effective way to get the information they needed.

"As repulsive as it may seem," she said, "find a way to see his point of view. Build rapport."

Mann asked, "Can it be done in a hospital room? With interruptions and machine noises and other people around?"

"It's far from ideal, but we take what we can get."

"I've got Mayfield's booking photo," Brix said. "I'll email it to all of you in case you need it."

"There's something else we need to look into," Vail said. "Robby had a friend in town. I think his name was Sebastian. I don't know anything about him. Actually—he gave Robby a bottle of delicious Madeira two or three months ago. All I can remember is that it was a winery that began with a *v* and it was a short bottle with red wax dripped across the top—"

"V. Sattui," Brix said. "Good stuff."

Vail pointed a finger at him. "Yeah, that's it. It's a long shot. Maybe they remember him, if he's a regular customer."

Various members of the task force cocked their heads or licked their lips, nodded slowly . . . clearly, they didn't hold high expectations for this "lead."

"Trying to find a guy who bought a bottle of Madeira is not much to go on," Brix said. "Some wineries have a thousand people come through every month."

"We don't have much to go on, period," Dixon said. "We've gotta do our best with what we've got."

"Assignments," Brix said.

Dixon, the task force lead investigator, nodded. "Okay. Let's grab a few hours of sleep and hit the trails as soon as people start getting to work. Mann—track down Sebastian, our V. Sattui Madeira drinker. Brix—follow up with Matthew Aaron, see what forensics he's gotten from the B&B room Karen and Robby were staying in. Gordon. Coordinate with Napa Special Investigations Bureau and start showing Robby's photo around. Never know, someone may give us something we can use. Karen and I will go pay Ray's wife a visit, wake her up, and give her the bad news. See what she knows about a disc or John Mayfield. Hopefully something."

"'Minor' detail," Gordon said. "You got a picture of Robby?"

Vail frowned. "On my old phone."

"The one that burned in the fire?" Dixon asked.

"Yeah, that one." Vail checked her watch. It was just after 1:00 AM. "I'll have something for you in the morning. Brix, you got another one of those contact sheets with everyone's phone and emails? I gotta enter it all into my new phone."

Brix found the correct manila folder and removed a sheet of paper. "Let's not leave it lying around."

Vail took the paper, folded it, then rose from her seat. "Thanks, everyone, for your help. Robby—he's very important to me."

"We'll find him," Brix said.

Vail made herself smile. "Thanks." She wished she was as confident as Brix. At this point, she could not delude herself into thinking they had anything worth pursuing. That meant no viable place to start.

And that's what bothered her most.

4

—

A gent Vail!"

Dixon and Vail, having just left the task force conference room, turned in unison. It was the sheriff—Stan Owens.

"A word?" As Owens approached, his eyes flicked to Dixon, then back to Vail. "Alone."

Vail and Dixon exchanged glances. With Owens's stepson, Detective Scott Fuller, having been murdered less than forty-eight hours ago—and Vail still in the sheriff's crosshairs as the likely suspect—their silent glance was like shouting in a quiet room.

"Go on," Vail said to Dixon. "I'll be fine."

Dixon nodded, then headed off down the hall as Owens approached.

"Sheriff." Vail bit her lip. "Again, I'm very sorry for your loss."

"Let's go in here and talk." He motioned to the nearby interview room. While it would certainly give them quiet and privacy, the irony was not lost on Vail; this was where she had interviewed Walton Silva, Scott Fuller's alleged conspirator in setting the fire designed to kill her.

As Vail pushed through the door, she caught sight of Brix lurking down the hall.

He tilted his head ever so slightly. "Everything okay?"

Vail shrugged. "Yeah. Sheriff just wants to talk. In private."

Brix squinted but didn't reply. He headed toward her as she disappeared into the room.

Owens was already seated at the small faux marble table. He left vacant the seat facing the concealed wall camera. *On purpose?* What *was* his purpose?

Was he hoping to elicit a confession? Was he fishing for information? Or was this meeting something more benign?

"What can I do for you, sheriff?"

Owens squirmed in his chair. Leaned back, loosened his tie. But didn't look at her. "Scott did set that shed on fire. At the school, when he was a kid."

Interesting. "I know. We got hold of the sealed file."

"Yeah." He looked around at the table, the walls. Licked his lips. "We got him help. Therapist said it wasn't a problem with him loving fire. It was just his way of acting out, of rebelling. He was the right age."

Vail wondered why he was telling her this. Because he'd made such a scene of accusing her of Fuller's murder? Because he had vehemently denied his stepson was capable of arson?

"Even therapists can be wrong."

Owens snorted, then finally made eye contact. "Apparently he wasn't just wrong. He didn't know shit." He waved a hand. "Aw, that ain't fair. I didn't see it, either. I thought Scott was a good kid, had straightened out his act. He wasn't my blood, but he was my son. You understand?"

"Of course I do." And she did.

"He had come from a broken home. His mother . . . Anita's a good woman, but that bastard she married wasn't worth the shit that came out of his ass."

"I've known a few like that. It's not necessarily Anita's fault."

"I'm not saying it was."

He said it hard, sharp, like he resented what Vail had implied. But she wasn't implying anything.

"I thought that because I got hold of Scott at a young age, I could fix him. Shape him. He had a rough streak that started when his father walked out on them. But I knew Anita before then. She worked at the Sheriff's Department as a legal clerk. That's how we met. When we got together, I just thought I could make a difference in Scott's life."

"You did. He became a cop. A detective."

"He was a good kid."

Maybe I'm just old-fashioned, but someone who sets fires and then conspires to kill an FBI agent doesn't deserve the "good kid" label. Instead, Vail said, "You gave him a lot of love, sheriff. Stuff he needed."

"Not enough, apparently."

"Sometimes there's only so much we can do. We're wired a certain way as individuals. We may learn, change, adapt, but when pushed—or if the stress gets too great—peer pressure or whatever—we fall back into our old bad habits. Because it's familiar to us, even comforting."

Owens sighed, deep, hard, and uneven. "I'm gonna miss him something terrible." His eyes canted toward the ceiling, filled with syrupy tears. "Is that wrong?"

"Of course not. He was your boy. Just remember the good times. Focus on those."

Owens tightened his lips, then nodded. He lowered his eyes to hers. "Thank you, Karen." He rose from his chair. "I hope you find Detective Hernandez. A guy like him, he's hard to lose. He's one big motherfucker. I know that firsthand. He sure put me in my place."

Vail flushed. "Sorry about that."

"Not at all. I deserved it." He shrugged. "Anyway, my point is, I doubt anyone could get the drop on him."

Vail forced a smile. "Let's hope you're right."

Owens held out a hand. "Anything—you need anything to help find him, you just let me know."

"Thanks. I will."

Owens pulled open the door. Brix was standing there.

"You need something, Redd?"

Brix's eyes flicked over to Vail. He seemed to read her expression, then shook his head. "Nope. All's good."

5

Vail met Dixon in the break room. She was reclined in a yellow plastic chair, her eyes closed and her mouth open.

Vail gently shoved her foot with a shoe. "Hey. Wake up."

Dixon rubbed two hands across her face. "Yeah, okay. Let's go." She pushed herself out of the seat and stretched. "This is gonna suck big time."

"Yeah. 'Sorry to wake you, Mrs. Lugo, but your husband's dead. Oh, and by the way, we think he was working with the serial killer we just caught.'"

Dixon patted Vail on the back. "I think it'd be better if I do the talking when we get there." They made their way into the stairwell, then down the two flights. "Regardless of what Ray was involved in, we owe it to the badge to do it right, so his wife gets news of his death from us rather than some reporter when the story breaks in the morning."

As they walked to Dixon's Ford Crown Victoria, Vail pulled the task force roster from her back pocket and unfolded it. "Can you drive with the light on? I want to enter this stuff into my phone on the way over."

"Not a bad idea. The light may help keep me awake."

They arrived at the Lugo home a bit past 2:00 AM. It was a modest but well-maintained two-story stucco in a planned development. A kids' basketball standard was evident just over the sturdy wood fence.

As they approached the house, bright halogen lights snapped on. "Motion sensors," Dixon said.

Vail nodded at the eave. "And surveillance cameras. Designed to come on with the lights."

"Look at the windows," Dixon said.

White decorative wire "sculptures" covered the glass.

"I don't think those were installed for their aesthetic value," Vail said. "If I didn't know who lived here, I'd say the people who own this house are scared of something."

"Or someone."

They stepped up to the front door and stood there, staring at it, both alone with their thoughts. Finally Vail said, "Roxx, we've gotta just do it."

Dixon sighed, then leaned forward and pressed the button beside the door. The deep bark of a large dog started up as if activated by the doorbell. "Ray had security in place, that's for sure."

"Goes with what he told us in the van."

They stood there, waiting, bathed in light with the surveillance camera rolling. Finally, footsteps. A voice spilled out from a speaker. "Who is it and what do you want?"

"It's Roxxann Dixon and Karen Vail. We're friends of Ray's from the major crimes task force."

"Where's Ray?" the voice asked.

"Mrs. Lugo, it'd be real good if you could open the door. We have a message from your husband."

Vail looked at Dixon. They didn't truly have anything from Ray other than bad news—but by the time they got finished telling her why they were there, Merilynn Lugo wouldn't be asking what the message was.

"Go ahead. I can hear you just fine."

Vail heard a child's voice in the background. It sent a shiver down her back. *Shit, I hate this. Absolutely hate this.* "Mrs. Lugo," Vail said, "I'm afraid we've got some bad news."

Dixon looked at her. Vail lifted her hands to say, *She left us no choice.*

The door swung open. Merilynn Lugo was a thick Hispanic woman with delicate features. Her mouth had fallen agape and her hands drew up to her cheeks as she searched the faces of the two cops. No doubt hoping she had heard wrong.

"I'm sorry," Dixon said.

And in that moment of realization, Merilynn Lugo burst into tears. That's when Vail saw the young boy behind his mother, holding on to her leg. Merilynn reached out—her face had lost all color—and Dixon grabbed her, helping her gently to the floor.

"What's wrong, Mommy?" the boy asked. The dog started barking again.

Merilynn pulled her son close. "Mommy's not feeling too good." She took a deep breath. "But I'll—I'll be okay. You want to go let Bart into the backyard?" She nodded at him and forced a smile. "Go on, Mario."

When the boy walked out, Merilynn turned back to Vail. Tears streamed down her face. "How," she finally asked. "How did it happen?"

Vail sat on the floor beside Merilynn. "A gunshot wound," Vail said. "We'd captured a serial killer the task force was after. We think it was the guy who kidnapped you and Mario—"

"You—you caught him?"

Vail regarded Merilynn's face before answering. "We did. And Ray . . . Ray was a big part of that. But while I was interrogating the suspect, Ray . . . Ray came into the room and shot him. One of the rounds ricocheted and hit Ray in the neck. We tried to save him. We rushed him to the hospital, but . . . " Vail stole a look at Dixon. "He asked that we make sure to look out for you and your son."

Merilynn swiped a hand across her wet cheeks, balled up her nightgown and used it to blot the tears. Vail and Dixon waited, Vail keeping a hand on Merilynn's shoulder to support her.

"Ray told us about what happened. With the kidnapping—"

"Is he still alive?" Merilynn asked. "Did the bastard die?"

Dixon and Vail shared a glance. Dixon said, "All we know is that he's out of surgery."

Merilynn straightened up. "Then I need to get out of here."

"'Get out,'" Dixon said. "What do you mean?"

"He's going to come after us. He will."

"Why?" Vail asked.

"We need protection," Merilynn said. "Or we need to leave."

"We'll make sure you're taken care of. Don't worry about that. But tell us what happened. When you got kidnapped, what—"

"I think you need to leave us alone right now," Merilynn said. She clumsily pushed herself up from the floor.

Vail and Dixon rose as well.

"Look," Vail said, "I know this is a tough time. But we've got a lot of unanswered questions, and someone else's life might depend on those answers."

"I can't help you. Sorry." The dog began barking again.

"A disc," Vail pressed. "Ray mentioned something about a disc. Do you know what he was talking about?"

Merilynn swung her head toward the yard. The barking continued. "No." She faced Vail. "I don't know anything about a disc."

"But—"

"He's going to wake the neighbors," Merilynn said as she hurried out of the room. "Please let yourself out. And lock the door behind you."

WALKING TOWARD THEIR CAR, Vail said, "Something's not right. We need to come back. After the initial shock fades. Tomorrow. We have to find out what the hell's going on. What she knows."

"Meantime, I'll have the Sheriff's Department post a deputy. Until we know what the deal is. For all we know, Mayfield had an accomplice."

Vail stopped. Her head swung hard to Dixon. "I hadn't thought of that. I should have, but I didn't."

"None of us considered that possibility. We've been going almost 24/7 for days. Who had the time to step back and think things through?"

Vail rested her head on the Ford's doorframe. She was exhausted emotionally and physically drained. Her life the past two months had been bordering on disaster, and she needed a vacation. Badly.

But with Robby missing, she knew a respite to recharge was not going to be coming soon.

6

After the sheriff's deputy arrived to baby-sit the Lugo household, Dixon headed toward Highway 29, the main drag that worked its way through the various business districts of the Napa Valley. She turned to Vail, who had gone silent. "Let's swing by the B&B, pick up your clothes, and head over to my place. We'll get some sleep, eat something, and approach this with a fresh perspective."

Vail leaned back against the headrest. "Yeah."

They drove without further discussion until they pulled into the B&B's small compacted gravel parking lot. Dixon shoved the shift into park and got out.

Vail followed and met her at the door to the room, fifteen feet away. She reached her hand into the front pocket and pulled out the key. Stood there staring at it. "What if we never find him, Roxx? What if Mayfield—"

"Stop," Dixon said. "We need to keep an open mind; let's try not to let the negativity creep in. Until we know, it's all speculation—and that's not going to find him." She leaned forward and they embraced.

A long moment later, Vail said, "Thanks, Roxx. I needed that."

Dixon sniffed back tears. "I needed it, too."

MORNING CAME and Vail pried open her eyes. She and Dixon had sat on her living room couch and finished a bottle of Peju Cabernet, Dixon lamenting the loss of Eddie Agbayani and Vail . . . trying to be a good friend, listening to the stories of Dixon and Agbayani's intense but less than smooth relationship.

And trying not to let Robby's absence consume her. The wine helped with that.

Dixon's white standard poodle, Margot, lay in her owner's lap, sensing her emotional void and seeking to fill it as only a dog can do. Her black one, Quinn, stepped gently onto the couch and sidled against Vail's body.

"They think they're lap dogs," Dixon had said as she stroked Margot's curls of cotton-soft fur.

Vail swallowed a mouthful of Cabernet, set down her glass, and began rubbing Quinn. "But they're huge."

"Don't tell *them* that. But it's very comforting. I don't mind."

"Apparently they don't, either."

Margot remained in Dixon's lap—Quinn had settled his front legs across Vail's thighs—until Dixon drained the last drop from the bottle and decided they should try to catch whatever sleep either could get.

Vail lay awake until sometime in the early morning hours. And now Dixon was knocking on her door. "Yeah," Vail said. She swung her legs off the bed. "I'm here. Sort of. I think."

Dixon pushed open the door and the usually head-turning blonde was a disheveled mess. "Slept like shit."

"Me, too."

"Can you be ready in twenty? I just got a call from Matt Aaron. He's at the B&B, and he found something "

MATTHEW AARON'S forensic kit was splayed open. A bottle of luminol was on the bathroom vanity and a square of carpet was missing from an area partially beneath the large overstuffed bed.

Vail and Dixon stood in the doorway. *Oh, shit.* Her mind added it up in milliseconds: *Luminol. A sample cutout. He found blood. Robby's blood?*

"You want us to put booties on?" Dixon asked.

Aaron waved a hand, welcoming them in. "Maid already cleaned it, right? So forget about it being a useful crime scene. But I vacuumed anyway, did a full workup, just in case. I'm about ready to close up shop."

They ventured in, Vail stopping by the conspicuously defiled carpet. "You found something."

"I did. I covered the place in luminol—the proprietor probably isn't going to be too happy with me—but I'm glad I did. I got a hit right there." He nodded to the area beside the bed. "So I cut away the carpet and sprayed again. When you have heavy blood loss, it seeps down into the carpet fibers—"

"And into the pad," Vail said.

"And into the pad. It lit up like a purple battlefield. So I took the pad, too. We'll run it for DNA and see what it shows."

Vail's shoulders slumped. She sat cross-legged on the floor beside the void in the carpet. "It could be from something else. It might not be Robby's."

"That's what the DNA will tell us. Do you have an exemplar we can use for comparison?"

"I can get you one." Vail's eyes remained on the carpet. "Whatever happened here, there was substantial blood loss."

"Not enough that someone bled out," Dixon said. "Right?"

"Probably not. But the sooner you can get Detective Hernandez's DNA—"

"Whoever caused that wound didn't want anyone finding it," Dixon said. "They cleaned it pretty good. We didn't see anything."

"Nothing," Aaron said, "until the luminol."

Vail nodded slowly. She pulled her BlackBerry and tapped out an email to Bledsoe, asking him to go over to Robby's house and get some hair from his bathroom, as well as his toothbrush. She told him to overnight the hair to the Sheriff's Department, and to bring the other sample to the FBI lab.

"Can you send a section of the carpet pad to the FBI?" Vail asked.

Aaron, who had begun packing his case, froze. His set jaw and narrowed eyes said all that needed to be said.

"I want a second set of eyes looking at this. No offense."

"You know," Aaron said, "whenever someone says, 'No offense,' it's usually preceded or followed by an offensive remark. And why shouldn't I take offense that you don't trust my work?"

"Matt," Dixon said. "Please. Just do it." She tapped Vail on the shoulder and extended a hand. Vail grabbed it and Dixon pulled her up.

Vail sighed deeply, then looked around the room. She had only stayed there a couple of nights, but they held intense memories of Robby. Her eyes lingered on the bed, where they had spent their last hours together.

No. Not our last. Please, not our last.

7

As Dixon drove back to the Sheriff's Department, Vail left a voice mail for her son Jonathan to call her when he took his lunch break, or between classes if he had enough time.

They used their electronic proximity cards to enter the secured section of the building and headed to the task force conference room, where Brix was seated beside Merilynn Lugo. The woman's face was streaked and flushed.

Vail sat beside her. "I'm glad you came. We sure could use your help."

Brix shook his head. "She's here because she wants *our* help."

"Of course," Dixon said. She remained standing, across the conference table from Merilynn and Vail. "Anything."

Brix cleared his throat and curled his face into a squint.

Reading Brix's expression, Vail guessed they were thinking the same thing: blindly offering "anything" was dangerous.

"She wants witness protection," Brix said. "*Federal* witness protection."

There was a long silence as Vail and Dixon processed her request. Merilynn kept her gaze on the table, apparently content to let Brix do the talking for the moment.

"To get that," Vail finally said, "to even get consideration, you'd have to level with us. Tell us everything you know."

"I can't live like this anymore," Merilynn said. "I need protection."

"Protection from what?" Dixon said.

"WITSEC, the witness security program, isn't something that's given out lightly," Vail said. "There are procedures and requirements. It has to be approved."

"You're the FBI, you can make it happen."

Vail shook her head. "It's not like that, Mrs. Lugo. The FBI doesn't administer WITSEC. The Department of Justice does. Application has to be made to the Office of Enforcement Operations, and it has to be approved by DOJ headquarters. Then you're interviewed by the U.S. Marshals Service, which oversees the program, to determine if you're a good fit."

"You have to understand the reason why WITSEC exists," Dixon said. "Witnesses are given protection because of testimony they agree to provide against another criminal the government's trying to build a case against. In exchange for that testimony, the government relocates you, gives you a new identity and financial backing to make it work."

"Don't take this the wrong way," Brix said, "but you don't have any testimony we need. John Mayfield, assuming he survives, is never going to see the light of day, and will very likely get the death penalty."

"Trust me," Merilynn said. "I've got information you need. "But if I give it to you, I want something in return. The safety of me and my son. That's the price."

Vail and Dixon shared a look.

Dixon said, "If we're going to submit a request for WITSEC, we really need to know what you've got. And we need to know what Ray was involved with, what was going on between him and Mayfield."

"While you're at it," Vail said, "you might also want to tell us why you think you need protection." She didn't mean for it to come off as sarcastic—but given all she'd been through recently, her tone wasn't a top priority. She knew that wasn't a healthy approach, but she was too tired and emotionally drained to care.

Merilynn set her jaw. She either did not appreciate the weight of her request, or she didn't believe that getting into the WITSEC program involved anything more than stating that you needed it.

With the silence growing, Vail knew she had to do something to get Merilynn talking. She had to treat the woman as if she was a suspect being interviewed. If she could establish a rapport and break down the barrier, the information they needed might come tumbling out.

"I was kidnapped once," Vail said. "I was drugged. When I woke up, I was in handcuffs in a small, dark place. Is that what happened to you? Did Mayfield drug you?"

Merilynn tilted her head and studied Vail's face.

Is she trying to determine if I'm lying to her?

"It was a couple months ago," Vail said. "I've had some . . . issues trying to get past it."

"He didn't drug us," Merilynn said. "He came up behind my son, grabbed him, and held a knife to his neck. Ray said it was all about control." She swiped at a tear. "With that knife at Mario's neck, what was I gonna do?" Her face spread into a wan smile. "Anything he wanted, that's what."

"I can't even imagine what that's like," Dixon said.

Vail shivered imperceptibly. *I can. I know what it's like to have your son used as a pawn against you, powerless to help him.*

"It was paralyzing," Merilynn said. "The guy, he was big and mean and serious. He just had this look about him. He said to keep my mouth shut. I kept it shut, didn't even breathe." She sat there a moment, staring at the table. "Everything was like a tunnel. All I could see was my son with the knife at his neck. All I could hear was that man's voice."

"The man was John Mayfield?" Vail asked.

Merilynn bent forward and pressed on both temples with her fingers. "I didn't know who he was back then. Ray kept asking me what he looked like, but I couldn't remember. I was so freaked out, I never looked at his face."

"What happened next?" Brix asked. "After Mayfield kidnapped you, did he take you somewhere?"

"He had a van. He put us inside and made us wear blindfolds. We drove for what seemed like an hour. He made so many turns I had no idea where we were."

Even though John Mayfield was in custody, knowing the location of his lair was important. Serial killers often did not keep their trophies, or keepsakes from their victims, at their homes, but at some other location that either had meaning or geographic and logistic convenience for them. With unanswered questions lingering, his base of operations might yield additional information to the unnamed victims Mayfield had listed and included in his communication with the police. And possibly even forensic clues relevant to Robby.

"Did you smell anything?" Dixon asked, clearly on the same wavelength. "Hear anything?"

"The train, I heard the train whistle. It was off in the distance, but I heard it." She closed her eyes. "And I smelled must."

Vail cocked her head. "Wait—what did you say? Must?"

"A by-product of the early stages of making wine," Brix said. "The un-fermented juice of grapes from crushing or pressing them, before it's converted into wine. If she smelled must, she had to be near a winery, or at least a facility that processes grapes."

"How do you know what must smells like?" Vail asked.

Merilynn scrunched her face, as if she resented the question. "I spent eleven years working at San Miguel vineyards. I worked the fields, I worked with the grapes. I know the smells of a winery."

Vail turned to Dixon. "Does this smell help narrow it down?"

Dixon chuckled. "Not really. The Napa Valley Wine Train covers al-most twenty miles before turning around. She heard the train, which means, what? How far can you hear a train whistle? Another two or three miles in either direction? That's a huge area. And this is the Napa Valley. You know how many wineries or grape processing facilities there are in this region?"

"The train sounds the whistle at crossings, and when it leaves the sta-tion," Brix said. "That might help narrow it." He turned back to Meri-lynn. "What happened after you were kidnapped? How long did he hold you?"

"I'm—I'm not sure. I think Ray said we were gone two days, but I can't remember. I didn't really want to talk about it." She stared off at the wall, as if reliving the ordeal. "He kept us in a dark place. I couldn't tell if it was morning or night. We were blindfolded and gagged most of the time."

Vail scooted her chair closer, then leaned toward Merilynn. "Mrs. Lugo, I'm truly sorry you had to go through that. But . . . what did Ray do? Did he report it? Did the St. Helena PD go searching for you?"

"Ray got a phone call from the man—from this guy you're calling John Mayfield. He said he had taken us and if Ray cooperated, he'd re-turn us unharmed. But if Ray didn't, and if he tried to find us or told any-one—anyone—about this, he'd kill us immediately. And it wouldn't be pleasant."

Vail looked at Brix.

"Ray never reported anything to anyone," Brix said. "If he had, St. Helena PD would've brought us in. Something like that is a major crimes task force deal, and way beyond St. Helena's capabilities."

Merilynn said, "Mayfield told Ray that if he ever told detectives

about him, he'd know. And he'd find us again, when we were out shopping or at day care. Or at school. He knew a lot about us. His point was
there was no way to escape him. There'd be no safe place."

Dixon sighed long and hard, then said, "But Mayfield returned you
unharmed."

Vail glanced at Dixon, then shook her head. "Wait a minute. You
said that if Ray cooperated, he'd release you. What did Mayfield want
Ray to do?"

Merilynn sat back, folded her arms, then looked at Vail, then at Dixon,
then at Brix. "If you want to know, get me and my son protection."

Vail brought a hand to her forehead and rubbed vigorously, as if doing so could calm the building anger. The lack of sleep had weakened
her internal checks and balances, and her frustration was threatening to
bubble over. "Mrs. Lugo," she said firmly. "Someone I care about a great
deal is missing. John Mayfield may have taken him. He may have him
blindfolded and gagged in that same dark place, just like he did to you
and Mario. But even if we get to talk to Mayfield, I doubt he's going to
be a good citizen and tell us what we want to know. If that's the case, my
friend—a cop, like Ray—might not have much longer to live. Without
food, water—"

Merilynn squared her jaw. "I'm sorry. But I have to think of my son. I
will help you. If you help me first."

Vail rose from her chair, spun around, and stormed out of the task
force conference room. She walked down the hall, then stopped, leaned
against the wall, and slunk down to the ground. She sat there, her forehead leaning against her knees. Vail was being totally honest with Merilynn: she had no sway over who was accepted into the witness protection
program. The Justice Department decided that. And based on what
Merilynn had told them, Vail doubted she was a candidate. While it
might comfort Merilynn and support her parental instincts, there did not
appear to be a clear threat that would require protection.

A moment later, Dixon left the conference room and located Vail
down the corridor. She sat down beside her but remained quiet.

Finally Dixon said, "That thing you said about Robby in there.
I hadn't thought of that."

"I didn't either. It just kind of came out. And then it hit me. Hard.
When she wouldn't budge, I had to leave before I said something we'd
all regret."

"We need to mobilize NSIB," Dixon said, referring to the Napa Special Investigations Bureau. "We can sketch out the radius on Bing maps and get them canvassing the area ASAP, see if we can locate Mayfield's hideout."

Vail got up suddenly. "Let's go."

"Where?"

"Mayfield. I want to see him."

8

D ixon tried discouraging Vail from making the hospital visit, but Vail would have nothing of it. En route to the medical center, Dixon called Brix and informed him where they were headed—and asked him to map out the area Merilynn Lugo had described and to engage NSIB assistance with the canvass.

They made their way into the ICU of the Napa Valley Medical Center. *I can't believe it was only yesterday that Mayfield was brought here after his arrest. Yesterday that Robby went missing.*

They pushed through the doors into ICU. An open and spacious nursing station occupied the center of the floor, with individual patient rooms lining the periphery. Large sliding glass doors sat sandwiched between translucent walls that could be curtained off by powder blue full-length drapes.

Vail and Dixon showed their credentials to the nurse sitting closest to them. Her name tag read "Helen."

"John Mayfield," Vail said. "How's he doing?"

Helen, a fifty-something woman whose chestnut hair was due for a dye session, consulted a chart, flipped a page, and said, "Looks like he's in pretty grave condition."

"Which room's he in?" Dixon asked.

Helen chuckled. "I'm afraid he's not in any condition to talk. They've induced a coma to stabilize him and increase his chance of recovery."

"Okay," Vail said. "Which room?"

Helen's gaze flicked between Vail and Dixon, clearly confused—her reply should have been adequate to assuage their desires.

Vail, for one, knew her facial expression was not conveying an air of calm and acceptance.

"Three." Helen's eyes slid left.

Vail and Dixon thanked her, then moved toward the room. "Shouldn't there be cops posted?"

Dixon rubbernecked her head. "There's supposed to be someone. Don't see him."

"Only one?"

"I'm guessing they don't expect a comatose patient to be much of a problem."

"He's huge and he's killed a lot of people," Vail said. "I think there should be a decent presence, don't you?"

Dixon raised a shoulder. "Budget's always an issue." She stepped forward and grabbed the door handle. She slid the large panel to the side and they walked in. Lying on the bed to their left, hooked up to flexible tubes and lead wires, was John Mayfield.

Vail moved to his side and had to summon the will not to reach out and grab him by the gown and shake him, slam his psychopathic head against the bed frame. Demand to know what he did with Robby. *If* he did something to Robby.

Instead, Vail stood there staring at him. Finally Dixon said, "I don't mean to be callous, but the nurse kind of had a point. What are we doing here?"

Vail pulled her gaze from Mayfield and looked at Dixon. "I don't know, Roxx. I needed to see him, what kind of state he's in." She looked down at Mayfield again. "Do you know what I feel like doing?"

"Shooting his brains out?"

Vail hiked her brow. "That would work, too." She leaned in close, put her face against Mayfield's left ear. "Should I do that, Johnny boy? Should I take my Glock and put it in your mouth?"

"Karen—"

Vail was not deterred. "If you manage to survive, I'm going to enjoy watching you get the needle. I'll be there in the death chamber, along with the families of all the people you've killed."

Dixon sighed audibly, then put her hands on her hips and turned away.

Vail leaned back and studied his face. "So tell me, Johnny, will you be seeing your mother in hell when you get there?" *There—what was that—did his face twitch?* "Roxx, you see that?"

Dixon turned. "See what?"

Vail continued scrutinizing Mayfield's expression. It was now blank.

Had she really seen something? "Tell me, John. What did you do with Roberto Hernandez? Did you kill him?"

Nothing, not a shudder or a quiver.

Vail moved in closer. "Do you have him tied up somewhere?"

"Does he have who tied up?"

Dixon and Vail swung their heads toward the door. Standing there, an icy expression on his face, was a man dressed in a white lab coat, stethoscope draped around his neck.

"You are?" Vail asked.

The man stepped into the room. "I think the question is, who are you?"

"I asked you first," Vail said, not yielding her ground.

The man stared at her. "Do I have to call security?"

Dixon held out her badge. "Investigator Dixon. This is Special Agent Vail. FBI."

"I'm Mr. Mayfield's surgeon. Dr. Koossey."

"Well," Vail said, "I guess that makes us related. We're *Mister* Mayfield's arresting officers."

Koossey threw his chin back. "So you're the ones who shot him."

"I wish," Vail said. Koossey didn't like that answer. *Tough shit, doc. You don't know who your patient is.*

He folded his arms across his chest. "Are you two about done here?"

Vail stepped closer to Koossey. With a smirk, she said, "Doctor, if I was done here, Mayfield would be flatlining."

"Karen." This from Dixon, whose face was a deep shade of red. Vail had to admit that was a stupid thing to say. One thing to think it. Another to speak it to the patient's physician. Certainly not when she wanted answers. Her "pleasantness filter" was failing her. Lack of sleep, stress . . . she was pissed off and, frankly, she just didn't give a shit.

"Sorry about that, Dr. Koossey. My partner's sleep deprived, she's not exactly exercising her best judgment at the moment."

His eyes flicked down to her holster. "Yet she's still carrying a loaded weapon. Very nice."

This guy's got a set of balls. Wonder if he's from New York. "I think I've heard just enough out of you, doctor. But I'll tell you how you can make yourself useful. How about telling us when *Mister* Mayfield here is going to be able to answer questions?"

Koossey snorted and tossed a look at Dixon, as if to say, "Is she for real?"

Dixon must've read the same thing from the man's face, because she said, "Look, doctor. Your patient is an extremely dangerous serial killer. He's murdered several innocent men and women. Including a couple local cops." Dixon yanked down on the collar of her blouse and craned her neck back, exposing her throat. The remnant of Mayfield's work was apparent in blood red, with emerging hints of eggplant-shaded hues. If it had been a sunset, it would've been memorable. It wasn't a sunset, of course—but for Dixon, it would forever remain a memory. To Koossey, she said, "Mayfield tried to kill me."

Vail likewise exposed her neck. "I'm a member of that club, too." *Whaddya think of that, doc?* "We've got another potential victim of his out there somewhere, a detective. Until we can question Mayfield, we've got no way of finding him. And we're hoping to find him alive." Vail folded her arms. "So."

Koossey worked his jaw from side to side. "We've induced a coma. Do you know what that means?"

"I know about comas," Vail said, flashing on her son's recent experience with the condition. "But only traumatic ones."

"Drug-induced coma is used these days to treat refractory cases of status epilepticus and in some cases of neurosurgery."

Dixon held up a hand. "Status ep—you mean epilepsy?"

Koossey looked annoyed at being interrupted. "Yes. Mind if I continue?"

Dixon and Vail stared at him. *Maybe it's not just me. The guy's a little arrogant. Probably would have something in common with Mayfield. Maybe they'd have been buddies.*

Koossey apparently got the message. "Its use in traumatic brain injury is a bit more controversial. The idea behind it is reduction of intracranial pressure and metabolic activity, to allow the brain to heal."

"How about we bring him out of it long enough to answer questions?" *And then put him under again, this time permanently. Wait, did I say that last part aloud?* Vail's eyes flicked from Dixon to Koossey. No reaction. *Phew.*

Koossey lifted the metal clipboard from Mayfield's bed. "It's not like that. I put him in the coma because his brain is too ill to function properly. The injuries were quite severe. So even if I were to bring him out of the coma, it's unlikely he'd awaken."

"How long are you going to keep him under?" Dixon asked.

Koossey canted his eyes toward the clipboard. He looked over the progress notes, flipped a page, then said, almost off-handedly, "A medically induced coma is incrementally lightened as the patient demonstrates elements of recovery. And that, Agent Vail, like it or not, depends on Mr. Mayfield. He's in control of the situation now."

He was in control of the situation before, too. That was the problem.

"We'll be monitoring his electroencephalographic patterns and intracranial pressure, as metrics to help determine when to lighten the coma. More than that, I can't help you." Koossey replaced the clipboard, then turned toward the door. "Miss Dixon, you seem to be the level-headed half of your duo. Can I count on you to keep your partner in check so I can finish the rest of my rounds?"

Dixon ignored his comment, but said, "Will you call me as soon as he's potentially capable of answering questions?" She pulled a card from her pocket and offered it to him.

Koossey frowned.

"Because of Mayfield's extremely violent nature," Dixon said, "if we have adequate notice, it'll enable us to increase security. To prevent him from murdering you and your staff."

Koossey gave Dixon a long look, then took the card and walked out.

Dixon moved around the bed to Vail, placed a hand around her shoulders, and said, "C'mon."

They stopped at the nurses' station. Helen glanced up from her file. Dixon handed her a business card as well. "I'd appreciate if you'd leave instructions for all the staff to notify me when you're preparing to bring Mr. Mayfield out of his coma."

"He's violent and extremely dangerous," Vail said. "He's murdered several people. And mutilated a number of women. Sliced off their breasts."

Helen glanced over at Mayfield's room. Vail figured she was about to piss her pants, if she hadn't already.

"Okay?" Dixon asked.

Helen, still looking in the direction of Mayfield's room, said, "Yeah, yeah, of course."

As they walked away from the nurses' station, Vail's BlackBerry buzzed. She reached to her belt and yanked it off. It was Jonathan. "Hey, sweetie, how you doing?"

"You okay, Mom?"

Vail sucked in a deep breath and stood up straight, as if Jonathan could see her, 2,500 miles away. "I'm fine. Why?"

"I—I don't know, you just sounded different. Unhappy."

"I've just got some stuff going on here I'm trying to deal with. How are things at home? Aunt Faye treating you okay?"

"Fine, she's fine. I'm actually having a good time with her."

"You are? I mean, that's great—I'm glad you're getting to know her better."

"Listen, Mom, I gotta get to class—"

Vail shifted the phone to her other hand. "Right. Okay—but I need you to do something for me."

"Wow, if you're making me late for class, must be important."

"I need a photo of Robby. You remember that one you took of me and him at the academy a couple weeks ago? Can you cut me out and email it to me?"

"You mean crop it?"

"Yeah, that. Crop it."

"Sure. I can do it after next period."

"No, I don't want you going home and missing school." *Actually, given the circumstances, maybe that'd be a good idea.*

"I upload all my pictures to my SkyDrive account. I can go into the computer lab and grab the photo."

"SkyDrive?"

"Free online storage. Don't worry about it, Ma, I can do it. I'll crop it and email it to you. You'll have it in like an hour."

"You're a lifesaver."

"Yeah, whatever." He hesitated a second, then said, "Is everything okay? With Robby? Why do you need the photo?"

Shit. It hadn't occurred to her that he would ask, but now that she thought of it, of course he would. Despite the short tenure, Robby had been the most positive male figure in her son's life—in years. *So how do I answer that one? I can't lie to him. He'd never forgive me. But I don't want him worrying.*

"I just need it for a case." *Okay, that's only partially true—but it'll have to do for now.* "Email it to me as soon as you can, okay sweetie?"

Jonathan seemed to accept the explanation—and the diversion—but he was no dummy. He would know something was wrong, but he probably also knew his mother wouldn't tell him much about a sensitive issue.

Vail hung up, reholstered her phone, and joined Dixon at the elevator.

It slid open and a uniformed officer stepped out.

"You assigned to John Mayfield?" Vail asked.

"Who—"

"Your prisoner." Vail held up her creds.

"Yeah. Why?"

"Because you weren't at your station."

"I had to use the head. I was only gone a few minutes. Guy's in a coma."

Dixon shook her head. "No good. Coma or not, he's extremely dangerous. Don't underestimate him. And don't leave your post again unless you've got coverage."

The cop gave them both an exaggerated frown, then pushed past them.

Dixon turned and watched him amble away. "Let's do something productive. Yes?"

Vail rubbed her face with two hands, then nodded.

9

They took the stairs, avoiding the elevator. Vail pushed through the metal fire door and moved onto the textured gray steel steps. "Merilynn said that Mayfield warned Ray that if he told another detective, Mayfield would know."

Dixon's shoes clanked beside Vail. "That would seem to fit with the fact that Mayfield had an inside source."

"Or," Vail said, "it merely means he had a way of getting into the Sheriff's Department and finding out that information. Since he had the cover of a pest control technician, he could move about with impunity."

Dixon pushed through the door that led into the first floor lobby. "I think we should tell Brix, have him sniff around to make sure there wasn't someone communicating with Mayfield behind our backs."

"Couldn't hurt."

Dixon pulled her phone and typed out a text with her request. The Crush Killer case was in an unusual gray area—it had been solved but remained active because, like a CSI puzzling over a broken pane of glass, pieces were scattered about but had yet to be gathered up and reassembled into a whole. As a result, Dixon was still the lead investigator.

"We should also dig into who John Mayfield is," Vail said. "Maybe something from his house will lead us to his lair. We might find a trove of information and forensics there."

Dixon closed her phone, then stopped short.

"What is it?" Vail asked.

Dixon turned to Vail, her mouth partially open. "Cannon."

Dixon was referring to James Cannon, a bodybuilder friend of Mayfield's whom Dixon and Vail had met at the gym. He had hit on Vail, then took offense to something Dixon had said. Shortly before they had identified John Mayfield as the Crush Killer, Vail thought Cannon might be the offender.

Vail shook her head. "Ray tried to locate him. He searched for that start-up winery where Cannon was supposedly the winemaker. Herndon Vineyards. Nothing came up."

Dixon narrowed her eyes in thought. "I'm not sure we can trust anything Ray told us. We don't know how he's wrapped up in all this. We need to look into Cannon and Herndon Vineyards ourselves."

"Best we start with someone who knows the operations of a winery up close and personal. Brix."

"Silent partner. But I'm sure he can hook us up with his brother or sister, since they're the ones who run the place. And I'll see if he can have NSIB get us Cannon's home address from DMV."

While Dixon made the call and told Brix what they needed, Vail wandered over to their car and rested her forearm on the passenger window, then dropped her head against her arm. Thoughts of Robby flittered through her mind . . . and came to rest on yesterday morning when she was leaving for the Sheriff's Department. She had kissed him good-bye and he stirred.

"See you tonight," he had told her.

She replied, "Yes, you will."

Except that she didn't. He was gone.

"Okay," Dixon said, pulling Vail from her reverie. "Brix is gonna touch base with NSIB, then have his brother call us."

Vail pushed away from the car door and nodded.

"Look, I know you wanted to put Mayfield six feet under back there—believe me, I would like to have helped you do it—but that's not what this is about."

Vail looked away. "Yeah."

"We'll find him, Karen. Eddie's gone. But Robby . . . We'll find him. You have to believe that."

Vail felt a tear roll down her cheek. She flicked it away. "Let's get going." As she climbed into the car, she realized she wished she knew where to go. She wished she knew where to go to find Robby.

10

The clock was ticking; Vail kept track of the seconds as they melted into oblivion.

She knew better than most that the initial twenty-four to forty-eight hours in a missing person's life were crucial. Even Robby, a homicide detective, was subject to the same rule. Because cop or not, at the end of the day, stripped of gun and badge, he was just a human being, a vulnerable civilian. When bound and gagged, or being held captive—if that's what was going on here—the victim was usually powerless to help himself.

The image of Robby being powerless was incongruous with his imposing physical presence: a thick but trim six foot seven. She had seen him vulnerable only once before—the result of a stun gun attack. And that had nearly been disastrous.

But if Robby was not injured or under someone else's control, a remaining option was one Vail could not bring herself to consider. Whenever her thoughts meandered in the direction of Robby's death, her subconscious yanked away her mind, much like old Vaudeville acts were pulled from the stage if they bombed.

As they entered the task force conference room, Vail took a deep breath and realized that her anxiety was causing her to grind her molars. Her dentist would peer inside her mouth at her next cleaning and, once again, admonish her for wearing down her teeth. She would, once again, give him a sharp retort—something like, "If you think stress has worn down my teeth, you should see my arteries."

But of course none of that mattered at the moment.

"You hear from my brother?" Brix asked.

Brix sat huddled over a stack of documents, a legal pad off to his right filled with scribbled notes. Stan Owens was on the phone, his own

40

comments scratched out on a page at his elbow. Gordon and Mann were not in the room.

"Not yet," Vail said.

Brix twisted his wrist and consulted his watch. "He was in a meeting. He should be out soon. Just so you know, I did a search for the place online. Nothing. Searched for Cannon. Nothing again."

"So Ray was telling the truth," Dixon said.

"About that, yeah."

Brix's dig was not lost on Vail. She opened her mouth to comment, but both her BlackBerry and Brix's phone vibrated. She pulled hers and read the display.

"My son just emailed me a photo of Robby."

Dixon pointed to the BlackBerry. "Send it to all of us. I'll print copies for everyone."

Owens looked up. "Include me in that. Time being, I'm gonna sit in on the task force, help you people out." His eyes found Dixon. "If that's okay with you, Ms. Dixon."

Dixon's expression was neutral. "Thanks, sheriff. We can use any help we can get."

The door swung open and Mann and Gordon walked in.

"That's my point," Mann said to Gordon. "Who woulda thought." They both took a seat at the conference table.

"Who woulda thought, what?" Vail asked.

Using his prosthetic hand, Mann deftly pulled a notepad from his pocket. "I didn't think it'd be the case, but there's a fair number of Sebastians in the area. Between first names and surnames, we've got over forty in the greater region. I mean, *Sebastian*? I wouldn't have expected it to be that popular. We got a list of names and numbers and started dialing, the ones closest to Napa city limits first. So far, no one knows a Robby or Roberto Hernandez. We asked a couple guys from NSIB to work the rest of the list."

"I just emailed all of you the photo of Robby," Vail said. "Can you forward it to the NSIB investigators?"

Gordon pulled out his phone. "Done."

Brix disconnected his call, then sat down in front of the laptop perched in the middle of the conference table. "NSIB got Cannon's home address from DMV, an apartment on Soscol. But it's old. They're there now. Landlord said he hasn't lived there for two or three years." He struck some keys and brought up Robby's picture, then sent it to the color LaserJet in the corner. "They're gonna see about getting a forwarding address."

"Who's Cannon?" Mann asked.

As Dixon made her way to the printer, she said, "We're looking into the possibility that a guy who was friends with Mayfield may be involved in this. James Cannon. Karen and I met him a couple days ago. Said he was a winemaker with a start-up called Herndon Vineyards. Anyone hear of it?"

Owens, Mann, and Gordon shook their heads.

Brix pushed his chair back from the table. "Herndon's supposedly not releasing their first cases for another couple years, so they're not putting out any promo materials. No product, no press. I'm hoping that my brother, with his wine industry contacts, can get us a twenty on Herndon."

Dixon scooped up the photos from the printer tray. "That's assuming that Herndon is real. Could've been a bunch of crap."

"We'll find out," Brix said, again stealing a look at his watch. "If it's legit, we may end up locating the winery before we get Cannon's current home address."

"I can give Ian Wirth a call," Vail said, referring to a vintner in the Georges Valley region, where the Crush Killer had a propensity for choosing his victims. "Ian would probably know just as much as your brother about how new winery applications are handled."

Brix shrugged. "Go for it."

Dixon handed a copy of Robby's photo to each of the task force members.

After leaving a message for Wirth, Vail said, "What happened with the media? Last night we had TV and print reporters here. When that Microsoft techie gave you Mayfield's name and you took off for my twenty, what'd the reporters do?"

"No idea," Brix said. "We left through the back. We didn't want to get stuck answering questions, and we certainly didn't want them following us down the road and getting in the way of a high-speed chase."

Stan Owens leaned forward. "I told them it didn't pan out, that I'd call them if anything broke."

"Did you?" Dixon asked. "Call them?"

"I've been a little busy."

Dixon held up a hand. "I didn't mean that as a criticism, sheriff."

Dixon glanced at Vail, who inched her chair closer to the table. *Tread lightly here* . . . "No one knows that John Mayfield, the man lying in a coma at Napa Valley Med Center, is a serial killer, and that he's killed a bunch of people here."

"Not this again," Owens said.

When the Crush Killer had started taking lives, Vail had lobbied hard to publicize his existence, which would've played into his narcissistic needs and enabled them to open a dialogue with him. Though she was vetoed for political reasons, their silence on the issue now might work to their advantage.

"No, no," Vail said, holding up a hand. "This is a good thing, sheriff. This guy, James Cannon, if he's an accomplice of John Mayfield's, then he doesn't know Mayfield's been caught. If he *is* involved, he's got no reason to be concerned."

Brix splayed both hands palm up. "Until he tries to reach Mayfield and his buddy doesn't answer."

"Right," Vail said. "So we've got a limited window to act. We've gotta move fast."

Dixon rose from her seat. "Okay." She looked down, brought a hand up to her chin, seemed to be lost in thought. "Burt. You and Austin see if you can locate Herndon Vineyards. Sheriff, coordinate with NSIB and let us know if anything comes up with either Robby's photo or his friend Sebastian. Karen and I are going to pay a visit to Superior Mobile Bottling. Redd, can you get a copy of Mayfield's phone records, home and cell, and see if there are any unusual connections we can make? We know there'll be calls to Cannon—they were buddies—so even if we have to call every number in his logs, we might find Cannon that way."

Vail snapped her fingers. "Wait a minute—Cannon was a member at Fit1. Maybe we can grab their records without a warrant."

"That'd be good, because we don't have near enough yet to get a warrant," Dixon said.

Vail rose from her chair, then reached over and unbuttoned the top two buttons of Dixon's shirt. She leaned back and appraised her partner. "Yeah, but I think we've got enough to get what we want."

11

The twenty-something tight-shirted front desk attendant smiled when Dixon and Vail stepped up to the counter. Vail looked pretty damn good for thirty-eight—especially considering all she had been through of late. But Dixon, several years younger, not only possessed a natural beauty but worked hard to keep herself in shape. Eddie Agbayani, her former boyfriend, had called her "Buff Barbie," a description Vail would've been hard-pressed to dispute.

And the dude behind the desk took notice, too.

"I haven't seen you around here," Dixon said, a coy smile spreading her lips and a straightening of her shoulders spreading her blouse.

"Rolando," the guy said, his eyes drifting down to the last fastened button as he extended his hand.

Dixon took it and squeezed, which got Rolando's attention. "There's a guy who works out here," she said. "He asked my friend here out on a date and she lost his number. Can you look it up for us?"

Rolando's eyes finally focused on Dixon's face. "His phone number?"

"I'll take his address, too," Vail said, "if you've got it."

Rolando squinted, hesitated, then moved to the computer at his right. In a low voice, with a glance over his shoulder, he said, "No go on his address. But I can give you his phone. Just don't tell anyone." He hit some keys and looked up. "Guy's name?"

"James Cannon."

"Cannon . . . " Rolando said as he scrolled down the list.

"Know him?"

Rolando typed, frowned, then typed some more. "Big dude?"

"That probably describes half the guys in this gym," Dixon said with a grin. "But, yeah."

"All we've got is a cell. That work?"

Dixon pulled out a pad and pen, then craned her neck to look at the screen. "You're a lifesaver, Rolando."

Rolando leaned back, but his eyes remained riveted on Dixon's well-defined cleavage.

Vail cleared her throat. She could've sworn Rolando gave her a dirty look—but it worked, because he momentarily diverted his eyes.

"How long has he been a member?" Vail asked.

He consulted his screen. "Looks like it's been a while. Couple years."

Dixon clicked her pen shut. "Thanks, Rolando. Maybe you wanna spot me some day."

"I'd—yeah, I'm sure I'll spot you." He chuckled. "The minute you walk in the door."

Dixon returned a wink. "Catch you later." She held up the pad. "Thanks again."

As they headed toward the parking lot, Vail said, "You realize he's gonna be all over you next time you come in to work out."

"I'll worry about that later. At least we got a number for Cannon."

"Address, too?"

Dixon smiled devilishly. "Of course. But it's the apartment on Soscol. Same one DMV had."

Vail blew some air out the side of her mouth. "Okay. So how do you want to play this?"

Dixon glanced around at the cars in the vicinity. "I'll text the cell to Brix, let him have NSIB follow up and try to grab an address from the wireless company. You call Cannon, remind him who you are, and tell him you've got some extra time. See if he wants to do lunch. He hit on you once, he'll probably say yes."

"He knows we're cops. If he was working with Mayfield, why would he want to meet with me?"

"You tell me," Dixon said as she reached into her pocket for her keys.

Vail looked off at the mountains. "If he's like Mayfield, he's a narcissist. In which case, this would be like a conquest for him. I initially rejected him, reconsidered, now I'm calling him. Crawling back is the way he'd see it. But," Vail said, "that's if he's a narcissist. We can't assume he is just because Mayfield was—but it would make sense. There's a reason why they found each other. Kindred spirits. They understand each other's needs, they think alike."

Dixon started tapping out her text to Brix. "Given the conversation we had with them, it's possible he is a narcissist."

Vail considered that and replayed the meeting they had with the two men. "You were there for more of it than I was, but yeah, it's possible. It could also be we're reading into it, seeing what we want to see."

"Guess we'll find out." Dixon popped open the doors and they got in.

Vail pulled her BlackBerry and dialed. Voice mail. Waited for the beep. "Jimmy, this is Karen Vail—we met a couple days ago in the gym and . . . well, I kind of blew you off. Sorry about that. I was there with my friend, and I couldn't accept your offer with her there. I'm seeing her brother back in Virginia. Anyway, if you're interested in catching lunch or dinner, or *something else* . . . " she said, suggestively, "I'll be here another few days. Give me a buzz back."

She disconnected the call. "Hopefully he'll respond. And if we're lucky, his wireless carrier will come through. If he really is a wine maker, this can't be a throwaway phone. And unless he thought to update the Fit1 records, which is unlikely, he's had this number at least a couple years."

Dixon shook her head. "Doesn't make sense that he'd be involved with Mayfield. He's got no cover. He's totally exposed."

"Could be he never intended to live that type of life," Vail said. "But the way this relationship might go would be he meets Mayfield, Mayfield makes some comment that's well received by Cannon, and they feel each other out to make sure one didn't misunderstand the other. They find they're of like mind. Cannon assists Mayfield in one of his kills and he gets off on it. He likes killing, it gives him a rush like nothing he's ever experienced. Maybe they even talk about planning kills as a team."

"What does that mean for Cannon with Mayfield temporarily out of the picture?"

Vail eyed a decorative stack of wine barrels by the parking lot entrance while she formulated an answer. "Until Cannon finds out about his buddy being caught, we're probably safe. But once he hears Mayfield's incapacitated, he may start killing on his own, at first just to prove to himself he can do it. Once he discovers he can, the only thing that's gonna stop him is us." Her BlackBerry began vibrating. She glanced at the screen. "This can't be good." Vail's gaze flicked to Dixon. "My boss." She answered the call and pressed the phone to her ear.

"Karen," Thomas Gifford began. "I realize this comes at a bad time, but I'm afraid I have to interrupt your vacation."

Vacation . . . oh, yeah. That's what this was.

"In fact, Hernandez is gonna kill me for this," Gifford continued, "but I need you back here ASAP—"

"Yeah," Vail said. "About that. We've got a problem here, sir. I shoulda called you this morning, but it's been a nightmare."

"Don't tell me you're still working the Crush Killer. I specifically told you you're off the case, and you assured me, Karen. You *promised* me—"

"It's not what you think, sir."

His volume leaped a notch. She could picture his face turning red through the phone. "It's never what I think, is it?"

"Sir, listen to me—"

"No, you listen to me for once."

"No sir. Just—just stop. You need to hear me out." She took a deep breath, then felt Dixon's hand on her shoulder. "Sir, give me a minute to explain. And if you still wanna go off on me, fine." He was silent, so she continued. "We caught the Crush Killer last night. He was shot in the process and underwent surgery. He made it through but he's in a coma."

"If you think that's an excuse—"

"During the day, I kept trying to reach Robby. But he wasn't answering. Late last night I went to our room at the bed-and-breakfast. He wasn't there. No sign of him at all. We've been looking for him since."

"Have you alerted the local field office?"

"No. We've been following up leads on the Crush Killer."

"Wait a second," Gifford said. "Just hang on a second. You've lost me."

His tone calmed, which was a good thing. Maybe he would understand. Help her out.

"I don't get it. What's the Crush Killer got to do with Hernandez?"

Vail closed her eyes. "Things weren't adding up. I kept feeling we were missing something. But I didn't know what. When we arrested him, I did the interview. He said to me, 'There's more to this than you know.' And then one of the sergeants on the task force, Ray Lugo, burst into the room and shot him. A ricochet caught Lugo and killed him. During transport to the ER, he said John Mayfield, the Crush Killer, had, at some point in the past, kidnapped his wife and son. Lugo apparently cut a deal of some sort with Mayfield to keep his family safe. What kind of deal, what he was doing, we don't know. And with Robby missing, and Mayfield saying there was more to this than we know . . . we can't rule out the possibility his disappearance is somehow related to Mayfield."

"And?" Gifford asked.

"We're already running down a lead that suggests Mayfield may've had an accomplice. If we find this guy, we may find Robby. Or at least some info that might lead us to him."

Gifford sighed audibly. She could see him at his desk, head bowed, free hand on his forehead, rubbing it.

"The task force is working this?" he finally asked.

"What's left of it, yes. They've got the assistance of the Napa Special Investigations Bureau."

"I'm going to call the ASAC in San Francisco. And the RA in Santa Rosa. See if we can coordinate efforts. How long has he been missing?"

"No way of knowing. My last contact with him was 8:30 yesterday morning."

Dixon leaned closer to Vail's free ear. "The carpet."

"Oh," Vail said, nodding. "The CSI here found blood on the carpet in our B&B. He's running it—"

"Blood. You sure? Any other signs of struggle in the room?"

"It'd been cleaned by the maids before we got there. So we have no idea. The crime scene—if it was one—was probably destroyed. The CSI did a full workup, just in case."

"Have a sample of that carpet sent here, to our lab. I want our guys looking at it, too. And we'll need an exemplar from—"

"Done. Paul Bledsoe's at Robby's place getting his hair and toothbrush. You should be getting one of them soon."

"Fine." There was a pause, then he said, in a softer tone, "This makes what I'm about to tell you even more difficult. But I need you back here. We caught a high-profile case. I can't talk about it on an unsecure line."

Vail pulled the phone from her ear, her face contorting into sarcastic disbelief. Fortunately Gifford couldn't see her—it'd most likely set him off. She brought the handset back against her head. "Sir," she said in a measured tone. "I'm sure you can understand that I've got my mind on finding Robby. I can't just leave here. Assign the case to someone else."

"What I *understand* is that I still have the behavioral analysis units to run and that's my priority. What I *understand* is that you're in a tough way right now. And I also *understand* that we've got a task force there working the case, and a well-equipped San Francisco field office ready to step in that can do the job just fine."

"With all due respect, I disagree."

"Not the first time, is it, Karen?"

"Frank. Why can't Frank take that new case?"

"Del Monaco left yesterday to teach a seminar at New Scotland Yard that goes for another week, then he's due to consult on a case they've been asking for our help on for two months. And Hutchings is on sick leave with an ulcer. Van Owen's wife was diagnosed this morning with ovarian cancer, so he's out on bereavement leave. Boozer just retired and we've got no one to take his place. I tried pulling Art out of arson and bombing, but they just caught a big case the White House wants them to consult on that might involve a trip to Iraq. And Director Knox isn't about to tell the president no."

"So get me the crime scene photos, autopsy photos, victimology—and I'll look it all over when I get back. Give me a week."

"Karen . . ." He paused, no doubt to gather himself, to phrase it in a way that kept him from exploding.

She realized now she had pushed him as far as she could. But for Robby's sake—she felt justified.

"Karen, this is close to home and the crime scene is fresh; it's the perfect opportunity to see things as they are. I don't have to tell you it's a world better than photos and reports. No, that won't cut it. Not for this case."

Vail slunk down in her seat. *I've got no choice. Short of resigning, I have no leverage, no valid reason for staying behind.*

"Karen. You probably know I'm fond of Hernandez. I knew his mother."

After a long silence, Vail asked, "How soon?"

"How soon, what?"

"Till I have to leave. How soon?"

"Lenka is booking your flight as we speak. You leave tomorrow morning, a 6:30 connecting flight out of SFO. She's arranging a car to pick you up at 4:00 AM. She'll email you the flight info."

Vail set her jaw. "Anything else, sir?"

"We'll find him, Karen."

"Yeah. Okay. Thanks." She disconnected the call and let her hand drop into her lap.

"He wants you back," Dixon said.

"I'm leaving at 4:00 AM tomorrow morning."

"We'll handle it, Karen. I'll stay in touch with you. We'll be your eyes and ears. We won't let you down. Okay?"

Vail nodded out the windshield at no one in particular, numbly and blindly. "No. Not okay. We've got several hours." She turned to Dixon, her face hard. "Before I leave, god help me, I'm gonna have some answers. We'll find Cannon. We'll find out what Merilynn Lugo knows. And we'll know if César Guevara is involved in Robby's disappearance." She pressed a hand against her pocket, which contained the photo of Robby. "You with me on this?"

Dixon did not hesitate. "Yes."

"Good. Then start the fucking car. Let's get the hell out of here."

12

Vail and Dixon's first stop was Superior Mobile Bottling, located in a light industrial area of nearby American Canyon

The company was a local concern that brought equipment-laden semis to wineries throughout the region to perform bottling and labeling functions. It was a cost-effective approach for many wineries, as they didn't have to expend resources and take up prime space for production machinery used only once a year.

The facility was overseen by César Guevara, a man who supposedly served as its CFO but appeared to be much more. Vail, Dixon, and Ray Lugo had questioned him a couple of days ago. Vail had picked up on strange body language—silent communication between Lugo and Guevara. It was an observation that led the task force to aggressively investigate Guevara as the Crush Killer. The likelihood of him being their UNSUB, or unknown subject, shriveled like a desiccated grape when John Mayfield emerged as the offender.

But Lugo's involvement with Guevara remained in Vail's craw, though with the harried pursuit of Mayfield, it became a lost seedling among a forest of concerns.

On the drive to Superior Mobile Bottling, Vail explained their rationale for pursuing Guevara: if Lugo knew Guevara, and Lugo was involved somehow with Mayfield, there was an outside chance that Mayfield and Guevara knew one another . . . Lugo being the common link. At the very least, Guevara might know something—or might even have had something to do with Robby's disappearance.

Dixon had remarked that there were a lot of suppositions factored into that reasoning. Vail could not dispute her point, but felt they needed to pursue the lead.

"Ray claimed he only knew Guevara when they were teenagers, working in the vineyards," Dixon said.

"That is what he said. But sometimes I've got to rely on my intuition. And I sensed there was more to it than that."

Dixon navigated out of Napa proper toward American Canyon, and the landscape changed from wineries to a more urbanized backdrop. "What Ray said. It's not an unlikely story."

"*If* it's true, I'd bet it's only the first chapter. Working the vineyards is probably how they met. But what happened after that? How did their relationship develop? That's what we need to find out. That could be a key."

Having arrived at Superior Mobile Bottling, Vail and Dixon slammed their car doors and headed toward the back of the warehouse-type structure. Bypassing the front entrance—and the interference-running administrator—they entered through the side roll-up steel door. Highly polished chrome and burgundy rigs sat stoically in their stalls in the spacious facility, like fine racehorses waiting for their turn to perform.

Mounted on the wall, at least a dozen feet off the ground, was the largest LCD high-definition television Vail had seen outside a professional sports stadium. The volume was turned down, but it was tuned to what looked like the replay of a vintage baseball game.

A medium-build Hispanic man appeared from behind the far end of one of the rigs. He wore a blue dress shirt with rolled-up sleeves and held a long screwdriver. César Guevara. He made eye contact with Vail, then looked away in disgust. "Not you again."

Vail glanced sideways at Dixon. "Wonder why we always have that effect on people."

"More questions?" Guevara asked.

Vail nudged Dixon with an elbow. "I told you he was smarter than he looked." She reached into her pocket and pulled out the photograph of Robby, keeping it shielded from Guevara's view until she was ready. She needed to watch his face carefully for the slightest of tells: a flicker, a sudden flutter of his eye, a squint, a hardening of his brow or a lift of his Adam's apple.

Vail flipped the photo over and handed it to him. "Know this guy or seen him around? Name's Roberto Hernandez. Also goes by Robby."

There—a narrowing of his eyelids.

"Should I?"

Vail tilted her head and leaned forward. "I'm a federal agent and I asked a question. That usually means you give me an answer, not another question."

Guevara held his gaze on the photo a long moment, then lifted it closer to his face and studied it.

"What is it?" Vail asked.

"Obviously," Guevara said, "he's someone important to you. A witness?"

"A friend and colleague. He's gone missing. I figured you might know something about it. Do you?"

He handed back the photo to Vail. "And why would that be?"

Vail stepped forward. "See, there you go again. Answering my question with a question."

"Is that a crime?"

Vail looked over at Dixon. "What we're investigating is."

"Really," Guevara said. "And what is it you're investigating?"

Dixon craned her neck around. "Where's the ladies' room?"

Guevara held Dixon's gaze for a beat, then said, "In the front. Toward the office." He cricked his head back over his right shoulder. Dixon walked off in that direction.

"We're investigating the disappearance of Roberto Hernandez," Vail said. "I thought that's obvious, since I told you he's missing, I'm showing you his photo and asking if you've seen him."

"Yeah, well, I haven't. Haven't seen him and don't know him."

Vail stepped closer. "I don't believe you."

"Oh yeah?" Guevara asked. "That's a shame."

In one motion, Vail reached for her Glock and cleared leather in record time. Stepped forward and slammed the muzzle not so gently against Guevara's prominent forehead, driving him back into the fender of the adjacent rig.

Guevara's eyes bugged out—but he wasn't afraid. Vail sensed anger, not fear.

"Are you fucking out of your mind?"

"You know what, Mr. Guevara? Yes, I am out of my mind. I'm god-damn pissed. My friend is missing and I think you had something to do with it."

"What does it take to get through to you? I told you, I didn't know the guy."

Vail held the Glock in place. "We'll see about that."

Guevara laughed. Mocking her. "I think you should remove your gun from my face, Agent Vail. I haven't done nothing wrong. And you've got no proof I have, or we wouldn't still be standing here. Would we?"

Vail's eyes narrowed. She felt her blood pounding in the arteries of her head. *What am I doing? What can I possibly gain?*

"How did you know Ray Lugo?" she asked.

Guevara's eyes narrowed. "Past tense? Is Sergeant Lugo dead?"

Vail cursed herself silently for being so careless. At present, until they knew who all the players were, it was best everyone thought that Lugo was still alive. "Answer my question. How well do you know him?"

"What makes you think I know him?"

Vail clenched her teeth and dug the Glock's barrel into Guevara's forehead. "Don't fuck with me. I'm not in the mood!"

"He's a cop. First time I saw him was when you walked in here couple days ago."

"Bullshit." Vail twisted her wrist, the Glock's metal now digging into the skin and muscle of Guevara's face. He winced and wriggled in pain. If she didn't draw blood, he would have a substantial bruise there by this evening.

"Why don't you ask him?"

"I did. He said you two knew each other when you were kids, teens working on vineyards. He's a good man. I believe him."

"Fine. Yeah, I think that's right. I knew he looked familiar when he walked in. I couldn't place the face."

"You're such a piece of shit," Vail said. "And you suck at lying."

"Did you know, Agent Vail, that I have security cameras hooked up all over this warehouse?"

Vail had seen the cameras in the parking lot on her last visit, but she hadn't noticed any inside. But it made sense. With so much invested in the rigs—and without the trucks there was no business—of course Superior would have instituted interior surveillance measures.

She stood her ground. There was nothing she could do now, in the eyes of the law—or in those of her ASAC, Thomas Gifford—that would worsen her situation. Short of pulling the trigger.

In a low voice, Vail said, "If I find that you had anything to do with Robby Hernandez's disappearance, I will find you. Where there aren't any security cameras. And if any harm comes to Robby, harm will come to you." She added pressure to her weapon. Guevara squinted away the pain. "You understand me?"

"You got it all wrong, Agent Vail." He locked eyes with her. "But I hear you. Loud and clear."

Vail splayed open her free hand, placed it against Guevara's chest, and pushed herself away from him. She kept the Glock in her right hand, her index finger hovering over the trigger rather than in a safety position by the outside guard.

"Everything okay in here?"

It was Dixon, walking toward her from the other end of the warehouse, down the aisle between the trailers.

Vail hadn't taken her eyes off Guevara. "Remember what I said."

Dixon's eyes seemed to find Vail's Glock in her right hand, which she now held at her side.

"Did I miss something?"

"Unfortunately, no." Vail started to back away. "'Let's go."

But Dixon stopped suddenly, her eyes pinned to the ceiling. Vail turned. No, not the ceiling—at the wall-mounted television, where a banner reading "Special Report" was scrolling across the bottom of the screen. An attractive female reporter was standing in front of the Sheriff's Department, motioning animatedly into the camera.

"Turn it up," Dixon yelled at Guevara.

He squinted anger, then reached for a shelf beneath the adjacent rig and lifted an elaborate remote. A green slider appeared onscreen and wiped across its surface, the volume rising proportionately.

" . . . refuses comment at this time. But KRSH-4 has learned that a man, who's been identified as John Wayne Mayfield, has been arrested in the deaths of several Napa area residents. According to informed sources and witness accounts, KRSH has learned that Mayfield is a serial killer who's been operating in and around the valley in recent weeks. Apparently, a number of individuals who have passed away under suspicious circumstances during the past several days may've actually been victims of John Wayne Mayfield. Attempts at obtaining verification have been unsuccessful, with the Napa County Coroner's Office declining to confirm or deny whether or not the bodies of these victims are even in their morgue. The FBI is reportedly on the case as well, though they, too, have declined comment.

"We'll bring you full coverage as soon as more information becomes available. But one thing is certain, Fred: the police kept the public in the dark that a dangerous killer was loose in our community. Impossible to say yet just how many lives that decision has cost the valley. And the killer? After an apparent shootout with cops, he's lying comatose in the intensive care unit at Napa Valley Medical Center.

"Reporting live from the Napa County Sheriff's Department, this is Stephanie Norcross."

The news anchor appeared onscreen and began talking.

Vail and Dixon shared a concerned look and then left the building.

13

W ell that sucks big time," Dixon said.
"What are the odds that Cannon saw that?" Vail asked.
"Who the hell knows? But the bell's been rung. It's just a matter of time before he hears, if he hasn't already." They got back into the car and Dixon started driving north, toward Napa. "What happened back there with Guevara?"

"I lost control. Just enough to get his juices flowing. Hopefully he wet his pants. But I doubt it. Cool customer." Vail looked off, alone a moment with her thoughts. "Too cool."

"You think he's involved."

"I know what I saw, Roxx. When he kept looking at Ray, something was going on. It was more than recognizing a guy you knew when you were a teen." She watched a huge Walmart-anchored shopping center flash by as they headed north. "The look he was giving Ray. It was . . . anger, maybe. Like he was pissed that Ray brought us there. As if Ray should've found a way to stop us from going."

"You sure?"

"Now that I have a free minute to clear my mind and think about it, yeah. That's what his look said."

"Okay," Dixon said. "Let's go with that a moment. They knew each other. They were working together in some criminal enterprise. We already know Ray was doing something he shouldn't have been, as part of his deal with Mayfield to leave his wife and son alone."

"Let's look into Guevara. Deeper this time. Let's try to get a warrant, poke around his financials. Phone logs. Superior's business. Look for patterns. Standard police grunt work."

Dixon was shaking her head. "Seriously, Karen. Maybe you'd find a judge in Virginia who'd sign off on something like that. But our case is so thin you can shine a light through it. It won't fly in California."

"You get a good look around?"

"I poked around here and there. It's a pretty clean facility. Not a whole lot there other than their rigs and machinery." She leaned to the left and dug into her pocket. "Found this. In the corner, behind a stacked case of wine." Dixon handed it to Vail.

Vail took the tissue and unraveled it. "A wine cork?"

"Yeah, but the real question is, is it real or is it synthetic?"

Vail refrained from touching it. She tilted the tissue cradled in her hands as she examined the item from all angles. "Synthetic." She rolled it back up and handed it to Dixon. "And this helps us, how?"

"No idea. I'll give it to Matt Aaron, see if the lab can find something."

The vibration of her BlackBerry sent her heart racing. "Shit." She grabbed for the phone.

"Jumpy?"

Vail grumbled. "How could you tell?" She looked down at the display. "Text from Cannon. He's out of town, but says he would've loved to get together." She turned to Dixon. "He said, 'Maybe your next visit out here.'"

"Interesting. Is he really out of town?"

"We're getting sloppy. After what we learned about texting and cells, we should've had a tracer put on his line before I made that call."

"But we've still got these little problems called 'probable cause' and 'a warrant.'"

Vail shook her head and looked off at the countryside, which had once again transformed into the Napa Valley she had come to know: plots of well-tended vineyards merging with rolling hills and mountains in the distance. Wineries on both sides of the road.

Vail's phone buzzed again. "Ian Wirth. Returning my call."

"Maybe we'll get some answers about Herndon."

Vail brought the handset to her ear. "Ian, this is Karen Vail. We . . . yes, we saw the news. And yes, that's the guy. So you can rest a little easier now. But what I called you about was information . . . No, a related case. Are you available to meet for a bit?" Vail rotated the phone away from her mouth and faced Dixon. "Taylor's? Know where it is?"

"Tell him we can be there in twenty-ish."

Vail relayed the info, thanked him, then hung up.

"Taylor's is a straight shot down 29, in St. Helena," Dixon said. "Owner renovated an old, dilapidated hamburger stand and started serving Ahi and halibut burgers. And, of course, for the health challenged, good old artery-clogging red meat and mouth-watering shakes."

"Sounds like a place I should visit before I leave town." *Which isn't that far off now.* The mere thought made her curl her fingers into a fist. "Are we wasting our time with this, Roxx? I mean, I've gotta find Robby. And it's down to hours now."

"It's not down to hours, not while I'm on the case. I'll keep working it. Remember, I used to be a detective. I know how to do this shit."

Vail tried to smile, but the thought of leaving town before finding answers brought tears to her eyes. She turned toward the window and let her forehead rest against the glass.

14

Taylor's Automatic Refresher was as Dixon had described it. A half dozen red picnic tables were arranged in front of the hamburger joint, where a long line of customers stood staring at the menu or chatting among themselves.

Dixon parked and found Ian Wirth near the front of the line. They ordered, then grabbed a table.

Wirth set down his glass of iced tea. "So you found the killer. The guy who murdered Victoria Cameron, Isaac Jenkins—"

"John Mayfield," Vail said. "The Crush Killer. Now you see why we couldn't be straight with you about what was going on." Vail and Dixon had told Wirth the causes of death had been strokes, but Wirth's father had been a cop, so he was wise to their subterfuge. They admitted there was more to what was going on, and advised him to be careful.

"The victims' names haven't been released yet," Dixon said, "so keep that info to yourself till we can deal with the families."

"Of course." He tilted his head. "But you didn't ask me to lunch to talk about John Mayfield."

"No," Dixon said. "We need some information on setting up a winery."

Wirth glanced from Dixon to Vail. "You two thinking of going into business?"

Dixon laughed. "No. And I can't say any more because—"

"Because it's an ongoing investigation," Wirth said. "Why do I get the feeling this Crush Killer thing isn't quite over?"

Vail sighed. "You know we can't say any more. But as to Investigator Dixon's question . . . "

"Obviously I know a fair amount about it. What'd you want to know?"

Their food was ready: Ahi tuna burger, rare, with ginger wasabi mayo for Dixon; Wisconsin sourdough burger, with bacon, mushrooms, and cheddar for Vail; marinated grilled mahi mahi in corn tortillas for Wirth.

And a double rainbow chocolate shake for Vail. *Hell with the calories. I need the chocolate. No, I need Robby. The chocolate will have to do for now.*

Dixon lifted the bun and examined her burger, seemed pleased, and continued. "Ever hear of a start-up, Herndon Vineyards?"

Wirth held his tortilla with both hands. "No. Should I?"

"Not necessarily," Vail said. "But it would've made our jobs a little easier. So here's the deal. We want to find the owners of this start-up. They're supposedly due to release their first wine in a couple years. Wouldn't they have to file paperwork to get approval to operate a winery?"

"Your easiest call might be to the valley appellation organization, in this case the Napa Valley Vintners, who regularly announce new winery members. That's assuming that this new winery decided to join the organization. It's not mandatory. So if you hit a goose egg there, you have to go the more bureaucratic route. Operating a winery is regulated by the TTB, the Alcohol and Tobacco Tax and Trade Bureau. For some reason, it's part of the Treasury Department. As you can imagine, it's the government, so there's a ton of paperwork to fill out and regulations to follow." He leaned back a bit and looked at Vail. "No offense." Wirth bit into his tortilla.

"None taken."

"Herndon Vineyards," Wirth said, "would have to go through the federal application process."

Dixon brought a napkin to her lips. "Just a guess, here. But unlike the Napa Valley Vintners, the federal application part is mandatory."

Wirth grinned. "That'd be correct. And because of that, they'll know everything there is to know about the owners. But you'd also need the state's approval. ABC—Alcohol and Beverage Control. Heck, even if you just change or modify the name of your winery, you have to file new applications. You're not officially a winery until they approve your apps and say you are."

"When do you have to file the paperwork?" Vail asked, then sucked deeply on her shake. The dark chocolate high washed over her.

Wirth tilted his head in thought. "That's tricky to answer. The owners could purchase land and get everything drawn up and ready to go.

Architectural plans, engineering studies, and so on. But there's a gray area. I spoke to the TTB once and they told me I was supposed to have the applications in place before I purchased equipment. But I wasn't about to spend two hundred grand until I knew I had a viable and approved winery. So I called back, got someone different, and received a totally different answer. A colleague of mind said the same thing. Different people, different information."

Dixon sighed. "Nothing's ever simple, is it?"

Vail vacuumed out the last of her shake with a sucking sound. "Let's take one step at a time. See if we can get something from the Napa Valley Vintners. If not, Plan B is TTB. That fails, Plan C would be ABC."

Dixon smirked. "You trying to be funny?"

"I'm not in a laughing mood," Vail said.

Wirth lifted his napkin and wiped his hands. "Anything else I can answer for you?"

Vail rose. "If there is, we'll give you a call. Thanks for lunch. Mind if we run? We're up against a deadline here."

"Not at all." Wirth stood and shook both their hands. "Good luck."

As Vail headed back to the car, she thought, *A little good luck sure wouldn't hurt*.

15

He did not have long. For twenty minutes, he had been driving around searching for the perfect setting. If he was going to make the splash that he felt he deserved, which meant preventing the police from containing news of his kills, he had to place the body where it would be seen by the average passerby. After much thought, he settled on just the spot.

The body in the trunk would stiffen, that much he was sure of. It would make his task that much more difficult, if not impossible. How long until rigor mortis set in? He wasn't sure. Best to get there quickly, do his deed, and leave.

Zipping along Silverado Trail, he passed a string of wineries—Clos Du Val and Hagafen on the left, Luna on the right—before the road dead-ended at Trancas Street. He swung right and followed it over the Napa River, then approached the traffic light and hung a quick turn onto Soscol Avenue, barely beating the yellow.

But apparently the Napa police officer behind him observed otherwise.

He glanced at the flashing lights in his rearview mirror, then considered his options. He had a fresh corpse in his trunk, and he had murdered a cop—though he doubted they'd already found her body. It couldn't be about that, not yet.

Floor it? That was one option—try to evade capture. But if he acted normal and polite, there'd be no reason for the cop to search his vehicle. All he had done wrong, in the eyes of the law, was run a red light. Marginally, at that.

He turned right into the adjacent parking lot and brought the old Mercedes diesel to a stop. The cruiser pulled in behind him. He watched as the cop shoved the gear shift into park, then brought the radio to his mouth.

Good thing he hadn't driven the minivan. By now it could be listed as stolen—and besides, there was no place to hide a dead body.

He looked up. The cop was still chattering away on his radio. He tapped his fingers on the dash. Come on, get out and move this along. Ask for license and registration and send him on his way. Simple. Easy. He'd pay the fine without dispute. He had an important appointment to keep, before the body in his trunk went stiff.

He waited, took a few deep breaths to calm his escalating nerves, and watched as the cop finally—finally—got out of his car and headed toward his window. He rolled it down, stuck his head out, and grinned broadly.

"Morning, sir. Any idea what you did wrong back there?"

Absolutely, he did. Why play games? "I assume I didn't quite make it through that yellow in time."

"Correct. License and registration, please."

He handed them over. "Sorry, officer. Guess I wasn't paying attention. Won't happen again."

"Napa 2X1," the man said into his shoulder-clipped radio.

The dispatch operator responded: "2X1, go ahead."

The officer read the pertinent information into the handset. He received a response of no wants or warrants. "I'm going to give you a citation," the cop said. "Be more careful when you approach an intersection, and pay attention to those yellow lights. Yellow means slow . . . "

He smiled and nodded. Just a polite citizen with a dead body in his trunk who made an honest mistake and committed a moving violation. "Yes, sir. Will do, sir." He sat back and waited while the officer completed the ticket. Wiped a collection of sweat beads from his forehead.

The cop walked back to his vehicle and retrieved something, then stopped. He was staring at the trunk.

Oh, shit. What could he possibly see? A smear of blood? A sliver of pink material hanging out that got snagged by the lock?

He started running scenarios by in his mind. He could hit the cop hard and fast, then leave and make as many turns as possible. But his license plate had already been called in. That was a problem. Not to mention his unwilling passenger. "Assault" would instantly turn to "murder." No matter how he parsed it, there was no good excuse for a violently executed woman to be crammed into his trunk.

As he began to perspire profusely, the officer returned to the window.

Here it was. If the cop asked him to open the trunk, he would have to take his chances. Clobber him, then leave town.

"Here you go," the officer said. "Your left rear brake lens is cracked, but the light's working. Keep an eye on it. Water gets in, it'll short out."

"I'll get right on it."

The cop squinted and twisted his body to face him. "You all right, sir?"

He faked a hearty laugh. Too hearty? "Just hot, is all. I'm also late for an important appointment."

The officer eyed him a moment, then nodded and handed him the ticket. "Obey the speed limit. And watch the traffic signals."

"Yes sir. Thank you, sir." He watched in his rearview as the cop headed back toward his cruiser, then poked his head out the window. "Have a great day!"

He didn't know about the officer, but his own prospects for doing just that had improved immeasurably.

16

For Karen Vail, good luck was not on the horizon. Before they had gotten out of the parking lot, Dixon's phone buzzed. She hit the hands-free Bluetooth speaker and answered. It was Brix.

"You're not going to fucking believe this," he said.

"Uh-oh," Dixon said. "I'm not sure I like the sound of that."

"Trust me. You won't. There's a new vic."

Vail shot forward in her seat. "What?"

"Maybe the vic's from yesterday," Dixon said, "before we grabbed up Mayfield."

"My first thought, too," Brix said. "But no. According to first-on-scene, she's fresh."

Dixon looked over at Vail, who was staring out the windshield. Thinking . . . *what the fuck is going on? How could this be?*

"Sounds like the same MO," Brix said. "I mean, same ritual. Gotta be a copycat, right?"

I'll be the judge of that, thank you very much. Vail's phone buzzed. She absentmindedly pulled it from her belt and glanced at the display. "Is this the address?" she asked Brix.

"I had Mann text it to everyone."

Vail rotated her phone to face Dixon, who, after digesting the location, turned the car around and headed back down 29, toward downtown Napa.

Unfortunately, even Vail knew the address.

DIXON PULLED TO A HALT at a makeshift barrier created by haphazardly parked Sheriff's Department cruisers blocking Third Street. Deputies and Napa Police Department officers milled about. A news van sat skewed at the end of Brown Street, where it intersected with Third: at the Hall of Justice complex, where the courthouse and the Napa jail were located.

Dixon parked behind Brix's vehicle, and she and Vail made their way toward the clot of detectives surrounding a quad area nestled between three large gray buildings. As Vail picked her way through the crowd of law enforcement bodies, she caught sight of Matthew Aaron holding a digital SLR up to his face. The burst from his flash illuminated the area of interest: a black square water fountain that sat atop two concrete rectangles.

And seated on the lower step was a woman, posed in such a way to make it appear as if she was reclining against the stone, her right leg extended in casual repose. Except that a trail of diluted blood cascaded down from her hands. A set of handcuffs dangled from her left wrist and her head was canted back, hanging at an unnatural left-leaning kink. The water from the fountain was lightly spraying her head, which now featured stringy-wet brunet hair.

"Can someone shut that fountain down?" Dixon asked.

Brix pushed his way toward her. "Working on it. Called Public Works. They're en route."

Vail stepped closer, to within a couple feet of Matt Aaron. "Was she— is her trachea crushed?"

"Haven't gotten to that yet, but my money's on it."

"I'm not interested in betting," Vail said. "Just give me goddamn answers."

Aaron hardened his jaw, then said, "There's bruising over the trachea. It *looks* like it's been crushed. But until I can get my hands on her, I can't really answer your question." He pointed at the body. "That said, the toenail's missing. Right second toe. And her wrist has a transverse gash."

Emerging from the far end of the quad was Austin Mann and Burt Gordon. And a haggard Sheriff Stan Owens. Brix motioned them to an area near the twin flagpoles, a few feet from the jail building's facade. Owens remained at Aaron's side—something the forensic technician probably wasn't too pleased with, but would no doubt keep to himself.

The remainder of the task force gathered between the flag poles and stood there staring at one another until Brix spoke up. "Okay, what the fuck are we dealing with here?" He looked at Vail. "Karen—did we or did we not arrest the Crush Killer?"

Vail brushed a lock of red hair behind her ear. "John Mayfield's the Crush Killer. We didn't release any details of the murders to the press, so the only people who know what Mayfield did with the bodies would be Mayfield himself—which isn't possible because of the timing—or he had a partner. That wasn't evident at any of the crime scenes, so if I had to guess—and that's what I'm doing here—he was mentoring someone, teaching him how to kill. Someone with a similar personality. Narcissistic."

"James Cannon," Brix said. "Mayfield's bodybuilding buddy."

"That'd be the first place I'd look."

"Cannon's out of town," Dixon said.

"Says who? Cannon?" Vail turned to the others. "I called him a little while ago and left a voice mail, told him I was sorry for turning him away, that I wanted to grab lunch or dinner with him. He texted back and said he'd love to, but he's out of town."

"Which could be bullshit," Brix said.

Vail kicked at a dead branch by her feet. "If he's our guy, yeah, it'd be bullshit."

Gordon shifted his thick legs. "Do you think your call tipped him off?"

"Anything's possible," Vail said. "But if he's a narcissist, he probably wouldn't permit himself to think we're on to him so soon. He thinks he's smarter than us, and my message was a little suggestive of some sexual rendezvous, which would play right into his mind-set. I think we're okay." She thought a moment, then added: "If this body is fresh—and it looks like she is—then clearly, he's comfortable killing. And he's comfortable bringing the body to a public place."

"What do we know about the vic?" Austin Mann asked.

"Not a whole lot," Brix said. "We didn't want to disturb the scene till we got that water shut." Thirty feet away, as if on cue, the fountain stopped bubbling. Heads turned. Aaron moved toward the woman's body.

"We should have a few answers soon," Burt Gordon said.

"Why here?" Brix asked. "Why did he dump the body here?"

"He didn't just dump the body," Vail said. "He posed her. And he placed her facing the street. Posing is a very different behavior. The Crush Killer left his victims out in the open where they'd be found, for sure. But this woman wasn't just left in public. She was placed at the Hall of Justice, right in the front, posed. For all to see. You can't get much more insulting to law enforcement, much more 'in your face' than leaving her right on our doorstep. He's sending a message."

Mann shifted his gaze beyond Vail to the area around the fountain. "And that message would be?"

"That he's better than us, smarter than us. That he can kill this woman right in front of the Hall of Justice and get away with it. That he's above the law, that we can't stop him. That he's in control."

"You talked to this James Cannon," Gordon said. "Based on what you saw, is he capable of doing that?" He gestured with his chin toward the victim. "I mean, is it possible?"

Vail and Dixon shared a look.

Dixon answered. "Yeah, I think so. His demeanor when Karen rejected him. He took it personally, almost as if he was so far superior to any other man—how could she reject him?" She held up a hand. "Now, that's looking at it in hindsight, maybe with a slightly skewed view. But you're asking if it's possible. I think it is."

"I agree," Vail said. "But it could also be more complex. By doing the kill this way, he could be saying, 'I'm my own guy. I'm my own killer. So I'm going to do things differently.'"

Mann said, "Differently meaning the posing, the location of the victim."

"Yeah."

"What about the handcuffs?" Mann asked. "Gotta be some meaning behind that."

"For sure. It's part of the message. He left her at a police station."

"Nothing deeper?" Dixon asked.

"Who can say at this point? Is it a taunt? That we're prisoners to his reign of terror? Yeah, okay. At this point, it's just a guess." Vail pulled her Glock, stepped forward, and carefully lifted the cuffs with the tip of the barrel.

"What are you doing?" Gordon asked.

"All cuffs have serial numbers, manufacturers and model numbers, right?" Vail leaned in close. "Serial number should be just below the key post. Four-five-three-five-one-one."

Brix typed the numbers into his phone.

"Model number's a seven hundred. Peerless."

Brix looked up. "Peerless. That's what we use. The Sheriff's Department."

"That's what most law enforcement agencies use," Mann said.

"You can buy a set on Amazon for thirty bucks," said Aaron, who'd moved beside Vail to look at the cuffs. "I wouldn't make too big a deal out of it. Security guards use 'em, too."

Vail frowned. "Track the serial number. You keep records at the department, right? Who gets which set of cuffs?"

"Yeah," Brix said. "I can check it against the database, see who they belong to. If it's one of ours. But we gotta do it manually. It's not computerized. We can also ask around, see if anyone's lost a pair."

"Keep it low-key," Dixon said. "In case."

"In case the killer's a cop?" Gordon asked.

Dixon rocked back on her heels a bit. "I'm just saying. Let's be smart about this. In case it is, yeah. I doubt it, but you can't unring a bell."

"I don't mean to be all doom and gloom," Mann said. "But could these be Robby's? Did he bring a set with him?"

"On vacation?" Vail asked. She shrugged. "No idea. I didn't see any. But I just don't know."

"Before we go down that path," Brix said, "let's first see if the serial number matches any used by LEOs in the area. If you really think it's possible, call Robby's PD and see if they keep records on which detectives get which cuffs. Or, we can check with Peerless and see if they know which organization or retailer they shipped that set to."

"Good luck with that," Mann said under his breath.

"Let's also get an ID on the vic. Find out the usual stuff. Who she is, who'd want her dead. Who had access to this quad." Brix swiveled his body and looked around. "Which is pretty much anybody. Security cameras?"

"I'll look into it," Gordon said. "I doubt they're aimed at the street. That fountain is damn close to the sidewalk. The cameras, if there are any, would be turned in toward the building. I think this guy knew what he was doing."

"But," Dixon said, "how do you kill a woman out in the open, during the day, in a public area, and have no one see it?"

Vail shook her head. "You kill her offsite. Crush her trachea, if that's what he did, then bring her here. Get her out of your van in such a way that it looks like you're walking arm in arm. If it is Cannon, he's easily strong enough to support her weight and carry her alongside him for fifty to a hundred feet. He sets her down beside him at the fountain, makes two quick slits to her wrists, and then he walks away and melts into the street and cars. The blood drains slowly due to gravity. Some washes away in the fountain." She examined everyone's face. "It can be done."

Dixon rubbed both hands across her eyes. "All right. So where are we?"

"We ran Mayfield's home phone LUDs," Brix said, referring to the local usage detail printout of calls made and received. "And we got a log of his mobile calls. His cell was one provided by his employer and only had work-related calls to and from the county mosquito and pest control abatement division. And a few to wineries and public buildings. We cross-checked, and they all corresponded to jobs he had—places where he sprayed and whatever the hell else he did with his time when he wasn't killing people."

Vail's attention was split between Brix and what Matt Aaron was doing with the victim's body. "And his home phone?"

"Nothing popped out at us. We were still sifting through it when this call came in. We're going further and further back in case he wasn't as careful early on."

"Any calls to James Cannon?"

Brix pulled his phone and began pressing buttons. "We've still got some unidentified numbers to track down, a few unlisteds. We should have an answer soon on that. And we should've also heard back from NSIB on whether they got a home address from the wireless carrier. I'm gonna see if I can scare them up right now."

"We spoke with Ian Wirth," Dixon said. "He gave us a rundown on the application process for starting a winery."

"My brother texted me on the way over here minutes ago. He's done with his meeting and should be calling me soon. Get anything from Wirth?"

Dixon filled them in on what she and Vail had learned.

"After I follow up with NSIB," Brix said, "I'll get someone started on calling the TTB and ABC ASAP, just in case the vintners organization is a dead end. If my brother gets us anything we don't already know, I'll give you a shout." He pressed SEND on his phone.

Vail's BlackBerry vibrated: a Virginia number, one she recognized as Detective Paul Bledsoe's. "I've gotta take this," she said, then moved off toward the Hall of Justice entrance, beneath the address sign that read "1125" in large silver decals.

"Hey," Bledsoe said. "I just wanted to check in with you. You get anywhere?"

"Treading water. You?"

"I got Hernandez's DNA sample over to the FBI lab and I've also got a sample coming your way, to the Sheriff's Department."

"Very good, thanks. And—you think you can keep your guy on Jonathan till I get home? I—this Mayfield thing may not be over. And it could be related to Robby's disappearance."

Bledsoe hesitated. "I think I can swing it. But are you sure? You think Mayfield had an accomplice?"

"Or a 'student.' I'm not sure, but it's possible. And until we can rule it out, and until we find out what happened to Robby, I can't take the chance it's personal."

"I'm working on something on my end," Bledsoe said. "A guy I know, someone who owes me."

In the background, Dixon continued her conversation with Gordon and Mann. Vail plugged her left ear to mute their discussion. "Who is this guy and what do you think he's going to be able to do for us?"

"Name's Hector DeSantos. I met him on another case a couple years ago; this guy's involved with a bunch of people who've got access to information no one else has. I think he's some kind of spook. But if there's info tucked away somewhere in a police or hospital database that can give us a clue as to Robby's whereabouts, DeSantos will be able to find it."

"Awfully nice of him to help us out."

"I haven't asked him yet," Bledsoe said. "But he owes me, and if he's stateside, I think we're good. I'll see if I can set something up for when you get back."

"I'm on a flight tonight—actually, I guess it's tomorrow morning. Anything changes, I'll let you know. And Bledsoe . . . thanks again. For everything." She hung up and rejoined the group.

Brix said, "Wireless carrier had the same Soscol address. They emailed his bills, which were paid by direct debit to his credit card. NSIB's now trying to get the address from the credit card company."

"Without a warrant?" Gordon asked.

A forensic technician handed Brix a bag containing the handcuffs. "Maybe we'll get lucky," Brix said. "Be surprised what customer service reps will tell you."

"It's not against the law to ask for information," Dixon said. "It's not even illegal to lie about who you are—as long as you don't say you're James Cannon."

"We'll see what we can get," Brix said.

Dixon took Vail's elbow and led her toward the street. "That call. Good news or bad?"

"My friend, Bledsoe. He wants me to meet with someone back home who might be able to dig up info on Robby."

Dixon unlocked her car doors with the remote. "Take any help we can get."

"Where we headed?" Vail asked.

"Mayfield's place. That's one warrant we didn't have a problem getting."

17

Vail and Dixon arrived at John Mayfield's house, a small Victorian-style two-story with a compact footprint on a postage stamp lot. The grounds were immaculately cared for, and the shingle siding seemed to be the recipient of a recent coat of brick red paint.

Parked out front, neighborhood cars. A large hockey net with a noticeable rip in the polyester mesh, shoved up against the curb.

Vail and Dixon were the first to arrive. They walked up to the front door, tried the knob, and found it locked. "Kick it, pick it, or call for a battering ram," Vail said.

Dixon slid sideways and slammed her left foot against the jamb, just below the lock. It burst open with a splintering pop. "Much more satisfying that way."

"Can't argue with that."

They moved inside the quiet house. Whenever Vail entered an offender's residence, a strange feeling washed over her. All the evil this killer conjured was conceived here. Like the behaviors the killer left at his crime scenes, his home was a diary of sorts: unedited, the raw idiosyncrasies and habits of human nature lay bare before her. The way he folds his towels, his laundry, his clothing. Are his shirts on hangers in closets? Neatly arranged on shelves? Are there dishes in the sink? Does he hoard newspapers, magazines, odd trinkets?

Everything she saw before her was like words in a novel; each room a chapter. Overall, that book told an important story about this offender. Who he was, at the core of his daily existence, unfiltered. Because he never expected to get caught, he had no reason to hide who he was.

And Vail was not disappointed. She had anticipated a neat, orderly living environment. Possessions well cared for. Trophies and framed certificates of his accomplishments. And nothing to suggest anyone else was responsible for, or had contributed to, his achievements.

After walking through the living room—dominated by an intricately carved walnut table with matching formal chairs—she moved into the hall and then the family room.

Dixon called out to her from the den. On a couch in the corner was a box containing an unopened pay-as-you-go phone. "No surprise there. I'm sure the one he'd been using is here somewhere, if he didn't already dump it before we grabbed him up."

"Even better," Vail said, heading toward a desk along the far wall. "His PC."

Dixon joined her by the window, which looked out at the mountains.

"Does the Sheriff's Department have a cyber crime division that can go through the hard drive?"

"Yeah, but I don't know if it's as good as what you've got at the Bureau. You want to wait, or do you want to see if there's anything on here about Robby?"

All questions should be that easy. Vail turned on the monitor and flicked the keyboard. The computer fan whirled to life and the screen read, "Windows is resuming." She looked over at Dixon. "It was on standby."

"How'd you know?"

"Narcissists tend to leave their computers asleep so they can get right to work when inspiration stirs them."

Dixon squinted. "Really?"

"No," Vail said. "I just made that up."

Dixon suppressed a smile, then nodded at the desktop, which had loaded.

"But narcissists think they're immune to the consequences of their own actions, functioning on almost a delusional sense of omnipotence."

"Meaning?"

"Meaning," Vail said, "I didn't think his PC would be password protected. He never expected to be outsmarted. To be caught." She sat down and moved aside a bottle of half-drunk Cakebread Cabernet. Moused over to the Computer icon and opened Windows Explorer. The familiar file tree appeared and she scrolled to Documents.

"You think there'll be anything incriminating on here?"

Vail leaned closer to the screen. "Count on it. Because he didn't expect us to catch him, there's no need to take safeguards or use deceptive
techniques to protect his information from the police. Besides, if it got
to the point where the cops were doing what we're doing and poking
around his house and computer, he'd be in deep shit. In which case he
wouldn't care what we found."

Vail used the document preview feature in Explorer to quickly scan
the files without opening them. She pointed at the screen. "Here's the ad
he sent to the *Press*." Then she remembered reading something in an
FBI forensics bulletin. "COFEE."

Dixon looked at her. "Now?"

"No, no, not the drink. COFEE's an acronym for a forensic tool
Microsoft developed for cops, so they can copy evidence off a computer
before it's turned off and moved to the lab. Once a computer's shut
down, this kind of data vanishes."

"You have any idea how to use it?"

"It's just a thumb drive. You plug it in and a few minutes later, it's captured all the data. Aaron's on his way over; he can do it and send it to the
FBI's cyber crime unit." She gestured at the PC. "Who knows what's on
here? What websites he's visited, who he's been communicating with.
From what I remember reading, some of that stuff is stored in temporary files. We don't want to lose it."

"Fine. I'll make sure he has this COFEE thing with him." Dixon
pulled her phone, walked outside, and called Matt Aaron while Vail continued to poke around John Mayfield's files.

Dixon returned a minute later. "He'll be here in a few minutes. But
he doesn't have that COFEE device. He knows about it, but he never
got one."

"You're shitting me. They're free."

"He said to leave the PC on. He's gonna make a call and see if he can
have one overnighted." Dixon pointed at the screen. "Check his email.
He use Outlook or web-based email?"

Vail looked down at the taskbar and saw the Outlook shortcut.
Clicked and watched as the logo splashed across the screen while the
software loaded. It immediately began downloading Mayfield's mail.
While it negotiated with the incoming server, Vail went to the Sent items
folder, where she found a couple of the messages he had sent them. Seeing them again, and sitting at the keyboard he used to send them, sent a
shudder through her shoulders.

"You okay?" Dixon asked.

"Now *there's* a loaded question if there ever was one." Vail chuckled. "Believe me, you don't want an honest answer." She clicked on the Start button, then typed "Napa Crush Killer" in the search field. It was the title of the first PowerPoint slide in the gruesome document Mayfield had sent the task force. A few seconds later, a series of results appeared. The one she was interested in—the PowerPoint document—was at the top of the list. Having received what was, in her mind, the ultimate confirmation, Vail rose from her chair and said, "I've seen enough. The techs can do the rest."

They walked through the house, pausing long enough in each room for Vail to take it all in, the contents, their layout, and orientation. Last stop: the two-car garage. The first thing Vail noted when she pulled open the door was a potpourri of grease, oil, and gasoline odors hanging on the stale air.

Dominating the occupied bay was an older, highly polished Audi. She knelt down to examine the immaculately swept gray floor, which featured painted lines indicating where the car was to be parked. And the wheels were lined up exactly where they were supposed to be. "Interesting."

Vail rose from her crouch. Against the far wall, across the empty parking slot, stood a six-foot-tall red Craftsman tool chest, the compartments all neatly closed. She walked over beside Dixon, who was pulling open each of the drawers. An assortment of tools and hardware stared back at them. Nothing suspicious or helpful.

In the empty car bay, atop a generous workout pad, was a barbell set and bench, cradled in V-brackets. A Platypus water bottle lay on the floor beside the weight stack. Vail stood there staring at the awkwardly shaped plastic container. "I've seen that recently."

"The water bottle?"

Vail nodded. "Yeah."

"Okay. So what?"

Vail hiked a shoulder. "So nothing." She gave a final swing around the garage.

Car doors slammed on the other side of the roll-up door. Vail pressed the wall-mounted opener and the sectional crept upward with silent precision. Standing there was CSI Matt Aaron, booties on his feet and tool kit in hand, with Brix and Owens bringing up the rear.

"Glad to see you two were totally fine with contaminating my crime scene."

"We've still got someone out there who could be in distress," Dixon said. "Waiting around didn't seem to be in his best interests. Not with another killer out there, who could be related to Mayfield in some way."

"We'll have that COFEE device tomorrow morning," Aaron said. "We can post an officer outside the house to make sure no one touches the PC before it gets here." He set down his kit against the wall. "Find anything that'll help you locate your missing guy?"

"No," Vail said. "Doesn't look like it."

"Shame."

"You know what," Vail said, advancing on him, before Dixon grabbed her arm with an iron grip.

"Let it go," Dixon said. "We've got more important things to deal with."

Vail shook off Dixon's hand, then spun and headed past Brix, out of the garage. *No, we didn't find anything that'll help us find our missing guy.* She craned her neck skyward. A passing cumulus cloud stared at her as it blew by. *I leave in a matter of hours and we're no closer to finding Robby than we were before.*

Vail leaned her back against the Ford's door and faced the house.

That's when she saw it.

A leather jacket. She pushed off the car and walked forward, eyes focused on the coat. It hung on a hook on the wall behind the Audi, innocently draped across a wood hanger. She stopped in front of it and stared at it. A shiver ran the length of her spine.

"Roxx," she called out, unevenly. "I may've just found Robby's jacket."

18

Dixon and Matt Aaron joined Vail a moment later.

"This?" Aaron asked, nodding at the lone coat hanging from the hook.

"No," Vail said, "the *other* jacket."

Aaron set his jaw and gave Vail an icy stare. The two had established a relationship as smooth as grit-studded sandpaper, and it was apparently destined to remain that way.

Aaron broke the standoff by retrieving his fingerprint kit, then applying dust.

"Full workup," Dixon said. "DNA, too. We've got a sample of Detective Hernandez's DNA en route." She waited a second for Aaron to reply, got nothing, and continued. "Give me a buzz as soon as you know something. Most important thing is, does this jacket belong to him, or not?"

Aaron dropped his hands to his sides and turned to Dixon. "I'm plugged into what's going on, Ms. Dixon." He moved his fingerprint brush back to the jacket. "You can go. I'll let you know what I find."

"You got a TOD on the Hall of Justice vic?"

Without looking at Dixon, he said, "Prelim estimate is approximately 1:00 PM. Give or take an hour."

Dixon turned away from Aaron. "If she was dropped there, that means she was killed before he arrived at the Hall of Justice complex, right?"

Vail folded her arms across her chest. "Right."

"So let's say she was there for what, ten minutes before someone saw her and reported it? Fifteen?"

"Okay, sure."

"That means if we're thinking she was killed between noon and

1:00, and we discovered her at 1:20, she was probably killed about thirty minutes from downtown Napa."

Vail nodded slowly. "You're establishing the radius of the UNSUB's kill zone."

Dixon shrugged. "Makes sense. We could map it out and see if we can focus our efforts. But give or take thirty minutes in any direction is a lot of real estate."

"Not as much as not having the radius."

"True," Dixon said.

Brix burst through the door leading into the garage from the house, holding up his cell phone. "Roxx—TTB came through. We got a twenty on Herndon Vineyards."

19

The needle on Dixon's speedometer zipped past 65—in a 50 zone. After Vail had stuck the light cube atop the car, they were silent, intent on what they might find—and what they would ask if, and when, they found James Cannon.

Leaving Owens at Mayfield's house, Brix was following behind them in his own vehicle. As they zigged around slower-moving tourists, Dixon took a call from Gordon and Mann. NSIB had secured Cannon's current home address—and four investigators were en route to meet Gordon and Mann as backup.

Before they hit the frenzy of their pending arrival at Herndon, Vail's thoughts turned to what they had found at Mayfield's place. "The jacket, Robby bought it a few days ago."

Dixon slowed behind a limousine. "You sure it's his?"

Vail worked it through her mind. Closed her eyes and tried to remember him walking into Bistro Jeanty, the restaurant where they'd eaten only a couple nights ago. "Yes." She shook her head. "No." She sighed. "He bought a jacket just like it when he went to the outlets to buy us new clothing after the fire. I only really saw it once. And Robby and Mayfield could be about the same size." She bent her head forward and massaged her temples. "I don't know."

"Hopefully Aaron will be—"

Vail snapped her fingers and sat up straight. "Wait a minute. That funky water bottle. The one in the garage. The Platypus. I'd seen it recently but couldn't remember where." She turned to Dixon. "At the gym. Fit1. Cannon had it when we were there working out. What's it doing in Mayfield's garage?"

Dixon zipped around the limousine and moved back into her lane. "They're big and hold a lot of water. Mayfield and Cannon were friends, they worked out together, maybe they both had one."

"But Mayfield *didn't* have one. At least not both times we saw him at the gym. What if the one at Mayfield's house is Cannon's, and they're more than just workout partners. They're killing partners. Or mentor/mentee."

"Whoa. No offense, Karen, but you're grasping—"

"At straws. Yeah. I'm scooping up the whole pile. I'm desperate."

"I think we're close to getting some answers. We'll be there in a few minutes."

Vail started bouncing her knee. "A few minutes" wasn't soon enough.

20

Herndon Vineyards was located in the hills above St. Helena, in the Spring Mountain district. Tucked away off a winding, ascending road that rose two thousand feet above the valley floor, the area was known for its rich volcanic soils that made it particularly favorable for producing exceptional Cabernet Sauvignon.

Dixon stopped the car a dozen feet before a metal security gate fitted with an electronic keypad-speaker device. Brix pulled in behind them. He raised them on the radio.

"I don't think a straightforward approach would be a good idea," Brix said.

"Agreed," Dixon said. "Let's go in as inspectors with TTB, to do a routine check of the facility. You should take the lead. If Cannon's in there, he's seen us; he knows who we are."

"Copy that. Pull back."

Dixon moved her car aside and parked; then she and Vail got into Brix's Crown Victoria. Brix maneuvered beside the intercom and pressed the button, then explained the purpose of the visit. There was some hesitation, followed by a "Let me check" comment.

"And we'll need to speak briefly with your wine maker. Is he in?"

Another pause. Then, "Yes. He's here today." The metal gate swung inward.

"You want me to go in, scout the place, feel out the owners?" Brix asked as he drove down the eucalyptus tree–lined, hard-packed gravel road that curved gently up a steady incline. Young, well-tended grapevines rose and fell on the rolling land.

"No," Vail said without hesitation. "We go in strong. Roxx and I know what the guy looks like. I say one of us hangs back. That should be you, Roxx, since you're the most mobile of the two of us. Brix, you should fast-badge them and ask a lot of wine-related questions TTB inspectors might ask, to keep them off balance. I'll stay right outside until I can be sure Cannon's not there—or until you've engaged him."

Vail swung her head in all directions to take in the landscape. Atop the mountainous countryside, redwoods in the distance framed the symmetrically planted vines that undulated with the terrain. *It's gorgeous around here.* She turned back. "Looks like there's only one road in or out. If he goes on foot, it'd have to be through the vineyards. Easy to see a huge guy running through small grapevines. Good?"

Dixon seemed to be mulling Vail's comment.

Brix slowed the car to 5 miles per hour as he approached the building. "How sure are you that Cannon's affiliated with Mayfield? As a killing partner or a mentee or anything like that?"

"We're not," Dixon said. "I'd call it an educated hunch."

"An 'educated hunch,'" Brix repeated. "That's a new one on me."

Vail crept forward in her seat to get a look at the building as Brix swung left into a parking spot. "I'm pretty damn sure Cannon is wrapped up in this."

Brix slipped the gear shift lever into park, then shook his head. "That's great. I'm glad we're in full agreement here."

He slipped the keys above the driver's visor, then grabbed his phone, which was vibrating. "It's Gordon." He turned on his Bluetooth device. "Go ahead, Burt. Got you on speaker."

"We're at Cannon's. Nobody's here. We were able to grab a look through the kitchen window. Dishes in the sink, that's about it. But a quick canvass of the property brought us to a shed he had out back. We found blood, so we went in."

"Blood? How much?" Brix asked.

"Enough," Mann said.

Vail gritted her teeth and closed her eyes.

"But here's the thing," he said. "There's a few matted-down fibers stuck around the edges of the puddle. One of the NSIB guys here's a hunter. Says it looks like it's from a deer."

Vail grabbed the seatback and pulled herself forward. "A deer? You think a deer was killed in that shed?"

"Looks that way. Fairly recently. Within days, would be my guess. But we'll know more once we get a CSI out here. I made the call. He's a half hour out. The guys just cleared the house. We're gonna go through it now."

Brix said, "Keep us posted," then ended the call.

"That would fit the profile," Vail said. "If he was learning from Mayfield, he decided it was time to try one himself. Started with an animal to
prove he could actually kill something, to see how it felt. I wouldn't be
surprised if he started with something smaller, like a squirrel or a dog,
but that deer could've been his first."

"Hopefully he's here and we can find out once and for all what the
deal is." Brix unholstered his SIG, checked it, then shoved it back into its
leather pancake. "Roxx?"

Dixon patted her side, where her sidearm was affixed. "Yeah. Go in
with Karen. I'll keep watch. He shows his face, he won't get far."

Leaving Dixon positioned thirty yards back of the front entrance, giving her a view of the entire facility, Brix and Vail headed across newly
laid sandstone tiles, toward oak barrel plank wood doors.

The building was a recently constructed stone structure—sporting
workmanship that took substantial time, and money, to complete. Inside,
boxes were stacked high atop one another. Carpenters were huddled
around half-built bare wood counters. Sawdust coated every surface, and
floated freely in the air. The whine of a drill rose and fell.

Looking though the front window, Vail took in as much as she could, as
rapidly as she could. How many people were there, and where. Her right
hand hovered near her holster, poised for quick access to her Glock 23.

"I don't see Cannon."

"Me either," Brix said. "I'll go in, let you know." He pulled open the
wood door and entered.

Vail watched as he surveyed the interior, tapped a worker on the
shoulder, and exchanged a few words. He then faced the window and
motioned Vail inside.

As she entered, a man with rolled-up sleeves walked into the lobby,
holding blueprints. A pencil was tucked between his lips.

"Excuse me," Brix said. "We need to talk with someone in charge."
He flashed his badge, then slipped it back into his pocket.

The man studied Brix's face, then Vail's. He pulled the pencil from
his mouth and stuck it behind his ear. "I'm one of the managing partners.
Cap. Cap Krandle."

Vail said, "We've got some questions about the TTB application you
submitted. Is your wine maker here?"

"Should be in the back. Haven't seen him in a while."

Vail's gaze continued to roam the shadowed crevices of the room.
"We're going to need to know how long 'a while' is."

"I don't know. He was out in the vineyard this morning—"

"Did he tell you he was out in the vineyard," Brix asked, "or did you observe that?"

The man tucked his chin back. "Is there a problem?"

Vail rested her hands on her hips. "Would we be here asking these questions if there wasn't 'a problem'?"

Krandle chewed on that a moment. Then he glanced over his shoulder, turned back to Brix and Vail and said, "He told me. I got here, I was busy with the guys here, working with the carpenters to make sure we had the day's work laid out before us. We're expecting a delivery and they need to make sure things are cleared out of the loading dock before the truck comes." He shrugged. "I went back down into the barrel room and he was there. He told me he'd been out in the vineyards all morning."

Brix and Vail stared at each other. Their faces were firm, but they each knew the impact of the man's statement.

"Anyone else here who might've seen Mr. Cannon?"

Krandle scanned both their faces. "*Cannon*. Jimmy Cannon?"

Vail tilted her head. "Yeah. That's who we're talking about, right?"

"I thought you asked about our wine maker. Eugene Hannity."

"Hann—so what does James—Jimmy Cannon do here?"

"Jimmy's our inventory manager. He applied for the wine maker position, but he had no experience and we wanted someone who'd been there, done that." Krandle chuckled. "We told Jimmy, 'Maybe someday. Learn the trade, then maybe we'll talk. But that's years down the road.'"

The muscles in Brix's jaw shifted. "Then let's back up and start the fuck over. Where's James Cannon been all day?"

"No idea," Krandle said. "But I did see him about fifteen minutes ago."

"Where?" Vail asked, her fingers inching closer to the Glock's handle.

Krandle thumbed an area over his shoulder. Just then, the whites of two eyes appeared in the distant darkness. And then they vanished.

Vail saw them, threw her left hand back, and slapped Brix in the shoulder. And then she took off, shoving Cap Krandle into the wall and heading past him, down the hallway into the shadows. She yanked out the Glock, keeping her back against the rough stone of the corridor as she sidled into the darkness.

Brix was behind her, presumably with his SIG drawn.

They moved quickly through the sawdust-fogged air, toward a larger area lit by a single compact fluorescent bulb. They both cleared the room, eyes scanning the walls, looking for an exit.

DIXON STOOD IN THE COOL AIR, looking out at the mountains a few miles away, thinking how serene and scenic the landscape was up here.

She swiveled back toward the stone structure and blew some air out her lips. Was this a waste of time, or was James Cannon really a killer? The deer blood Gordon and Mann found may or may not be significant; Cannon could merely be a hunter.

Dixon thought back to the conversation at the gym. He was cocky and seemed to bully Mayfield—not what she would expect if Mayfield was Cannon's mentor. It came off as playful banter between two friends, but was there something going on beneath the surface? Or were they playacting?

As she mulled her previous exchange with Mayfield and Cannon, her phone vibrated. She pulled the handset from her pocket without taking her eyes off the building. "Yeah."

"Roxx."

Brix's voice.

"He might be on his way out toward you. Cannon isn't the wine maker, he's a wannabe. Currently the inventory manager. We didn't get a good look at him, but someone made us and took off."

"Got it." She snapped her phone closed and drew her SIG.

"ANYTHING?" VAIL WHISPERED.

Brix used hand signals to indicate he was moving toward the door. He wanted her to cover him.

Brix stepped to the side, grabbed the knob, and pulled it open. Vail was in a crouch, Glock out front in a Weaver stance. The area beyond the door was vacant. Brix motioned her through.

Vail slid forward, cautious yet determined not to let Cannon escape their grasp. At best, they had a scared employee who saw cops and, for whatever reason, didn't want to hang around to chat. At worst, they had a murderer in their sights, someone who might be able to provide clues about Robby.

Vail moved onward, through another room and down a different hall-way. She was beginning to think they were going to lose him. He knew the layout of the winery, much of which wasn't even finished, and there could be an exit they hadn't seen during their approach. Some downwind access, a loading dock or delivery port that would take him away from them without their ever seeing him.

She was about to turn to share her thoughts with Brix when her phone rang.

DIXON STOOD THERE with her SIG at the ready, clasped in both hands, knees slightly bent, forearms taut.

And that's when she saw him: James Cannon, the size and shape, the face. No doubt. They locked eyes—and his gaze dropped to her hands, where she was holding the chiseled metal pistol.

"Hold it right there, Jimmy," Dixon shouted.

But he didn't "hold it right there." He spun and ran.

21

He's headed—" Dixon craned her head skyward, but the sun wasn't far enough in one direction to estimate east or west. She glanced toward the mountains, estimated where Highway 29 sat, and pressed the handset back to her mouth. "West, I think. Down behind the building. Positive ID."

"As soon as we find our way out," Vail said, "we'll have your back."

Dixon shoved the phone in her pocket and increased her pace, headed around the sharply sloped left side of the building. She shifted the SIG to her left hand and stuck out her right, using it as a third leg against the hillside. Her feet slipped in the loosely tilled soil, but she maintained her balance.

Fifty feet ahead of her, Cannon was doing much the same, ambling as fast as he could. But was he running away from her or toward something?

A yell behind her—Vail's voice. Dixon dared not turn around or she might lose her balance and slide down the hill into the vines that lay less than ten feet away. Cannon was approaching level ground.

"Jimmy—" Dixon called. "We just want to talk! C'mon, man, why are you running?"

The dumb cop routine didn't work—Cannon kept moving. He climbed over a short wrought iron fence, more decorative than functional, and broke into a dead run. Dixon struggled with the soil, and the faster she tried to go, the more she slipped and slid.

Goddamn it, come on!

VAIL TOOK ONE LOOK at the sloped ground and knew she could not traverse it. She had undergone knee surgery two months ago, and had already stressed it more than was wise. Vail waved Brix by her and told him she'd circle around. But as she turned to head back toward the front of the sprawling, multilevel building, her eye caught sight of an ATV parked in the shadows of a utility garage built into the far end of the structure. It was a tier below them, and Cannon was headed toward it.

That's his endgame.

DIXON GRABBED a protruding root and yanked hard, using it to leverage herself up and over the fence. But as her feet hit the level ground, the rev of a rough outboard engine snagged her attention. She looked up to see James Cannon on a three wheel vehicle blowing out of an open garage. He twisted the throttle and the ATV burst forward, over the far edge of the hill.

And out of sight.

22

Vail reached Brix's Crown Victoria out of breath—not so much because of the run but due to the stress of the moment, piled atop the strain of the past week. So much on her mind, so much had gone wrong. So little had gone right.

And now a killer within her grasp, about to slip away—unless she prevented it. She yanked open the door. But she was out of sync. She stuck her right leg into the car just as the door hit the endpoint and swung back into her face. *Fuck!*

She pushed it open again, felt her bottom lip swelling, then grabbed the keys from atop the visor. Backed out and headed farther down the road, around the other side of the tasting room building. But the road stopped—dead-ended as they had originally thought it did.

For an ATV, however, roads were unnecessary. That was something they had not anticipated.

The Ford's engine was idling, her foot was shoved up against the brake—and she was filled with indecision. Forward? Or back, the way they came in? Which way would Cannon go? Toward the road? No—that'd make no sense. On the road, the cops had the advantage. Off road, the ATV was king.

Ahead were vines and beyond that, evergreens. Mountain. Uphill. Behind her, if Cannon was not headed for the road, he could go down through the vineyard and then into the forest. They wouldn't be able to follow and he had acres upon acres to roam.

She swung the car around, floored the pedal, and drove past the winery building, which flew by on her right. And then, as she surmised, in the distance, a plume of smoke billowing behind him, was James Cannon and his ATV.

Vail climbed out of the car and started on foot after Cannon. It was hopeless, really. She knew that. But to just stand there and watch as the killer who had posed the woman in front of the Hall of Justice got away was more than she could stomach at the moment. Cannon's mind game of leaving the vic on law enforcement's doorstep had worked: Vail's anger was close to boiling over into a red zone of danger.

She tore the Glock from her holster and headed into the vineyard.

23

Vail ran down an aisle, knowing the risks to her knee. Knowing it was something she had to do.

Behind her somewhere, Dixon and Brix were shouting.

She wasn't about to turn around—or stop. Now in the same vineyard row as Cannon, all she could see was the brown plume of smoke. She smelled the acrid gasoline fumes and tasted the dirt on her tongue. Her sweat-soaked face was coated with a fine film of soil.

Trying to keep the dust from infiltrating her lungs—already irritated from the fire a few days ago—she brought her left arm to her mouth and buried her nose and lips in the crook of her elbow.

And as James Cannon continued increasing the distance between them, the sheer futility of her efforts hit her full on. She slowed to a jog, then stopped, bent over at the waist, hands on her knees.

She looked up to see the cloud of brown dirt hooking into the dense blind of trees to her right. Just as she had suspected.

Vail straightened up, her eyes tracking Cannon's visible trail as she felt with her fingers to insert the Glock into its holster.

A moment later, she was joined by Dixon and Brix. She pointed toward the plume, somewhere in the distance, a location that was now only accurate in her imagination. She had no idea where James Cannon had gone. She just knew he wasn't lying at her feet, handcuffs encircling his wrists.

"Totally sucks," Dixon said.

"Saw it coming. Nothing I could do."

Brix stepped forward and peered out over the vines, into the forested land half a mile away. "I called it in. There weren't any choppers on alert. I think we just gotta face the fact he's gone."

"For now," Vail said. "Let's poke around his house, see what we can turn up."

Dixon sighed. "Somehow that doesn't seem . . . adequate."

Vail turned and headed back toward their car. "It's not." She spit a mouthful of grainy soil from her mouth. "Not even close."

CAP KRANDLE HAD CONTACTED Herndon's chief executive and asked him to pull James Cannon's employment application and hiring paperwork, which contained a home address that matched the one Gordon and Mann had obtained. If it had been as she suspected, that Cannon had not been looking to be a killer when he'd taken the job with Herndon, but had merely been someone capable of violence and had it unlocked through an association with Mayfield, then it made sense that he had not had the forethought to use subterfuge by listing false addresses and using disposable phones.

And if he was truly a narcissist like Vail believed, then Cannon probably felt he was smarter than everyone else and would be capable of eluding the grasp of law enforcement if the need ever arose.

Thus far, Vail had to admit, Cannon's plan—whatever it was, and though far from ideal—had kept him a free man. Just how long that lasted, however, was not something the guy should take to the track. If Vail had something to say about it, he'd end up being disappointed with the results.

Vail finished cleaning her face with the wet cloth Krandle had given her. "Something to keep in mind, Mr. Krandle. We've got reason to believe James Cannon is a violent individual. You'd be smart to avoid contacting him. And if he comes back here—which I sincerely doubt—play it cool. We didn't tell you anything and you don't know anything. But as soon as it's safe, call us. Better yet, text us so there's no chance of him overhearing you."

Brix handed him his card. "He calls, comes by, anything—let us know."

WHILE BRIX TENDED TO AN ERRAND, Vail and Dixon made their way to Cannon's house. Upon arriving, they saw three county vehicles parked out front at various angles, a haphazard job that suggested they arrived on scene in a hurry.

Through the front window, its blinds parted by the tip of a SIG Sauer handgun, Burt Gordon was motioning them in. He stepped back and the aluminum slats fell closed.

Vail led the way across the lawn, green and thick and robust—which did not surprise her. The medium gray house, set back and sandwiched between two equal size single-story homes, was located in what appeared to be a respectable middle class neighborhood.

Vail pushed the door open and entered ahead of Dixon. As expected, the interior was well-maintained and obsessively clean.

A series of reference texts on the art and science of enology lined the bookshelves of his family room. Dixon pulled one and thumbed through it. "He was clearly serious about being a wine maker."

"Lots of people have dreams," Vail said. "Just because he had books about the subject doesn't mean he would've been any good at it. But the point is, he didn't think there was much value in being an inventory control manager. It was a job he took because he couldn't secure the position he really wanted. To him, being a wine maker held the prestige he sought."

Dixon shoved the book back onto the shelf. "So he saw his job as a failure?"

Vail pressed on through the house. "That could've been a trigger. Frustrated in his ability to capture the position he really wanted, he saw the power and 'respect' Mayfield commanded by killing. He began to thirst for that power. Killing was a way for him to achieve that. Posing the body on the steps of the Hall of Justice put him front and center. Bang—he's got the power."

"PC?" Dixon asked.

They swiveled, did not see one, then split up and searched the two bedrooms.

"Got a laptop," Vail said. "It's unplugged." As Dixon joined her, she lifted the lid. The screen remained black. "Looks like it's off. Let's have Gordon and Mann bring it to the lab for the techies to comb through."

They moved into the living room. Bodybuilding magazines were stacked on the coffee table—and in the master bathroom, too. Empty MET-Rx canisters sat stacked atop the recycling bin in the garage, near an extra set of dumbbells and a weight bench perched in front of a mirror in the second, empty port. A half-filled Platypus water bottle stood on a chair by the far wall.

Mann appeared in the doorway to the garage. "Anything?"

"Got a laptop for you to take back to the lab." Vail then told him her developing theory on the trigger behind Cannon's suspected act of murder.

"We'll get a deputy posted here in case he returns," Mann said, "but I doubt he'll come anywhere near here."

"Where's that shed?" Dixon asked.

Mann led them out the backdoor into a medium-size yard. Through a stand of tall bushes and trees was an evergreen-painted structure that blended into the existing flora.

They stood inside, a ceiling mounted fluorescent fixture providing adequate light. Vail knelt and examined the dried, matted blood.

"The CSI took samples," Mann said, "so don't worry about messing it up."

"Did he agree—was it a deer?"

"He said that was a good guess, but you know those guys. They'd rather have facts than spend time debating possibilities."

They left the shed and stood in the yard.

"He knows we know," Dixon said. "We've set up roadblocks on all roads leading out of the valley, but he's on an ATV. He could be anywhere. Question is, how far can he get on that thing before he runs out of gas? And how far can he go before he hits a natural barrier he can't cross?"

"From what you described," Mann said, "sounds like he could get lost in those woods. Unless he's a survivalist, sooner or later he's gonna need food and water."

"There are plenty of houses to breach," Dixon said. "I say we go public, put the word out. Make everyone aware he's out there. We can circulate a photo. Go full blast."

Vail had to hold her tongue. If they had gone public a couple days ago with the Crush Killer's murders, John Mayfield might've been caught sooner. *And Robby might still be—*

She stopped herself. No sense in looking backward. It was time to move ahead, keep tending the path they had started clearing.

Dixon's phone buzzed. She lifted it, listened, and said, "Be right over. Have her wait—" Dixon's eyes rose from their focus on the ground and met Vail's. "Really. Okay, thanks."

"What?" Vail asked.

Dixon turned to Burt Gordon, who had just entered the yard. "Finish up here, then meet us back at the department."

"What's the deal?" Vail asked.

"Merilynn Lugo. That's where Brix went. She gave him a DVD for us."

24

Dixon and Vail burst through the second-floor doors of the Napa County Sheriff's Department and strode purposefully to the glass window. Dixon swiped her proximity card and the electronic locks clicked open.

They walked briskly down the hall to the task force conference room. Sitting on the table was a black DVD case with a Post-it note stuck on the front: "From Ray."

"I didn't say anything because it was a long shot and I didn't want to get your hopes up, but I made one last attempt with Merilynn. I took her on a little field trip to visit Mayfield in the hospital. He didn't look so threatening with all the tubes and beeping machines. I told her we'd submitted her WITSEC request and that we needed her to do something for us. Seemed like I was getting through, but I didn't want to push her. So I gave her a little time to think about it. Her place was on the way back from Herndon, so I stopped by."

"And she gave you a DVD?"

Brix scooped it up and handed it to Vail.

Vail pried open the lid and stared at the disc, which bore Ray Lugo's slanted handwriting. Did it hold some secret information that would give her clues as to what happened to Robby? Would it answer the question of what John Mayfield had meant when he taunted them with, "There's more to this than you know?"

"Karen," Dixon said softly, "We need to watch this."

Vail woke from her stupor. "Right." She plucked the disc from the plastic spindle, then placed the DVD in the laptop tray and watched as Windows Media Player loaded.

Brix, Dixon, Mann, and Vail stood around the computer. Vail felt Dixon shudder when the image of Lugo's living room filled the screen. Lugo then appeared and sat down on the couch. The angle of the camera and Lugo's proximity to the lens gave the impression it was filmed on a webcam.

He leaned in close, looked up at something off to his right, then turned back to the camera. "If you're watching this, something must've happened to me." He lowered his voice and his eyes danced from left to right, suddenly avoiding the lens.

"I . . . this is Sergeant Raymond Lugo of the St. Helena Police Department. Everything I'm about to tell you is the truth. If you're watching this . . . I have to assume you're law enforcement. I need you to . . . I need you to look after my wife and son. Please promise me that." He glanced up at the camera and then canted his eyes downward again.

He took a deep breath, covered his face with both hands, then dropped them to his lap and extended his neck. Staring at the ceiling.

"C'mon, Ray," Dixon said under her breath. "Get to it."

"In October, my wife, Merilynn, and my son, Mario, were kidnapped. I got a call. This guy said he had them, and he'd kill them unless I did what he wanted. He proved he had them. I—I had no choice."

Lugo looked away, licked his lips, kept his head down as he talked.

"He told me. If I tell anyone at work, he'd kill them. If I call in the FBI, he'd kill them. If I told the media . . . he'd kill them. And he said he had a way of finding out if I told anyone at work. He knew I was a cop. I couldn't . . . " He looked up at the camera. "I couldn't take a chance he was telling the truth."

His bottom lip quivered, and he bit down to arrest its twitch.

"He had them," Lugo finally said. "For two days. He called back and I, I made a deal with him. And he let them go. Left them by the side of the road in front of the fire station, near the Sheriff's Department.

"I looked at video, tried to figure out who this guy was. I spoke with Merilynn. And my son. Tried to get any information I could to find this fucker." He wiped at his face with both hands, sighed deeply, and sat back into the couch. He was far from the camera now, but his voice was still audible. "He told me not to look for him, that I'd never find him. And . . . and that no place was safe. If I did anything wrong—tried finding him, reporting it, he'd find Merilynn and Mario again. Only this time they wouldn't be coming home. He'd kill them. And it wouldn't be pleasant." His eyes narrowed in anger, then he sat forward, leaning closer to the lens in a way that distorted his facial features.

"I couldn't find anything, I got nowhere. But the deal I cut with him. I thought it might give me some clues as to who he was. I thought maybe there was some way I could track him based on the info he wanted me to get for him. Finally I found something. But he knew and he called me, warned me. The only warning I'd get, he said. Stop immediately or he'd kill them. And me."

Vail put her hands on her hips. "What the fuck were you doing for him, Ray?" she shouted, as if it would do some good. No one seemed to mind. They all wanted the same question answered.

"I thought that if I got that kind of a rise out of him, I must've been on to something. It had to do with a guy I knew, César Guevara."

Vail and Dixon eyed each other.

"The guy wanted info on César," Lugo continued, "from the police database. Not just ours, but the Sheriff's Department's, too. So I ran the stuff he wanted. Then I started looking into César's business. He runs a mobile bottling company out of American Canyon. I know César from when we were kids, working the vineyards. But the kidnapper is somehow tied in with him because he called me right after I went to see César and started asking questions. He said he didn't know what the hell I was talking about, that he didn't know a big white guy who drives a van. But that's all I had on the kidnapper. That's all Merilynn and my son could tell me. He spoke English like a native, no accent. And that was it.

"An hour after visiting César, the kidnapper called me. I knew I was on to something. What it was—I didn't know. But . . ." He turned away and said, "I was too afraid to look into it. He said he'd find us. Another state, another country, didn't matter. He'd track us down."

A noise behind him. Lugo twisted his torso. What looked like Merilynn in the background, entering the room. Lugo reached out his hand, splayed fingers covering the webcam, the screen darkening. Fumbling. Raised voices. Lugo's body leaned left, then the video cut off.

They waited a few seconds before Dixon blurted, "That's it? Please, tell me there's more."

They continued to stare at the screen, but the progress bar at the bottom struck the endpoint and then the video started from the beginning. Brix stuck out his index finger and clicked the mouse. Windows Media Player closed.

Vail looked up. Her eyes searched the conference room and came to rest on the clock. It was now almost 5:00 PM. *Damn it*. She grabbed her temples, took a deep breath, and coughed. Then she sat down heavily on a nearby chair.

Burt Gordon walked into the conference room. His eyes scanned the others in attendance and seemed to have no difficulty reading their body language. "Bad?"

"I'm not sure how to characterize it," Brix said.

"Bad sounds about right to me," Austin Mann said. He filled Gordon in on what he'd missed. "There's no good way to look at it. Question is, what did Ray know, and when?"

Dixon swung a chair from beneath the table and sat down. "You mean, did he know Mayfield was the guy who took his wife and son?"

"I think the question is *when* he knew it," Vail said. She slid forward in the chair and leaned back, letting her arms fall free over the chair's sides. "At some point he figured out that Mayfield was the kidnapper. And if I had to guess, I'd say it was before Roxx, Lugo, and I went to see Guevara."

Brix walked over to the white board and examined the timeline he had drawn for the prior week, which documented the major breaks in the Crush Killer case. "Maybe, maybe not. I mean, I wasn't there so I didn't see the looks Ray and Guevara were giving each other, but Guevara simply might've been pissed at Ray for bringing five-o onto his premises. May have nothing to do with Mayfield and the murders. Maybe he's cheating on his taxes. Whatever it is, good bet it's illegal— but it's not the answer to our problems."

"No," Vail said. "Hold up a minute. Ray thinks Guevara's involved in some way with the kidnapper—who turns out to be Mayfield—because right after Ray goes to Guevara and starts asking questions, the kidnapper flips out and goes off on Ray for not leaving 'it' alone. That's a pretty irrefutable connection."

"But we don't know what Ray asked Guevara. I guess we might assume it's got to do with him, with Mayfield." Dixon nodded at the laptop. "But Ray didn't say. Seems to me we've got lots of holes and only a few facts, and we're trying to fill in the holes with assumptions. That's a recipe for a failed investigation. At best."

"I agree," Mann said.

Vail held up her hands in surrender. "Fine. I'll give you that. But we can't ignore the connection. There's no obvious reason for Guevara to even know the kidnapper unless they were affiliated somehow. Guevara's involved in this. On some level."

"I got Guevara's LUDs and cell logs earlier this afternoon," Gordon said, moving to a stack of papers at the far end of the conference table.

"Haven't had a chance to go through them yet." He licked his index finger and thumbed through the pile. He stopped, glanced around the room, then snuck a pair of reading glasses from his shirt pocket. "Here." He yanked a sheaf of pages free and tossed the first aside.

"Just so you all know," Vail said. "I'm on a flight out of here in a few hours. I leave for SFO at 4:00 AM."

Brix ground his molars. As he looked at Vail, his stress and frustration were evident for all to see.

"My boss is gonna have agents from the San Francisco field office pick up the investigation."

Dixon shook her head in disapproval.

"Any chance I can get him to reconsider?" Brix asked.

"Beyond our control," Vail said. "I tried. But the unit's shorthanded and they caught a big case."

"Got something," Gordon said, his stubby finger poking at a spot on the phone logs. "Calls from Guevara to Ray. Ray's cell. Starting two days ago with a text message, followed by a three-minute call."

Vail gathered herself and rose slowly from her seat. She moved beside Gordon and looked over his shoulder. "That was after we'd met with Guevara, which makes sense. Guevara was pissed."

"At some point," Mann said, "Ray knew Mayfield was the kidnapper."

"He could've suspected it all along," Vail said, "but didn't get positive confirmation until yesterday. Maybe it was something in the interview. 'Cause that's when he pulled his gun and shot Mayfield."

Dixon shook her head. "He purposely left his backup piece in its holster when we all stowed our side arms in the lockers. So he either knew or strongly suspected."

"Or he needed us to find Mayfield so he could kill him. Payback," Vail said.

Dixon stood and began to pace. "Not payback. Security. He said he tried finding the kidnapper, but he couldn't. And when he did try, Mayfield was all over him, with more threats. He'd already proved he could operate at will, so Ray couldn't chance it. What if he had an accomplice? Friends on the outside who'd take care of business for him? When Ray put two and two together, and realized that his kidnapper was our serial killer, he knew the opportunity would come for him to get the guy out of his life—and keep his family safe—when we caught him."

"If we caught him," Gordon said.

"Well, we did catch him. And soon as we did, Ray shot him."

"We're missing an important point," Vail said. "We got a vital piece of information from Ray's video."

Brix kicked at the chair in front of him. "Really? Might as well share it with us, because I didn't fucking see anything that'll help us."

"Mayfield's in a coma and who knows when he'll come to or what he'll tell us. Ray's dead. Cannon's in the wind. But we've got someone who's tied into this somehow right in our backyard."

"Guevara," Dixon said.

Mann nodded slowly. "Guevara."

Vail glanced at the clock again. *Running out of time.* "Seems to me, makes more sense to lean on Guevara and see what he knows."

"So . . . what?" Brix asked. "Bring him in, sweat him?"

Dixon began pacing in front of the windowed wall. "A guy like that, we bring him in, I think he clams up at best and lawyers up at worst."

"Agreed." Vail thought a moment. "We get a warrant, we go to his place and start going through his rigs."

"His rigs," Gordon said. "Those mobile bottling trailers? What do you expect to find in there?"

"Nothing," Vail said. "But once we start putting our hands on his precision machinery, talk about tearing it apart to look for evidence, he'll flip out. It's his profit center. He may start talking just to make us stop."

Dixon flipped open her phone. "I'll start the wheels moving for getting a warrant."

"How long do you think?" Vail asked.

"I'll need someone to draw up the probable cause statement."

"Got it," Mann said. "Plenty of experience with that." He pulled a chair in front of the laptop.

"Redd," she said to Brix. "Get NSIB over to Ray's house. If Merilynn won't cooperate, get a warrant. Impound his computers, every goddamn thing you can find. Ray made a video; maybe he kept an insurance policy."

"Insurance policy. Like copies of records, phone calls, video, stuff like that? Wouldn't he have mentioned it in the DVD if he had?"

"Not necessarily. Looked to me like Merilynn interrupted him and he didn't finish it." She pointed at the laptop. "Wait a sec. Look at the DVD Ray made. The file, when was it created?"

Mann opened Windows Explorer, clicked, and scrolled. "The DVD was burned two months ago. As to when it was filmed . . . I don't know."

"Close enough," Dixon said. "My guess is he filmed it, then burned it to disc. No reason I can see to film it and leave it in the drawer. A lot of shit could've gone down in the past two months. But maybe things didn't heat up till we found Victoria Cameron in that cave. Mayfield's first vic." She turned to Vail. "Is it possible Ray knew Mayfield was the killer from day one?"

Vail played back the events of the past week in her mind. "I doubt it. But now that we know there was something going on between Ray and Guevara beginning at least two months ago, I don't think we can rule it out, Roxx."

"Goddamn him." Dixon looked at the screen, where the image of Ray Lugo had stared back at them moments ago. "Karen, with me. Let's go pay a visit to Guevara. You tried rattling his cage before. Maybe we need to try a different approach."

25

The sun's March burn melted behind the mountains like wax over a bottle of Madeira: beginning with a smoldering deformation, then accelerating as the heat built, spreading, losing definition, and enveloping all.

They arrived at Superior Mobile Bottling without a warrant in hand, and little time to kill. But kill it they must . . . because going in strong against a César Guevara without the ammunition to back it up had already failed. And at present, their best ammunition was not filled with gunpowder but with written words.

Dixon pulled the Ford Crown Victoria against the curb, down the street from Superior's facility in American Canyon, and shoved the gearshift into park.

"How long?"

Dixon glanced at the dashboard clock. "No way of knowing."

"Your judges?"

"Not always sympathetic."

"At least you got a look around last time we were here."

"I didn't have much time," Dixon said. "It was a quick once-over. We really need to tear the place apart."

Vail turned and looked at the fading light in the distance. The sky behind her was a purplish black, like a fading bruise on an otherwise pleasing landscape. Ahead, there was still a yellow hue, dissolving to dusky charcoal as the minutes ticked by.

"You okay?"

Dixon's question pulled Vail from her reverie. "I'm not going to see the sun in Napa again for . . . who knows how long."

"Did you ever see the sun in Napa?"

Vail chuckled.

Dixon's phone vibrated. She tapped the Bluetooth receiver. "Dixon."

"Roxx." It was Brix's voice. "You want the good news or the bad news first?"

"I'll take the good."

"Just spoke with Timmons from NSIB. He's taken over as point for us so we have a consistent contact, since it seems we're going to need them long-term. Or longer-term than we originally thought."

"Yeah, no shit."

"So Timmons says he's got a list compiled of all the potential locations where must is produced within earshot of the Napa Valley Wine Train whistle. There's a margin of error because it's not scientific or anything like that. But this is like a freaking needle in a haystack, anyway."

"How many potential sites are there?" Dixon asked.

"Sixty-plus. NSIB's got some guys looking into the whole list, just to see if there are any that can be eliminated based on some set of criteria Timmons and his team are developing. You want to be plugged into what they're thinking?"

"No, we've got enough to do. Let them do their jobs. Touch base with him from time to time, and if they sound like they've landed on the wrong planet, let me know and we'll meet with them, set them straight. Otherwise, let's see what they turn up." Dixon threw Vail a sideways glance. "Redd—I said I wanted the good news first."

"By comparison, that is the good news."

"I'm not sure we want to know," Vail said, "but what's the bad?"

"Search warrant was denied. Mirabelli rejected our argument. Said there was no direct connection between . . . well, between anything. Get him something that's more than just a series of coincidences and he'll reconsider. What we've got doesn't even rise to reasonable suspicion."

Dixon shook her head. "Well, that's just great."

"And for what it's worth," Brix said, "DOJ wasn't too excited about our WITSEC request for Merilynn."

Vail said, "We didn't give them anything particularly compelling, and that video Ray made didn't help her case any."

"One other thing. The Hall of Justice fountain vic has an ID. Kaitlin Zago. They're putting together a backgrounder on her but there doesn't appear to be any obvious connection to Mayfield's vics. And—the manual search through the handcuff database is taking longer than I'd hoped. I put a call into Peerless in case they can tell us who they sold that serial number to. But they're back east, so we probably won't hear from them till tomorrow. Where are you two?"

"Sitting a block away from Guevara's place. Waiting on the warrant that's not gonna come. We'll check in with you in a bit." Dixon reached up and disconnected the call, then leaned back hard in her seat. "Now what?"

Vail pointed ahead. "Let's go take a look around. See what we find."

Dixon did not hesitate. She kicked over the engine and proceeded down the street into Superior Mobile Bottling's parking lot. Standard sodium vapor lamps illuminated the area in front of the building where about a dozen spots sat empty. Except for a fluorescent fixture in the office, everything appeared dark.

Dixon stopped the car and craned her neck to look through the front glass door. "What do you think?"

"Go around back. Let's see if there are any cars in the lot or lights on in the warehouse."

Dixon pulled up to an iron gate that blocked their path approximately halfway along the right side of the structure. "Was this here last time?"

Vail sat back. "It was rolled all the way open." She popped her door, got out, and stepped up to the fence. Grabbed the upright wrought iron struts, peered into the back region of the property, didn't see anything.

She turned and headed back to the car. "Nothing. We got a location on his house?"

"I can get it." Dixon pulled her phone, made a call, and was soon jotting down the address. Twenty-five minutes later, they were pulling into the Sonoma neighborhood where César Guevara lived.

From what Vail could see in the complete darkness, it appeared to be an immaculately cared for community, with houses that almost looked out of place, possessing an eastern Victorian grandeur.

"Nice neighborhood," Vail said, straining to get a look at the passing homes.

"Oh, yeah," Dixon said. She held up her pad and caught the headlight of a trailing car. "Millions. Each one of these homes. Five mil, maybe more." Dixon glanced one more time at the address, then looked left at the house. "This is it."

"You said 'millions' and 'this is it.' Almost in the same sentence. César Guevara lives here?"

Dixon hiked her brow, then nodded. "Looks like mobile bottling is quite lucrative."

Vail grabbed the handle and pulled. "Quite."

Dixon and Vail walked down the cobblestone path, passed through a short white picket fence, and stepped up to the hand-carved hardwood door. Dixon stuck out her hand to knock, then pulled it back. "What are we doing?"

"We're about to see if this is Guevara's current address. And if it is, if he's home."

Dixon stepped back from the door, out of the porch light. "Let's sit on the house. Watch for a bit. See who comes and goes."

Vail glanced behind Dixon at the house. "I don't have a lot of time left, Roxx."

"We can't run an investigation based on what your schedule is."

Vail turned away and rested her hands on her hips. "I know. Let's at least talk to him, confront him with what we've got, see what gives."

"You've done that. Didn't work."

"We've got something now," Vail said. "We can bluff him."

"We don't even have enough to get a warrant. You've gone toe to toe with Guevara. Is he the type of guy who can be bullied or tricked?"

Vail sighed. *What does she want me to do? I'm leaving in a few hours and I'm nowhere on finding Robby. No leads. Except—maybe— Guevara.* "Probably not. But I need to try."

Dixon held up her hands. "Fine. I can't see it putting us in a worse position than we are now."

Vail frowned. "No shit." She quickly rapped on the door before Dixon could change her mind. Seconds passed, then the door swung open. Two men stood there, both wearing large-caliber pistols and making no effort to hide them. "Those legal?" Vail asked, nodding at their hardware.

"Who the fuck are you?" one of the men asked.

Vail held up her creds. "FBI. Who the fuck are you?"

"I got it." A voice in the background. César Guevara. The door swung farther open, revealing the man of the house. He was wearing a sport coat and a black silk shirt. Dressed to go out, perhaps. And in the distance, Vail could make out the tips of high heels. Smelled floral perfume. *Wife—or girlfriend. Definitely going out on the town. This may work out better than I thought.*

"Sorry to bother you on your way out," Vail said. "But we've got a couple questions."

"Come by my office. Tomorrow." Guevara started to close the door, but Vail stuck out her foot and the heavy wood hit against her shoe. Guevara turned back and eyed her with a narrow gaze. "What do you think you're doing?"

"We won't take much of your time—"

"I guess I should cooperate. At least you're not sticking your gun in my face this time. Very decent of you, Agent Vail. By the way, I've got that videotape all ready to go to your . . . what do you call it? Your behavioral analysis unit?"

Vail felt Dixon's gaze bearing down on her. *Ignore it. Guevara's trying to get under your skin. Block it out. Don't let him make you do something you'll regret.* Vail grinned, which helped diffuse her anger. "We just need a couple of minutes of your time." Plowing forward without pausing, she said, "Ray Lugo told us you two were more than just friends who worked the vineyards together as kids. He said he was helping you out. You and John Mayfield." Vail stopped, watched the creases in his face. There was decent illumination from the porch light, and some ambient brightness pouring in from the entryway. His face twitched, the eyelid fluttered, much in the same way it had this morning when she had questioned him and shown him Robby's photograph. "And that interests us, Mr. Guevara, because John Mayfield is a serial killer. He's done some bad things. And that means you . . . " She shrugged.

"I don't know what you're talking about," Guevara said. "And it's probably all bullshit anyway, because if it wasn't, we wouldn't be standing here chatting. You'd be sweating me out in some hot interrogation room. Isn't that what you people do? But then I'd call my lawyer, who charges seven hundred bills an hour, and, well . . . we both know how the game is played." He turned away from the door and called to one of his men, "Vaya a la limusina. Ahorita llego." *Go to the limousine. I'll be there in a minute.*

"A limo. Very nice." Vail let her eyes demonstrably roam the interior of his home. "Guess the mobile bottling business pays well."

"Good evening, Agent Vail. We're done here." He moved back from the door. And it slammed closed in their faces.

26

Vail pushed her head back into her severely reclined seat. They were parked a block and a half away, across the street in a neighbor's driveway. "That looks like a Hummer limo. What do you think?"

Dixon lifted her head and took a peek. "Yeah."

"You think his bodyguards are going with them?"

Dixon kept her eyes forward, watching the lights of the vehicle move away from them. "They wouldn't be very effective bodyguards if they didn't . . . guard him. Would they?"

"Good point." The lights faded and then disappeared. "Ready?"

"You sure you want to do this?"

Vail reached up and turned off the dome light. "Are you really asking me that question?" She opened the door and pulled herself off the reclined seat, then turned to Dixon. "Better move it onto the curb. In case the neighbor complains."

Dixon propped up her seat, started the car, and moved it. Then she joined Vail as they made their way toward César Guevara's house.

"Karen, I'm gonna say it again. Because you're not hearing me."

"I heard you the last three times. Breaking and entering. Not like I'm a goddamn dimwit. I know what I'm doing. You wanna save your ass, stay back. Go take a drive. Pick me up in twenty."

"You know I'm not going to do that."

"Then stop reminding me what we're doing is wrong. But I'm leaving, Roxx. And Robby could be in trouble. John Mayfield's in a coma. Lugo's dead. And the only person we know of who knows anything about anything is this asshole. And the goddamn judge won't give us a warrant. Do you think we've got a choice?"

"There are always choices, Karen."

Vail gave Dixon a hard look. But she kept moving, stepped over the low picket fence, and made her way to a dark side of the house, bordered by manzanita hedges. "If you're with me, watch my back. And if you see any security cameras, let me know."

"I didn't see any when we were talking to him."

"Me neither," Vail said, keeping her back against the bushes and shuffling forward. "Doesn't mean he hasn't got any."

"What about dogs? I didn't hear or see any, but—"

"They'd be on us by now." *Am I insane? What the hell am I doing? Robby would do the same for me. There's no choice.*

Vail moved to the back of the house and pointed at security lights mounted above the large ivy-covered arbor. "Motion sensors. Follow me." She made her way in a circuitous route that took them beyond the reach of the infrared lenses. Seconds later, they stepped up to the door without having tripped the sensors. "You don't happen to have a lock picking kit with you."

Dixon glared at her—a look Vail could make out as hostile even in the moonlight. "I don't even own one, Karen."

"Don't look at me that way. I don't own one, either." Vail examined the glass panels that made up half the wood door. She did not want to enter forcefully, but she didn't see a choice. She wrapped the bottom of her shirt around her right hand and tried the knob. Locked.

"You didn't think he'd leave his house unlocked, did you?"

"I learned a long time ago to check."

Dixon leaned back. "How many times have you done this?"

Vail looked over her shoulder to the left, then to the right. By landscape and architectural design, they were well blocked from any neighboring houses. With her hand still wrapped in her shirt, she thrust her fist forward, through the lowest glass square.

"Oh, Jesus," Dixon said. Her eyes canted up, then left, right, and back to the house. No movement inside. "Can't believe we're doing this," she whispered.

Vail stuck her left hand through the opening, unlocked the door, and pushed it open. Then she wiped the inside knob with her shirt. "Okay. We're in."

"And now what?"

"Now we look around. Fast. In case we tripped some kind of silent alarm."

Dixon closed her eyes. "Oh, that'd be fucking peachy."

"C'mon," Vail said, then moved forward. "No fingerprints, okay?" It was an obvious comment, but when you're working fast and stressing over the fact you're breaking and entering, it's easy to reach and touch without thinking first about every action you take.

Had she known they were going to do this, she would have brought gloves. But crossing over the line was not something she planned on doing—ever. Yet in the here and now, it seemed like the best thing to do . . . certainly the desperate thing to do.

Most of the house was dark. A light was on by the entryway, where they'd been standing—legally—about an hour ago. "Look for an office of some kind. A place he'd keep papers, business stuff."

"Wouldn't that be at the warehouse?"

"Not necessarily. Depends on the nature of the documents. Does it have anything to do with Superior Mobile Bottling?"

"What exactly is 'it'?"

Vail moved through the darkness. "Anything related to Robby, Lugo, or Mayfield." She pointed Dixon toward a room off to her left while she went right. They worked slowly in the dark, until Vail found a flashlight in a drawer in the kitchen. She used it judiciously, holding two fingers across its lens to restrict the beam in case a neighbor could see in through a second- or third-story window.

She pulled her BlackBerry and glanced at the display. She figured they'd broken the seal to the backdoor two minutes ago. How long did that leave them before the police arrived? She had no idea—except that a typical response rate was around nine minutes. But there were so many variables in that figure it was nearly useless to her. Were cruisers nearby when the call came in? Were there private security guards employed by a neighborhood watch group? How far was the closest Police or Sheriff's Department substation?

Dixon joined her in the hallway. "Nothing. How long do you want to keep pushing our luck?"

"Keep looking down here. I'm going up. You wanna get the hell out, I totally understand."

Vail took her flashlight up the curving staircase to the second floor. Unfortunately César Guevara lived quite well, and this home had three stories. She would have to move more quickly.

Master bedroom. Bathroom. Checked beneath the four-poster, shone her light behind cabinets, through closets. Guevara was a dapper dresser when he wasn't working in the warehouse, with dark double-breasted suits that looked like designer cuts. Allen Edmonds and Bruno Magli shoeboxes lined the middle shelf in the cavernous walk-in closet.

This is where she would concentrate her efforts. She grabbed a new pair of black Gold Toe dress socks and slipped them on her hands. It made for awkward groping, but the trade-off was worth it.

She brushed aside his suits, then his shirts, pants . . . looking for a concealed wall safe. Pulled open the drawers of the built-in ebony cabinetry, felt around for a false bottom. Got down on all fours and crawled along the floor, her Gold Toe–clad fingertips probing for a break in the carpet, a concealed seam that might be an invitation to buried treasure. Nothing.

Checked the clock on her BlackBerry. They'd now been in the house nine minutes. At this point, with each passing second, the likelihood of a law enforcement response to their entry bordered on unacceptable risk.

As she started down the stairs, Dixon came running at her. "I got something—but we gotta get outta here. Now. Sonoma PD's on its way—"

"How do you—"

Dixon turned and led the way out. "Brix. When you went upstairs, I called him, told him to monitor the radio."

They hit the ground floor and were heading toward the backdoor. Vail wiped down the flashlight and placed it back in the drawer. "Did you touch anything?"

"Don't know—don't think so. Maybe a few things—"

Vail, hands still protected by the socks, grabbed for the doorknob. "Does he know? Brix?"

They followed the same roundabout route toward the hedge line, avoiding the motion sensors. "Did I tell him? No. Does he know? Of course, he's not an idiot."

As Dixon followed Vail back to the car, Vail pulled off the Gold Toes and shoved them deep into her pocket.

"Neat trick with the socks," Dixon said. "I get the feeling you've done this before."

"Nope. First time." *And hopefully the last.*

After they had climbed into the Ford and slammed their doors, two Sonoma Police Department cruisers pulled up to the Guevara estate, light bars flashing. Vail and Dixon laid their seats back. To any of the cops who cared to look, theirs was an empty vehicle parked at the curb a block and a half away. While their Ford was somewhat out of place in a tony neighborhood like this one, it was dark and empty. The police were more likely focused on the object of their concern: the compromised house, with a peripheral eye peeled for fleeing suspects.

"How long do you want to hang out?" Vail asked.

"Let's wait for them to get inside, then I'll fire her up and we'll back away slowly. Hopefully they didn't grab our plate."

"Too far away."

Dixon lifted her head and peered over the dash. Apparently satisfied the area was clear, she reached forward and started the engine, then backed away as planned, using the side view mirrors as a guide. When they had gotten another two blocks, Dixon angled around a corner and swung the car around, headed away from the scene of their crime.

"You gonna show me what you found?"

"It was dark and I didn't have a whole lot of time, but I thought it might be important."

"Let me see it."

Dixon pulled to the curb, then flicked on the dome light. She stuck her hand inside her blouse, extracted a piece of folded paper, and handed it to Vail.

Vail unfurled it.

"It's just an address," Dixon said. "I think it's Ian Wirth's. His home." Dixon thought a moment. "Wirth, Victoria Cameron, and Isaac Jenkins were the only three people who were against Superior getting that bottling contract. Cameron and Jenkins were killed. If I'm right, and this is Wirth's home address . . . we may be on to something. There'd be no reason for Guevara to have it. Right?"

Vail sat there staring at the page. Off somewhere in the distance she heard what Dixon was saying. But she was seeing—and *thinking*—something else. Because in front of her was an address, all right.

But what caught her attention was that it was in Robby's handwriting.

27

"A re you sure?" Dixon asked. "Robby's handwriting?"

Vail wiped away the tears that had pooled in her lower lids. "No doubt whatsoever."

Dixon looked away, facing the windshield. The interior dome light made the glass into a mirror from which their distorted reflections stared back at them. Neither one looked pleased at this news.

Vail glanced at the clock. "I leave for the airport in six hours. How the hell am I gonna solve this in six hours?"

"I know this is hard for you, Karen. It'd be hard for me, too. But have faith in us. This case doesn't have to be wrapped up before you get on that plane."

"The longer Robby is missing, the less chance we have of finding him. And if he is around here—in Napa, in California, on the West Coast—the thought of flying twenty-five hundred miles away is . . . " She shook her head. "It's like I'm abandoning him. I don't know if that makes sense."

Dixon placed a hand on Vail's forearm. "Of course it does. I'm sorry. But I promise you, I won't give up. We won't give up."

Vail looked down at the paper bearing Robby's handwriting. "What does this mean?"

"At its most basic level, Robby wrote someone's address on a piece of paper and it ended up in César Guevara's possession. At the moment, that's all it means."

That's not all it means. There's something here. But as has been the case this past week, nothing adds up. Nothing makes sense. We catch the serial killer, who says, "There's more to this than you know." And he's being truthful. So what's wrong with me? Why can't I figure it out?

Dixon pulled her phone and started tapping away. She stopped, dropped it into her lap, and waited. A moment later, it buzzed and she lifted it to her ear. "Yeah." She listened a second and then said, "Okay. Meet you there." Dixon hung up, then yanked the gearshift into drive.

Vail, however, was still staring at the paper.

BRIX SUGGESTED THEY MEET at a restaurant, since none of the task force members had eaten anything for several hours. Dixon pulled into the parking lot, where a large landmark sign read "Brix - Restaurant Gardens Wine Shop." Had this been another time, she would've thought Brix's choice of eating at the Brix restaurant curious, but with the burden of the past few days weighing heavily, she was only concerned about getting some glucose into her brain and figuring out what the hell was going on.

As they approached the entrance along the dark walkway, patio chairs and coffee tables were occupied by a couple of women toking on cigarettes. Behind them, a wall of windows showcased a brightly lit gift shop stocked with tasteful artwork, wine racks, and clothing.

Near the large wood plank entry doors stood three men huddled in a circle: Brix, Gordon, and Mann.

Dixon and Vail greeted them, then Mann held open the door and they all filed in. The interior was well-appointed in warm woods and a wine motif. Oversize half barrels fitted with red upholstered seats lined the aisle to the left, serving as individual booths. Above, dozens of Chardonnay-shaped bottles jutted out from a central light fixture. Off to the right, on the far side of the restaurant, marble-topped oval tables sat in front of intimate two-seater couches. Perfect for the romantic couple winding down a day of wine tasting and sightseeing.

The kind of Napa experience Vail and Robby had envisioned when they went wheels up at Dulles.

Dixon took in the décor and said, "I'm not sure I can afford this."

"Yeah, make that two of us," Gordon said.

There were only a few couples scattered throughout the restaurant, a function of the late hour. Brix greeted the hostess, who was sporting a wide grin and hugging menus across her chest. She motioned for them to follow her.

Gordon jerked a thumb over his shoulder. "I need to hit the head."

"Ditto," Mann said. "Meet you at the table."

"Karen," Brix said as they continued past the bar to their right, "about a week ago when you got here, you asked me if I owned this place because of my name. I don't. But I'm part owner of a winery, remember? I don't do police work because I have to, I do it because I want to. So don't worry about the cost. I got it handled."

Brix led them alongside the barrel-walled booths and stopped opposite the servers' pickup window, then reached out and pulled open a wood door to a private room. "The reserve wine cellar. It's cozy and gives us the ability to talk about serial killers without disturbing the customers."

"Good thinking—but this room is . . . "

"Gorgeous. Elegant. Exclusive. I know."

To their right, three windows looked out onto the main dining area. But the remaining walls—and ceiling—were lined with side-lying wine bottles encased in hardwood wine racks with dramatic top-down low-voltage lighting, creating an air of showcased uniqueness to each vintage.

"This is my first time in here," Dixon said, perusing the magnum bottle of Anomaly Vineyards Cabernet. "Probably my last, too."

Vail and Dixon settled down in chairs facing the windows. Brix took a seat opposite them, then engaged the waiter with a nod as the man entered the room. "Bring us a spread. Whatever you've got prepared. We're hungry and we need some time to talk undisturbed. There'll be five of us."

"Yes sir," the server said.

After he had left the room, Brix turned toward Vail and Dixon. "I know we're under the gun. I realize you're leaving in a few hours. And I know Detective Hernandez is still AWOL. But what the hell were you thinking? The warrant—" he lowered his voice and glanced around, even though they were in a private room. "The warrant was denied. You're both vets here, you know the deal. I mean, what the fuck?"

"It was my call," Vail said.

"No, Karen, it wasn't your call. There was no call to make."

Vail leaned back in her seat. She wasn't in the mood for this. "What's done is done. If it matters, it wasn't a waste."

"It doesn't matter, because anything you think you may've gotten, it doesn't count for shit."

"Legally," Dixon said, "that's true. But it is significant."

Mann and Gordon entered the room and, in unison, craned their necks to take in the décor.

"It's nice," Brix said. "We've covered it. Have a seat."

As they settled in, Gordon said, "I take it you're ripping them a new one."

"I was just getting started."

Dixon set both her elbows on the table. "Before you get too upset, the address we found was Ian Wirth's."

Gordon stuck out his pudgy hands, palms up. "So Ian Wirth's address was found in Guevara's house. Guevara's company had a contract with the Georges Valley AVA board. Victoria Cameron was a board member and Isaac Jenkins's business partner was on the board. Are you saying we're back to thinking Guevara was involved in the Cameron and Jenkins murder? I thought we settled that when we caught Mayfield."

"Not the least of which," Brix said, "is that if Guevara's wrapped up in that, there's nothing we can do about it because you broke into his fucking house!" He took a breath, calmed himself, and lowered his voice. "Do you see what—"

"It's not that," Vail said. She brought both hands to her face and rubbed her bloodshot eyes. "The address. Yes, it was Wirth's *home* address. But . . . " She reached into her pocket and pulled out the paper. Laid it on the table in front of them. "What bothers me is that it's written in Robby's handwriting. And yes, before you ask, I'm sure."

There was silence at the table. The waiter must've sensed the opening, because he slipped in with plates cradled across his left forearm. He deftly set them down across the center of the table and said, as he pointed, "Halibut wrapped in prosciutto. Grilled lamb chops with creamy spinach. Artisanal cheese plate with apple slices, spiced almonds, and dried dates. Clams, served with a warm sauce drizzled on top and presented on a bed of sea salt. Finally, fennel sausage pizza. Need anything else, please let me know." He turned and left.

Austin Mann looked at Brix, who held up his hand. "I got it covered. Honest."

They all stared at the food. Poking out from between the halibut and lamb chops was the Wirth address. It served as a barrier to the decadent treats in front of them.

"So what does this mean?" Mann finally said.

Vail sat back. "I'm at a loss. I'm too close. I can't see it objectively. The obvious questions are, Why did Robby know César Guevara? Why did Robby write down Wirth's home address? Why did he give it to Guevara? What's Guevara's relationship to John Mayfield?"

Dixon shook her head. "You're getting ahead of yourself. We don't know Robby knew Guevara. All we know is that Guevara was in possession of a piece of paper containing something Robby had written."

"That's true," Brix said. "So let's all calm down a minute." He motioned to the food. "Eat. We need to get something in our stomachs."

They hesitated until Brix himself grabbed a slice of pizza. Then Gordon, Mann, and Dixon dug in. Vail was the last to toss some food on her plate. She reluctantly stabbed at the halibut and scooped the fish into her mouth. But despite the promise of heavenly flavors, she didn't taste anything.

"The pressing question," Dixon said, "is why Robby had Ian Wirth's home address. There's just no obvious reason for that. Robby was on vacation. He didn't know Wirth. He had no *reason* to know him." She put down her fork, pulled out her phone, and scrolled through the log. "I need Wirth's phone number."

"He's on the Georges Valley board, right?" Mann asked.

"Yes. And if Robby had any contact with Wirth, I want to know why."

Brix leaned to the left and pulled a sheaf of papers from his right rear pocket. "You gonna call him now? Kind of late—almost 11:00."

"It's about his dead colleagues. I don't think he'll care."

Brix read her the number. Dixon dialed, then rose and stepped outside the room.

"I wish Mayfield was conscious," Vail said. "I'd like another crack at him. I didn't do such a good job the first time around."

"Bullshit," Brix said. "You did great. That shit with making him talk to his mother, that was fucking brilliant. If your phone hadn't rung—"

"If Ray hadn't unloaded on him," Gordon added, "things would be different."

Vail lifted a shoulder, played with her food. "But my phone did ring. Ray shot Mayfield. And Robby went missing." Saying the words, at the late hour with her flight looming, finally hit. She dropped her head to keep from bursting into tears—but it didn't work.

"Ah, shit," Brix said. He got up and moved to the other side of the table, beside Vail. Took her in his arms and let her bury her face in his chest. Her shoulders lifted and shuddered, and she grabbed his arms, wanting to escape the embarrassment, the pain, the stress, the strain of the past week.

Dixon walked back in and said, "What happened?"

Vail lifted her head, pushed away from Brix and grabbed her napkin. She stuck her elbows on the table and wiped the thick, rough cotton against her eyes. "I'm sorry. That shouldn't have happened."

"Nonsense," Mann said. "Probably best that it did. You needed that release. We're not robots, Karen. We go about our jobs seeing all sorts of shit—violence, greed, death, you name it—and we try to bury it. Well, sometimes, especially when it's personal, it just fucking gets to you."

She nodded, then reached for her glass and swallowed a mouthful of water.

Brix straightened out his shirt, then left the room.

"Thanks," Vail said. "I—You're right."

Dixon held up her phone. "Wirth didn't know a Robby or Roberto Hernandez, and said he didn't remember having any contact with him."

Gordon frowned. "Worth a shot."

"But . . . he did receive a call a few days ago, a voice mail from some unidentified caller. Warning him that his life was in danger."

"Why didn't he call us?"

"He did," Dixon said. "But Wirth didn't get the message right away because they called a line for a small subsidiary of his. He doesn't check it daily. Once he retrieved his messages, which was yesterday, he called the number on the card I gave him."

"Which is your office line," Mann said.

"Right. And I haven't been to the office, and I haven't checked my voice mail. I've been a little busy. He's beefed up his security, just in case it wasn't a prank."

"He didn't recognize the voice?" Vail asked.

"Nope."

"So he's got a guardian angel."

"That guardian angel could be the key to all this. Someone who knows what's going on—which is more than we can say for ourselves."

"A guardian angel?" Brix was standing in the doorway holding an open bottle of red wine.

Dixon briefed him on the Ian Wirth phone call.

"Let's get the audio over to the lab," Brix said. "Have it analyzed."

"Already asked him to save it."

"Whaddya got there?" Gordon asked, wagging a stubby finger at the wine.

"Kelleher Cabernet," Brix said, spinning the bottle to display the label.

"From the owner's own vineyard. Out there," he said, gesturing out the windows. "Good stuff." He reached across the table and poured a glass for Vail. "You need it."

Vail took it and swallowed a mouthful. It was "good stuff," as Brix said. By the second gulp it was hitting her bloodstream and she could feel the relaxation flowing through her arms, her legs, and her face.

She put down the glass and leaned back in her chair.

"Now get some more food into you," Dixon said.

Rather than filling her plate, Vail said, "Aside from this mysterious guardian angel, there's only one source of information right now."

Brix held up a hand. "Stay away from César Guevara. We'll need to take it slow with him. Put some guys on him, build a case. Get a warrant. Do it right."

"Sounds like a plan." Dixon glanced over at Vail, who was staring at her plate. Nudged her elbow.

"Yeah," she said, at the prompt, "no problem."

"Let's look at what we've got so far," Mann said. He lifted his prosthetic left hand and tapped the fingers on his right. "Blood evidence on the carpet of your B&B. A fair amount, but not really enough if he'd bled out. But enough if he'd been shot or stabbed, then moved. No results yet on matching the DNA to Hernandez. Then we've got the leather jacket found in Mayfield's house. Hernandez's?"

"I'm not sure," Vail said.

Brix pulled his phone. "Aaron should've had something on that by now. Prints, DNA. Something." He began thumb typing.

"We got Mayfield's boast," Mann continued. "'There's more to this than you know.'"

"And," Dixon said, "Robby's phone logs were deleted. That might or might not mean anything. If he was the kind of person who regularly emptied out his phone, means nothing. But if someone did it for him, it could tell us a story: who called him or who he called before he disappeared."

"Any way we can recover that data?" Gordon asked.

Vail swallowed another sip of wine. "I sent it back to the FBI. Theoretically, the lab should be able to read the memory. They were also supposed to get his logs from the wireless carrier. Haven't heard anything yet."

"That's a big one," Dixon said.

"I know, Roxx." Vail's tone was short. "I should've thought of it earlier, when I could've called the lab. I fucked up."

Dixon placed a hand on Vail's forearm to calm her. It worked.

Mann glanced over at Vail and said, "Where are we in finding Hernandez's friend? The Sebastian dude."

Brix shook his head. "Last I heard from NSIB, none of the names checked out. And we hit a zero with V. Sattui, the winery that sells the Madeira that Sebastian supposedly drinks. Customer listing, charge receipts, nothing. No one's recognized Robby's photo, either."

"And," Gordon said, "there's the fact that Robby's gone off the grid. No credit or debit card use. No hotels. Nothing at area hospitals or—excuse me, Karen—or at morgues. No plane, train, car rentals."

"He had a car rental," Brix said. "He would've just taken it if he left of his own choosing." The sudden vibration of the phone in his hand nearly sent it careening to the floor. Brix angled his gaze down to read the text message. "Aaron—analysis of the leather jacket. He's able to account for 14 out of 16 latents as—" He scrolled down and continued: "as belonging to Mayfield. The others were unidentifiable partials. Nothing on DNA. Too soon."

"Doesn't look like it's Robby's coat," Vail said. She let her head fall forward into her hands and rubbed her temples. "I'm not sure if that's good or bad."

"It's good," Dixon said. "Anything that removes, or weakens, a connection between Robby and Mayfield is good in my book."

Brix set down his phone and piled a few squares of cheese on his plate, followed by a couple of clams and a lamb chop. "But it does bring up the issue of James Cannon. He's still in the wind. We've got about two dozen deputies and investigators looking for him. His photo has been sent around to LEOs in a hundred mile radius. I've even snagged a chopper to scour the woods with infrared. So far, nothing."

"So it comes back to Guevara," Mann said. "He's got skin in the game, but we can't prove it and we can't nail it—or him—down."

Vail sat there, the wine stirring her head in pleasant waves. Her lids felt the weight of a lack of quality sleep and an overabundance of stress. But through it all, the broad outlines of a plan began to form. It wouldn't be something she could share with the others because they would explicitly forbid her from carrying it out. With time disappearing like a painter rolling a primer coat on a wall, covering all beneath it, she didn't see a choice. They were beating their heads against a wall. At least, that was how she felt.

Vail pushed her chair back from the table. Her body had the heavy

and sloppy movements indicative of high blood alcohol content. "I'd totally understand if you guys wanna knock off. Go catch some sleep. We
haven't had a whole lot of it lately."

Brix and Dixon locked eyes, silently weighing the offer.

"Seriously, guys. I'm leaving for SFO in like four hours. Unless we've
got something pressing to follow up on that's not already being done,
there's no reason to work through the night. Again."

Brix hiked his brow. "I guess you're right. Let's go catch forty winks,
start fresh at 8:00 AM. Roxx?"

As the lead investigator, she had to make the call.

Dixon turned to Vail and read her face.

Shit, she knows I'm up to something. Here it comes.

"Yeah. Let's call it a night. Keep your cells by your beds. Just in case."

Make that a definite. She knows.

Brix wiped his napkin across his mouth, then threw the soiled cloth
on the table. He stepped around the table and spread his arms. He gave
Vail a firm hug, then leaned back. "Karen, I never, ever thought I'd say
this . . . that first day we met we kind of got off on the wrong foot. But
I've really enjoyed working with you. You challenge me—all of us. You
make us better."

Vail tilted her head. "I don't know about that."

"I mean it. It's been an honor."

"Same here." She turned to Mann and Gordon. "All of you. Thanks
for putting up with me. My attitude."

"Hey," Mann said, "you just wanna get the damn case solved. We may
go about it in different ways, but . . . Well, Redd's right. Thank you. If
there's anything we can do on our end—"

"We'll keep working this," Brix said. "Tomorrow morning, we'll be
right back at it. We're gonna find Robby and we're gonna find Cannon."

Vail tightened her lips, then nodded appreciation.

"C'mon," Dixon said. She led Vail away, back toward the car. Neither
of them said a thing until they got inside. When the doors closed, Dixon
pulled away and let loose.

28

I know you, Karen. You're thinking of doing something stupid." She turned to face Vail, her eyes hard and wide and angry. "And don't fucking lie to me."

"So after all we've been through these past seven or eight days, working in close quarters and dealing with all the shit we've dealt with, all you can say is that you know me and that I'm going to do something stupid?"

Dixon extended the fingers of her right hand, which remained on the steering wheel. "That didn't come out right. I'm sorry. I just think, well, I think you're reacting emotionally. I'm sure I'd be the same way if this had happened to me, with Eddie. If I could've prevented his death, had I known he was in danger . . . " She curled her hand around the wheel. "So let's cut through all the shit. Can you do that for me?"

Vail sat there a long moment. "Drop me at Guevara's house, a couple blocks away—"

"See? That's what I mean!"

"What do you expect me to do, Roxx? Guevara's the only one who knows what the hell is going on."

"And you've already tried prying information out of him."

Vail turned and looked out the black side window at the quiet countryside. "So I'll try again. And this time I won't be so nice."

"You weren't very nice the last time around, either. Yesterday, when we stopped at Superior."

"You mean when I shoved my Glock against his head?"

"I think that qualifies, yeah. But look at it logically. He's got bodyguards. Even if you can neutralize them, they're witnesses. So when his high-priced attorney files a complaint—which he will—there'll be corroboration of his story. And the worst part is, he'll be on the right side of the law. And you'll be on the wrong side."

"Just take me there. Let me worry about it."

Dixon pulled the Ford hard right onto the shoulder. Gravel flew up and kicked around the wheel wells.

"What are you doing?"

"It's goddamn obvious, Karen. I'm not going to let you throw away your career. You're not thinking clearly."

Vail turned away and again peered out the window. Rolled it down. The cool air blew against her face. Stole a glance in all directions. Pinpricks of light here and there. But it was dark, too dark for her to figure out where she was. She grabbed the handle, opened the door, and swung out her legs.

"Where do you think you're going?"

Vail did not reply. She flung the door closed and trudged off, ahead of Dixon's vehicle, the headlights cutting through the damp air and slicing around her body, throwing it into silhouette.

At this time of year, it was still nippy at 12:30 or 1:00—or whatever time it was now. She wasn't going to stop to look.

But what was she going to do? It wasn't like she could hail a cab—not in the middle of the Napa countryside. She didn't even know where she was. She stopped walking, put both hands on her head, and leaned her neck back. Her body swayed—the wine was still in her bloodstream. *How did this happen? How did I get to this place?*

She heard Dixon's door open. She turned and saw that Dixon was talking to her through the windshield. No, not to *her*—to her Bluetooth visor.

Dixon stuck her head out the door and rose from her seat in one motion. "Get in the car!"

"What is it?"

"We got a twenty on Cannon."

29

Vail ran back to the Ford but nearly flew out of the seat when Dixon floored the accelerator. The tires spun in the gravel, then squealed as they gripped asphalt.

Vail settled herself in and then snapped the seat belt closed. But the blood was pounding in her temples. The wine? The sudden dump of adrenalin? "What's the deal?"

"Our chopper got an infrared hit in the area about three miles from where Cannon disappeared. They were tracking him at a high altitude through the mountains, and then he stopped moving. Based on the restrained motion within a confined space and the IR signatures of other bodies in the structure, it looks as though he entered a secluded house in the woods and might have hostages."

"So what's the plan?"

The speedometer needle effortlessly slipped past 72. Dixon, two hands on the wheel, said, "SWAT's en route. We're closer. Chopper's surveillance only, it won't be dropping anyone or landing."

Vail rubbed her face and tried to excise the mounting pressure from her thoughts. She closed her eyes and audibly blew air through her lips.

"You okay?"

"Actually, pretty shitty. Thanks for asking."

Dixon drove in silence, deftly negotiating the winding mountain roads—and Vail, remembering the challenging landscape from their last visit out this way, was not about to distract her with interruptions.

Dixon pointed skyward. "See if you can find the chopper. I think I know where this road is, but if we can use the chopper's spotlight as a beacon to pinpoint the house's location, it may keep us from driving off the side of the mountain."

Vail craned her neck back, forth, and side to side—but couldn't make out what looked like a helicopter. She rolled down her window—

and within three minutes, in the distance, she saw blinking lights hovering against the inky blackness. "There she is, two o'clock. No beacon."

"Probably best if Cannon doesn't know we're on to him. Grab the radio," she said, tossing a nod at the glove box. "Primary channel. See if you can raise the pilot."

Vail found the secure radio—it was only three days ago she'd handled this very device while they were in pursuit of John Mayfield. That had turned out well; if they replicated those results, it would be a hell of a send-off back east.

She glanced at the dashboard clock. *Running out of time. Two and a half hours. Nothing's ever easy, Karen, is it?*

"What's their call sign?"

"H-30. Flown by CHP."

"CHP H-30, this is FBI Special Agent Karen Vail and Investigator Roxxann Dixon with the major crimes task force. We have you in sight. Do you have us? Over."

"That's affirmative, Agent Vail. This is Ken Orent commanding H-30. SWAT is en route. ETA eighteen minutes."

Vail managed a chuckle. "A lot of shit can happen in eighteen minutes." She thought back to a time many years ago when she had uttered a similar comment over an open radio channel, then sweated the likely ridicule from colleagues. Here and now, she didn't give it a second thought.

"Pull over, Roxx. I need your full attention."

Dixon stopped the car.

"What's your procedure out here?"

Dixon shoved the gear into park. "H-30 will circle the area until ground units set up a perimeter. The patrol sergeant has already requested that SWAT respond. The SWAT team's made up of officers from the Napa sheriff and the Napa city police. But because we're an unincorporated county, the Sheriff's Department runs the show. They'll draw up a tactical plan, which'll probably include setting up a perimeter closer to the house. We'd bring in our hostage negotiating team to attempt phone contact with the suspect."

"Doesn't sound like eighteen minutes to me. It'll take them at least as long to get themselves set up and plugged in. Besides, James Cannon doesn't want to talk to us, Roxx. Right now, he's tired and freaked out and hungry and on the run. The people in there with him are in extreme danger."

"No argument there. Your point?"

"What do you want to do?" Vail asked.

Dixon stole a look at Vail. It was fast, but it said, "Are you fucking kidding me?"

Vail brought the radio to her mouth. "Commander Orent, how many heat signatures do you have?"

"We count five. Four are stationary, one is mobile. Judging by their movements, we assume Mr. Mobile is our suspect. He seemed to clear all the rooms and herd the occupants into a main area in the center of the house."

Vail swung her gaze over to Dixon. "You think Robby's one of those hostages?"

Dixon shook her head. "No idea. Either way, no matter who he's got—"

Vail keyed the radio. "What's he doing now? Over."

"He appears to be pacing back and forth. Over."

"We're going in. Copy?"

There was a long pause. Vail was ready to rekey the mike to repeat when suddenly Orent said, "You are instructed to wait for SWAT. Over."

Vail let the radio fall back to her lap. "Do we need them?"

"I don't want to go in with drawn guns and start a shootout because of a mistake. We don't even have the street address. And these people who live in the mountains . . . who knows what kind of rifles they might have?"

"How would you normally handle something like this?"

"Assuming they'd run it the same way they take down pot farms, the H-30 will use GPS to give us the coordinates, and the ground units would plug them into their portable GPS devices. That's how."

"You have a GPS?"

Dixon started to shake her head, then stopped. "Let me check."

She jumped out of the car and rummaged around the trunk. A moment later, she returned with a small canvas kit. "I usually don't have one, but I borrowed one a couple weeks ago from a buddy in the department and forgot to return it. Fire it up."

Vail did so, then keyed the mike. "Commander, we're concerned about the wait. That's a very violent offender in there. But my purpose is not to debate this with you. We understand you will not assist. Thing is, we're going in and we need the GPS coordinates. We don't have the address. It's dark out and these houses don't have neon signs out front that say 'suspect's in here.'" She paused, waited, then said, "Of course, I'd totally understand if you refuse."

As the seconds passed, Vail and Dixon stared out the windshield be-fore finally turning to each other. "Maybe he's thinking about it," Dixon said. "Or calling for approval."

"Unable to comply, Agent Vail," Orent said. "Over."

Dixon shrugged. "It was worth a shot."

"May've been worth a shot, but it didn't get us anywhere." A second later, Vail said, "There!" and jabbed a finger at the windshield, indicating a house about a hundred yards away. Moving slowly across the roof tiles was a pinpoint green laser beam.

Dixon was about to jam the gear into drive, but Vail grabbed her arm. "Leave it here," Vail said. "We're too close. Let's go it on foot. If Cannon hears the car, we're cooked and so are those hostages. Unless he's aware of the chopper tracking him—which is possible but not likely. That ATV is a loud son of a bitch, and the chopper was purposely flying at a high al-titude. We're probably okay."

"So why'd Cannon stop?"

Vail checked the dome light to ensure it was off, then quietly opened her door. "He's been riding for hours. Probably hungry, tired. And his ass and balls hurt, I'm sure."

"You sure you want to go in? SWAT will be here in ten minutes."

"We both know we should wait," Vail said.

Dixon sat there with her door ajar—but didn't move. "Right."

A crackle from the radio. "Agent Vail, we've got activity. Two individ-uals moved toward the rear of the structure and it appears that one ex-ited the premises."

"Copy," Vail said. She leaned forward and shoved the radio in her back pocket. "Well, that solves that." And off they went.

30

Traversing the steep mountainside in the dark made moving along the hilly terrain at Herndon Vineyards seem like child's play. Vail slipped and slid on the damp forest floor, pine needles and low-lying ferns serving as snow discs that propelled her down and forward.

This would do wonders for her knee. At the moment, it didn't matter.

They were moving reasonably well as they approached the house, which sat below street level in a large gulley carved out of the mountain. The rear of the home was suspended on pilings, leveling out the structure. A muted dimness from within suggested it emanated from one of the inner rooms, where light had a tough time escaping the confines of walls and doors.

Vail had moved thirty feet ahead while Dixon moved more deliberately. As Vail evaluated the area behind the house, Dixon lost her footing on the incline and slammed against a narrow eucalyptus stalk, chest first.

"Shit," she said between clenched teeth.

Vail pulled her gun from its holster. "You okay?"

"Fine. I've got another boob on the other side." Dixon pointed. "There's the rear of the house. You see any movement?"

Vail shook her head. "Without night vision, we're not gonna see much. I can't even make out how many fingers you're holding up."

"I'm not holding any up."

"My point exactly." Vail moved forward, then stopped. "Hang back, cover me. Just in case Cannon sees me before I see him. No sense in giving him a shot at both of us."

"You think he's armed?"

"I wasn't speaking literally, but then again, who the hell knows? It wouldn't be his style—he killed his last vic up close and personal, which means he gets off on that, just like Mayfield. But does he have a gun? We know so little about him, it's impossible to say." Vail bent over. "Cover me."

She scurried ahead, scampering as fast as she could without slipping and going down on the slick terrain. As she approached, what she saw made her pull up, which sent her into a slide—right into the slumped body of a male. In a leather jacket.

Vail felt a lump the size of a baseball blocking her throat. *Robby?* In the dark, it was hard to say. His body was folded and crumpled, almost fetal in its curve. She steadied herself, leaned over the man, then felt for a pulse. Not only did she not feel anything, but her fingers slipped on the unmistakable thick and slick liquid she knew as only one thing: blood.

She grabbed the jacket lapel and yanked—nearly slipping down the incline—and shined her BlackBerry light on the man's face. *Around the same age. Smaller. Not Robby.* Actually, the guy's face shared a resemblance with Dixon's former boyfriend, Detective Eddie Agbayani, a victim of John Mayfield's violence a couple of days ago. Vail hoped Dixon wouldn't notice.

Dixon was now by her side. Vail looked up at and caught the whites of her partner's eyes.

"It's not Robby," Dixon said.

"No."

"Dead?"

"Dead. Trachea crushed. Wrists slit. My guess," Vail said, "is that this is the man of the house, the father. The only true threat to Cannon. Take out your threat, then you can do whatever the hell you want. Common tactic among disorganized offenders who enter a house or apartment and find a boyfriend or spouse. Blitz attack, get 'em out of the way." Vail reached into her back pocket and pulled the radio. Lowered the volume, then keyed the mike. "H-30," she said in a soft voice. "This is Agent Vail. That heat signature you picked up exiting the building's rear is a dead body. Early thirties male Caucasian. Looks like Cannon killed his only threat, to get him out of the way. Over."

"Copy that. Relaying same to SWAT. Over."

Vail leaned over to Dixon's ear. "He could kill the others. And soon."

"Why?" Dixon asked. "I thought he only killed this guy to get him out of the way."

"Point of getting the male out of the way is so he can have his way with the women. On the other hand, if he knows the chopper's located him, he's under extreme duress."

"Then in a matter of minutes, he's going to be knuckling down, waiting for the police assault. And the chances of getting the hostages out alive will plummet like a bear market."

Vail looked at the backdoor. "A bear out in the woods. Nice analogy. But SWAT's less than ten minutes away now. At this point, I think we should let them handle it."

Dixon looked at the man lying on the ground at their feet. Vail saw the way she appraised at the victim's face, the way her lips tightened.

"It's not Eddie," Vail said.

"Fucking looks like him."

Vail glanced at the house, her eyes checking things out. Then she leaned down to catch Dixon's gaze. "Roxx, listen to me."

"What's his reaction going to be to an armed assault?"

"He won't surrender, if that's what you're asking."

"That is what I'm asking," Dixon said. "Those hostages inside are in a heap of trouble. We have a window, before this escalates. I don't think he knows we're here. This is the best shot we're gonna have. Right?"

Vail bit down on her lip. "Probably. Yes."

Dixon rose from her crouch. "Then I'm going in. We approach from opposite angles, we've got him. He doesn't have a gun."

"How do we know that?"

"Because he didn't shoot this guy. Looks like he did what Mayfield did: crushed his trachea, slit his wrists. That's the way he kills."

"We think that's the way he kills. We don't know enough about him to reach definitive conclusions about his behaviors, about his identity as a killer."

"I've got all I need right here."

"Roxx, don't—"

Dixon started climbing the slick hill. "I'm going in the front. If you're gonna help me out, count to sixty, then go in the back." She stopped and turned. "You with me?"

Vail rubbed her forehead with the back of her hand, the one holding the Glock. *I hate situations like this. You know it's the wrong thing to do, but you have no choice.* "Don't get me killed, Roxx. I still have to find Robby. And I've got a kid, remember?"

"Then we'd better be careful. Sixty seconds. Fifty-nine Mississippi, fifty-eight Mississippi, and so on. On my mark. Ready?"

Vail nodded.

"Mark." Dixon turned and scurried away. Into the darkness.

31

Vail made her way up the slippery wooden steps onto the deck that led to the backdoor. At least with wet wood there was less chance of a board squeaking under her weight.

Counting. *Forty-five. Forty-four.*

There were two windows, one on either side of the door, which was partially constructed of glass. She crept along, keeping herself low. Inspected the jamb and considered where she would need to strike the door to blast it inward. Because of its construction, she knew she could do it—using her good leg.

Thirty. Twenty-nine.

She put her ear to the crack in the weather seal, down below the window line. Listened. One, perhaps two, female voices whimpering. *Maybe Roxx was right. Going in now before he killed someone else made sense. Didn't it?*

Seventeen. Sixteen.

Vail tightened her grip on the Glock. She would kick in the door, then go in low. It was always risky when you did not know the floor plan of the house you were infiltrating. Where was your target? Would you be immediately visible to him upon entry? And most disconcerting . . . did he have a weapon? In close quarters combat like this, a knife was often more dangerous than a handgun.

Infiltrate, rapidly assess: Was your immediate environment safe? Were your hostages in imminent danger? Had your appearance *placed them* in imminent danger?

Five. Four.

Vail stepped back—she was now in view of the home's occupants should they choose to look—and brought her right leg up and then thrust it forward, just below the knob.

The jamb cracked and splintered, and the door flew open. Vail dropped to the floor and clambered into the room—it was the kitchen—and brought her back up against the wood cabinets. Listened.

Shouting—screaming.

Vail spun around the edge of the wall, Glock out in front of her, and moved down the carpeted hallway toward the light—and the commotion. There! In the family room, three females. One woman. Early thirties. Two girls, about eight and nine, sporting tear-streaked red cheeks.

No sign of James Cannon. Not good—he could be behind me, or he could be choking Dixon, right now—

Slamming noise. Loud. something smashing into a wall Again, and again.

Vail followed the noise and stopped in front of the three women, whose wrists and ankles were bound with duct tape. A taut strip stretched across their mouths. "I'm gonna get you out of here, okay?" She quickly pulled off the mother's gag, which elicited a whimper. Vail ignored it. "Scissors?"

"In the drawer," the mother said. "The desk—"

Vail swung around and found the piece of furniture three strides away. Grabbed the scissors, cut the ankle bindings. "Out the back," she said. "Go!"

She would be sending them where the woman's husband and the girls' father was lying dead—but their physical safety was of paramount importance. Their mental health could be addressed later.

Now. Find Dixon.

A loud thump. A groan.

Vail slipped out of the family room, then moved down the hallway toward the front door. There, laid out face up on the carpet was James Cannon—and Dixon astride him, pounding away at his face. "Roxx!"

Another punch.

Vail ran forward and grabbed the back of Dixon's shirt. "Roxx, enough!"

Dixon's shoulders rose and fell with rapid heaves as she got up and stumbled backward. Vail almost gasped when she saw her partner's face: red welts over the left eye, which was already swollen half shut. A bruise across her right cheek.

Cannon didn't look much better: his mouth, which hung open, was bloody, his teeth coated a slasher-film burgundy.

"Cuffs," Vail said, then swung her Glock into her holster. As Dixon handed them over, Vail asked, "Where's your SIG?"

Dixon looked left, then right, then paced up and down the hallway. Vail knew she would want to locate it before SWAT arrived on scene. Having your sidearm taken from you in a confrontation was embarrassing—and bordered on incompetent.

Vail pulled the radio from her back pocket. "H-30, this is Vail. All secure. Repeat. All secure. Suspect in custody. Request ambulance."

"Roger that, Agent Vail."

Dixon came up to her, SIG in hand. She slipped it into her holster without offering a word.

"So what happened?"

"I came through the door, and he was on me as soon as I stepped through. We both landed some good shots, but I think I got the worst of it. I went down and he came at me, but I landed a hard kick in his steroid-shrunken balls. That was all I needed. I got to my feet and kneed him pretty hard in the face. Broke his nose, for sure. He staggered back and I landed a few good blows. He went down, and a couple punches later, you appeared."

"A couple punches?"

Dixon flexed her swollen right hand. "Maybe a few more."

Red, blue, and white lights strobed through the drawn window curtains, projecting a nervous energy onto the far wall. The thumping beat of the H-30's rotors intensified, indicating that the chopper had dropped to a safe distance above the house. Vail felt the vibration in her chest, and she fought the urge to cough or bang it to dislodge the discomfort.

She made her way to the backdoor and saw the helicopter's white beacon bathing the rear yard in light. A CSI Vail hadn't yet met was slipping and sliding toward the dead body lying on the wet bed of pine needles and mud.

"Karen!"

Dixon's voice. She made her way back to the front door. The SWAT commander would no doubt be entering the house any minute. But as Vail approached, she realized that wasn't why Dixon had called her. James Cannon was regaining consciousness.

Dixon was standing a few steps away from him, her SIG drawn and in her right hand, extended and pointed at his chest. Inviting him to make a threatening move.

He pushed himself backward against the front door and now sat half reclined, canted left, his shoulder pressed to the wall. His hands were cuffed behind his back. He did not look comfortable—or pleased.

Vail approached and stopped ahead of Dixon, at Cannon's feet. She crouched and rested her forearms on her thighs. "Jimmy, Jimmy, Jimmy. You fucked up real bad. You had everything going for you. Working at an up-and-coming winery, possibly slated to be the wine maker in five to ten years if you learned the business well and proved yourself. Forgive me for asking, but what the hell were you thinking?"

Cannon's right eye narrowed. "You're not as pretty as I thought you were when we met in the gym. Asking you out . . . yeah, what the hell was I thinking?"

Vail grinned. "That's good. I believe in giving credit where it's due. But we don't have a lot of time here, Jimmy. So I'm gonna come straight with you. I'm serious—was the wine thing a cover or did you really have intentions of being a wine maker?"

Cannon's gaze fell to his lap. "I took enology in college. I wanted to be a wine maker."

"Until John Mayfield came into your life. Then you saw something that interested you more. Right?"

Cannon pouted his lips and nodded imperceptibly. A concession without an embarrassing admission.

"Okay, Jimmy," Vail said. "I understand."

Jiggle of the door knob. Pounding knock. "Napa County Sheriff's Department. Captain Dave Nash. Open up!"

"This is Special Agent Karen Vail, FBI. We're okay in here. Suspect is secured. We'll be out in a minute."

"If the suspect is secured, open—"

"My partner's coming out," Vail said. She gestured to Dixon, who made her way toward the garage. She would run interference with Nash while Vail finished her interview.

"Jimmy. How much did you work with John Mayfield? Did you know what he was doing?"

Cannon firmed his lips and turned away.

Okay, he's not ready to answer that one. "Here's what I think happened. You two found each other in the gym, and Mayfield tested the waters, told you about some animals he'd killed when he was young. And you were interested. More than interested. Intrigued. So he took a risk and told you about some people he'd killed. And it excited you. So he told you more. And it made you feel different, alive, like something woke up inside you. That sound about right, Jimmy?"

Cannon glanced quickly at Vail. "Something like that."

Vail knew, even with Dixon out front running cover, she didn't have much time. Time to get to the nuts and bolts.

She reached into her pocket and pulled out the photo of Robby. "You recognize this guy?"

Cannon looked at the picture. His gaze remained steady. "I've seen him, but I don't remember where."

Vail leaned in closer—unwise, for sure, but she couldn't help herself. "You've seen him? When?"

Cannon turned away, his eyes rolling left, then right, then up. "Can't remember. Recently. Past couple days, I think."

"What was he doing? Where'd you see him?"

Banging on the door. "Agent Vail, open up. Now."

"Suspect is wedged against the door. Come in through the garage." She turned back to Cannon. "Where'd you see him?"

Cannon closed his eyes. "I feel like shit. My head's gonna explode. Can we do this later?"

Vail clenched her teeth. *I'm getting on a fucking plane in about ninety minutes. No, we can't do this later.*

"That's my last question, Jimmy. Answer it and I'll see to it they give you something for the pain in the ambulance."

He let his head fall back against the door.

"Agent Vail."

Voice behind her. Stern, deep. No nonsense. The guy from the other side of the door. Dave Nash.

She did not turn around. Her eyes were stuck on Cannon's face like epoxy.

Captain Nash grabbed Vail by her shoulder and moved her back. She lost her balance and fell on her buttocks.

"Can you get the hell out of the way so we can do our jobs?" Nash asked.

Vail pushed herself up. *Please, just answer my question. I need this piece to the puzzle.* "Where'd you see him?" she yelled.

Cannon tightened his face. "I can't remember. Now leave me the hell alone. My head's fucking killing me."

Vail felt a hand on her arm, leading her away. It was Dixon.

"C'mon," she said by Vail's ear.

Vail followed her outside. A mist, foglike and thick, hovered around the first responder vehicle lights. The cool moisture prickled Vail's cheeks.

The SWAT Peacekeeper, a military-modified Dodge Ram truck sporting an armored shell, was parked in front of the house. Several men milled about, one smoking a cigarette, another leaning against the vehicle. The helicopter hovered above, much louder outside than it had been inside. As Vail craned her head skyward, the H-30 began moving off, the beacon becoming weaker and more dispersed as the craft rose.

Two paramedics, standing beside an ambulance that was parked a dozen feet back of the Peacekeeper, snapped into action and wheeled a gurney to the front door.

"He said he saw Robby." Vail was watching the scene unfold and spoke so softly Dixon almost didn't hear her.

"You showed him the photo?"

"He said he'd seen him. Couldn't remember where."

Two headlights appeared in the distant darkness, speeding down the street toward them. The vehicle screeched to a halt behind the ambulance. Brix and Stan Owens poured out of the car and headed toward Vail and Dixon.

"Nice of you to tell me," Brix said to Dixon.

"We were kind of busy responding to the situation. He killed the father and dumped the DB out the back. So we went in."

"You went in? SWAT was en route."

"We didn't think there was time. There were three other hostages."

Owens folded his arms. "Obviously we're gonna need to discuss that. Later. What's the current status?"

"Cannon's in custody."

Vail said, "I showed him Robby's photo. He said he'd seen him, but he couldn't remember where."

"You believe him?" Brix asked.

Before Vail could answer, Dave Nash joined their circle. "Sheriff," he said, with a nod at Owens.

"Report."

"Victim's in the rear of the property being processed by CSI Bruno Rancelli. Suspect James Cannon's being treated and readied for transport under guard to Valley Med. He's in and out of consciousness.

Medic's concerned he might have a subdural hematoma." Nash glanced sideways at Vail and Dixon. "He apparently took a beating."

"Necessary force to bring down the suspect," Dixon said. "And self-defense."

Owens seemed to notice the bruises on Dixon's face for the first time. "I don't think there'll be a problem with that. But before Rancelli takes off, have him snap some photos of you. CYA."

"Also," Nash said, "Cannon wanted me to deliver a message to Agent Vail." He turned to her and said, "Before he lost consciousness, he mumbled a name."

Brix nearly shouted, "What name?"

Nash scratched at his temple. "I don't know if this makes any sense, but sounded like he said, 'Sissy Guava.'"

32

"César Guevara?" Vail asked.

Nash lifted his hat and brushed back his hair. "Yeah, could be. But that's all he said. Mean something to you?"

Brix grunted. "You could say that."

"Why would he say Guevara's name?" Owens asked.

The doors to the ambulance slammed shut and its light bar began swirling as it pulled away from the house, James Cannon tucked into its rear compartment.

Vail watched another piece to the puzzle being whisked away down the road, evaporating into the dark fog, the siren remaining long after visual contact had been lost. "I showed Robby's—Detective Hernandez's—photo to Cannon, and he said he'd seen him but couldn't remember where. I guess he's saying he saw him somewhere that's associated with Guevara."

Dixon began to gently massage her inflamed hand. "We're missing the bigger picture. Why would James Cannon know César Guevara?"

"Obvious answer," Brix said, "is that Cannon is a manager at a start-up winery, and they were talking with Superior Mobile Bottling about contracting for their services."

"That's one explanation," Vail said, stifling a yawn. "Another might be that there's a connection somehow between John Mayfield, James Cannon, and César Guevara. A connection we haven't figured out yet."

Dixon stretched her arms above her head. "We know there's a connection between Cannon and Mayfield. Mentor and student. And Ray said on the DVD that he thought there was some kind of connection between Mayfield and Guevara."

"So what does all this mean?" Owens asked.

Dixon looked up at the black sky. The air was calmer now, without the beating rotors of the helicopter whipping at the treetops. "It means we don't know enough to figure it out yet."

Brix pulled his phone. "I'll get Mann over to Valley Med, so he's there when Cannon arrives. If he regains consciousness, maybe we can get some clarification. And I'll talk with Cap Krandle at Herndon in the morning, see if they'd had any discussions with Guevara about using Superior."

"Nothing left for us to do here," Dixon said. While Brix was waiting for the line to connect, she said, "We'll pick up Karen's stuff at my place, then head over to the hospital until she leaves for the airport."

"Yeah, Austin, it's Brix." He nodded at Dixon, and Dixon and Vail said good-bye to Owens, then climbed into their vehicle.

Vail snapped her seatbelt then let her head fall back against the seat. Yawned wide and loud. "I'm so damn tired. And we've got so little to show for all our time and effort. I'm out of here in—" she checked the dashboard clock—"about an hour fifteen."

Dixon turned over the engine and brought the Ford around to head back the way they had come. "For the moment, you're still here. The fat lady ain't singing just yet."

"You'll let me know when, right?"

Dixon managed a grin. "Yeah. I'll let you know when."

33

They arrived at Dixon's house twenty minutes later. Vail scooped up her measly belongings—her clothing and personal effects greatly reduced in number and volume by the fire Scott Fuller and his conspirators had set a few days earlier. As she gathered everything into a pile, her thoughts shifted to a few nights ago, when John Mayfield had injected Vail with BetaSomnol, a powerful sedative, then used her Glock to kill Fuller. It set off a major confrontation with Sheriff Owens, which Robby squelched by tossing Owens onto his rump.

Scott Fuller vanished from her thoughts when she felt a nudge on her forearm. She turned to see Margot looking at her, wanting attention. Vail sat down on the floor and Margot jumped into her lap. Quinn came running over, and having lost the "prime real estate" to Margot, took up the next best location—alongside Vail's thigh.

With a hand on each dog, Vail felt soothed by their curly fur. She got as much comfort from stroking them as Margot and Quinn seemed to be getting from the human contact.

Dixon walked into the room and gathered Vail's soiled towel and bedsheets.

"Maybe I need one of these," Vail said as Margot reached back and gave Vail a lick on the cheek.

"Standards are terrific dogs. Extremely smart, very athletic and physical, and they live for the human connection. Great companions—and excellent watchdogs. A lot of upkeep, though. Trimming their coats, keeping their fur free of tangles—"

"Seems like it's worth it."

"I don't regret it for a minute."

Vail patted Margot's chest and the dog disengaged herself from Vail's lap. Vail pulled herself off the floor and grabbed what amounted to an overnight bag.

She said good-bye to Margot and Quinn, then left the house with Dixon. En route to Napa Valley Medical Center, Vail called the car service that Gifford's secretary, Lenka, had arranged, and gave them the new address where she was to be picked up.

When they arrived, Vail sat in Dixon's Ford, staring out the windshield at the ER bay. "When were we here with Mayfield?"

"A couple days ago?"

Vail brought both hands to her face and rubbed at her eyes and cheeks. "This has been a week from hell."

Dixon popped open her door. "Look on the bright side. When was the last time you caught two serial killers in one week?"

Vail gave Dixon a weary look. "Nice try, Roxx. But until I find out what happened to Robby—or find him alive—I won't consider the past ten days a success."

Dixon got out and closed her door. "I think you're being too hard on yourself."

They made their way into the ER and found the charge nurse. Cannon had been brought in, triaged, and sent directly to the OR. "Brain surgery. No telling how long he'll be in there."

"What was wrong?"

"Subdural hematoma. That's bleeding in the brain due to traumatic—"

"Yeah, we got that part," Vail said. "Thanks."

"Roxxann."

Behind them, Austin Mann was approaching. He looked surprisingly fresh for nearly 3:30 in the morning.

"Cannon's in surg—"

"We know," Vail said. "You get a chance to talk with him before they took him back?"

Mann twisted his mouth. "No such luck. Came in unconscious."

Vail looked around for a seat. Ahead and down the hall was the waiting room. She led the way and wearily lowered herself into a chair. "So that's it."

"Hey, we're not giving up," Mann said. "Just because you're gettin' on that plane doesn't mean this is 'case closed.' We're still gonna work it. Soon as Cannon is conscious, he and I will have a chat. We learn anything, we know where to find you."

Vail's BlackBerry buzzed. She sighed, then lifted it out of its holster. "Vail." She listened a moment, then said, "You're early." She pulled herself straight in the chair and said, "I'll be right out. Yeah, in the back, by the ambulance bay."

Vail shoved her phone onto her belt, looked at Dixon and Mann, then stood up. They rose as well.

"There's nothing more to do here," Mann said. "At this point, ten, fifteen minutes isn't going to make a difference."

"I don't want to leave."

Dixon gave Vail's shoulder a squeeze. "It's time to go."

Vail smirked. "I think the fat lady is singing, Roxx."

Dixon gave her a firm hug. "The fat lady doesn't sing under my watch, Karen. She's not even here."

Vail turned and shook Mann's hand, thanked him, then headed off to grab her bag from Dixon's car.

As the cool night air struck her cheeks, she thought back to when she and Robby landed at SFO. The time ahead full of promise, fun, play, and relaxation. And now, as she settled into the rear seat of the black Towne Car, she wished she could have a "do over."

If only I hadn't insisted on working the Victoria Cameron case. If only I'd taken Robby's advice and let it go. If only she had done nothing that she had done.

Things would be different. Robby would be here with her. And she wouldn't feel the empty void that now enveloped her like a straitjacket.

PART 2

TRACTION

Washington Dulles International Airport
Fairfax & Loudoun Counties
Dulles, VA

The flight home was uncomfortable. Vail hadn't expected to sleep, but the woman next to her seemed to have bathed in some horrendous floral perfume—enough to perfuse every passenger on the plane. It irritated Vail's nose and she launched into a sneezing fit multiple times throughout the flight. And there was nothing she could do about it. There were no vacant seats—but she wasn't sure any seat was far enough away to evade the offensive scent.

After landing and powering up her phone, Vail e-mailed Dixon to ask if anything had broken while she was in the air. Dixon replied immediately: "Cannon's no help. Amnesia. Hang in there."

Now, standing in a Dulles restroom before heading out, she caught a glimpse of her face in the mirror. It may not have been a red-eye, but she exhibited all the manifestations of it. Add in the bruises and cuts, and she looked like a boxer who'd gone twelve rounds and lost. Felt like one, too.

She passed a coffee kiosk and grabbed a shot of espresso—full octane to get her brain and body moving—and went out to the curb, where Detective Paul Bledsoe was due to pick her up.

It was a quarter past five and the early evening was masked by a gray, depression-draped sky. Vail was not dressed for the weather, which she estimated at around 45 degrees. She waited just inside the doors until she saw Bledsoe arrive out front. She tossed her overnight bag into the backseat and climbed into his department-issued Crown Victoria.

"Where's your luggage?"

"It ended up being reduced to fine dust and aerosolized into the Napa air."

Bledsoe pulled away from the curb and entered the airport traffic, which was headed en masse toward other terminals—and the exit. He looked at her for additional explanation.

"Long story."

"With you, I know better than to ask." He merged left and followed the exit sign. "So, this case your boss brought you back for. Know anything about it?"

"Not a whole lot. I wasn't paying much attention, other than trying to get out of having to come home. Robby's still missing and when I left, we still had a lot of unanswered questions."

Bledsoe leaned forward in his seat to check his mirror, then changed lanes. "Make any progress?"

Vail bobbed her head from side to side. "I guess 'progress' is a relative term." She summarized what had transpired the past ten days with surprising detachment.

"Hopefully your luck's gonna turn," Bledsoe said as he entered the interstate. "I'm taking you over to meet my guy, name's Hector—"

"DeSantos. I remember. You really think he can help?"

"Don't know. But he's got access to people and information most law enforcement agencies don't even know exist."

"Hope you're right. I'm tired and pissed off and desperate."

"Good," Bledsoe said with a grin. "So nothing's new."

That brought a smile to Vail's face. "I guess, in a sense, it's good to be home."

He elbowed her, then accelerated.

DESPITE THE RUSH HOUR TRAFFIC, they arrived at the D.C. location of Clyde's a quarter past six. They started to put their names down, but Bledsoe made a point of brushing his sport coat back, which had the effect of flashing a little brass of his badge. Whether or not it made a difference, Vail didn't know, but they were seated within ten minutes. From what she knew of Clyde's at prime dinnertime, that was pretty damn good.

They were ushered up the grand staircase, past the hostess station, and into the strikingly ornate dining room. Elaborate blown glass dish–shaped light fixtures hung from the walnut wood ceiling, suspended by multiple wires that splayed out from a central point, providing just enough illumination to be romantic without being dark. Square columns rose throughout the room, dividing it into private dining areas.

Plate clanks, utensil clinks, and inspired chatter rose from the patrons. It was either a good place for a covert conversation or a bad one: you might not be able to hear what the other person at your table was saying—but neither would an eavesdropper hovering nearby.

They settled into a booth along the far wall, where gold leaf frames hung suspended adjacent to one another, covering the expansive wall. A busboy delivered a flat aluminum pitcher, embossed with black letters that read "Filtered Water."

"You ever been here before?" Bledsoe asked.

Vail was still taking in the décor. "First time."

"Everything's good. The sandwiches fit my budget and are delish. Especially the Reuben and the grilled Portobello."

Vail peeled open her menu and her eyes caught sight of the crab cakes. Her stomach growled. Without looking up, she asked, "So where's Mr. DeSantos?"

"Call me Hector. I won't tell you what my friends call me."

Vail looked up. Standing there was a man a couple inches over six feet, impeccably dressed in a dark pinstripe suit with small-rimmed designer glasses.

"Where'd you come from?"

"Originally?" DeSantos asked. "That's classified."

Vail frowned. "Look, Mr.—Hector. I'm in a real shitty mood. I've just had the week from hell chasing down two serial killers. My boyfriend's missing. More than that, believe me, you don't want to know."

Bledsoe slid over in his seat. DeSantos sat, then folded his hands on the table in front of him.

"You think you've got a lock on shitty weeks? Believe me, you don't want to hear some of mine." He looked hard at her, his eyes boring into hers, reinforcing what he had just told her.

Vail had no urge to push him on that assertion.

Bledsoe, apparently concerned over the icy start to their conversation, said, "I've asked Hector here because he can help."

DeSantos held up a hand. "We don't know that."

"Yes," Bledsoe said firmly, "we do."

DeSantos shook his head and looked away to his left, into the open end of the room. "I'm only here because I owe you. There are no guarantees I can offer you anything of value."

Vail closed her menu and looked at Bledsoe. "This is a waste of time."

"No, it's not. Just tell Hector what you know."

Before Vail could answer, the waitress appeared, ready to take their order. DeSantos, who hadn't even looked at the menu, ordered first. "You have steak?"

The waitress pointed at the closed menu in front of Bledsoe. "We've got a grilled sixteen ounce rib eye with—"

"Perfect."

"I'll have the Rueben," Bledsoe said.

Vail handed over her menu. "Salmon for me."

The woman asked a few more questions, then left.

Bledsoe gestured to Vail to pick up the conversation.

"Robby—Roberto Enrique Umberto Hernandez. Thirty years old, detective with Vienna PD."

"Little Vienna? They have detectives on their force?" He looked at Bledsoe. "I'm serious."

"Yes, Hector, they're a real PD and they've even got real detectives."

"So Robby and I were in Napa," Vail said, "and I was working the Crush Killer case, and he was out sightseeing and wine tasting."

DeSantos held up a hand. "So if Robby wasn't working the case with you, why did he tag along to California?"

"I didn't go there to work. It was supposed to be a vacation for both of us. But it didn't work out that way." Vail felt a pang of guilt in her abdomen. Heck, it was more than a pang. It was a lancing wound.

"So from what little Bledsoe told me," DeSantos said, "your friend's gone."

"That's about it. Cell left in the room, log deleted. Everything there, even his car. A bloodstain on the carpet, near the bed, cleaned up. We're awaiting DNA on the blood. We did the usual workup, but no one had seen him around. He had a friend, some guy named Sebastian, but we couldn't find a Sebastian in the whole freaking region who knew Robby. Wait, that's not true—what I said before, about no one seeing Robby. Someone had seen him. The serial killer we grabbed up last night recognized Robby when I showed him a photo. He wasn't sure where he'd seen him, but then he left me a message that seemed to suggest he'd seen Robby with a guy named César Guevara." Vail then provided further details, including background on César Guevara and his Superior Mobile Bottling business.

DeSantos leaned back, his head tilted, processing all the info. He looked at his water glass, lifted it, and took a drink. Finally he said, "This is some fucked up shit, Agent Vail. I don't know what to make of it. Or where to even begin."

"Call me Karen. And I know very well what we're dealing with. Thanks for your expert assessment." She looked at Bledsoe, thinking, *So far this has been real helpful.*

"You don't even know if he's still alive. Chances are good he's not. Are you prepared for that?"

"No, Hector, I'm not prepared for that. Would you be prepared to accept the death of a loved one if she went missing, without doing everything in your power to find her?"

DeSantos seemed agitated. He glanced at Bledsoe but did not look at Vail.

Bledsoe said, "Hector went through the death of a loved one. He knows what it's like. I don't think he made that comment lightly."

"I didn't," DeSantos said "And the facts are that after the first forty-eight hours—"

"I'm not some ill-informed civilian. I know what the deal is with missing persons. That's why I've been running myself ragged. Because I know that every minute that passes, the likelihood of finding him, if he is still alive—" She felt her throat catch and stopped.

DeSantos sucked on his cheek a moment, then said, "I've got some materials Bledsoe put together for me. I'm going to review them tonight and poke around. But I want to be totally honest with you. I'm probably going to have to dig deeper, use resources that should only be used for sensitive government work. Robby going missing is a personal case. At best, it's a local case for Napa County to deal with."

"That's not tr—"

DeSantos held up a hand. "I deal with issues where national security's at risk, where thousands, tens of thousands, or millions of lives are at stake. To use my resources for one life . . . "

"Rewind a bit, Hector," Bledsoe said. "If you were sitting in Karen's seat—"

"I get your point," DeSantos said firmly. "I already said I'd help and I'll honor that. You know me, you know I'm good for that. But you've gotta understand there are limits. That's just the way it is. Because if I step too deep into the shit, the director will be on my ass. I know him personally, and I try to keep my relationship with him in a good way."

Their food came, and Vail looked at the salmon in front of her. The presentation was exquisite and the aroma rising from her food did not disappoint. But she had lost her appetite. Robby was on her mind. She thought of all the serial killer victim families she had met over the years. Most at least knew the fate of their loved ones. Robby was gone. Alive? Injured? Dead? Tortured? Inhumanely disposed of? Not knowing was an internal torment she would have to deal with for now. It would fuel her hunger for finding him. Or finding answers to what had happened to him—and why.

Then she would catch whoever was responsible. And make him pay.

35

Bledsoe dropped Vail at home. She said a few words to the cop Fairfax County had assigned to watch over Jonathan, and then trudged up to her front door.

The porch light was out, making the area darker than usual. She made a mental note to change the bulb. For safety's sake, it's the least she could do. Lighting and trimmed shrubs were as important as locks . . . they acted as deterrents and indicated to a would-be offender that the occupant was aware of her environment and personal security.

Before Vail could bring up a fist to knock, the wooden door swung open. Her Aunt Faye was standing there, a dishrag in hand. "Well, well, well. I was beginning to wonder if you were ever going to come home."

Vail pulled on the screen door, then gave her aunt a hug. "It's good to be home."

Faye squinted, looking around Vail at the dark stoop. "Where's your luggage?"

Vail lifted her arm, revealing the day bag. "I packed light."

"Nonsense," she said, looking intently into Vail's eyes. "I remember you leaving with a large suitcase."

Vail moved into the house and tossed her bag onto the couch. "Let's just say it's a long story and leave it at that."

"Did your friend drop you off? Robby, isn't it?"

"He's—no, another friend of mine brought me home."

Faye leaned in closer, then turned on the living room light. She made a point of studying Vail's face. "What on earth happened to you?"

"Me?" *You don't want to know. Trust me.* She forced a phony smile. "All in a week's work. There's nothing I won't do for the Bureau."

"Uh-huh." She turned her head away, viewed Vail from the corner of her eyes. "So what was it, really?"

"A case. It got a little rough. Good thing is the bad guy got the worst of it."

"Your work is so dangerous, Kari. I don't know why you do it."

Vail wasn't going to be baited into this discussion. She was not in the mood to discuss it. Instead, she stepped into the hallway. "Jonathan home?"

"In his room."

Vail took another few steps to his door. Knocked. No answer. Napping? Not likely at 8:00 PM. Tried the knob—unlocked—so she walked in. Jonathan was sitting at his desk, his back to her, large black gaming headphones covering his ears and his Xbox 360 controller in his hand.

She came up behind him and tapped him on his shoulder. He twisted his neck quickly up and back—saw his mother—and set the controller down and pulled off the headset in one motion.

He rose to give her a hug but stopped an arm's length away. "What happened to your face?"

"All in a day's work. No big deal. Looks worse than it is." She took him in her arms and gave him a squeeze. "How was Aunt Faye?"

"Fine."

Vail sat on the edge of his bed. "I hope you two spent some time together. It was awfully nice of her to come out here to stay with you. Did you make her feel welcome?"

"We went out to dinner. And we caught a few movies."

"Good, good. Did you get to know her?"

He bobbed his head. "Yeah. We talked. She's easy to talk to."

Vail's brow rose. "Good. That's good to hear. I'm glad you two connected. She hasn't seen you in, well, a good five years. I doubt you remember her."

"We went to some state fair with her and she took me for ice cream. That's pretty much all I remember. She said we used to go to her house for a barbecue on the Fourth, but I don't remember any of that." He leaned back in his chair. "So is Robby coming by? I just unlocked a new character and I wanted to show him how I did it. He's gonna be so fucking jealous."

"Watch your mouth, please." She felt hypocritical—she was admittedly free with the expletives at times, but tolerating it from her son was a different matter. Of greater concern was what she should tell Jonathan about Robby. The truth was always best. But in this case, was it? Was lying to her son the lesser of two evils? "I don't think Robby's coming by, sweetie. Not for a while." There we go. Spoon it out until he stops asking questions—and maybe he'll satisfy his curiosity before she has to go into detail.

"You two broke up?"

Vail waved a hand. "No, nothing like that. We had a great time in Napa." *Of the time we had together. Before he vanished.* She rose from the bed and swept a hand across his cheek.

"Hey," he said. "What's up with that cop who's following me around? It's annoying."

"Just a precaution, sweetie. I don't want my work spilling over into my personal life." *Now there's a novel idea.* "Shouldn't be too much longer." She pointed at his Xbox. "Get back to your game. I'm going to go unpack." Jonathan slipped on his headphones and Vail walked out.

36

C are to tell me what really happened in California?"
Vail let go of Jonathan's doorknob and turned to see Faye
standing in the hallway, hands on her hips.

She was tired and mentally drained. Now was not the best time. Still, she owed Faye some explanation. And she needed to ask her for a favor.

Vail walked back toward the living room and they sat down next to each other on the couch. Not two months ago, she and Robby were making out on this sofa, headed toward a promising future, despite a brief interruption by the Dead Eyes killer.

"How was your visit with Jonathan?"

Faye's face brightened and broadened into a grin. "I wasn't sure what to expect, but I rather enjoyed it. We had some good talks. About his father. He had some unanswered questions."

Vail sighed. She had talked with Jonathan about what happened between her and Deacon but held back some of the details. She wasn't sure what the raw truth would do to a young teen and his place in the world. Then again, it was no secret to Jonathan that his father had turned into an abusive deadbeat. And Vail explained to her son that Deacon was a different person when she had met and married him. It was a good lesson as to the depths one can sink when a perfect storm of mental imbalance, medication indifference, and the spiral of depression conspire to bring down a person to the nadir of human suffering.

"How'd he take the answers?" Faye had a background in counseling, so Vail was not surprised that she had broached the topic with her nephew.

"Very maturely, I thought. He had a healthy perspective. I think he'll be fine. So—your trip."

"It started out wonderful and I stuck my nose where it shouldn't have been. I got involved in a case. And because of that . . . " She looked down at the coffee table. The short, squat bottle of V. Sattui Madeira she had shared with Robby was still there, a memory of their night together. A reminder of the start of a meaningful relationship. If she thought there was a chance it would hold Sebastian's fingerprints, she would've driven it directly to the lab.

"And because of that," Faye prompted.

"Because of that . . . Robby went missing a few days ago." She brought her eyes up to Faye's. Her aunt's mouth was open.

"What do you mean, 'went missing'?"

Vail got a couple glasses from the adjacent kitchen, poured some Madeira, and told Faye the whole story, beginning with their arrival in Napa. Soon the alcohol was flooding her bloodstream, making her head and arms feel like dumbbells.

"Do you think Detective Bledsoe's friend will be able to help?"

It was a question Vail had asked herself on the drive home from Clyde's. "I sure as hell hope so." She set her glass down on the table. "Aunt Faye, I have a favor to ask. And a proposition."

Faye leaned forward, apparently sensing the weight of Vail's request.

"Because of the nature of the investigation into Robby's . . . disposition, it may be necessary for me to come and go. Where, I don't know. But it could also entail long hours away from home." She put two fingers to the bridge of her nose. "Point is, I have no idea what's coming around the bend."

"You need me to stay," Faye said. Her demeanor was flat, neither excited by the idea nor turned off by it.

"And that brings me to my proposition," Vail said. "The room in the back. It's got a separate entrance, its own bathroom. There's even a plug for a mini fridge."

"Move here, move in with you."

"You'd be closer to me and Jonathan, and to Mom." Vail's mother, Emma, had Alzheimer's, and Vail had moved Emma from her childhood home in Westbury, New York, to an assisted care facility in Virginia.

"First things first," Faye said in a measured response. "Of course I'll stay for as long as you need me to. As to a longer-term arrangement, let me think about it. I don't have much keeping me in New York, but I just need to sit with the thought for a while. Okay?"

"Take as much time as you need." Vail barely got out the words before a yawn overtook her and flooded her eyes with fluid. "I've gotta get to bed. I haven't slept worth anything in days."

"Don't worry about anything here, Kari. You just work on finding out what happened to Robby. I'll handle the rest."

Vail said good night to Jonathan, walked into her bedroom, and collapsed onto the mattress.

37

*F*ollowing *their dinner at Bistro Jeanty, Robby ordered dessert to go, and when they arrived at their bed-and-breakfast room, he made her wait outside. When she protested, he smiled. "You said you trusted me."*

She tilted her head back and looked up into his eyes. "I do."

Inside, a room full of candles. And a night of passionate lovemaking . . .

Vail awoke from her dream curled into a tight ball. Her shirt was soaked, her hair matted to her face. Only this was not a nightmare—it was a memory. A memory of their last night together. The next morning, when she gave him a kiss on her way out, would be the last she would see of him.

Vail sat up in bed, wiped away the tears, and steeled herself. It was time to go to work.

VAIL WALKED INTO the behavioral analysis unit and found it a flurry of activity. Despite Thomas Gifford's claim that most of the profilers were out on leave, on assignment, or engrossed in vital projects, there was plenty going on.

Vail entered her office and sat down heavily. A stack of files on the corner of her desk was exactly as she had left it when she departed for California. A pile of messages was skewered on a pin to the right. She pulled them off, flipped through them, determined that none were time sensitive, and put them back on their holder. Except one: a reminder of her forthcoming counseling appointment with Dr. Leonard Rudnick.

She turned on her PC and watched as Windows booted up. While she sat there, she began to acknowledge the feeling she'd been fighting for days: that Robby had been murdered. The blood on the carpet in the B&B bothered her. If tests showed it was Robby's, it would increase the odds of a violent confrontation that Robby likely did not survive.

Though it was a fair amount of blood, it was not of sufficient volume to indicate a body had bled out in that spot. But if he'd been shot or stabbed—certainly possible. Then again, he could've been moved—he wasn't left there, so how soon after whatever violence befell him was he taken away? Or was that not his blood at all?

Vail opened Outlook and scanned through her mail. There was a message from Dixon, which came through yesterday around the time Vail was climbing into bed. As if Vail had sensed it, Dixon was writing her about a follow-up note regarding the blood on the carpet. She had spoken with the owner of the B&B, who said she knew about it, and claimed it was from a suicide attempt two or three years ago.

But the woman couldn't be absolutely sure it was the same room, and she thought it was on the other side of the bed—but whichever room it involved was cleaned with some sort of organic enzyme. They had thought of hiring a company that did crime scene cleanup, but it was costly and the chemical worked well enough that they did not need to replace the carpet. And the spouse, who had found her, did not want a police report filed, so the owner agreed to keep it quiet—which certainly was in the B&B's best interest, as well.

Vail replied, thanking Dixon and telling her she'd met with DeSantos and had no sense of whether or not it was going to bear fruit. As she hit Send, there was a knock on her open door. She swiveled her chair around and saw the stoic Art Rooney. She smiled and leaped from her chair, almost running toward him. She gave him a firm hug and told him she was glad to see him.

"Yeah, I got that from the greeting. Good to see you, too. Back home in one piece. Sometimes I'm concerned about you, Karen."

"If I had any sense, I'd be concerned, too."

"Got a minute?" he asked.

"For you? Always." She took her seat behind the desk and Rooney took the lone guest chair.

"I wanted to touch base with you on the Crush Killer. Gifford said you guys found him?"

Vail leaned back. "Yeah, he won't be plying his trade anymore. Ray Lugo shot him while I was questioning him, and he's now in a medically induced coma."

"What the hell was Lugo's problem?"

Vail told him. She described her interview with Mayfield, the shooting, meeting with Merilynn Lugo, the DVD, the Guevara connection and her less than legal foray into his residence, the discovery of the new victim, and the apprehension of James Cannon. And then she told him about Robby.

Rooney sat back in his seat and crossed his legs. His gaze roamed the small office as he worked through the particulars of the case. "So we're settled that Mayfield was a narcissist. And it sounds like Cannon was, to some extent, too—but his is an entirely different story. He was just learning to kill. Mayfield was his mentor. However it happened, they crossed paths and realized they had common inclinations. Mayfield took him under his wing and Cannon followed along, observing, learning. Then it was his turn to try his hand at the trade."

"That's probably why we caught him so quickly," Vail said. "He wasn't sophisticated as a killer. He rushed into it, had not planned his cover. He killed in the same community in which he lived—and not so anonymously. Even after crossing paths with a cop and an FBI agent, and making a pass at one of them, he still thought it was safe to kill."

"Remember, these killers don't think they're leaving behind markers for us to follow. We pick up on things they aren't even aware of."

"Yeah, thank god for all that. Makes our job possible."

"So that brings us to Detective Hernandez." His eyes roamed the room again. "There would normally be no logical reason to conclude there was a relationship of any kind to John Mayfield or James Cannon. Far as we know, they hadn't seen you with him. There'd be no reason why he'd have contact with either of them, no clear connection. So on the surface, I'd say you don't have to worry about Mayfield's comment about there 'being more to this than you know'—at least as it relates to Detective Hernandez. Maybe he was talking about Cannon's coming murders."

"I hadn't thought of that." She tapped her foot while she processed it.

Rooney pushed his chair back and rocked on the rear legs. "That brings us to the next question: what happened to him? Let's approach this as a typical missing persons case. A ton of people go missing each year. The possibilities include someone who disappears because of a criminal act he's committed and he drops under the radar. Another is because he's witnessed a criminal act and is afraid for his life. Or the most common, he's having an affair or escaping a failed relationship, and this is a less confrontational way out for him." He let the chair fall forward with a thump, then rested his forearms on his knees. "How are you handling it?"

"I haven't totally lost it. But I've come close."

Rooney nodded slowly. "If it was me, Karen, until I saw a dead body, I'd treat it as if he's alive; I'd need that in order to function."

"I now know what a victim goes through when her child is taken, presumed dead . . . but the body isn't found."

"Contrary to media myths, finding a body doesn't bring closure. It helps a little, I guess, but the pain never goes away." He waved at the air, as if dispersing smoke. "That's not what we're dealing with here. We'll find answers—and we'll find Detective Hernandez."

"Thanks, Art."

"I've got this thing the president needs me to deal with. Looks like I'm shipping off to Iraq in the morning, but I'll be in touch. You need something, call. If I go, I'll have a phone of some sort. Gifford will have the number."

"What number will I have?"

Gifford was standing in the doorway, a stealth entrance—as was his style.

"My winning lottery ticket," Vail said.

Gifford stared at her. "It's so nice having you back, Karen. I missed the sarcasm and dry humor. Then again, I've missed my hemorrhoids, too, so that puts you in the same class. Now—we had a 9:00 AM appointment, did we not?"

Rooney rose from his chair. "César Guevara. He could be the key. I'll give Austin Mann a call, touch base." He gave Vail a wink, then walked out. "You hang in there, you hear?"

"Loud and clear," Vail said. *But that's one of those things easier said than done.*

38

Thomas Gifford led the way to his office. Lenka, seated behind her desk, nodded to Vail as she passed.

Gifford sunk into his black leather chair, which sat in front of a large picture window on the building's second floor. He rolled the seat to the edge of his desk, grabbed a pair of metal-framed reading glasses, and stuck them on his nose. "This is your new case." He reached for a file folder, then flipped it open. "Vic is a twenty-eight-year-old player for the PFL, the Pro Football League. It's a start-up positioned to compete with the NFL. Vic's name was Rayshawn Shines. Played for the Redskins for five years before being cut and hooking up with the PFL." He stopped and removed his glasses. "Karen, you listening to me?"

Vail had to shake her head to dislodge the fugue into which she'd descended once Gifford began talking. "Yeah, of course. No. I'm—my mind's on Robby."

"Karen, I'm now talking to you as ASAC of the behavioral analysis units—"

"Since we don't socialize, sir, have you ever spoken to me as anyone else?"

Gifford ignored her jab. "Get your shit together. You have a new case here. I need you to focus. I need a productive profiler, not dead weight."

Dead weight? That hurts. "You have a way with words, sir." She may've understood, but she wasn't going to give him the satisfaction. She rose from her chair. "Who's the dick on the case?"

"He said he was going to touch base with you about it. Paul Bledsoe."

"Bledsoe? He didn't say anything—" But she immediately realized her mind hadn't been tuned to matters other than Robby's case. "I'll get with him right now." She turned and headed for the door.

"One other thing."

Vail stopped and turned.

"Your appointment with Dr. Rudnick. I expect you to keep it."

Vail twisted her mouth. "As if I don't have more important things to deal—"

"Look," he said, rising from his chair. "Your mental health is the responsibility of your unit chief and he and I have been concerned about all you've been through the past couple months. Dead Eyes, then the shooting at the White House, all that shit that happened to you in Napa—"

"No need for the recap. I know what my life's been like. I've lived it."

"Fine. Then look at this objectively. You may not be able to admit it to my face, but you know I'm right. Keep that appointment. That's an order."

"Yes sir," Vail said with a mock salute. She pulled open the door and left.

39

Vail called Bledsoe on the way back to her office and arranged to meet at the crime scene, John F. Kennedy Stadium, in thirty minutes.

Vail parked in the player's lot and badged the security guard, who told her he was expecting her. She was to meet Detective Bledsoe in the fitness facility, adjacent to the clubhouse.

The hallways were freshly painted and new industrial carpet had been laid recently, judging by the chemical smells that teased her nose. Vail pulled open the heavy metal door and stepped inside. An array of physical fitness equipment stared back at her, rivaling only the volume and selection of that found at Seattle's University of Washington facility, which she had visited once on a case. The FBI Academy's conditioning machines were impressive, but this was like an ocean compared to a lake.

"Karen. Over here." Bledsoe's deep voice from somewhere off in the distance was swallowed by the large room. The rows of equipment, combined with the floor-to-ceiling mirrors and awkward acoustics, made locating him a challenge.

"You didn't tell me we had a case together," she said.

"I started to last night, in the car. You weren't in the mood, so I left it alone."

"I'm still not in the mood. And I don't have a lot of time." She nodded at the bloodstained carpet, where white tape delineated the position and location of the corpse. "What's the deal here?"

"Rayshawn Shines, offensive lineman for the D.C. Generals of the Pro Football League. One of their stars. Found right there, garroted. Stabbed multiple times postmortem. No defensive wounds."

Vail stood over the bloody stain, as if looking at it would help her visualize the body as it lay the moment it had been found. It didn't.

"So why am I here? It's a homicide."

"His penis and balls were cut off."

Okay, that changes things. "So we've got a sexual homicide of a large male. How large?"

"Six-five, three hundred. They don't screen for drugs in this new league like they do in the NFL. Steroid and PED use is rampant. League's built on the concept of a narrower field, stronger armed quarterbacks, faster wide receivers. No huddles and more touchdowns."

"That glazed look in my eyes is boredom. But don't take it personally."

Ignoring Vail's remark, Bledsoe handed her a manila envelope. "Crime scene photos. Look 'em over in your spare time."

"What spare time?"

"Hear me out. The PFL had to give fans something more exciting, right? To compete. The average NFL game runs from ten to thirteen minutes of actual playing time. The other three hours is the clock running during huddles, commercials, replays, and time-outs. The PFL got it right—fewer time-outs. Twenty-nine to thirty-three minutes of action. Their games are very exciting, like a constant rush. But when you're up against a powerhouse like the NFL, you need a bigger gimmick. If a league wanted to grab attention, get a ratings bump, this might be a way to do it. Star player gets offed, that's big news."

Vail contorted her face. "Kind of a negative way to do it, don't you think? Bad publicity."

"I thought there's no such thing as bad publicity."

Vail considered the severed gonads and what bloggers would say if that fact were made public. "Your buff star player getting emasculated is good publicity?"

Bledsoe snorted. "Good point." Bledsoe picked at a spot on his forehead. "So what do you make of that sexual component?"

"That sexual component, yes." Vail sat down on a padded weight bench and thought for a moment. "First impression is that when we see male-on-male sexual homicide, we're looking at a homosexual offender. Or, it could be someone who's confused about his sexual identity, or someone who was sexually abused or exploited by a male figure as a child."

"That it?"

"If you're asking me to profile the offender, you know I can't do it yet—not accurately. There's only one vic."

"But there are behaviors here," Bledsoe said, craning his neck around.

Vail sighed. She wasn't in the right frame of mind to do this. She wanted to be putting the pieces of Robby's puzzle together, seeing if she'd missed something. She pulled herself up, took a deep breath, and cleared her thoughts. Tried to. She couldn't. "Look, I've got an appointment I have to get to. I really didn't want this case. Each minute that ticks by . . . "

"I know. But anything you can give me would help."

Vail checked her watch. "I think he'll kill again. This may not be his first kill. No defensive wounds on a big guy like Rayshawn Shines? Your UNSUB knows what he's doing. You can't do this and hesitate or you'll end up dead yourself. So he exhibited very high levels of confidence. He probably looks at this kill as an accomplishment. He did *this*, he can do anything. Unless this was a personal gripe, this killer enjoyed what he did. The garrote is an up close and personal kill. He enjoyed overpowering a big football star."

Bledsoe absorbed all this, then said again, "That it?"

"Until this guy kills again, there's probably not much else I can help you with." She held up an index finger. "Not true. If I can clear my head long enough to concentrate on this, I'll be able to give you more. Meantime, if you put together a list of suspects, I'll help narrow it down. And I can help map out an effective interview approach."

Bledsoe looked down at the blood-soaked carpet. "Okay."

"I know you don't want to hear this, but the more vics he leaves in his wake, the easier our job will be catching him."

"Yeah—not very comforting."

"It is what it is." Vail held up the manila envelope. "Here you go."

Bledsoe waved a meaty hand. "Those are yours."

"Oh, goodie. I'll put them in my photo album as soon as I get home. You know, the fancy leather one on my coffee table."

"Now there's the Karen Vail I know and love."

"The Karen Vail you know and love is officially on leave."

"DeSantos will come through," Bledsoe said. "I just got a feeling."

Vail twisted her arm and stole another look at her watch. "Gotta run. Doctor's appointment."

"Everything okay?"

"Bumps and bruises, but nothing that won't heal. This is for my mind. Mandatory."

"The shrink has to see a shrink. Ain't that a kick."

"You're being an asshole, Bledsoe. Don't ruin my opinion of you." She turned and headed out of the fitness room.

40

Vail had a hell of a time finding a parking spot on M Street, but finally walked into the tiered, gray marble–tiled lobby. She took the elevator up and entered the small, warmly lit waiting room of Leonard Rudnick, PhD. Well-maintained Persian rugs were arranged atop satin-finished mahogany floors.

Vail had just sunk into the seat when the office door opened. Standing there was a gaunt older man who barely broke five feet.

"Ah, Karen. Good to see you're back. I've been meaning to remind you that I've got a special entrance for agents." Rudnick thumbed an area over his shoulder. "It's around—"

"Why do I need a special entrance?"

Rudnick broadened his face into a forced grin, as if summoning patience for a petulant child. "Many agents I've treated over the years have preferred not to be seen entering a psychologist's office."

"I deal with the mind all day, doc. I'm not afraid to admit I have to see someone to get mine straightened out."

"But your ASAC sent you here. It wasn't a voluntary act."

"I was in denial. But Robby sat me down and we had a heart to heart. My boss was right in sending me here. Believe me, if I thought he was wrong—"

"You wouldn't have come?"

Vail let a smile tease her lips. "Something like that."

"Come," Rudnick said, motioning her in with both hands, a hyper-welcoming gesture. "Let's start."

Vail sat down in a firmly upholstered seat opposite an identical counterpart a few feet from her.

"So," Rudnick said, patting his thighs. "Tell me. How's the anger management going?"

Why'd he have to start with that? How do I begin to answer? Should

I tell him about my interactions with Scott Fuller—where I held my tongue but ended up in a fistfight—or about my confrontation with César Guevara, where I rammed my Glock into his forehead? Tough choice.

"You're hesitating. Does that mean it's been a mixed result?"

Vail grinned. "I couldn't have put it better."

"Well, then. That's okay, Karen. It's a work in progress. You at least have seen some improvement, hmm?"

"Definitely. I find I'm able to hold my thoughts without them spilling out. I'm getting better at filtering the sharp retorts. Except when it comes to my boss. I can't help myself."

Rudnick's brow rose about a foot. "You—you talk back to Mr. Gifford?"

Vail waved a hand. "All the time."

Rudnick nodded slowly but did not respond to that. "Yes. Well. Let me ask you—"

"It's not a big deal. I just—you know how it is with some people. You've got a different way of relating to them. Some people you can joke around with, others you can't. My boss, I can give him some abuse. I can usually tell when I push him too far."

"So this is humor? You poke fun at him?"

"I guess there are times when I do that. Mostly it's sarcasm."

"And he's okay with that?"

Vail shrugged both shoulders, a slow, demonstrative movement. "I'm still gainfully employed as a supervisory special agent. But—honestly, that's the least of his issues with me. He probably figures it's best to choose which battles to fight."

Rudnick chewed the inside of his cheek. It wasn't pronounced, but Vail could see his jaw moving, and a slight concavity in the skin.

"I'm scaring you, aren't I?" Vail asked.

"Scaring?" He laughed. A short burst. "Not the word I would choose, no. But you are . . . *concerning* me. Respect for a superior is a basic tenet of an organizational structure. Surely you have a feel for that. So when you purposely abuse your ASAC, it tells me there's more going on beneath the surface. Would you agree?" Rudnick tilted his head, sliding his chin slightly to his right.

Vail checked her watch. She couldn't help it. Robby was on her mind—no surprise there—and she needed to get back to his case.

"Someplace you'd rather be?"

Vail looked up. "Hmm?"

"Checking your watch. It tells me—"

"Yes. You want me to be honest with you, so I'll tell you what's going on. Robby went missing. While I was in Napa—"

"During your vacation?"

"Yeah, well, things didn't really work out the way we'd planned." She sighed, rubbed hard at her left eye. *Do I have to go through this again?*

"Did you and Robby have a . . . disagreement? Does that explain those bruises on your face?"

Vail sat up in her chair. "No, no. Nothing like that." She took him through the events of the past ten days, realizing it was going to eat up a good portion of the remaining appointment time.

Rudnick listened with riveted interest. When she finished, he leaned back and seemed to absorb her pain. His eyes were glazed with nascent tears. "You've dealt with cases where families never learn the fate of their missing loved ones, yes?"

Vail nodded almost imperceptibly.

"Then this episode, at its very least, will make you a better agent. It will give you instant credibility when confronting a similar situation. That type of empathy can't be faked or created. It's genuine or it's not there." He paused a moment, studied her face, then continued. "As to you personally, how are you dealing with Robby's disappearance?"

Vail wrapped a lock of hair around her right index finger, then pulled it behind her ear. "Not very well. That was one of those times when my anger management counseling didn't help."

"Understandable," Rudnick said. "What else?"

"As you'd expect. I'm on edge. I'm not sleeping well. When I get the chance to actually sleep." She turned toward the wall where the doctor's numerous certificates and licenses hung in ornate gold leaf frames. There was even a commendation or award of some sort bearing the Bureau seal, but at this distance she couldn't make it out.

"I see. And how will you feel should you find out that Robby has died?"

Vail felt a ball in her throat, blocking her airway. She coughed, a dry rasp that cleared her trachea but didn't completely dislodge the lump. "I refuse to accept his death. Not now. When I see a body," she nodded. "Then I'll accept it. Then I'll deal with it. Until then, he's alive."

"I think we may need to eventually discuss at what point you stop looking and possibly accept a fate we don't want to acknowledge."

Vail started to answer but Rudnick held up a hand.

"That's not for us to discuss right now. I'm planting a seed. At present, you have a goal. You're driven to find someone who means a great deal to you." He tilted his head, looked her face over, side to side, then top to bottom, before coming to rest on her eyes. "But don't let it consume you, Karen. You have a son who depends on you. From what you've told me, he's developed a special relationship with Robby, that Robby fills the void left by your absent and ill-intentioned ex-husband. Yes?"

"Yes."

"Then remember that Jonathan will be hurting, too."

Vail dropped her gaze to her lap.

"Does Jonathan know? About Robby?"

"He asked me if Robby was coming by. I danced around the question but didn't say anything about his going missing."

"There'll come a time when you realize it's best to level with your son. And he's going to need you. You can bring him with you, if you'd like. And you can break the news to him here."

Vail looked up, pursed her lips. "Thanks. I think I'd rather do it. At home." She shook her head, as if waking from a trance. She balled her right hand. "But that's not going to be necessary because I'm going to find Robby. Alive."

Rudnick sat back. "Keep your head, Karen. Rational thought will help you find answers. Stay within yourself. Remain focused. And remember: emotion will cloud your thinking, blind you to what's there in front of you."

"I see you know me quite well."

Rudnick lifted both hands palm up and smiled. "I'm a student of behavior, Karen. Just like yourself."

"Everything's a learning experience."

"That's true," Rudnick said. But his face stiffened and he leaned forward with an index finger raised. "Just make sure you take away the correct lesson."

41

As Vail made her way back to her car, she mused on the lure of counseling. Talking through your feelings felt good, if you had a skilled therapist who put you at ease. Still, the lure had to be tamed, because if you were not careful, it could become a crutch. And she prided herself in being able to solve her own problems. That was part of what made her a good field agent—instead of always asking for directions or assistance, she knew the constructs of her rules and regulations—and she acted accordingly. *Fine, sometimes I act outside those regs . . . but, fuck it. Aside from my visits to Guevara, I never strayed too far and OPR's investigations always cleared me.*

The drive back to Aquia, Virginia, where the behavioral analysis unit was located, allowed her to be alone with her thoughts in a relaxed, posttherapeutic state, for the first time she could remember. She had been in motion, in meetings, and in confrontations for eleven days straight, with little sleep. The amount of adrenaline her body had manufactured and released over that time period would be precedent setting. *Does Guinness track world records for biologic fluid production? Probably not.*

Vail took the 143A exit off I-95, then swung her car into the unit's parking lot. Two minutes later she was walking the hall to her office. The lure of her boss's door was too great. She grabbed the knob, pushed through, and greeted Lenka. "Can I have a minute?"

"Let me see if he's free." She lifted her phone and pushed a button. A moment later, she said, "You can go in."

Vail took a seat in front of Gifford's oversize desk. "Anything new from the San Francisco field office on Robby?

Gifford peered at her over his reading glasses. "Nothing. They were just given the case yesterday, Karen. Cool your jets."

"Who's the lead agent?"

Gifford held up his hands. "No. I'm not going to tell you. I want you hands-off. Let them do their jobs. They don't need Karen Vail giving them the third degree every day."

Vail opened her mouth to object.

Gifford pointed at her across the desk. "And don't tell me that wouldn't happen."

Vail swallowed her words and shrunk in her seat. *Oh, yes it would happen. Yessiree. I'd keep them on their toes. I'd drive their asses to work the case hard.*

"Do you know if they've at least gotten hold of Robby's cell phone logs? I haven't heard back from the lab about whether or not they've been able to recover the call data off his phone. I haven't even gotten his logs from the wireless carrier."

"All of that's going directly to the agents out of San Francisco."

Vail clenched her jaw. "If you don't mind me asking, sir—"

"Whenever you start a sentence like that, my answer should be, 'Yes, in fact, I do mind,' so don't bother asking."

Vail ignored the remark. "I don't get why it was so important for me to abandon Robby's search. Yeah, the PFL vic looks like the work of a sexual predator, and the UNSUB is likely someone who could become serial, but it's not a serial case. Not yet. If ever."

"I told you—not that you were listening—but it's a high-profile murder. I had no one else to assign it to and I wanted to get out in front of it ASAP."

"But the body's been moved. Another few days wouldn't have mattered."

Gifford removed his glasses. "Another few days. Really. When do you think you'd have been ready to come home, Karen? If you hadn't broken Detective Hernandez's case, you'd still be stalling, hoping you'd find something. And I'd be short an agent."

Vail felt her blood pressure rising. "You'd be short an agent? Big fucking deal. Robby—Robby could be holed up in a shed somewhere in Napa, without food and water. He won't survive much longer."

"And he could already be dead." Gifford looked away and rubbed a hand across his forehead. "I'm sorry. I shouldn't have said that."

He met Vail's eyes, and she could see his face was flushed, his remorse genuine.

"I'm as concerned about Robby as you are," he said in a low voice.

"There are agents working the case. If there's something to do, something that only you can do, I'll let you know. But you've got other work. I have three units to run. And your unit chief's not a happy camper, trying to juggle cases with a skeleton crew. It's my job to make sure he can do *his* job."

"Well then." Vail pushed herself up from the chair. "I guess that means I should get back to work. I don't want my unit chief to be *unhappy*. Thanks for keeping me in the loop." She walked out and closed the door behind her a tad harder than was necessary.

42

Vail sat down heavily at her desk. Finding out which agents were assigned to Robby's case would not be difficult. A quick call to the field office would give her the information in a matter of minutes. She reached for her phone and noticed the light was blinking. She lifted the receiver and retrieved her voice mail.

The automated faux persona said, "Message left at 8:46 AM, today."

A familiar voice boomed across the little speaker.

"You know who this is, Agent Vail. I thought you should know that by now, your friend is dead. Don't ask how I know this because I'll never tell you and you'll never find out. But I have my sources. You see, I may not always operate within the law, but apparently neither do you."

Click. The computer voice said, "Next message."

She dropped the handset at her side and sat there, attempting to absorb what she had just heard. *Think! Concentrate. The voice. The voice sounded like César Guevara's. Robby is dead? He's screwing with me. Revenge for breaking into his house. How did he know I was back in Virginia? Is Roxxann at risk?*

"Hey." Knock at the door. "Hey—"

Vail pulled her face up toward the voice.

"You okay?" Hector DeSantos asked. He walked toward her, but she did not move.

Think, can't think, Robby is dead? Can he be trusted, how do I check if he's right—

"Karen." DeSantos had moved around her desk and was pulling her up and out of the chair. "Look at me. What's wrong?"

Vail hung there in his arms. Her gaze swung down toward the phone. *Talk. Tell him.* She licked her lips. Dry mouth, tongue thick, sticky. "Call. Guevara's voice. He said—he said—" She pulled her eyes toward his. "He said Robby's dead."

"The guy's a scumbag, Karen. He's just fucking with you. Ignore what he said." He looked at her, then gave her a gentle shake. "Karen, focus on my voice. Listen to me."

She closed her eyes tight, then opened them.

"Think for a second. Reason this through. Why would Guevara do something as blatant as leave you, a federal agent, a voice mail like that when he's already under suspicion?"

Vail took a deep breath. DeSantos was trying to wring out her emotions, make her think. *Back to logic. My comfort zone.* "Because Guevara's not a guy that's pushed around by anyone. Because I broke into his house and went through his things. Given who he is, that's a huge insult. Who the hell am I to do that to him and get away with it?"

"Leaving you a message like that may not be smart," DeSantos said, "but he's got a huge ego and he needed to strike back at you. Psychological warfare can be very effective."

Guevara's showing me he's above the law. He wanted to get inside my head. And it worked.

DeSantos tilted his head, studied her face. "You look like you're spacing out on me."

Vail shook her head. "Yeah. No. I mean I'm here."

"Good. Because I did some digging around, and I found out some shit you're not going to like."

She looked at him but did not answer.

"Come with me."

DeSantos led Vail by the arm out of her office and down the hall. She was still numb, in a fugue like none she had ever experienced. Things moving by her, noises in the background. *Robby's alive. It's not true. Just psychological warfare. But what if it's not, what if—*

"I accidentally came across something. It was classified and filed in a way that made my nose twitch." He looked at her, then stopped walking and pushed her up against the wall. "You with me? I need your full attention, Karen."

"Yeah. Yes." She took a deep, uneven breath.

"I came across something unusual. So I sniffed under the rock, one thing led to another, I made a few phone calls . . . and I ended up at the deputy administrator for the DEA. But I hit a brick wall. I couldn't get shit. Before I started calling in favors and getting the FBI director involved, I took another look at what I had, dug a little more, and found another name associated with all this, someone accessible who we'd be able to speak with."

Vail straightened up, pushed away from the wall. Like smelling salts under the nostrils, her brain whipped back awake. "Who is it? I want to talk to this guy."

DeSantos looked at her a long moment, then said, "I thought you might. Let's go."

Vail followed DeSantos down the hall—and into Thomas Gifford's office.

"Can we have a moment with Mr. Gifford?" DeSantos asked.

Lenka hesitated, glanced at Vail, then at the sharply dressed DeSantos. "And you are—"

"Hector DeSantos, DoD." He pulled a credentials wallet and held it in front of her face.

"What's this about?"

"Agent Vail and I need a moment with ASAC Gifford."

Vail shook her head. "Hector, we're wasting time. Let's just go and see this guy. I don't need permission from my ASAC to leave the building." She turned toward the door, but DeSantos grabbed her arm. "We don't need to leave the building. The person you need to talk with is right here."

Gifford's door opened. Vail and Gifford faced each other. Gifford's gaze flicked over to DeSantos.

"Hector De—"

"I know who you are," Gifford said.

"We're here about Detective Roberto Hernandez," DeSantos said, then stepped forward and pushed past Gifford into his office.

Gifford stepped aside. "Sure, just come on in," he mumbled. He turned toward Vail and said, "Are you coming, too?"

43

Gifford sat down in his chair. Very official and stiff. He folded his hands in front of him and rested them on the desk. "Is there something I can help you with?"

DeSantos leaned forward. "Oh yeah, I'd say there is."

"Is there a problem, Mr. DeSantos? I detect an attitude."

DeSantos seemed to study Gifford a moment. Vail watched the warring male egos, relieved that she was not part of it.

"I was asked to assist in locating Detective Hernandez and—"

"I thought I told you there were agents working this case," Gifford said, his hard brow and stern voice aimed at Vail.

"*I'm* talking to you at the moment," DeSantos said.

"Excuse me? Listen here, Mr. DeSantos. I'm the assistant special—"

"I know what you are. Acronyms aside, you're a goddamn liar."

Gifford sat there, his entire head shading red with anger.

"Hector," Vail said. "Back up a second. Please. Let's keep this civil. What are you talking about? You said you found some information on Robby's case."

"Yes." He turned to Gifford. "I got into a classified DEA file. I spoke with Deputy Administrator Donaldson but he wouldn't tell me shit. But there was another name there. Yours."

Gifford did not move. "So?"

"The other name in the file was Roberto Enrique Umberto Hernandez. Now I don't know about you, but there aren't two people I know of with that name. And I also know there isn't a good goddamn reason why Roberto Hernandez's name should be in a classified DEA file."

Gifford leaned back in his leather chair. Bit his bottom lip and examined the ceiling.

Vail and DeSantos shared a glance as Gifford began speaking.

"Detective Hernandez—Robby—wanted in to the FBI. But he

didn't want any help. No favors, no strings, no one on the inside making it happen. He wanted to earn it."

"I already know that," Vail said. "He and I have been down that road."

"He has a friend in Napa. Sebastian—"

"We tried tracking him down," Vail said. "Sebastian doesn't exist."

"His name's Antonio Sebastiani de Medina. Goes by Sebastian."

Vail cursed under her breath. *Hadn't seen that coming.*

"Sebastian is a veteran undercover DEA agent working to infiltrate a violent Mexican drug cartel. Sebastian's partner was killed in a freak car accident a couple weeks ago and he needed a quick replacement who could step in for one transaction."

Vail felt her stomach beginning to turn. She closed her throat, fearing she might vomit.

"Sebastian recommended Robby because he knew him and he figured they'd work well together. For Robby, it was an 'audition' of sorts— if all went well, he could turn it into a permanent position with DEA. We've done this before, but it's usually with task force members who are federalized as DEA task force officers. There wasn't any task force in place, but Sebastian was both desperate and insistent. And his ASAC, though reluctant initially, gave in because Robby fit the bill and they needed him."

"But—"

Gifford held up a hand to silence Vail. "That's not all. Behind the scenes, Robby mentioned this job to me. He and I had talked a few days earlier about applying to the Bureau. But there are problems with that. With the budget deficit, we're on a hiring freeze and shifting personnel around toward antiterrorism efforts, and . . . the biggest problem, and which I didn't know until I happened to ask, Robby never got his B.A. He stopped a few credits short, so he has to finish that out and get his degree before he can apply."

"I didn't know that."

"He didn't realize it was an issue until he got the app. It's not something he talks about." Gifford leaned the chair upright. "Robby doesn't know, but I reached out to Sebastian's ASAC, Peter Yardley, with the understanding that he didn't tell Sebastian, because I didn't want Robby to know it came from me. Yardley wasn't going to do it, because he was being a prick and if it went south he didn't want his ass getting whipped.

But when I called, I told him Robby was a good fit because of his background growing up in LA, in gang areas. He grew up around the drug trade and spoke Spanish fluently. Yardley was still noncommittal, but I asked him to do me a favor. I vouched for Robby, and Yardley said he'd review the file again. Next thing I know, Robby tells me Yardley's giving it a 'go' based on Sebastian's recommendation."

"So this undercover op was in Napa?" Vail asked.

"Your trip to Napa was a setup from the start. When I ordered you to take a vacation, I'd already planned to tell you to get out of town, based on all you went through with Dead Eyes. But when the shootout happened in front of the White House with Danny Michael Yates, it was an added bonus because it gave me an obvious and immediate reason to tell you to take time off."

"Going to Napa was Robby's idea," Vail said, half to herself. "And Sebastian arranged those wine cave tickets . . . "

"Certain details of his op, what he was doing, who he was meeting with, were classified," Gifford said. He stopped, looked down at the desk.

"You knew all along and you didn't say anything," Vail said. She rose from her seat and leaned both palms on the desk. "Do you know what I've been through? And this—this bullshit about coming home for the Rayshawn Shines case—"

"That was true. Sort of. We do need you working the Shines case, and we are shorthanded. But I also didn't want you poking around anymore. You're too damn good, Karen. I was afraid the longer you were there, the greater the chance you'd figure out what was going on."

"Son of a bitch." Vail held his gaze, refusing to blink.

"Karen," DeSantos said. "Take a breath."

"Sit down," Gifford said, one word at a time. "And get yourself under control."

Vail ground her molars but didn't move. DeSantos placed a hand on Vail's forearm, but she shook it aside, then took her time returning to her chair.

"You could have trusted me," she said. "You could've told me what was going on."

"All I know is that it was dangerous. I didn't want to take any chances. It's undercover, for Christ's sake. I shouldn't have to explain this to you."

Vail sighed deeply. "But if we hadn't found that vic in the wine cave, if the Crush Killer hadn't—"

"Robby said he had it all worked out. There were times when you'd be busy. He told me he booked a massage and some spa time for you. During those hours, he was off with Sebastian meeting their contact. According to Yardley, he also got called out during the night—he left, met with Sebastian and the contact, and was back before you woke up."

Vail shook her head. "If only you'd told me you knew where he was and that everything was okay . . . "

"Would you really have been satisfied with that?"

Vail took a moment to answer. "No. But at least I would've known."

DeSantos shifted himself in his chair. "If all he had were those two meets, where was he when Karen was trying to reach him the day they caught John Mayfield?"

"According to Yardley, the meet with their contact went extremely well," Gifford said. "The guy took to him. So Yardley let him continue. And since you were busy with the Crush Killer, he knew you weren't going to be a problem."

"So that's what I was, a problem?"

"For an undercover op," DeSantos said, "yeah, you'd be a problem."

Vail shook her head. "I can't believe this. He lied to me. Robby lied to me."

Gifford leaned both elbows on his desk. "Karen, be realistic about this. Robby was prepped to make one appearance, to meet with this one contact. He hoped it could lead to something permanent with DEA so he could build his resume. But he did a great job and it worked. Yardley was impressed. All I know is that he was granted emergency TFO—task force officer—status. My guess is that circumstances dictated that he go deep. And when you go deep undercover—"

"He left, without telling me. He disappeared."

"More than that I don't know."

Vail shook her head slowly. Almost to herself, she said, "That would certainly explain the delay in getting Robby's cell phone logs."

"Don't expect those records anytime soon," Gifford said. "Obviously, there'll be calls to and from sensitive targets. DEA's got that data locked down tight."

Vail brought a hand to her mouth. "Oh my God. Oh my God—" She rose from the chair and nearly knocked it backward. She grabbed both temples.

"What's wrong?" DeSantos asked.

She turned to Gifford and pointed. "Get the name of the contact, of the guy Robby and Sebastian were meeting."

Gifford chuckled. "Were you not listening? I can't get that information. It's classified."

"Bullshit. Call Yardley, tell him you need to know."

"He won't tell me, Karen," Gifford said. He shrugged. "He won't."

"I'll get the name," DeSantos said. "You have a secure line I can use?"

Gifford reached over and pulled a phone from a drawer. He handed the receiver to DeSantos. "Who are you calling?"

"The director. He'll have a chat with the DEA administrator, and he'll get us the name."

Gifford held up a hand. "Above my rank. Good luck with that."

DeSantos punched in the numbers. "Keep your fingers crossed."

44

Vail watched while DeSantos began his quest to track down FBI director Douglas Knox. As he waited for Knox to take his call, Vail's BlackBerry buzzed. She thought about whether to answer, noticed it was Dixon, and grabbed it as she moved out of Gifford's office. Dixon . . . pretty early in California. Must be important.

"Roxx," Vail said, "you're not going to believe—"

"Are you near a computer?"

"I can be. What's going on?"

"Don't laugh," Dixon said. "But I want you to go to YouTube."

"No, wait. I've got some news for you."

"Listen to me. Open it up and type in 'Lugo confession.'"

Vail continued down the hall and slipped into her office. Sat at her desk and tapped on her keyboard. Opened YouTube. "Okay, typing in 'Lugo confession.'"

"Scroll down. See Ray's face?"

"Scrolling," Vail said. "Wait—did you say Ray's face? Lugo *confession*?"

"Just find the video."

Vail passed the thumbnail that displayed Lugo's image, then fingered her mouse wheel and clicked on the video. "Got it."

"Turn up your speakers."

Vail pressed Pause, then said, "Wait, what am I watching? Where'd this come from?"

"WITSEC approval came through for Merilynn Lugo. Surprised the shit out of me—out of everyone. Just guessing here, but maybe they figured that since Mayfield and Cannon are still alive, there was still a reasonable threat against her. When I met the U.S. Marshals Service at her place, she handed me a piece of paper with the name of this video written on it. Now just watch it."

As she moved her mouse toward the link, she noticed that it said, in fine print, *4 days ago*. "This was uploaded four days ago?"

"Yes, right before we caught Mayfield. Press Play."

Vail did as instructed. As on the DVD, Ray Lugo's face appeared on-screen, in a dimly lit room. The image jerked a bit, the result of a low-quality webcam. "If you're watching this, it means I'm dead. Hopefully, I was successful in taking out the man who's made my life a living hell. I don't know his name, but he's someone who kidnapped my wife and son five months ago. I guess Merilynn already gave you the DVD I left with her.

"If she didn't, she and my son were returned unharmed, but with a warning that he'd kill them unless I did things to help him out. At first it was just getting some information for him. Then it became addresses, home addresses, and other information about people that I needed to use the Police Department and county database to look up. And then he wanted me to get him a prox card, which would give him access to the Sheriff's Department."

Vail closed her eyes. *Shit, Ray, you should've told us all this. We could've done something. And it would've helped us.*

"I didn't realize what he was doing with the card, or all the info I was getting for him, until he asked for stuff on someone I knew, a friend of mine." He bit his bottom lip and looked away from the camera. Seconds later, he turned back and tears were streaming over his lower lids onto his cheeks. "Our first vic, Victoria Cameron. Honest, I didn't know what he wanted with her. I tried to ask him about it, but he told me to shut up and do as I was told. A couple days later, Vicky was dead. And I knew we had a problem.

"I tried. For months, I tried finding him. Son of a bitch was good. Too good. I got nowhere, and when I poked around, he knew. He *knew*." Lugo tightened his jaw, then took a breath and blew it out.

"I should've said something. I'm sorry, I should've leveled with all of you. But there was nothing we could've done. I didn't know who the guy was. I had nothing on him that would've helped catch him. But . . . " He wiped at his eyes, looked off to his right, then back to the camera: "As we kept finding new victims, I felt like I should've been able to do something. I felt responsible. But I was just trying to protect my family. I had no idea what he was doing . . . "

He wiped his face across his sleeve. "I had no idea he was using some of this information to locate and kill people. I—I don't know what I would've done if I'd known. I truly believe he'd come after my wife and son—no matter where we went.

"So if you're watching this, my wife has told you where to find it. I assume she's safe. And I assume I was successful in killing this goddamn fucking monster who's made the last five months of our lives a living hell. Wondering if he's watching us, if he's going to keep his end of the deal . . ."

He paused, dropped his chin down—it looked like he had fallen asleep—but there was still timeline left on the video.

Lugo's head came up and he said, "César Guevara is tied into this somehow. I don't know how, but I've just got a feeling. There's gotta be something. If he is somehow affiliated with our killer, I don't want him skating by. Again, I'm sorry. But know that I gave my life trying to keep my family safe. And, yeah, mix a little revenge into that too. A lot of revenge."

He sat there looking at the camera, then said, "Take care. I feel honored to have served with all of you."

Vail closed the window.

"Open Live Messenger," Dixon said.

Vail clicked and signed in, then added the Sheriff's Department email address. A moment later, a request for a video call popped up. Vail accepted, and Dixon's face filled the screen. The sight of her friend's image made her feel good. There hadn't been many moments like that of late.

"So Ray was more deeply wrapped up in this than we thought," Dixon said. "That explains why he was so agitated and stressed out. He knew what was going on but wasn't telling us."

"Don't be so hard on him, Roxx. He thought he was doing what he had to do to protect his wife and son. It's a horrible choice to have to make."

"Still . . . he could've pointed us in the right direction."

"What direction was that? We were already looking at Superior and Guevara. The only thing we might've been able to do is to put a tail on Ray so that when Mayfield contacted him, we could track it. But that would've run the risk that Mayfield would've found out or detected it somehow. And Ray probably wasn't willing to take the risk that we'd be able to adequately protect Merilynn and Mario." She shook her head. "We still don't have the whole picture."

"I'm going to talk with Brix about putting some undercovers on Guevara. It'll be tough, because the street-wise SOB may pick it up. But we still don't have enough for a search warrant." She brushed her blonde hair off her face. "Let me switch gears a minute. I haven't heard any-thing from the San Francisco field office about Robby. If they're working the case, I'm in—"

"That's what I was going to tell you," Vail said. She rested both fore-arms on her desk and said, "You're not gonna believe this, but Robby's working undercover. I can't go into it over an unsecure line. But that ex-plains why he suddenly disappeared. He went dark."

Dixon's eyebrows rose. "No way!" She sat back in her chair. "That's a huge relief. But Jesus, I can't believe he didn't tell you. I mean, doesn't he realize what he put you through?"

"I just found out a minute before you called, so it hasn't really sunk in. Let's just say I feel betrayed. Bottom line, he didn't trust me."

Vail's desk phone buzzed. "Agent Vail," Lenka's voice said over the speaker. "Mr. Gifford wants you in his office right now."

"On my way." Vail faced the webcam. "Roxx—"

"Before you go. Aaron's analysis of those fibers they found in the blood in Cannon's shed turned out to be deer, as we thought. They combed through his house and found the body buried in his yard. Clearly a brutal act. Nothing tentative about it."

"Not surprising."

"I thought you'd want to know."

"You thought right. Gotta run. I'll call you later."

Vail disconnected the call and ran out, back toward Gifford's office.

45

Vail didn't have time to put further thought into Cannon's door killing, but she felt as if she already knew everything she needed to know about it, and the man—at least for the purpose of her current task.

When Vail walked into her ASAC's office, DeSantos and Gifford were standing and arguing—and stopped the moment she entered. They turned to look at her.

"What's going on?" she asked.

"Robby's undercover contact," DeSantos said. "His name is César Guevara."

Vail processed that a long second, then reached back for a chair and sat down heavily. The discovery of Robby's handwriting in Guevara's house suddenly came into focus. "Shit. Shit. Shit." She dropped her head into her hands. "I'm not feeling very well."

"What's the problem?" DeSantos asked.

Without raising her head, Vail said, "When Robby went missing, I went into a frenzy. I looked everywhere. The task force and the Napa Special Investigations Bureau mobilized. I gave them Robby's photo to show around town." She grasped her hair in both hands. "And I . . . I showed it to Guevara."

But that wasn't the worst of it. Vail yanked her phone and pulled up the photo Jonathan had sent her. The image struck her like a slap to the cheek.

DeSantos must have seen her reaction, because he reached over and grabbed the BlackBerry from her hand. "Ah, shit."

Vail watched as he handed the phone to Gifford, who took a look, then sat down slowly in his chair.

"Hector, get the DEA administrator on the line—and have him conference in Yardley."

DeSantos paged to the number, then lifted the secure handset.

"I've got some more disturbing news," he said as DeSantos made his call. "We've lost contact with Robby and Sebastian. They missed their last three check-in times."

Vail felt panic rising in her throat like bile. She steeled herself, tried to settle her nerves. *Now's not the time to freak out.* As Rudnick had said, she had to keep her emotions in check. This wasn't exactly what he was referring to, but it certainly applied.

"Yes, Mr. Administrator, I'm here with ASAC Gifford and Agent Vail. I'm putting you on speaker." DeSantos listened a moment, then gestured to Gifford, who pressed a button. "He's bringing Yardley online."

A moment later, DEA administrator Bronson McGuire's voice filtered through the speaker. "Yardley and I are here. What's the problem?"

"Sir, Karen Vail. I've just been briefed on Roberto Hernandez's undercover op." *Would've been nice to put me in the loop, asshole.* "I was with him when we—"

"Yes, yes, Agent Vail. I'm familiar with the op. What's the problem?" he repeated.

Vail clenched her jaw. *Emotions in check.* "When he went . . . missing, the Napa County major crimes task force began an all-out search. I obtained a photo to distribute to the LEOs for them to show around the community. I needed a picture fast, and I used one I had from a few weeks ago. We took it at the FBI Academy." She paused, as if the next sentence was too painful to utter. But she pressed forward nonetheless. "We took it in front of the academy sign."

There was silence, so Vail continued.

"You could see the large 'FBI' lettering." She closed her eyes. "I showed the photo to César Guevara. And I may've referred to him as 'a colleague of mine.'" At the verbalization of those facts, Vail began to perspire. No, dammit, she was *sweating.* The implication was clear: she had inadvertently blown Robby's cover. And the fact that they had lost contact with their undercover agents could only portend a less than optimistic result.

"Well," McGuire said, "this is just fucking goddamn great. Nice work, Agent Vail."

"Now hang on a minute, *sir,*" Gifford said. "Agent Vail was not privy to what was going on. She did what any of us would've done if a fellow officer went missing. The . . . unintended consequences are very bad, no question. But to blame her—"

"Sorry if I hurt Agent Vail's *feelings*," McGuire said. "But tough shit. We've got a situation here, and it's a fucking bad one. Thanks for all your help."

The call disconnected.

DeSantos put his hands on his hips and began pacing. Vail sat there seething. And Gifford stared at the silent telephone.

"We've gotta find him, Hector." Vail was now on her feet.

DeSantos looked at her. The resigned tilt of his head reflected his thoughts: it was probably too late.

Gifford said, "It's not your fault, Karen. If I hadn't done this favor for him, he never would've been on this op. If anything, it's my fault."

"Assigning blame isn't going to help anyone," DeSantos said. "No one could've foreseen this." He stopped pacing. "This is a DEA operation. They've got assets in place that could find him a lot faster than we could."

"Are you saying we shouldn't try?" Vail asked, then turned to Gifford, who was still lost in thought. "Sir, please."

Gifford pulled his gaze to Vail. "Find him. Whatever it takes, bring him back. Preferably alive."

Vail looked at DeSantos. "You with me?"

DeSantos licked his lips, hands still on his hips. "Yeah."

"Then let's go. We're wasting time."

46

Once they'd cleared the stairs outside the BAU, Vail stopped. She grabbed the railing. "I blew it, Hector. Do you think— did I get Robby killed?"

DeSantos put his arm around Vail's shoulders. "I sure hope not. I'm not gonna lie to you. This is bad. His cover's been compromised. We're behind the eight ball on this. But you've got friends on the task force in Napa?"

Vail nodded.

"Call them. Have them find Guevara. Take him somewhere, legal or not, and sweat him. Will they do that? Will they grab him up without a warrant?"

She hesitated. "Maybe."

"Convince them. Whatever it takes, they've gotta find out what he knows. It may be our only chance. Meantime, I'm gonna reach out to some people and see what I can do."

He pulled his phone, then turned back to Vail. "Now. Make the call."

Vail mentally slapped herself. *Get with it, Karen. Freak out later.* She called Dixon. Brix was in the car with her, so he could hear what she had to say.

"I'm about to ask you a favor, and it's going to jeopardize your careers. But I've got nowhere else to go."

There was a moment's hesitation, then Dixon said, "Go on."

"Brix, have you been briefed—"

"I'm up to speed."

"Okay. Listen to me. César Guevara was the target of a DEA operation. Robby was brought in by his friend Antonio Sebastiani de Medina—Sebastian—to work the case with him. He was only supposed to handle one transaction, but Robby's meet with Guevara went well, and his role expanded."

"I thought Robby was a detective with some small town in Virginia," Brix said. "Venice?"

"Vienna. Long story, and it's unimportant. He got this gig with DEA, hoping it'd lead to a permanent position. So now we have the connection between Robby and Guevara. That'd explain Ian Wirth's address in Guevara's house, in Robby's handwriting. Robby was probably helping Guevara at that point. Maybe it was a test. I don't know—I don't know if we'll ever know. But you've got to find Guevara. Before it's too late."

"I'm turning the car around right now. We'll check Superior first."

"There's still not enough for a warrant, so you're going to need to grab him up and take him somewhere." Vail realized she was on an open cell connection—but there was no time. Robby's life was of paramount concern. If she lost her career but saved him, it'd be worth it. Then again, if she lost her career and he turned up dead—*no, I can't think that way. He's alive. He's alive.*

"I'm texting Mann," Brix said. "Get him over to Guevara's house. Just in case."

"One thing you should know," Vail said. "Robby and Sebastian missed their last three check-ins with their DEA case agent. And Guevara left a voice mail for me a little while ago that said Robby was dead. He made it sound like he wasn't responsible, but that he knew who was."

"Don't believe that scumbag," Dixon said. "If he's got information, we'll get it."

"Thanks, guys."

"Hang in there," Brix said. "We'll be in touch."

Vail looked up. DeSantos was ending his call. "C'mon. We've got a meet with a guy who's gonna get some info for us."

"Who is he?"

"Don't ask, don't tell. Best that way."

Vail pulled herself up from the steps. "If he's got the info we need, I couldn't give a shit who he is."

47

Dixon took the turn too fast, and the car dovetailed. Brix grabbed the dashboard with his right hand but couldn't keep his shoulder from pushing up against the door.

"Sorry," Dixon said. "Make sure your seat belt's fastened because I don't intend on going the speed limit."

"How hard do you want to push this?"

"I intend on coming away with answers, Redd. Simple as that. This guy's wrapped up in this. He might've had something to do with the Lugo kidnapping. He may've had something to do with aiding John Mayfield. And he apparently has something to do with Robby's disappearance. I don't plan on giving him a Coke and a slice of lime and treating him like he's at a spa."

But Dixon was well aware that Brix had recently given her and Vail a hard time about entering César Guevara's home without a warrant. Now she was expecting Brix to join her in leaping off the career-ending legal precipice with her.

"Once we cross this line," he said, "there's no going back."

Dixon took a quick glance in Brix's direction. Their eyes locked. A silent answer.

They pulled onto the street where Superior Mobile Bottling was located. "It's 7:00 AM," Brix said. "I doubt he's here."

"He gets to his office every morning at 7:15," Dixon said, pulling into the adjacent parking lot. She slid the car into a slot behind the building, hidden from the street. "Up ahead, by that brick wall," she said, pointing. "We'll have a view of the front entrance and the side driveway. We'll be able to see him when he arrives, but he won't see us."

Brix nodded and then followed Dixon on foot to their perch. The air was crisp and the sky was brightening to their left, in the east.

The time ticked by without activity. Finally, at 7:40 AM, Dixon sat down on the ground, her back against the brick wall.

"What do you think?" Brix asked.

"I don't know. My source only knew what time he came in each day. I don't know how prompt he usually is." Dixon pulled her phone, called Austin Mann. "Anything?"

"House is dark. By now I'd think someone'd be awake and moving around. I've got the front, Gordon's got the back, and I've got two other guys from NSIB placed at various other points of interest. Nobody's seen anything."

"Guevara's usually at his office by 7:15," Dixon said. "It's possible he's out of town. If he is, that'd be very convenient timing."

"You want us to go up and knock?" Mann asked.

Dixon thought about that. "No, let's give it a little longer. Maybe he's running late. I'd rather take him at his office. There isn't a whole lot around here. But in a residential neighborhood . . . lots of potential eyes and ears."

"Okay," Mann said. "We sit and wait."

48

V ail followed DeSantos to his car, a low-slung black Corvette.
"You're kidding me," Vail said.
"What?"

"You want me to drive around in that?" She wiggled a finger at the highly polished sports car. "I have claustrophobia. Let's take my Ford."

DeSantos unlocked the Vette. "I don't ride in Fords. Get in, you'll be fine."

And a moment later, they were speeding out of the lot, en route to I-95.

Vail looked around. She was sitting lower than she had ever sat in a car. But so far, there was no crushing anxiety. Her psyche was probably so overworked with stress from Robby's situation that it had nothing left to give. *Take your mind off it and you'll be fine.*

A spark of sunlight glinted off the highly polished chrome of De-Santos's stylish watch band. "Is that a bicycle chain you're wearing?" She nodded at the timepiece on his wrist. "Your watch."

"It's a Dēmos. Same one the president wears."

Vail twisted her lips. "And you would know that, how?"

DeSantos frowned. "You'll soon learn not to ask me questions like that." He gunned the accelerator and they rocketed across three lanes of traffic to the far left of the interstate.

Vail felt her stomach vault into the backseat and she reached out for something—anything—to grab onto. Perhaps she got too comfortable in this vehicle too soon. She licked her lips, trying to restore moisture to her suddenly dry mouth. "This guy you've hooked us up with. Who is he? I don't like going into any situation blindly, let alone a meet with a CI."

"He's not a CI," DeSantos said. "He works for DEA. Let's just say he has access to files and information. That's how I got what I got that led me to Gifford."

"And I'm not supposed to know any of this."

"If you did know it, he'd have to kill you."

At the moment, Vail did not find that funny. And despite both Gifford's and DeSantos's admonitions, she did feel responsible for blowing Robby's cover. *Dammit, if he had just trusted me, if he had just confided in me and told me he had a mission and that he'd be gone awhile. What would the harm have been?*

"You went quiet on me," DeSantos said. "Where were you just now?"

Vail turned toward her window. "Nowhere."

"Bullshit. You were thinking about Robby. You feel guilty."

Vail did not respond.

"For all we know," DeSantos said, "he's fine and lying low until it's safe to resurface. He could've talked his way out of it."

"Anything's possible," Vail said. "Either way, I'm going to find him. And if something's happened to him, I'm going to find whoever's responsible. I can be a real bitch when I'm crossed."

"You understand he had to leave without you knowing. He couldn't tell you."

"No, I don't understand any of that. What I understand is that he lied to me. I kissed him good-bye in the morning and he told me he'd see me later that evening. But he had no intention of seeing me, did he?"

DeSantos zipped past a car that was doing ten over the speed limit. She glanced at the speedometer. They were going 95 miles per hour.

"We don't know what happened. Maybe he expected to have dinner with you. But something might've broken on the case, and he had to leave. Don't judge him until you know the facts."

"Bottom line. He was doing this and chose not to tell me. Omission of facts is the same as lying, Hector. He deceived me. How can I trust him the same way ever again? Trust is one of the most important things in a relationship."

"I'm married, Karen. I understand where you're coming from. But until you give Robby a chance to explain, you're not being fair. You're taking this personally, not looking at it as a federal agent who has an in-depth knowledge of deep cover work."

"You don't know what I've been through. A failed marriage. A spouse who went from loving husband to abusive drunk who refused to take his medication. I needed someone I could trust, someone I could lose myself in and not worry about whether or not he was lying to me." She shook her head. "As far as I'm concerned, there are no excuses. When we find him, Hector, I'm going to kill him."

THEY ARRIVED AT THEIR MEET with the contact, whom DeSantos called "Sammy." It wasn't his real name, but it was safer this way for all involved.

DeSantos pulled his Corvette up to the curb in front of Professors Gate at The George Washington University on 21st Street NW. He shoved the shift into park and popped open his door.

"I don't think we can leave it here," Vail said.

"Not a problem. If they start to write up a ticket, they'll run my plate and everything'll be fine."

Vail looked at him. "You're not really serious."

DeSantos slipped on his wraparound sunglasses. "Really, I am." He dropped the keys into his suit pocket. "You worry too much, Karen."

He walked through the decorative wrought iron arch, which was supported by two squat concrete tile columns. "GW" was prominently lettered in gold on black above the apex of the curve.

"Why here?" Vail asked as she followed him along the red brick pathway.

"Why not? It's my alma mater. I donate every year when they call me, so I may as well get some use out of my donation."

"Yeah, I don't think that's the point."

"It's not, but so what?" They walked past a black circular sculpture seated on a square cement emplacement within a slightly elevated grass strip: three circles intertwined within one another. They continued past it toward Kogan Plaza and stopped near a miniature concrete gazebo topped with a copper dome. A man in jeans and a navy sweatshirt leaned against one of its ionic columns, pulling on a cigarette.

"Kogan Plaza," DeSantos said, nodding at a brick-laid square ahead of them. "Bart Kogan's a big donor to the school."

"You know him, of course."

"Matter of fact, I do. Friend of mine introduced me to him once, when he was in town. Had coffee. Nice guy."

DeSantos stopped short of the structure and took a seat on a weathered wooden bench to his left, positioned beneath a row of medium-height trees. Vail sat beside him.

Vail tilted her head toward the gazebo. "That Sammy?"

"It is," DeSantos said. "He'll be over in a minute." He turned to

Sammy, removed and replaced his sunglasses, then put his arm across the back of the bench behind Vail. "Let me do the talking, okay? He'll be nervous enough with you here."

"He's got a baseball hat on, sunglasses and a beard. I'm guessing the beard's fake. Is he really worried I might ID him?"

"A guy like this doesn't take chances." DeSantos pulled out a pack of Juicy Fruit. "And neither do I." He flipped open the gum and removed a stick, then offered Vail a piece. She declined.

As DeSantos folded the Juicy Fruit into his mouth, Sammy joined them on the bench, to DeSantos's left. He did not look at them.

He lowered his chin and said, "Your friend was working on an op known as Velocity. The op's been active since 2006 and heated up this year when we caught a break. Things were moving nicely till one of our guys had an accident. Your friend filled that void."

"What was the op?" Vail asked.

DeSantos turned to her and gave her a look.

Tough shit, Hector. I'm here. I'm going to ask questions.

Sammy tilted his head back, his aviator sunglasses reflecting the glary sky like a mirror. "It's far-reaching. But bringing down a cartel's one of the primary objectives."

"Which cartel?" Vail asked.

Sammy's mirrored glasses flicked over to Vail. It was evident he was not pleased with her intrusions. His gaze slid over to DeSantos. "Cortez."

"Cortez—" Vail said, then stopped herself. *Holy shit. That's the big leagues.*

Sammy craned his head around, searching the immediate area. "I've said enough."

DeSantos dipped his chin. "Appreciate it."

"Wait," Vail said. "That's it? How does César Guevara fit into this?"

Sammy looked at DeSantos. His expression was as unreadable as stone. "See you around."

He rose from the bench and turned in the direction of the gazebo. Vail started to get up, but DeSantos clamped down on her arm with vise-like strength.

"Let him go, Karen."

She pulled away—to no avail. "But he knows more than he told us."

"If he does, he'll let me know. He said what he felt he could say in front of you. Let's run with what he gave us."

DeSantos released his grip. Vail turned and watched Sammy dissolve into the moving mass of students. Vail put a hand to her forehead, then rose and began to pace. "This is worse than I thought, Hector. Carlos Cortez, Jesus Christ. Cortez is one of the most violent and aggressive cartels."

DeSantos looked off and, for the first time, Vail saw a look of concern on his face.

49

H e's not coming," Brix said.

Dixon twisted her wrist and consulted her watch for what felt like the fiftieth time. Sitting and waiting, when so much was at stake, was a difficult skill to master. She still hadn't perfected it. Her knee was bouncing and she felt the need to scream—anything—to burn off the excess adrenaline.

Brix stood up and brushed off his pants. "What do you want to do?"

Dixon got to her feet and looked up at the sky. It was bright and warm. It would be unseasonably hot today. "He's not home and he's not at work. Let's poke around and see if anyone knows what's going on. He has a secretary. It's 9:00 AM, start of normal business hours. Why isn't *she* here?"

Brix pulled his phone. "You got the number for Superior Mobile Bottling?" Dixon gave it to him, and he dialed. A moment later, he closed his handset. "They're closed for annual maintenance. What do you think, bullshit?"

"I don't know. But let's go talk with someone who might."

DIXON'S LAST VISIT to Wedded Bliss Vineyards seemed like weeks ago— but it was only a few days. She led Brix up to the glass structure built into the face of a mountain. Brix marveled and made all the appropriate gaping movements with his mouth.

"Makes Silver Ridge look like a shack."

"You should be proud of your winery, Redd. I wanted to own a winery once."

"Yeah? What happened?"

"Money happened. It was expensive back ten years ago. Now it's just plain ridiculous."

"It's business. Supply and demand. Napa's a very valuable brand.

That means the value of the finite amount of land goes up. We were lucky our family got in when land was cheap." He tilted his chin up toward the glass roof, beyond which lay the soil and roots of the mountain that towered above them. "But even if I'm not actively involved, I am proud of it. It's ours. And we turn out high-quality wine." He gestured at the pristinely lit glass structure around them. "But then you see a place like this, it feels like a different league."

"Up the stairs. Crystal's waiting for us."

They walked into Crystal Dahlia's all-glass office and dispensed with the pleasantries. Crystal grinned. "And how's your friend. Agent Vail?"

"Back in Virginia."

"Did she enjoy her stay out west?"

Dixon and Brix shared a knowing look. Dixon said, "Not particularly."

"Oh," Crystal said, her smile fading. "I'm sorry."

"Couldn't be helped," Dixon said. "Circumstances beyond our control."

"So how is Silver Ridge, Lieutenant Brix?"

Brix threw out both hands, palms up. "Who can complain? The economy sucks, sales are down a bit. But the wine is great. I'm told this will probably be a good year for the grapes if the weather goes as expected."

"I'm told the same thing."

"If you don't mind," Dixon said. "We've got some pressing business. No pun intended." She waited a beat, then said, "Your board—the Georges Valley AVA."

"I told you, my presidency is almost over."

"Yes," Dixon said. "But we need some information about Superior Mobile Bottling. César Guevara, in particular."

Crystal placed well-manicured red nails on her desk. "Our contracts VP has dealt with him more than I have."

"That's Ian Wirth?"

"Good memory. If you wait a few minutes, Ian will be here if you'd like to talk with him. I'm due to hand over my file as part of the transition to the new president."

Dixon checked her watch yet again. "A few minutes?"

"Any minute now." Crystal picked up her phone and dialed an extension. "When Mr. Wirth arrives, please send him up to my office . . . He has? Excellent." She placed the receiver back in its cradle. "Ian just came in the front doors."

A moment later, Wirth was in Crystal's office, taking a seat beside Dixon.

"Ian, good to see you," Crystal said, eyeing him with a lingering gaze.

The look was not lost on Dixon, who recalled that Crystal was Wirth's ex-wife.

"Ms. Dixon, good to see you again," Wirth said. He held out a hand to Brix. "Ian Wirth."

"Redmond Brix." He stood and shook firmly, then retook his seat. "Good that you're here. We've got some questions and Crystal thought you might be able to help us out. We know you were your board's primary negotiator in its dealings with Superior Mobile Bottling. But how much did you interact with César Guevara?"

Wirth smirked. "Quite a lot. I negotiated our last contract with him and had ongoing discussions with him about its potential renewal."

"And was he aware that you were one of the three on the board who was against him getting this contract?"

Wirth leaned back in his seat. "If he was, he never let me know it. And I played my cards close to the vest. Besides, I was speaking and negotiating for the entire membership, not me, or Victoria, or Todd."

"I know you're aware that the two others who opposed this contract are dead."

"Hold it a second." This from Crystal, who was suddenly paying attention. "What are you saying?"

"Victoria Cameron and Isaac Jenkins were the victims of a serial killer," Brix said.

"I heard something on the news—"

Brix held up a hand to quash Crystal's panic before it could work itself into a frazzle. "He's been caught, and he's no longer a threat."

"Yes, that's what they said." Crystal's gaze shot from Brix to Dixon, and back. "But I thought Victoria had a stroke."

"We didn't want word getting out until we had things under control," Brix said. "The victims' names still haven't been released, so I'd appreciate if you'd keep that to yourselves until we've had a chance to meet with the families."

Dixon said to Wirth, "Did you ever have any indication that Superior was engaged in anything other than legal activities?"

Wirth's chin jutted back. "No. Should I have? I mean, our business with him was strictly related to bottling, and nothing else."

Dixon placed a hand on his forearm. "Ian, I don't want you to get the wrong idea about this. We're not accusing you of anything. Like I said at lunch, we're still investigating something that may or may not be related to John Mayfield."

Wirth's shoulders relaxed a bit. Brix asked, "Was there ever a time when Superior closed down for annual maintenance?"

"Annual maintenance. You mean on his rigs?"

"On anything," Dixon said.

Wirth thought a moment. "Nothing I'm aware of. But our business with them is seasonal, so it's conceivable he went off line. I'd have no idea." Wirth sucked on his top lip. "But he did periodically make trips out of the country. There were a couple times when our appointments got rescheduled because he had to leave unexpectedly for a week or ten days at a time."

Dixon said, "So there may be a perfectly reasonable explanation for him being gone."

"Maybe," Brix said in a low voice. "I'm not so sure."

A thought wormed its way into Dixon's head, but she didn't want to discuss it until she and Brix were in private.

"Is there anything else you can tell us about Guevara?" Brix asked.

Wirth did not hesitate. "He's a shrewd businessman. He understands his product and what it saves his customers. At the same time, he does what it takes to get our business. And I have to admit, even though I was resisting the renewal of his contract, it wasn't because they didn't do a fine job. There were other forces at play."

Dixon smirked. There were, indeed, other forces at play—more than Ian Wirth knew. "Has he ever been to your home, know where you live?"

"No, why?"

"So he wouldn't have a need for your home address."

Wirth eyed her cautiously. "No."

Dixon slipped a hand inside her pocket and pulled out Robby's photo. "Ever seen this man?"

Wirth studied the picture, then shook his head. "Should I have?"

Dixon tucked away the photo. "I honestly don't think so." She rose and extended a hand to Crystal. "Once again, Ms. Dahlia, a pleasure. Thanks for all your help. "Ian, thank you. We'll call you if we have any other questions."

She hurried out of the winery, anxious to share her thoughts with Brix.

AS SOON AS DIXON hit the front door, she said, "Add it up, Redd."

Brix glanced back over his shoulder at the glass structure embedded in the mountainside. "Already have. Guevara's involved with a drug cartel. He owns several rigs that can easily be attached to large trailers and used for long haul transport."

"I think we've got enough for a search warrant."

"If we get the right judge. Let's work on it, see how far we can get. Whether Guevara's there or not, it'll get us in the front door so we can take a closer look around."

"If we're going to find Robby, I don't think that'll help us. We need Guevara. And we need to find him without going down the usual roads because I doubt they'll lead anywhere. APBs and subpoenas on his credit card transactions will be useless. He's too sophisticated for that. But somehow we need to find out what he knows."

Brix sighed. "You know what my brother would say?"

Dixon shrugged.

"He'd say, 'Good luck with that.'"

"Yeah," Dixon said. "But here's the thing. Luck hasn't once factored into this investigation. I don't think it's something we can count on."

50

D eSantos gunned the Corvette. Vail, once again, grabbed for something to hold onto. The repeated whiplash was starting to get to her.

Four minutes earlier, DeSantos had received a call from ASAC Yardley telling him that Antonio Sebastiani de Medina had surfaced and was being debriefed at the DEA's facility at Quantico.

Vail showed her creds and was admitted to the base. DeSantos zipped along the road past the FBI Academy and five minutes later pulled into the parking lot of the DEA's decade-old training academy complex.

Inside, after being informed that they were on the premises, Peter Yardley walked out into the hallway. "He showed up at the front gate. No ID, no money, and he hadn't eaten in two days. Apparently he babbled enough credible information that the guard got me on the line."

"Can we see him?" Vail asked.

"He's had a rough go of it. Normally, I'd say we should give him some time. But—"

"We don't have that luxury," Vail said firmly.

Yardley frowned. "No, we don't. Follow me." He led Vail and DeSantos down a long corridor. The building still had a new construction feel to it, even after a decade of use. Multicolored blue, red, and gray industrial carpet led up to glass administrative doors. "Undercover agents are not normally debriefed at the Quantico facility," Yardley said. "It's used primarily for training, but he was in a bad way and I didn't want to risk transporting him. The nurse has him hooked up to fluids and he's perking up. But we haven't gotten a whole lot out of him yet." Yardley pushed through a wooden classroom door and held it open for them.

Inside, a trim-bearded man with an olive complexion sat at a table with an IV snaking from his left hand.

Antonio Sebastiani de Medina.

"I'm Karen Vail," she said. "This is Hector DeSantos."

Sebastian's gaze flicked between them. "You're Robby's girlfriend," he said softly.

"Do you know what happened to Robby?"

Sebastian sucked in a healthy dose of air. "I know what happened, yeah. But—"

"Tell me."

Sebastian's gaze moved around the room, then came to rest on the ceiling, as if the answers were printed on high. "We were undercover. I'd gained the trust of César Guevara, a lieutenant in the Cortez cartel. Things were going good. Robby was a godsend because the agent I was working with had an accident and I was afraid that'd fuck up everything we'd worked for." He looked at Vail. "But he took a liking to Robby right away. Robby's a natural UC. He's got a sixth sense for it. Guevara's not an easy mark."

Vail scrunched her lips into a frown. "I noticed."

"But the asshole bought it. Robby got him talking, and he started taking us inside his operation, how they operated. And I thought we were finally going to blow it all wide open." He stared off at the table a moment. "Then it all went to hell. Somehow our cover got blown. I don't know how," he said with a shake of his head. "We were so careful."

Vail cleared her throat, then took a seat at the table opposite Sebastian. DeSantos remained in the back of the room, beside Yardley. "I'm afraid that might've been my fault." She proceeded to explain what had happened, then sat back, her eyes in her lap. Embarrassed. "I'm deeply sorry. Obviously this isn't what I wanted to happen."

Sebastian chewed on that a long moment, then said, "Jesus Christ, of all our goddamn luck." He sucked in some air, took a swig of Powerade, made a show of swallowing it. Then he set the bottle down harder than necessary.

Vail figured he was considering if he was going to go off on her and stop answering her questions. No doubt wondering how this FBI agent had destroyed months of high-risk, hard-won work.

But instead, Sebastian waved a hand. "Wasn't your fault, Karen. Just the way it went down, is all. Besides, how can I get angry at you? Robby thinks you're the best thing that ever happened to him."

"Do you think—" Vail had to choke back the emotion threatening to tighten her throat. "Is it possible he's still alive?"

Sebastian looked away. He seemed to follow the IV tube from his hand up to the bag hanging from the stand. He answered without looking at her. "Years ago, a friend of mine once told me that anything's possible. So, yeah, I guess it's possible."

DeSantos walked up to the table and took a seat beside Vail. "Sebastian. We know this was an op that's been in process since '06. What's the objective?"

"What do you know about César Guevara?"

"CFO of Superior Mobile Bottling," Vail said. "Superior does mobile bottling for the greater wine country in northern California. Big operation."

"Guevara is more than the CFO," Sebastian said. "And Superior is more than a mobile bottling company. They've become a major arm of the cartel."

This just keeps getting worse. "You're kidding," Vail said. "How so?"

"Brilliant operation, actually. It wasn't until a few days ago that we got a handle on what they were doing. Guevara outlined everything for Robby and me." He leaned both forearms on the table, seemingly infused with a renewed sense of energy. "That bottling deal. Yeah, it's a business, and yeah, they make good money on it. But its real purpose is to function as a front for a major smuggling operation. They need contracts with area wineries to keep their bullshit business running, which gives them the cover to do what they're really in business to do: bring huge amounts of illicit drugs into the U.S. from Mexico."

"Using the rigs?" Vail asked.

"Yeah, but there's more to it than that. A lot more." Sebastian took a long gulp of Powerade. "There are a few aspects to it. First, you got the corks."

A shiver sparked across Vail's spine. *I knew there was something going on with that.* "The synthetic corks."

"Right. They truck in tons of them across the border. Only about a quarter of them are legitimate. The rest are hollowed out, then Fentanyl powder is compacted into the core. Fentanyl's unusual for Mexico, because they typically only move coke, meth, heroin, and their cash crop, marijuana."

"How much Fentanyl can they possibly fit in a cork?" Vail asked. "Hardly seems worth it."

Sebastian shook his head slowly, either disgusted at her ignorance or annoyed that she interrupted him. "Fentanyl powder is extremely potent. One gram can be cut into a thousand units, or tablets, or whatever. That's a thousand-fold return on your money. But these corks don't hold one gram, they hold about *four*. And if you're transporting a million corks in a semi, that's a lot of fucking money."

Vail tilted her head. "Isn't that detectable?"

"They seal off the cork, which is a chemically treated silicone shell, to help keep the drug scent from being detected by CBP dogs at checkpoints."

"And," DeSantos said, "NAFTA opened the door to allow Mexican trucks to cross the border into the U.S. It got worse last year because of the treaty Mexico strong-armed us into signing."

"What treaty?" Vail asked.

"There was pressure to allow Mexican truckers to travel on U.S. roads," DeSantos said. "It became a huge trade issue, and the Mexican government made a big deal out of it. U.S. unions didn't want Mexican trucks transporting product that could be transported by union drivers. Others thought Mexican trucks weren't inspected as often and posed a safety danger to American drivers."

"I remember reading something about that."

"They negotiated a compromise," DeSantos continued. "They carried out an experimental project with a small number of Mexican trucks traveling on U.S. freeways. They found that Mexican truckers got into fewer accidents than their American counterparts. The findings were challenged because it was such a small sample size and because those Mexican trucks went through more rigorous inspections than normal since they knew they'd be part of this study. But because of political pressure, they expanded the program."

"And because of that," Yardley said with a tinge of hardness, "the volume of Mexican trucks on U.S. freeways increased exponentially. Customs and Border Protection can't possibly inspect all of them. Guevara capitalized on that. And he took steps just in case."

"Like hiding the drugs inside the synthetic corks," Vail said.

Sebastian took another gulp of Powerade. "Yes. But that's not all. It wasn't just about the corks. These cartels, they're flush with money and time and imagination. They worked on ways of maximizing what they were doing while still taking advantage of the front of being a mobile bottler. And they came up with liquid cocaine."

Vail leaned forward. "*Liquid* cocaine?"

"That's what they transport in the wine bottles. Cocaine hydrochloride is soluble in alcohol or water. Cortez uses alcohol because it's easy to re-cover the drugs. You heat it to 50 degrees Celsius, or just let it sit out in the sun. The alcohol evaporates, leaving the coke."

Vail shook her head. "Damn."

"Damn effective is what it is," Sebastian said. "There are about eight thousand grams of coke in a case of wine. And if you've got a semi full of cases, that's a huge amount of contraband being moved around without being threatened or even challenged."

"Brilliant," Vail said. "They can move the cocaine around the country under the cover of shipping cases of wine, and short of opening the bot-tles and testing the liquid, we'd never be able to detect the drugs."

"Exactly. Even the random screening they do at certain border ports of entry can't pick it up. We generally use fluoroscopy, and fluoroscopy can't detect liquids containing illicit drugs. And if it's sealed inside a bot-tle, drug-sniffing dogs can't pick it up, either. So we've experimented with CT scans—computerized X-ray tomography—to measure the mean opacity of what's inside the bottles. Differences in the opacity of dis-solved drugs can be detected without having to open the wine and de-stroy the product if it's legit.

"But it's extremely expensive to deploy these CT machines. You'd really need a hospital nearby to make it work. But Guevara's already found a way around it. That liquid cocaine, it's got what's known as X-ray attenuation. The way he explained it to me is that when a case of wine contains identical liquid contents, the bottles have the same mean atten-uation when scanned with the CT equipment. If the attenuation read-ings of some bottles differed from the others, that'd set off a red flag. Filling the bottles with liquid cocaine gets around that."

"So he's a smart shit," DeSantos said.

"All these cartels are. You'd be surprised at the stuff they come up with. Baseball hats made of cocaine, chocolate bars, decorative globes, jet engine turbine gears—anything that can be innocently imported is a potential gold mine for them. It's only limited by their creativity."

Is that what John Mayfield was referring to when he said there's more to this than you know? But how is Mayfield connected to Guevara? And what's that got to do with the murders in Napa? Ray Lugo? And the Cortez cartel? C'mon, Karen, add it up.

"Then there are the labels," Sebastian said.

"Labels?" Vail asked. "How can there be drugs in the label of a wine bottle?"

A thin smile crept across Sebastian's face. "The adhesive that holds the label on the bottle is actually black tar heroin. Very sticky and an ideal glue. The label itself is made of LSD blotter paper. It's so fucking potent they have to cover it with a plastic film so they don't get it on their hands. And because it's so potent, one wine label can be sliced into multiple small pieces that are placed on the tongue. It dissolves, giving the high. Again, well thought out. Maximum yield."

Vail ruminated on that for a moment, then jumped from her seat. Sebastian flinched. "Sorry," Vail said. "Would you excuse me for a few minutes? I've gotta make a call."

DeSantos leaned back and looked at her over the top of his tiny glasses. His face said, "You've gotta be kidding me."

But Vail had an idea by the tail—and she needed to firm up her grasp before it had a chance to escape.

51

Vail pushed through the door while simultaneously pulling out her BlackBerry. Dialed Roxxann Dixon.

"I've got something, Roxx. You in a place you can talk?"

"I'm sitting in the conference room with the task force."

"Perfect. Call me back so you can put me on speaker."

Seconds later, her phone buzzed. "Okay," Vail said. "I think I've put a lot of this shit together. All these parts that were dangling out there, things I couldn't add up because they didn't seem to make sense. I think I've got it. Or most of it."

"Go on," Brix said.

"All of Mayfield's murders, I had such a hard time profiling him, because the more information we got the less sense it all made to me. Because male serial killers don't kill for profit. Right?"

"That's what you kept saying," Dixon said.

"One thing I've learned is there are exceptions to most of what we think is behavioral fact. There are general guidelines and tenets, but people are different. Circumstances are different. And when two converging powers find one another, they discover they have desires and needs that come together in a symbiotic relationship. That's what we're talking about here. Symbiosis."

"Karen," Austin Mann said, "you've lost me."

"John Mayfield killed because it filled a psychosexual need. He marked the bodies the way he did, severing the breasts, slicing the wrists, yanking off the toenail. He did those things for reasons he wasn't consciously aware of. He did them because they comforted him. And that made sense to me. It fit our paradigms of serial killer behaviors. But then he also did things that didn't make sense, that didn't add up. It was almost like he was a schizophrenic killer. The male victim, for one. That didn't fit."

"And you've figured it out," Gordon said.

"I think so." Vail thought another moment, then continued. "It seemed at times like he was killing for a profit motive, while at other times the victims appeared to be unrelated. So here's what I think was going on. John Mayfield was a bona fide serial killer, with classic childhood pathologies that shaped him into what he became: someone who was selecting victims that reminded him of his mother. But there was more to this than just the classic serial killer behavioral patterns. He was working with César Guevara. This is where the symbiosis comes into play.

"Mayfield was a psychopath, but the reason why some of his victims didn't match his ritual was because he was killing vics chosen for him, by Guevara. And they used his behavioral murder patterns as a cover to divert attention from the Guevara-ordered killings, so no one would suspect they were contract kills. And we fell into that trap."

"But what's Guevara's role?" Gordon asked. "Why did he choose these particular victims?"

"Guevara's a lieutenant with the Cortez drug cartel. They smuggle liquid cocaine in wine bottles all over the country. Heroin and LSD in the labels. And the synthetic corks—they have ultra high potency, very expensive Fentanyl hidden within them."

"That's why," Dixon said, "Superior almost exclusively uses synthetic corks—because they can hollow them out and fill the inside with drugs."

"Right. And they have the license to do all this because of their company, Superior Mobile Bottling. Key to Superior being able to do its thing is the bottling contracts it has."

"Because it's a front," Brix said.

"And because the Georges Valley AVA board is unique in that it negotiates bulk contracts for its member wineries. If Superior gets that contract, they bottle, label, and ship a shitload of cases of wine. That gives them the cover, should DEA or ATF or CBP question it, to be handling a large volume of wine shipments."

"That's goddamn ingenious," Brix said.

"Yes." Vail started walking down the hallway toward the building's entrance. "So look at our vics. Victoria Cameron, Maryanne Bernal, and Isaac Walker were AVA board members, or affiliated with board members who were decision makers on this bottling contract. And Victoria and Isaac, through his partner Todd Nicholson, were opposed to Superior's contract renewal. Bang, they turn up dead."

Vail flashed on something Robby had said to her: that if she dug some more, she'd find something that provided connections she wasn't expecting. It seemed like a generic pep talk at the time, but now in the context of all she had learned, he was trying to key her in on important aspects to her case.

"But Ian Wirth wasn't killed," Dixon said.

"Wasn't killed yet," Vail corrected. "Remember, we found Ian Wirth's home address in Guevara's house. Wirth was going to be Mayfield's next victim."

"Hang on a minute," Mann said. "You're saying John Mayfield was a contract killer."

Vail pushed through the doors that led into the parking lot. She squinted against the bright sun, which was analogous to what she was feeling: that she was suddenly enlightened as to what this case was all about. "A contract serial killer. First of its kind, far as I know."

"That explains Ray's state of mind," Dixon said. "He seemed so tightly wound at times. We took it as the same stress we were all feeling. But he'd internalized it. He took each of those murders hard because he felt partially responsible."

"Regardless of the circumstances surrounding his wife and son, if Ray was aiding and abetting John Mayfield in any manner, that wouldn't be far from the truth."

"That also explains why Ray felt so strongly that Miguel Ortiz was not our guy," Brix said, referring to an illegal vineyard worker who was, for a brief time, suspected of being the Crush Killer. "Because of Merilynn's description, he knew it was a physically large Caucasian male, not a Hispanic."

"But what about the other vics?" Mann said. "Ursula Robbins, Dawn Zackery, Betsy Ivers. And Scott Fuller."

"Ivers was one of Mayfield's first kills in the region." Ivers's body was found in 1998 at Battery Spencer, near Golden Gate Bridge. "No relation to Superior or the bottling contract. Just the victim of a serial killer. Zackery was probably killed because of me, so to speak. We thought at the time that Mayfield was in Virginia. Killing Zackery was his way of sticking his finger in our eye. Saying, basically, 'You dumb shits, I'm right here. And I've been here all along.' For a narcissistic killer, which Mayfield was, that's how he'd do it. Telling us wouldn't have been as dramatic as leaving us a body. It was the ultimate insult, his way of showing his superiority."

"And Ursula Robbins?" Gordon asked. "Cameron, Bernal, and Walker weren't included in that PowerPoint file he sent us. But neither was Robbins, which suggests a connection to the other three."

"Robbins was a Georges Valley winery exec," Dixon said. "I think that if we were to dig some more, we may find that she was against the board approving Superior's *first* contract."

"Very possible," Vail said. "Or she was merely another woman who matched certain characteristics that a serial killer needed to fulfill his fantasies and psychopathic desires." She ticked each name off her mental list. "And then there's Fuller. I'm not sure we'll ever know for sure what happened with him. But I think he was collateral damage. He was following me, with the intent to scare me. Or worse."

Vail didn't want to be too harsh on their colleague. Even though she felt he truly meant to kill her, she kept the thought to herself. "But things got out of hand, and we had that car accident. John Mayfield was also following me that night. Why? Who knows. Maybe he followed me more often than we knew. Regardless, that night, he was there. He came up behind me, injected me with a sedative, and shot Fuller with my gun. Maybe he intended to make trouble for me, to throw me off my game. I don't know."

"Almost worked," Brix said.

"People were really pissed at you over Scott's murder."

People. As in Sheriff Owens. The boss.

Brix said, "Let's be glad cooler heads prevailed."

"Cooler heads and forensics," Dixon added.

Vail closed her eyes and aimed her face at the sun. "What's Mayfield's status?"

"No change. The doc said he's not ready to be brought out of it."

"There's something else we can cross off our list," Brix said. "How Mayfield got the BetaSomnol that he injected you with. We got the pest control company's records, the one Mayfield worked for. He paid visits to the Napa Valley Medical Center five times in a four-month span. For ants."

"Sounds like he got more than ants," Vail said. "Any thoughts on how the arson figures into all this?"

Burt Gordon, the arson investigator for the Sheriff's Department sitting on the task force, explained: "I think that's exactly as we had it figured—that Tim Nance, Congressman Church's district director, and Walton Silva conspired with Fuller to get you, Karen, off their backs. Permanently."

"I don't know if your Bureau buddies told you," Brix said, "but the Feds found a bungled wire transfer this morning. They traced it to an account that appears to be controlled by Nance. They're still wading through everything, trying to find other transactions, other accomplices. But he's toast. So to speak."

Vail opened her eyes and watched a black sedan pull into the parking lot. "So Nance was taking payments to influence the outcome of an issue due to be ruled on by the Alcohol and Tobacco Tax Trade Bureau. They were using Nance to buy government legislation regarding the minimum grape requirement for the Georges Valley AVA."

"If Church became governor," Dixon said, "Nance, Fuller, and Silva all stood to take major posts in the administration. And you, Karen, threatened the power and prestige that went along with that because you wanted to bring the Crush Killer case public. That would've dirtied Church's congressional district and potentially damaged his chance at being elected governor."

Brix asked, "What about Robby? How does he factor into all this?"

"He doesn't," Vail said. "Not directly. Remember Sebastian? Real name's Antonio Sebastiani de Medina and he's a DEA agent. Robby was running an undercover op with him and their target was the Cortez Mexican drug cartel. César Guevara runs their front, Superior Mobile Bottling. So when Robby went dark, and we started looking for him and showing his photo around, I fucked things up big time. One of the people I showed Robby's photo to was Guevara. Not only was there a connection between me and him—I think I told Guevara he was my friend and colleague—but the photo was one we'd taken in front of the FBI Academy sign."

"So you blew his cover," Mann said.

"I blew his cover. Yeah." Merely saying it caused a stab of pain to Vail's stomach. "Sebastian escaped. I've gotta go back and ask him how it went down, but I suddenly put everything together and wanted to let you know how it all fit."

"Does he know Robby's disposition?"

Vail watched an FBI police SUV circle the parking lot. "No."

"Well, this all makes sense with what Matt Aaron just told us," Dixon said. "Remember that cork I found at Superior? They finally got around to running it. On the surface, he said that it appeared to be a thermoplastic elastomer. But after swabbing it and putting it through the mass spectrometer, he picked up a trace of cocaine."

"How much is a trace?" Vail asked.

Rustling of papers. "Here's what Aaron wrote: 'Looks like enough for identification. I got reproducible fragments at 303, 182, and 82, but below our quantitation limit.'"

"Did he happen to translate that into English?"

"Not enough to get a warrant, if that's what you're asking."

Vail chuckled. "I don't think a warrant's going to be a problem, Roxx. I was wondering about the cork. Obviously it's not one of the fake ones packed with Fentanyl."

"I'll make sure he slices it open and checks," Dixon said. "But he said this kind of minute dusting could be from someone touching it who'd handled powdered cocaine. That said, the elastomer material can retain natural oils, and there weren't any prints on the cork."

"All right," Brix said. "Get back to your interview with Sebastian. We'll keep working things on our end. Whether Guevara knows we're looking for him or he's on a regularly scheduled drug run, we don't know."

"Either way," Mann said, "with Sebastian's statement, we'll have enough for warrants. As soon as they're executed, we'll turn his place inside out."

"Too bad you can't join us," Dixon said. "Tossing his place would probably be therapeutic."

52

Vail disconnected the call and took a deep breath of March air . . . far damper than it had been in Napa. Had it been late summer or early fall, the chorus of cicadas and crickets in the nearby thicket of trees would be like a welcome home song. But it was silent now. She turned and headed back to Sebastian, toward—hopefully—more answers.

DeSantos was standing outside the room, touching the screen on his phone. He looked up when Vail approached.

"What's going on?"

"The nurse needed to adjust something. He wasn't feeling so good."

The door opened and Yardley motioned them in.

Vail and DeSantos sat at the table opposite Sebastian, whose face was ashen and his hair slick and stringy from perspiration. He was taking another swig of his Powerade.

"You okay?" Vail asked.

"Better."

"We won't keep you much longer." She leaned both forearms on the table and scooted her butt forward in the seat. "I'd like to go through what happened, what you saw. When you realized there was a problem."

Sebastian tilted the plastic Powerade bottle and picked at the label with a fingernail. "You sure you want to hear this?"

"I have to wear two hats here. I've got my business as a federal agent in pursuit of a missing colleague. And I have to acknowledge that I care deeply for what happens to that missing colleague. I'm doing my best to keep those two hats from interfering with each other."

"What she means," DeSantos said with a shake of his head, "is just answer the question."

Vail gave him a stern look. She didn't need him acting like her interpreter.

"Robby was already there. They sent me on an errand. At the time, I didn't think there was anything up. But then when I got back, Robby was surrounded by five guys. Guevara, a top Cortez lieutenant named Ernesto Escobar, and three others I didn't know. But they weren't friendlies."

"Why do you say that?" DeSantos asked.

"Because they weren't treating Robby very good."

"Don't mince words. What did you see?"

"I wasn't there when it started. But I heard the noise. I hid behind a car. What I saw . . . it was hard to watch, but I knew if I tried helping Robby, I'd either blow my cover or if I played along, they'd expect me to . . . I—I just couldn't do that." He closed his eyes. "I wouldn't have been able to hurt my buddy." He shook his head, then faced Vail. "I took off, kept a low profile, caught a ride with a trucker out of town. Figured, worse came to worst, I might be able to go back, make up some bullshit excuse for being gone."

"And," DeSantos said, "you figured, if Robby's cover's blown, yours was probably worth shit too, since you're the one who vouched for him. They might kill you before they killed him."

Sebastian didn't respond. He continued to pick at the Powerade label.

Vail was sure DeSantos's analysis was accurate, but she didn't want to move off topic. She swallowed hard. "What were they doing to Robby?"

Sebastian clenched his jaw, looked down at his Powerade. "Yelling at him in Spanish. Working him over. Kicking him. Worse."

Vail closed her mouth. She couldn't let anyone in the room see how much it hurt to hear that.

DeSantos placed a hand on her forearm. With a quick flick, she shook it off. She knew he meant well and she appreciated the gesture, but that wasn't what she wanted to project to the men in the room.

"A guy like you," DeSantos said, "you've got CIs with their ears to the ground. If there's something to be known about Robby's . . . disposition . . . they'd hear about it."

"I'm not going anywhere, not for a couple days. Believe me, I tried talking to the doc. He didn't want to have any of it."

"Then us," Vail said. "Set it up. We'll do the meet."

Sebastian leaned back in his seat. "That could work, I guess."

"No," Yardley said, stepping forward.

Sebastian looked up at the ASAC. "All I gotta do is call my guy, let him know—"

"Absolutely not."

Vail rose from her seat and faced Yardley, toe to toe. "You've gotta be kidding me."

Yardley, a few inches taller than Vail, stood his ground. "Soon as the doc clears him," he said calmly, "Sebastian will go. He's worked too hard, too long, to cultivate his CIs. Especially this one, who's got reliable roots right into the goddamn cartel. We screw it up, guy so much as smells something bad, we may never find a replacement."

"I realize Robby's 'only' a task force officer, but he deserves 100 percent effort on our part—all our parts—to get him out of danger."

"Agent Vail, we don't even know if he's still alive."

Body blow to the gut. *Don't take that shit.* "Listen to me," she said, bringing an index finger up toward his face. "With your help or not, I'm going to find Robby. Dead or alive. We owe that to him. I owe it to him. If my fuckup is responsible for blowing his cover, it's on me."

"I understand you don't like it," Yardley said, "but this is the way we handle these matters. Soon as we can, Sebastian will meet with the CI with regard to the issues at hand and then we'll get back to you."

Yardley started to turn away, but Vail grabbed his forearm. "When?"

He spoke while looking down at her hand. "We'll do what we can, *when* we can. But how we do it, and when, and what resources we use to do it, is our business, not yours." He brought his gaze up to hers. "I know you're concerned about Hernandez, but there are multiple lives at stake. You think he's the only asset we have in that organization?"

Vail dropped her hand. She was not prepared for that.

DeSantos was by her side. "Look," he said, both hands out in front of him, fingers spread, a calming gesture. "I can make some calls. Go over your head. Have one director talk to another director. And get that information. Or I can go to my sources and dig up who this CI is that Sebastian won't disclose. Either way, we will get what we want. Both ways are messy for you." He shrugged. "Your choice."

Yardley looked at DeSantos with a tournament-winning poker face. "Fuck you. And you too, Agent Vail." He turned to Sebastian. "We're done here."

Yardley walked to the door and flung it open. "This is a DEA investigation, Mr. DeSantos. Interfere, and I don't care what juice you can pour. I'll make sure it goes sour. So if it's a pissing contest you want, have at it."

DeSantos returned his poker face, then he and Vail started for the door—but not before Vail glanced back over her shoulder at Sebastian. He was biting his lower lip and picking at the Powerade label.

Vail had a sharp rebuke for him on the tip of her tongue, but held it. As DeSantos had implied, Sebastian abandoned Robby out of fear for his own life. But it was her fault, not his, that Robby's life was in danger in the first place. And now it was her responsibility to find him.

Before it was too late.

53

They got into the Corvette and DeSantos gunned the engine and peeled out of the parking lot. "You're doing your best to make my life difficult, you know that, Karen?"

Vail released her grip on the dashboard. "What?"

"I played our hand and I had nothing."

"What about 'I'll call the director'?"

DeSantos brought the Vette to a screeching halt. "Karen." He licked his lips, looked off into the distance as he gathered his thoughts. "I can't call the FBI director every time I can't get what I want. I don't even work for him—he's a . . . let's just say I've got a special relationship with him. Bottom line, I bluffed. Yardley called it. That's it."

Vail covered her eyes with a hand. *Great.* "What about working your resources?"

"My resources, my assets and CIs and everything else I use for terrorism-related intel, is valuable shit. I can't use it for stuff like this. One life . . . I don't want this to come out the wrong way. But I deal with threats that involve dignitaries or U.S. congressmen, thousands— sometimes *millions*—of civilians. I can't burn though valuable assets for this. I just can't."

"Wait a minute. Sebastian said something . . . " She thought a moment, then said, "He may've been trying to tell us something."

"Yeah. He and Yardley told us to go fuck ourselves."

"No, no. He said he could *call up* his CI."

DeSantos looked at Vail. "His phone records. If we can look through the calls he's made in the past, what, three months—we may have his CI."

"We'll never get access to his records."

"Legally," DeSantos said. "We'll never get his records *legally*. I've got other ways."

"Ways that won't burn your assets?"

"Exactly." He shoved the gearshift into drive and stepped on the accelerator. Vail flew back in her seat. Only this time she didn't mind. As far as she was concerned, the faster, the better.

54

At the Pentagon security booth, DeSantos spoke with the guard while Vail waited in the car. The telephone was lifted, words were exchanged, and a moment later DeSantos was climbing back into the Corvette.

"Give me your driver's license."

Vail handed it over, and DeSantos delivered it to the guard. Moments later, they were admitted into the parking lot. And moments after that, Vail was following DeSantos into the lower reaches of the Pentagon.

"No one can know what you see or hear. Are we cool?"

Vail nodded. "Yeah. Yeah." Her head rotated in all directions. "Where are we?"

"The bowels, where I work. No sarcastic comments, please."

He stopped at a door, placed his hand on a glass panel, and waited while a yellow light scanned his palm and a beam struck his retina. A computer voice said, "Scanning complete," the electronic click of a lock released, and DeSantos pushed through the door.

"What's OPSIG?" Vail asked. She thumbed a fist over her shoulder. "Sign on the door."

"Operations Support Intelligence Group. We're a highly covert team. And that's all I can tell you."

"That's all I think I want to know," she said.

Inside, an entire wall was subsumed by oversize LCD monitors, which displayed satellite imagery and blinking locator beacons. A worn conference table sat off to the side. An air-conditioned breeze whisked by Vail's ears, neutralizing the intense heat radiating from the wall of screens that buzzed her face as she passed them en route to a chair.

DeSantos sat down on one of the navy seats, placed his hands on a laptop PC in front of him, and stroked the keyboard. He leaned forward and a light from an external device scanned his retina.

"Okay," he said. "I'm logged in. Now, let's see what I can do." He reached over to a button on the table and pressed it. "Hey, man, can you come in here a sec?"

Vail moved to a seat beside DeSantos. "Who's that?"

"Let's call him Benny. My personal tech guru. I don't have a clue what I'm doing half the time. I'm TC." He glanced at her, must've seen her mind unsuccessfully processing that acronym, then said, "TC. Technologically challenged. My former partner could troll servers and penetrate secure databases like a true hacker. But me? I do Windows. That's about it." He struck a key. "When it involves delicate hacking, I need someone who knows how to hide our tracks."

In walked Benny, a bear of a man with fingers so thick they reminded Vail of bratwurst. She wondered how he was going to navigate the keyboard.

"Whazzup, boss?"

"Have a seat," DeSantos said. "We're going fishing."

BENNY, INDEED, HAD DIFFICULTY manipulating the computer keys—and as a result had to go slow, regularly correcting his mistyped commands. Finally, twenty minutes later, DeSantos retrieved a sheaf of papers from the LaserJet.

"Those are Sebastian's phone logs?" Vail asked.

He splayed them across the table in front of him. "Cell, home, and work."

"Scary that you can do that."

DeSantos chuckled. "This ain't nothing, my dear. You should see what we're capable of."

"Something tells me that if I did, you'd have to kill me."

Benny chuckled as DeSantos regarded the papers.

"Wouldn't be the first time," DeSantos said, "believe me."

Based on what little she had seen thus far, Vail certainly did.

Prior to printing the document, DeSantos had Benny sort the data multiple ways. He filtered out calls that were made to known people in Sebastian's life: his family members, girlfriend, known acquaintances, and of course, Robby. Established businesses and federal agency contacts were eliminated. And that left calls to individuals or businesses that were unidentified or suspect.

"We'll go from here, which is a lot more manageable." DeSantos turned to Benny. "Page three. Do a search and get me the names of all the owners of these phone numbers."

Benny turned back to the laptop and began poking at the keys. After a moment, he leaned back in his chair, which bent precariously close to the ground. "We'll have the results in a minute. So," he said to Vail, "I haven't seen you around here."

"I'm with the behavioral analysis unit."

Benny looked at DeSantos.

"She's fine," DeSantos said. "She hasn't seen anything and even if she did, she can be trusted."

Benny eyed her cautiously. His laptop beeped and he turned his attention back to the screen.

DeSantos rose and placed a hand on Benny's thick shoulder. He pointed at the color-coded display. "Sort it here and here. Give me a printout. That'll leave us with a manageable list."

Benny did as instructed, then left the room. DeSantos handed Vail the new, streamlined printout, which contained five names and numbers. "Let's eliminate the four non-Hispanic names. If I had to guess . . . " He placed a finger on the paper. "That'd be our guy."

55

Union Station was an odd place. Not the building—which was outwardly and inwardly architecturally pleasing, having been refurbished in 1988 into a modern transportation hub, shopping and restaurant destination—but the surrounding area. Located in the heart of the district and only ten football fields from the Capitol building, one might assume it sat in a premier neighborhood, the pride of the heart of U.S. government. Yet a wrong turn to the northeast landed you in a down-and-out section of D.C. that was best avoided.

And that was where DeSantos chose to meet Jose Diamante, purportedly a man who had insider information into the Cortez drug cartel, the confidential informant that DEA agent Antonio Sebastiani de Medina coddled and cultivated, paid and protected. Yardley knew the value of a high-level CI such as Diamante, which explained the resistance to providing his identity.

DeSantos foiled their plans, however, and now Diamante had agreed to meet his contact Sebastian. In another tech feat, a different OPSIG team member had cloned Sebastian's cell phone number, enabling them to send a text message to Diamante requesting the meet. After a tense ten-minute wait, the CI responded. He would be there.

Benny then hacked the DMV server and secured a photo and physical description of Jose Diamante. Now it was a matter of executing a get-together with a high-level CI who was, no doubt, a careful and suspicious sort.

"Me or you?" Vail asked.

"You mean the attractive woman approach? You think you can show a little cleavage and get closer than I can?"

"You don't think I can pull it off?"

DeSantos made a point of running his gaze from head to toe. "Probably best if I circle around, bring up the rear in case he runs."

Vail dropped her jaw. "Thanks a lot."

DeSantos broke a smile. "If he runs from you, the guy needs glasses. C'mon, let's go."

Leaving the car in the Union Station parking lot, they hoofed it down H Street NE. DeSantos stopped abruptly. "There used to be an Amoco station there, on the corner," he said, nodding ahead of him. "That's where I told him to meet us."

Ahead of them was an empty lot, filled with sprouting weeds and partial remnants of asphalt that was spider-cracked like a sun-weathered face. At the corner of 3rd and H Street stood three battered passenger bus-size cargo containers. It appeared as if construction was due to start and the crew brought the equipment onsite prior to initiating the project.

"Maybe he figured it out and is waiting by those storage containers," Vail said.

"Let's hope so."

They approached separately, DeSantos taking a detour between freshly constructed multistory brick apartment buildings, where he'd walk parallel to H, toward and across 3rd Street. He would then come up fifty yards behind the location where they hoped Diamante was waiting.

DeSantos was carrying the cloned cell phone—and all network traffic to that number was diverted to his handset. Like an arrested suspect, Sebastian's real phone would remain silent until DeSantos's team member released it for normal telephonic reception. If Diamante was not where he should be, DeSantos could contact him while retaining his cover.

DeSantos advanced from the rear. He signaled Vail, who began walking toward the front of the closest blue-gray cargo container. As she approached, she saw there was just enough room between the long structures for a person to fit—not comfortably, but it was possible to shuffle sideways through the opening. Just looking at the tight quarters made her chest tighten.

Along the exposed side of the shipping container was a smaller storage box. Roughly half the size of the other two, it was positioned approximately a dozen feet away. And leaning against its side pulling on a cigarette was Jose Diamante. DeSantos had spotted him too, as he was tipping his head left in the CI's direction. DeSantos stood frozen, waiting for Vail to advance so that errant footsteps wouldn't be detected before Vail could engage him.

She smiled and walked gaily toward Diamante, motioning at him until his head lifted and his body straightened. He was locked in.

"Excuse me," she said. "I'm totally lost. My phone battery's dead and I was looking for a pay phone. Someone said there was one in the gas station on the corner, but"—she spread her arms and made a point of swiveling her head from side to side—"there's no gas station."

"Looks like they tore it down," Diamante said, then sucked again on his cigarette, out the side of his mouth, like he was thinking of what kind of fun he could have with the attractive redhead who was approaching.

"I was looking for a street that had an 'NW' after it, but all these street signs say 'NE.' Is there a difference?" She laughed. *Stupid me, I'm a vulnerable woman in a bad neighborhood where a missing dimwit might go unnoticed for hours, if not days. Go ahead and try something.*

But he suddenly swiveled 180 degrees, and his body language suggested he caught sight of DeSantos and had read him as a cop. Not merely suggested—he tensed and coiled low and bent his knees and took off in Vail's direction. She was still a ditsy redhead and had not entered his threat zone. Yet.

Vail stepped left, into his path, and threw her arms around him. But he must've seen this move before, because he stuck an elbow into her neck, and she went down.

Diamante continued south, toward H Street.

Shit. She hustled to her feet—DeSantos was still thirty or forty yards away—and resumed her pursuit.

Diamante tried cutting a hard left and he went down, sprawling in a patch of loose dirt. As he gathered himself, Vail pounced, wrapping her arms around his back. But she was only 115 pounds and Diamante was—per the DMV—200.

And that seemed about right as he flung her off his back rather easily. But Vail was not about to let her sole connection to Robby go that easily. She had an iron grip on his collar and he dragged her forward through the dirt. She pulled with all her weight, choking him best she could. But he wouldn't go down.

She fumbled for the handle of her Glock, yanked it free, then swung it as hard as she could, clocking him across the back of his head. Diamante stumbled, then crumpled to his knees.

Vail landed atop him but maintained the grip on her pistol. She thrust it into the base of his skull and damn-near shouted, "Don't move.

Not one move—or I'll blow your goddamn brain all over the dirt, you hear me?"

DeSantos was pulling up behind them in full stride. "Karen! Karen, what are you doing?"

Ignoring DeSantos, she said into Diamante's ear, "We need some information. We're not here to hurt you. Understand?"

He nodded his head, and his face scraped across the ground.

She gave him a thorough pat down and pulled a .45 Magnum from his belt. She handed it back toward DeSantos, who snatched it away, anger pulling his face into a snarl.

They needed to move Diamante away from the main drag. People would be getting out of work soon, and it'd be best not to be in full view while they questioned him. In the era of camera phones—not to mention ATM cameras and security eyes recording everything within reach—they had to be careful.

"I'm gonna get off you now," Vail said to Diamante. "You're going to stand up. Slowly. Then we're going to walk to the back of this container and have a chat. You cooperate and no one will get hurt. Understand?"

He again abraded his face against the dirt.

Vail backed off him but kept her Glock at her side, against her pants, out of view of any passing onlookers—who'd already gotten a good show if any had cared to watch. Vail surmised that in this neighborhood, when shit like this happened, people either turned their backs—or got the hell away before bullets started flying.

They also needed to avoid trolling Metro police cruisers. Vail didn't have a problem with pulling her creds and explaining their purpose, but the last thing they wanted to do was make a show of being seen with Diamante; it could destroy him. Talking to cops was . . . frowned upon in this hood, and it would likely result in him no longer being a source of any value. Not to mention it'd probably get him killed.

Diamante, a coerced but willing party, walked alongside Vail, with DeSantos bringing up the rear. They continued about a hundred paces until they reached the far end of the long container. Two dozen feet away stood a line of parked vehicles. Realizing that these SUVs, pickups, and minivans could provide adequate cover while they talked, Vail headed in that direction.

Before they arrived, her phone buzzed. It was Gifford. She muted the ringer, then steered Diamante between two Suburban-type SUVs.

Vail got a good look at his face for the first time: not a bad-looking guy. She wondered what he was really like, why he had a connection to one of the most powerful drug cartels—and if he'd be a cooperating informant.

DeSantos stood with his hands in the back pocket of his jeans—no suit for this meet—and did not look pleased.

"Sorry about that back there," Vail said to Diamante. "I didn't think you'd run. I didn't have a choice."

Diamante turned to DeSantos. "Whaddya want with me?"

"It's like I said," Vail replied. "We need some information."

With his gaze still on DeSantos, Diamante said, "I don't talk to women who carry guns. It's one of my rules of doing business."

"What business are we doing here?" Vail asked.

But DeSantos held out his arm and eased Vail aside. "That's fine. Talk to me."

Vail bit down hard—the objective was to get information. How they did that did not matter. Now was not the time to allow her bruised female ego to intervene.

Diamante reached for his pocket. Vail raised her Glock.

And Diamante raised his hands. "A cigarette, *cabrona*, take it easy."

Vail knew that translated to "bitch"—but she let it pass. Dr. Rudnick would be proud.

DeSantos nodded for him to continue. He pulled a lighter and held it out for Diamante, who lit up. He puffed smoke into the air and said with a shrug, "I don't know nothing, so there ain't nothing to talk about."

DeSantos stepped forward and spoke in a low voice. "Cortez. We know you're connected. That's what we need to know about."

"You're loco, *amigo*. Fucking loco if you think I know something about drugs."

DeSantos grinned. "I didn't say anything about drugs. So you know enough to know what Cortez's business is. But okay, I get it. You had to say that. Now that we're past all that shit, I need to know what you've heard. About a certain guy."

"I told you. I don't know nothing."

Vail stepped forward, nudging DeSantos aside. "Bullshit. And I'm not in the mood to play games, so you *will* answer our questions."

Diamante spit in her face. A gooey, cigarette smoker's phlegm stuck to her cheek. Rather than wiping it away, she reached back and slugged him, right in the nose with the butt of her Glock. His head snapped back into the top of the car and he slunk down onto his knees, at her feet.

DeSantos turned away and brought a hand to his forehead. "Jesus Christ."

Vail crouched between the trucks. Her face was now an inch from Diamante's bloodied, crushed nose. "Now we're going to try this again. I don't know you and I don't know what you're involved in. But I do know you've got a line into Cortez. That's all I care about." She lifted the Glock to the man's face. He looked at it with groggy eyes, his head bobbing slightly to the sides. He probably had a mild concussion. Getting slugged in the face with a handgun will do that to you.

Vail tilted her head. "I want to know what you heard about an undercover cop whose cover was blown."

Diamante's eyes slid from her weapon to her face. "Yeah. Cortez and Guevara were pissed, big time. What was he . . . your partner or something?"

"Yeah. Or something." Vail glanced at DeSantos. A confirming look that this was working. "See?" she said to Diamante. "This isn't so hard, talking to a woman with a gun. Is it?" She wiggled the Glock in front of his eyes. "Where is this undercover cop now?"

Diamante's gaze rose skyward. "Don't know."

"I don't believe you."

"Hey, you don't believe me, shoot me. But you're a cop, you won't do that. So I guess we're done here."

Vail brought her hand back to strike him, but DeSantos grabbed her arm.

"He's lying," she said. "He knows more than he's telling us."

DeSantos frowned, then shook his head and knelt down in front of their informant. "See, the thing is, Jose, she's a bit of a loose cannon. And what we do, we do off the grid. So if you don't cooperate, we've got the option of killing you. Honest. I've done it before." He leaned forward and lined up his eyes with Diamante's. "Many times." He waited a long minute, then shrugged. "But I think we can come to some kind of understanding. I'm gonna be reasonable. You've got till midnight to get us the information we need."

Diamante shook his head.

DeSantos held up a finger. "Again, I understand how this works. I know that demanding that you get us some intel wouldn't mean much if I didn't back it by a threat. Right?" He grinned. "So here's the deal. If we don't hear from you, I'm going to spread the word, carefully, selectively, so that, in time, it'll make it back to Carlos Cortez himself that you're a CI for the DEA."

Diamante's jaw line tensed.

"On the other hand," DeSantos said with a shrug, "you give us what we want, and you'll never hear from us again. And that's a promise." He rose from his crouch—and Vail followed suit.

Diamante swallowed hard, touched his bloody nose with a finger, testing to see how badly broken it was—then threw Vail a dirty look. He pushed his back against the SUV and got to his feet.

A moment later, he was disappearing down the block, gone from view

56

D eSantos stood there glaring at Vail. She stared back.
"What the hell was that?" he asked.
"Oh come on. You know what it was. And don't tell me you never roughed someone up to get information vital to your mission. Or whatever the hell it is you do."

"That's different. Do you really need me to tell you that's not the way to go about this, that you're burning a CI? Sebastian's gonna be pissed as all hell if Diamante tells him to go fuck himself next time he contacts him for a line on Cortez. Not to mention your behavior's going to get us both killed." He lowered his voice and took a breath. "Do you usually go about your business like that? Because if you do, I've had the FBI all wrong."

Vail looked away at the deteriorating apartment buildings and duplex homes in the near distance. "No. Yes. Lately, I've lived on the edge. I've done things I've never done before."

DeSantos stood there looking at her before responding. "I'm no shrink, but I think you need help, Karen. Anger management."

"Been there, done that." She thought of Dr. Rudnick. "Still doing it, I guess."

"Yeah?" DeSantos stood with his hands on his hips. "Well, it's not working."

"You know what? If you're going to preach, you'd better be prepared to follow the advice in your own sermon. You can't tell me you wouldn't be doing exactly what I've been doing if your loved one's life depended on it."

DeSantos dropped his arms and turned away, placed both palms on the driver's side window of the adjacent SUV.

"I'm right, aren't I?"

DeSantos did not answer. But the fact that he hung his head sug-gested she was, indeed, correct in her assertion. Finally, DeSantos pushed back from the truck and walked away, back the way they had come, toward Union Station.

57

Vail had returned Gifford's call while they were en route to their car. She had nothing else to do, since DeSantos was in no mood to talk. At least he was in no mood to talk to her.

Lenka told Vail that Gifford was in a meeting but wanted to see her in his office if she was headed back to the unit. Vail could not think of other leads to track down, so going back to the BAU seemed to be the best move. If Rooney had not yet left for Iraq, she wanted to sit down with him and tell him all she had learned about Guevara, John Mayfield, and the drug smuggling operation. Perhaps he could recommend some unseen angles worth pursuing.

DeSantos said he had an errand to run twenty minutes from the BAU, so he dropped Vail at her office and told her to check in with him when she was done.

As Vail moved through the secure door to the BAU, a text came through from Dixon:

answer on audio of message left on wirths voicemail. guardian angel was robby.   :-)

She allowed herself a moment to grin. Robby may've been undercover, but after giving Ian Wirth's home address to Guevara, he found a way to send Wirth an anonymous warning.

While Vail was typing a reply, another text came through:

and got a hit on handcuffs serial nmbr. female cop napa pd. last seen at a bar downtown about 1am. didnt report to work today. this isnt gonna end well

No. This isn't going to end well. Vail typed back:

for what its worth she was probably cannons first victim

"Everything okay?"

Vail looked up. She was standing in front of Lenka's desk.

"Yeah, sorry. I was—" She held up her BlackBerry. "Got a text."

Lenka reached for her phone. "I'll let him know you're here. I'm not sure if he'll be glad or mad."

Vail tucked her chin back. "What's that supposed to mean?"

"My sense is that he's had a bad day. And right now, with the people in his office and the noises coming from inside, I think it's only gotten worse." She lifted the receiver and poked a button. While it rang, she said to Vail, "Not to mention he should've gone home fifteen minutes ago."

Vail's relationship with Gifford was odd, to say the least, for an ASAC and an agent. Profilers usually dealt directly with their unit chief. But Vail and Gifford always worked one-on-one. Her unit chief didn't mind—at least, he'd never said anything to her about it—although that could've been Gifford's doing. Maybe he labeled her a troublemaker and felt a more direct, hands-on approach would be the best way of keeping her reined in.

Am I a troublemaker?

Lenka set the handset back in its cradle. "You can go in."

Vail nodded, then turned toward the office door.

"Good luck."

Vail looked over her shoulder at Lenka, hesitated with her hand on the knob, then walked in.

And it immediately became apparent why Lenka had wished her luck. Gifford was behind his desk. Standing to his left was FBI director Douglas Knox. And to his right was DEA administrator Bronson McGuire. Gifford did not look pleased.

Knox did not look pleased.

Nor did McGuire.

In fact, they looked downright angry, like frustrated cougars who couldn't get at their meal. And Vail suddenly felt like a sacrificial lamb.

"Agent Vail," Knox said. "Good of you to finally join us."

"I just got word—"

"I received a call about an hour ago," Knox continued. "Do you know who it was?"

"I'm guessing it was Administrator McGuire," Vail said, and glanced at McGuire. *Is he salivating?*

"That's right," McGuire said. "I had a scheduled meeting with the president, which was supposed to be happening—" he consulted his watch "—right about now. Only once have I ever told a president I had to reschedule. And that was when I was in an ambulance on the way to an emergency appendectomy."

Vail licked her lips. *Something tells me I'm about to have some scars of my own.*

"Do you know what the problem is?" Knox asked.

"No sir, not exactly." *There've been so many things I've fucked up. Take your pick.*

Knox's eyes flicked over to McGuire before settling back on Vail. "I'm pulling you off this case. Effective immediately."

"You mean Rob—Detective Hernandez's case?"

"That would be the one," McGuire said. "You weren't officially authorized to be working it, anyway. And if you'd kept your nose out of things, we wouldn't be needing to have this discussion."

"Okay," Gifford said, lifting a hand. "Just hold it right there. We all know that's not true."

McGuire snorted. "We don't know it's not true. Agent Vail—"

"No need to rehash it," Gifford said. "I've heard your position."

McGuire's hard stare spoke volumes. Gifford, a subordinate, was standing up to the DEA administrator. *Ballsy. Risky. And—holy shit—it sounds like he's defending me.*

"Your actions," McGuire said to Vail, "have seriously jeopardized a years-long effort to take down the Cortez cartel. And while I understand your knee-jerk, ill-conceived, half-assed attempt to find your *boyfriend,* we are professionals. We all know the risks when we go undercover. Detective Hernandez certainly knew them."

Gifford shifted his feet, turned his head, and looked off at the wall. Vail couldn't help noticing. *Interesting body language—that statement made him uncomfortable. Why? Because he feels responsible for what happened to Robby?*

"This operation is far more important than absolving yourself of guilt over having blown his cover. And possibly costing him his life."

Vail clenched her jaw. She had reached her tolerance point for taking the bullshit McGuire was doling out. Respect for authority or not, she could not let his statement stand without a response.

"I resent the implication, sir," Vail started.

"I'm not implying anything. I thought I was pretty damn clear."

"Bronson," Knox said firmly, "that's enough. This has been a tragedy. For the DEA op, for Detective Hernandez—and, yes, for Agent Vail. Pointing the finger is not going to get us anywhere. Move on."

"Fine," McGuire said. He turned to Vail. "Then let's get something straight. If you ever get in the face of one of my ASACs, I'll make sure you're busted down from the BAU so you regret your behavior for a good long time." He faced Knox. "The Bureau is done here. Don't come near my operation. I'll let you know when we find Hernandez. Alive—" he turned to Vail—"or dead."

McGuire slammed the door on his way out. The room was silent.

"Don't worry about him," Director Knox said. "He's got no jurisdiction over Bureau personnel matters. I'll clean up the mess once he calms down. But me . . . that's another story. We are done with this case, and you do have to do as *I* tell you, Agent Vail. Because I do have the power to make your life miserable. And I *know* you're not even close to retiring from the Bureau, so let's be honest. Your work is exceptional but you tend to find yourself in deep shit more often than is acceptable. Don't think I've not been made aware of all your recent escapades. And for an FBI director to be made aware of the actions of a profiler in the BAU, that means something's wrong with its management."

Knox did not look at Gifford, but the implications were clear.

Shit. Gifford deserves a lot of things, but blame for my screw-ups is not one of them. "Mr. Gifford suggested suspending me by a crane over the Potomac to keep me out of trouble." *Levity. Did it work?*

Knox looked at her, an expression that said he was gauging whether or not she was serious. Gifford was facing away, clearly uncomfortable.

Gazing squarely at Vail, Knox said, "That may yet be a good idea." He turned to leave. "I'll take it under consideration."

When the door clicked shut, Vail found a nearby chair and fell into it. Hard.

Gifford stood there, staring at her, sucking his bottom lip. Seconds passed. "Damn it, Karen."

"Sir—"

"No. Just goddamn it. I have a love-hate relationship with you, you know that? You frustrate the hell out of me. I don't know what the hell to do with you sometimes. If you weren't so damn valuable to the unit, I'd recommend you be kicked out of the Bureau so far you wouldn't be able to find your way back."

Vail leaned forward and rested her forearms on her knees. This time, for once, she kept her mouth shut.

"What the hell were you thinking? Threatening Yardley, a DEA ASAC? What possible good did you think would come out of that?"

"We were trying to get information about Sebastian's CI," Vail said. "Yardley didn't want to help us out. I was just trying to save Robby."

"Yeah, about that. Your behavior might just have sealed your boyfriend's fate. Because we can't do anything to help find him now. And we're the ones who are most concerned about his well-being."

Gifford's voice was now so loud Vail was sure it could be heard on the other side of his door.

"Do you realize that? We are *fucked*. You heard the director."

"I heard him, but—"

"Robby's status—a task force officer—was some goddamn fabrication we created to help him advance his career because there *was* no task force. But it leaves him in no-man's-land. He's not one of DEA's own. Will they go to the end of the earth to save him? Probably. But do you see any written guarantees? Because I sure don't. I can tell you that this op is hugely important to them. They have to nail it to show the war on drugs is worth pumping more money into. With all federal budgets under pressure, you bet they need a home run on this. Normally, they'd do everything they could to get Robby back. But with all this in play, it's not a normal situation." Gifford hung his head and said, beneath his breath, "And it's my fault. It's all my fault."

"No sir. I'm the one who blew his cover."

Gifford's head snapped up. "And I'm the one who pulled strings to get him into that operation in the first place." He shook his head, leaned back in his chair, and massaged his face briskly with a hand.

Vail watched him. He was under unaccountably severe duress. Yes, a law enforcement officer was in danger. And some time ago, Gifford had promised Robby's mother he would look after him. Was that all there was to this? Or was there something more?

"Sir, we'll find him. Hector and I have got a line—"

"Karen, I don't want to hear this. I can't hear this. Did you *get* what the director just said to you? The Bureau's done, we're out of this. Our hands are tied."

"Your hands are tied, sir. I don't intend to sit by and wait for Robby's body to show up on a morgue slab, or worse—along the side of some Mexican highway. Not gonna happen."

Vail realized Gifford was not listening. He was staring ahead, at nothing in particular. Eyes glazed.

"I promised his mother I'd look after him. On her death bed, I promised."

Vail studied his face a long moment—and then it hit her. She should have seen it before . . . the information had been there, teasing away at her brain for months, but she never put it all together. Until now, the look in Gifford's eyes. Guilt—but not just guilt.

"Robby isn't just the son of a good friend, is he, sir? He's *your* son. Biologically."

Gifford's eyes found hers. But he did not reply.

Back when they were working the Dead Eyes case, Robby told her he suspected Gifford of having a fling with his mom. Vail assumed it was a recent occurrence, in the year before his mother died. But what if it had been a much longer relationship than Vail realized—than Robby realized? "You knew Alexandra a great many years," she said softly. "You had an affair with her. A long time ago."

Gifford rocked forward in his seat and dropped his gaze to his desk. In a weak voice as flat as Texas, he said, "I think it's time you left."

Vail sat there, debating how hard to push. But she realized she knew all there was to know—for now. Her time was best spent trying to find Robby. After what just went down, she had to operate under the radar of both the Bureau and the DEA.

It was then that she realized it was a good thing the man assisting her was Hector DeSantos. Under the radar was his specialty.

58

Vail met DeSantos at the World War II memorial. When she had called and told him she was officially removed from the case, he told her to put that thought on hold.

"I've got someone who wants to meet." He told her where and encouraged her not to be late.

She caught a cab and was there two minutes early. Vail got out and walked toward the towering southern entrance, the limestone block four-poster Pacific gateway. A giant stone wreath hung above, supported by eagles in midflight. Splitting off to both sides of the archway were dozens of freestanding pillars, each lettered in relief with the states' names, in addition to the various U.S. territories. The columns were dramatically lit from below and curved in a gentle semicircle, forming a recessed central plaza, where a large, active fountain sat. Carved in bas relief along two long walls were scenes depicting iconic milestones in the war.

Standing a few yards from the edge of the rainbow pool was Hector DeSantos. Several clumps of people milled about the water's periphery, including the usual contingent of tourists with cameras; older men reminiscing about the war and commiserating about how the world had changed in the intervening decades; children holding their grandfathers' hands, learning their country's history in a way that transcended textbooks and two-dimensional black-and-white photos.

Vail walked up to DeSantos and was about to speak when he tapped her arm, then turned to his right and began walking. He stopped twenty yards later, near a cutout in the pool's rim, midway between the Pacific and Atlantic gateways. A man sat at the water's edge, hands clasped around his knees.

Vail eyed him closely. It was Sammy, DeSantos's DEA contact.

DeSantos sauntered toward the man but kept a distance so that the two of them did not appear to know each other. Vail stood at DeSantos's left, between him and Sammy. She figured it was her job to stand there and make like DeSantos was chatting with her, when in fact he was talking across her to Sammy.

"What've you got?" DeSantos asked.

Sammy looked down at his lap and picked at a loose thread on his shirt. "I haven't heard anything about your guy."

"Who would you be hearing this from?" Vail asked. She glanced at DeSantos and noticed his tight jaw. But she couldn't help herself.

Sammy did not react. Calmly, he said, "We have more assets in place than just the two you knew about. They send us texts using clean phones, but contacting them is risky and not always possible. We prefer to keep it a one-way street."

DeSantos faced Vail, as if he was talking to her. "And?"

"They're gearing up for some big changes. Some new shit with real bad consequences."

"How so?"

Sammy looked out at the fountains a moment, then tucked his chin.

Vail realized he was probably hiding his face in case anyone was attempting to read his lips. Good tradecraft—but paranoid as shit.

"You know about the wine bottles? The labels?"

"The black tar heroin," DeSantos said. "The LSD."

"There's more to it. They're testing something new, something that could turn the drug trade on end. A potent drug with a revolutionary delivery system. No needles. Using the wine bottle labels."

"What drug?"

"BetaSomnol. Ever hear of it?"

Vail couldn't help but turn toward Sammy. "Fuck yes. I was shot up—"

"Honey," DeSantos said with a forced chuckle. "Please watch your language." He grinned at her, then said in a whisper, "Keep your eyes in my direction and lower your goddamn voice."

"I was injected with it," Vail said. "It put me to sleep. Why would 'our guy' think there's anything special about that?"

"Injecting the drug causes different effects," Sammy said. "But put the drug on a film—or a label—and then put the film on your tongue . . . and you've got a novel delivery system. Oral and transdermal. It releases part of its total drug content orally—which produces the nap you experienced with the injection. But the rest of the drug is transdermally released to produce the lasting high upon waking a few minutes later."

"Who'd want to walk around with this film in your mouth?" DeSantos asked.

Sammy shook his head, then examined something he was holding in his hand. A digital camera. He thumbed through the pictures on the display while he talked. "Transdermal delivery deposits the drug in the dermis, the tongue's top layers under the patch. When the patch is removed, the dermis continues to release the drug into the person's system. So the euphoria continues even though the film's been removed. It's a very intense, long-lasting high. The gift that keeps giving."

Vail looked out at the milling tourists as they snapped photos. "This is new?"

"Totally. BetaSomnol is used in hospitals as a powerful, fast-acting sedative—"

"I know how it's used."

"Then you know it's a growing problem. Abuse by physicians on long shifts. They take the drug and it induces a rapid nap. After they wake, they have an intense, momentary high—which doesn't last because they're not using the transdermal film—but it does make it seem as if they'd slept for hours, even though it's only been about twenty minutes. Helps on long shifts."

"And that's legal?" Vail asked.

"Not exactly. But it's becoming an abuse problem among hospital docs and nurses. Guevara found out about this. There was a doc at the hospital in Napa who nearly killed himself when he screwed up and misadministered the BetaSomnol to himself. Guevara heard about it, had an idea, took it to Cortez, and their chemist started working on it. Five months later, he came up with this transdermal film, modeled after a patented process that's currently used in the manufacture of Duragesic. Transdermal Fentanyl."

"And there's a market for this?" DeSantos said.

"Guevara wanted to bring something big to Cortez. Be a big feather in his cap. He'd already looked into using Propofol, the shit that killed Michael Jackson. But it was too damn dangerous. Too easy for some junkie to OD—that'd bring serious addict heat."

"Addict heat?" Vail asked.

"When addicts start dying, the police take notice and come down hard. The cops know they've got a big problem, so it gets more attention.

I'm not saying we look the other way when there aren't as many junkies dying—but it'd make the papers. And once that happened, word would get out the stuff's no good. Bad for business. So the cartels gotta keep their customers happy. And alive. Dead customers tend to stop buying stuff."

DeSantos took Vail's hand in his. He obviously wanted this to look believable. It didn't help that Vail turned and gave him a hard stare.

"Cortez wasn't totally convinced it was safe. Apparently skin permeability varies person to person and he didn't want to risk it. But a couple days ago, his chemists came up with a fix. They refined the product by processing the film with some chemicals. It worked. Word is that it produces a very intense, long-lived high—that's completely safe. And the return on investment's very high. The label can be sliced into multiple smaller sections, multiplying the doses per smuggled wine bottle. His goal is to create a whole new craze in the marketplace. And Cortez is the only one who's got it. He's the sole supplier. He'll clean up."

"Great," Vail said. "Not good enough we've got tens of millions of drug abusers in this country. Now he's gonna make it quick, easy, and safe to walk around stoned. Great goddamn world we live in."

"It's a credible threat," Sammy said. "We're taking it very seriously. Only solution is to take down his organization. Or cut off its head and weaken it."

DeSantos let go of Vail's hand and put his arm around her. "I think it's time we got back, honey."

Vail rolled her eyes. "Yes, dear. Let's get back."

DeSantos said, "Anything comes up on our guy, let me know." He turned to glance at Sammy—but the man was thirty feet away, heading toward the steps at the far end of the plaza.

59

Vail called Gifford to update him on what they had learned from Sammy—and Lenka informed her he had just left the office. She could reach him on his cell, as he was headed into Georgetown for a late dinner.

Gifford agreed to meet them at the restaurant provided they got there quickly and didn't stay long.

Georgetown Seafood Grill was located below street level in a marble-faced office building. DeSantos pulled his car to the curb, again with no regard for the district's parking enforcement laws and the five—*five*—stacked No Parking signs that towered in front of the restaurant's entrance.

"They have valet parking," Vail said, pointing to the A-frame sign at the curb.

"Won't be here that long. We're fine."

They walked past a handwritten "50 cent Clams & Oysters" sign locked inside a display case that featured the restaurant's menu, then descended the stone steps and pushed through the glass doors.

Vail moved past the bar and into the maritime-themed dining area. Clinking glasses and silver-on-ceramic clatter mixed with the rumble of idle chatter among the patrons. Polished cherrywood booths were separated by frosted dividers, neatly finished by crisscrossed wires that wove through riveted holes in the glass. Oars hung overhead, alongside inverted canoes and three sizable swordfish.

Gifford sat at a booth along the side wall, alone, a mixed drink in his hand and a menu propped up to his left. Vail slid in beside him. DeSantos stood at the end of the table, not wanting to invade the ASAC's space without asking permission.

Gifford motioned him in. "My friend should be here soon. Make it fast."

"We need to get the Bureau back in the game," Vail said.

Gifford set his drink down beside a metal porthole carved into the wall just above the table's surface. He removed his reading glasses and said, "No."

"Sir—"

"I realize 'no' is a hard concept for you, Karen. But this is a DEA op, and the FBI has no part in it. No jurisdiction."

"What about interstate trade? Crossing state lines? Kidnapping?"

Gifford was silent.

"Karen can be a pain in the ass," DeSantos said, "But I think she's right here." He proceeded to recap what Sammy had told them. When he finished, Gifford sat back. He lifted an oversize canister marked SEA SALT and absentmindedly rotated it in his hand.

"Sir?"

"Yes. Yes. Kidnapping." He set the salt container on the table. "This flies in the face of interagency cooperation. If we're running our own op and not coordinating with DEA, it's just bad. So let's do it right. Keep DEA in the loop."

"And just how are we going to do that?" Vail asked. "We have no contact on the case other than Yardley. I don't even know if Sebastian is still working it."

"He is. More than that, I don't know. But the docs have cleared him for duty as of tomorrow."

DeSantos pushed his glasses back up his nose. "As soon as you tell Yardley we're back in, he'll throw a fit."

"Let me worry about that. Meantime, work it as a kidnap case, not a drug case."

"And the difference is?" Vail asked.

"A matter of interpretation. But your objective is to find Robby—Detective Hernandez. It's not to bring down the cartel. Let the DEA handle that. That should clarify it for you."

Not really. It's not always possible to separate one string from a ball of yarn. You pull and yank and the whole thing starts to unravel.

"Start out by letting DEA know about this BetaSomnol thing."

"Yeah . . ." Vail said. "Can't do that. And what I told you has to remain in confidence."

Gifford threw up his hands. "Karen—"

"I'm sorry. It came from a very sensitive source."

"This isn't the way to start off our newly restored relationship with DEA."

"I think it's safe to assume the DEA knows all about Cortez's plans for BetaSomnol."

"And how is that?"

Vail bit her lip. *He's not going to like this.* "Hypothetically. What if I told you that our sensitive source is a DEA agent working the case?"

"Hypothetically, I'd have to say you're finding new ways to shorten my life. Just when I thought I'd figured out what to expect from you—"

"I got the info, didn't I?"

Gifford rubbed his face with both hands.

"As soon as you have information you can share with DEA, I expect you to do that. For now, consider Antonio Sebastiani de Medina to be your contact. I'll have Lenka text you his cell when I get in tomorrow."

Vail tossed a quick glance toward DeSantos. "I believe we've already got it, sir."

A woman dressed in a clinging violet dress and diamond drop necklace walked up to the table. The stress drained from Gifford's face like water through a storm drain.

DeSantos rose and nodded at the woman. Vail followed and excused herself.

"Remember what we talked about," Gifford said. "Both of you."

"Yes sir," Vail said. She bowed slightly, as if he were Asian royalty. "Absolutely, sir. You know that whatever you say goes."

As they moved past the bar, DeSantos leaned close to her ear. "What's up with that bowing thing?"

"Just trying to make him look important in front of his date. He and I have our moments, but overall he's a good man."

DeSantos grinned. "If you were his date, would you have bought that crap?"

"Me?" She chuckled. "Come on."

They emerged from the restaurant and ascended the steps. DeSantos stopped short and yelled. "Fuck!"

Vail turned to see what he was looking at—or, rather, what he was not looking at. The curb space was empty. His Corvette had been towed.

60

The morning arrived, a welcome occurrence given her futile attempt at sleeping. Earlier in the evening, Vail had spent a few hours with Jonathan, relating an edited version of her adventures in Napa and dancing around Robby's disappearance by explaining that he was working undercover.

They capped the evening by watching the latest Star Trek movie, during which Vail nursed a glass of bargain-priced Cabernet—a throwback to her pre-enological education. The inevitable comparison to the fine Napa Valley out-of-her-budget reds that she had recently tasted was a foreseeable disappointment.

Upon climbing into bed, instead of shutting down, her mind upshifted to a gear in which she had spent too much time lately. Images, thoughts, and ideas zipped and flowed for hours. Mayfield, Fuller, Owens, Lugo, Cannon. Her friendship with Dixon, even Brix. Every one paid a visit to her thoughts, except the sandman. But ultimately her focus was Robby. Not knowing if he was still alive . . . and if he was, what were they doing to him? She didn't have to ask the DEA how cartel members treated exposed undercover agents.

At four o'clock, in the desolate silence of the dark night, her pillowcase had absorbed an hour's worth of tears and needed to be changed. She rolled out of bed, retrieved the new linen, and walked into Jonathan's room. She sat down on his ottoman and watched him awhile. It was only a short time ago she had done this very thing—in a hospital, hoping to God he would regain consciousness. A huge battle among many in a war she was fighting at the time.

And now, still engaged in that war, just a different theater. Like Iraq and Afghanistan.

Vail grabbed breakfast with Jonathan and Faye, then sent her son off to school while Faye went to visit Vail's mother at the assisted care facility.

"I saw her before I left for California," Vail said as she cleared the table. "She seemed to be doing well." She stopped in front of the sink, a plate in each hand, lost in thought. "As well as someone can be with advancing Alzheimer's."

"I'll tell her you send your love," Faye said.

Vail shook the funk from her thoughts, then set the dishes down. "Give her a kiss for me, will you?"

Faye's grin conveyed empathy mixed with pity. She gave the back of Vail's head a thoughtful stroke. "Of course."

Vail spent the next hour in her den jotting down all she knew about Robby's disappearance. It was not much help, but it passed the time until DeSantos picked her up. She slid into his Corvette, which looked no worse for its trip to the impound lot.

DeSantos had summoned two cabs last night, one to take Vail home and the other to bring him to the tow yard.

"Your Vette looks fine," Vail said as he eased it onto the interstate. "I assume you got it all straightened out."

"Can we not talk about it?

Vail suppressed a grin. And then her belt vibrated. A text from Dixon.

can u get to a pc with internet?

She wrote back:

yes in about 15 min. K?

"What's the deal?" DeSantos asked.

"We need a PC with a broadband connection."

"We can do that. When? For what?"

"Got a text from Roxxann Dixon. Don't know what it's about." Her BlackBerry buzzed again.

dea bringing us on board. u and ur partner need to be plugged in. welcome to the dea

She replied and told Dixon they would be ready. "I think we're being added to a DEA task force." Another text, this one from Gifford:

expect a call. they've set up a jtf. pulled strings. u owe me. dont fu.

Vail chuckled.

DeSantos tossed her a sideways glance. "What's so funny?"

Vail shoved her phone into its holster. "Gifford. He pulled strings, got DEA to set up a joint task force. We're apparently on it. He told me not to fuck it up."

"Give me a break," DeSantos said. "With you on the case, does your boss really think things are going to go smoothly?"

61

A dark-skinned black man who fit the mold of a starting middle line-backer walked into the room. Sporting a shoulder slung beat-up leather messenger bag, unmoving confidence, and three day's growth of stubble on his face, he dumped his satchel on the table. "I'm the DEA task force coordinator from the San Diego field division." The man had the type of Brooklyn-specific accent that had faded somewhat with time and place, but still poked through on certain words. He stepped forward, found Dixon first, and extended a hand. "Guido Turino."

Dixon unsuccessfully suppressed a laugh.

Turino had just clasped her hand. He tightened his grip. Narrowed his eyes. "You got a problem with something?"

Dixon looked down at their conjoined hands, then at Turino. She squeezed back, matching his strength. "Just wondering. Is Guido your real name?"

"My unit calls me Guy."

"Seriously. Guido? I mean, that was a joke we had growing up. You know, somebody screwed you over, you'd threaten to send Guido after him."

Turino cocked his head. "What are we in, junior high?"

Dixon pulled her hand away, then dipped her chin. "You're right. I apologize. I haven't had a whole lot of sleep. It's been a tough couple of weeks. I'm a little giddy."

Turino eyed her a moment, then nodded. "Then I suggest you find an empty room and get some rest." He turned to the others. "We got a lot of work to do. Best we get down to it. First, I need to know who all of you are so I can match names in my file with faces." He nodded at Dixon. "The tired, ditsy blonde. You are?"

Dixon clenched her jaw. What the hell, she deserved that. "Roxxann—"

"Dixon. Yeah, got it. And who's Redmond Brix?"

"Redd is fine," Brix said. "And that's Burt Gordon and Austin Mann." He indicated each with a quick nod.

Turino folded his arms across his thick chest. "I've been briefed on everything that's gone down. The Mayfield thing, the Georges Valley AVA board stuff, Superior Mobile Bottling, and Guevara. You people've done a good fucking job on all that." He frowned a moment at Dixon, still registering his disappointment with her, and said, "You should all be commended. And it makes me feel good that I'll be working with all of you. Gets under my goddamn skin when I have to work with a bunch of rooks." He threw back the flap of his bag, reached in, and extracted a thick file folder. Held it up and said, "I've got all your reports here, and some classified reports from our deep cover op."

"You got copies for us?" Dixon asked.

"No. It's deep cover. You got questions, I may be able to answer them. If something's relevant, I'll let you know. And that's where I'm gonna start, if that's okay with you."

Dixon set her jaw. "Just so we're clear, *Guy*. I'm the lead investigator of this task force. So if I ask a question or make a request, I do expect you to make sure we have what we need to make correct and prudent decisions. We're all professionals, and we're all on the same side here. The information shared in this room stays in this room."

Turino sucked on his upper teeth. "I assume that doesn't include the documents you left on the table in this here room, the one the Crush Killer stole right from your own house."

Dixon felt her blood pressure building.

But it was Mann who spoke. "I completely understand your need to protect your assets undercover. If I was the guy with my balls on the line, I'd want a hard-ass like you protecting it. But there's a certain level of trust we need here if we're going to work together. That's not an ATF thing, a DEA thing, or a Napa County sheriff thing. It's just common sense."

"I'm glad we're getting all this out in the open. Better that way. And like you said, Roxxann: Let's be clear. We're all on the same team, and I trust you people. Otherwise, I wouldn't be here. But Operation Velocity is an extremely sensitive op spanning two continents and five countries, and might be on the verge of costing one of our men his life. So excuse me if I offend some of you. I'll take what you said under consideration.

But you have my word: I've been doing this a long time, and I have a real good feel as to what's necessary information to release and what's not. I'll make sure you have what we need to find Task Officer Hernandez."

Dixon, Mann, Gordon, and Brix shared looks. None of them had anything to say, so Turino opened his file and splayed it open.

Dixon's phone buzzed. Text from Vail. They were ready. "Hold up," Dixon said. "We've got Karen Vail and Hector DeSantos joining us by teleconference. Any of you know how to work that RoundTable thing we used the other day?"

"I got it," Mann said. He settled himself in front of the laptop that sat in the middle of the conference table, made sure they were logged into Live Messenger, then started the RoundTable device. "Are you there? Karen?"

Vail—and a male figure—appeared on the laptop and on the projection screen. On Vail's computer, she would see each of their likenesses strung along the bottom, with the person whose voice was loudest taking the top position as an enlarged image.

"Hi everyone. Long time no see. This cool-looking dude to my right is Hector DeSantos."

A sad-sounding chorus of grunts and greetings issued forth from the various task force members.

"Special Agent Guy Turino's joined us. DEA." Dixon knew that if she introduced him as Guido, Vail would likely have some smart comment—and Dixon already regretted subjecting Turino to that once.

"You logged on at a good time." Turino turned away from the screen and said, "All right. Picking up where I left off. This is a DEA operation, so DEA runs the show. We appreciate the cooperation of your respective agencies and we'll do our best to make sure everyone's kept in the loop. You're now officially federal TFOs—task force officers. As federal agents, you'll be able to carry your sidearms across state lines and we'll have jurisdiction to conduct our business."

Turino looked at the RoundTable camera telescoping up from the table surface and said, "Obviously, Vail and DeSantos, you don't have to worry about that." He reached into his file folder and spoke as he dug through some papers. "Because of Superior Mobile Bottling and Cesar Guevara's involvement, this area's been an important focal point for us—and might continue to be so."

Brix had a can of Coke Zero in front of him. He twirled it slowly as he spoke. "Since we're all being honest with one another, I'd like to throw something out on the table. With DEA San Diego coordinating Sebastian's and Hernandez's op, isn't it safe to say they wanted to be sure we're all on the same page, that they don't want us poking around without their knowledge? Seems to me, Guy, the easiest way to make sure they know what we're doing is by bringing us under your thumb. We're happy because we're part of the team, but in reality, you're just keeping us busy."

Turino scraped an open hand across his stubble. "I'm going to respect your intelligence, Redd. So the answer would be yes. And no. 'No' because I got better things to do with my time than be a baby-sitter. So yeah, they don't want you poking your dicks in places that could fuck things up. But this'll be an active, working task force. And because I'm in charge of it, you can bet your last dollar we're gonna be at the epicenter of anything that goes down. That good enough for you?"

"Absolutely," Dixon said with a glance at Brix.

Turino found the document he was looking for and set it in front of him. "Now then. I haven't had a whole lot of time to put stuff together for this task force, but its goals and objectives are pretty damn clear. First off, it's my job to get you up to speed on a few things you'll need to know about the drug trade and how these cartels operate. One or two of you may know some of this stuff, but you won't know all of it, so I'm going to go through it because I think the answer of where we focus our efforts is right here."

He glanced down at what was apparently his outline. "So. Illicit Drug Trade 101. Running the show these days are Mexican drug trafficking organizations. You've heard 'em called cartels. We also call 'em DTOs. Bottom line is, no matter what we call 'em, they *were* a big problem and have *become* a huge problem. They've set up shop in 230 U.S. cities, and are now expanding into suburbs and rural areas.

"To put this in perspective, in the past three years, Mexico's had over 18,000 drug-related murders. And the violence has started spilling onto U.S. soil. So let's go through how these DTOs get their drugs into our country. California ports of entry are the cartels' equivalent to an interstate highway that runs from Mexico into the U.S. The Arizona and Texas borders are just about as problematic. In California, Mexican cartels typically enter at or between the six land ports of entry along the U.S.-Mexican border: Andrade, Calexico East, Calexico West, Otay Mesa, San Ysidro, and Tecate." He pointed at the map, beginning west at San Ysidro and moving east toward Calexico.

"You got the obvious, stuff you've probably been briefed on at some point: trucks and cars bringing the shit in, hidden away in secret compartments. These cartels are extremely motivated and very wealthy, so they find all sorts of ways to get their stuff across the border. Spend a day at any port of entry along the border with Customs and Border Protection officers, and you'll see what I mean. Underneath the carriage, inside the dashboard, in the engine compartment, embedded in the seats, the tires. Name any part of a vehicle, we've probably seen it rebuilt or hollowed out and filled with drugs.

"Then you got drug mules, which you might've heard about. The cartels pay these people to carry drugs inside their bodies, in sausage link type packaging they swallow and then crap out when they get across. That is, if it doesn't burst and kill 'em before they reach their target. Or they carry the shit strapped to their bodies, in huge backpacks, across the desert or through the mountains. Real rough terrain. A lot of 'em don't make it. A lot of 'em do. May I?" He pointed at the large map hanging on the wall near the window.

"Go for it," Dixon said.

"You got a U.S. map?"

"Flip it. Third one down."

Turino did as instructed and found the chart he needed. He pulled a pen from his pocket and slapped the point against the map. "A majority of the illicit drugs coming into the U.S. are now crossing over the Arizona border. Right here." He indicated an area south of Tucson. "Problem is most of this border is wide open. No rivers or other natural barriers. Checkpoints only in the larger cities or along the major highways in and out. Actually, a lot of the border only has chicken-wire fencing, if that. Maybe sensors. But that's it. The border's more heavily regulated in bigger towns, so the mules take the routes of least resistance. Makes sense." He glanced up. "Any questions?"

"Yeah," Brix said. "How much are we talking about? I mean, so you got some poor guy you're paying to ferry drugs across the desert or on a plane. How much is he really gonna be able to carry, inside or outside his body?"

"Limited only by their imagination. Backpacks if they're coming across land. If they're coming on foot through a port of entry, or even on a plane, they'll stuff it in their underwear, their bras, or strap it to their bodies. They wear oversize clothing or baggy jeans to conceal it. Typically, a mule can hold up to 800, 900 grams, and maybe even a little more. They pack the coke into wax-coated condoms that the mule then swallows. Sometimes they use large capsules—10 to 20 grams per capsule, depending on the person. They practice swallowing large grapes whole until they can get 50 to 70 of them into their bodies. They ingest them prior to boarding the plane or crossing the border, then crap 'em out at the other end. But the measures we've got in place at airports—scanners, dogs, X-rays—nab a lot of 'em. Like I said, though, the capsules or condoms sometimes open and these people have gotta be rushed to a hospital for emergency surgery. A lot of 'em OD and die."

Dixon asked, "How much do they get paid for that?"

"Not a whole lot. Two to three grand, maybe even less."

"And what does it net the cartel?" Gordon asked.

Turino bobbed his head. "Twenty to twenty-five grand. Per kilo."

Vail piped in through the speaker. "How much can they carry outside their bodies?"

"That's a much bigger issue, from a law enforcement point of view. The land-based border. You might not believe it, but like the rest of us, they also ship their products in FedEx and UPS packages. Then you've also got trucks, tractor trailers, and containers. Not to mention maritime—boats, fishing trollers—"

"They're also using submarines," DeSantos said.

Turino pointed at the RoundTable screen. "Yes. That's a fairly recent thing. Semi-submersible vessels. But a far more dangerous threat, because of the volume they can move, is subterranean tunnels. It's a trick they borrowed from Hamas in Gaza. These tunnels can be anything from large diameter PVC pipes to well-engineered concrete structures equipped with electricity, ventilation, and rails for moving mining-type carts. Bad news is our GPR—ground penetrating radar—can't find these tunnels unless they're right below the surface, and they're usually much deeper than that.

"But by far, most of the drugs coming into the U.S. flow across the Arizona and California borders. San Diego's particularly bad, with San Ysidro and Tijuana leading the way. Ciudad Juárez/El Paso is another hotspot that's gotten a lot worse and more violent lately. There aren't any rivers to cross in these areas, so it's an ideal place to transport your load into the U.S."

"Isn't this whole goddamn thing simple supply and demand?" Brix asked. "I mean, we're a big part of the problem. If we'd stop buying this shit, the cartels would be out of business."

"Good luck with that one," Mann said, almost a grumble.

Turino nodded his head animatedly. "Exactly right, Redd. The U.S. is one of the largest consumers of illicit drugs in the world. And 90 percent of the coke entering the U.S. from Colombia comes in through Mexico. That's why the Mexican cartels there have become so much of a problem for us."

He stepped up to the U.S. map he'd pulled. "Take a closer look at the border regions we talked about a minute ago." Tipped his head back, found an area, and pointed a finger. "A lot of it is reservation land. And that's been a big fucking problem for us. Because a criminal band of Native Americans facilitate the drug trade."

"Native Americans? How's *that* work?" Mann asked.

"Pretty damn well, actually. You got mostly barbed wire along the reservation's border with Mexico. Not much of a deterrent—especially if you've got willing partners on the other side of the wire. And the smugglers are most definitely willing partners."

"Unbelievable," Gordon said.

"Gets better." Turino pressed a finger against the map. "See this here? The Tohono O'odham Nation territory has been a longtime problem for us. It's huge," he said as his hand traced the almost circular shape of the land, which covered a substantial portion of the Mexico/Arizona border. "Roughly the size of the state of Connecticut, 2.8 *million* acres."

"The size of Connecticut?" Vail asked over the speaker. "This is reservation land *within* the state of Arizona?"

"Right. And they've got only about eighty cops to cover nearly 3 million acres. You can see the problem. Mules can literally drive up to the border in trucks and hand over kilos of drugs across the barbed wire fence. Cartel-backed criminal bands of Native Americans take the hand-off and drive it to their buildings for storage before it's transported into Tucson or Phoenix in a stolen van. The locals like it because they get a thousand bucks or more per load. It's good money and a lot of 'em are unemployed."

Dixon blew air out her lips. "What are you guys doing about it?"

"We've beefed up our presence. The smugglers use radios with rolling codes and watch Border Patrol with night vision equipment so they can see when it's clear for them to move their loads. Border Patrol's countered with trucks outfitted with infrared cameras that can detect heat signatures. Bottom line, the land's in danger of turning into a militarized zone. But even with that, last year alone was a record year. Over 160 tons of marijuana were seized—and that's only what we *caught*."

"Don't be fooled by marijuana," DeSantos said. "The people trying to legalize it? Be careful what you wish for. Pot may seem harmless to some, but it's really the driving force behind the whole illicit drug trade. The cartels use the profit from pot to buy coke in Colombia as well as the ingredients for making meth and heroin."

DeSantos's image enlarged as he leaned closer to the webcam. "Take it a step closer to home. Almost half the foreign terrorist organizations—which are involved in investigations with a validated terrorist link—have ties to the drug trade and are responsible for our country's illicit drug supply. Groups like the FARC, the AUC, and the ELN in Colombia. And the proceeds from drug trafficking end up with groups like Hezbollah and Hamas. So in a perverse way, like Detective Brix said, the American drug user is the single largest funder of terrorism in the Western Hemisphere."

"Drugs aren't the only problem with these cartels," Turino said. "People. Lots of human smuggling, too."

There was a collective sigh from the task force. They leaned back in their seats, sensing the enormity of the situation. Everyone in the room had been briefed at one point or other about some aspect of the war on drugs. But Turino's presentation, and the fact that it was hitting close to home, made it suddenly more real—and overwhelming in scope.

"Biggest problem is that once they get these drugs into the United States, no matter how or where, they're transported on our freeways—Interstates 5, 8, 10, 15, 19, 805—they link the southwest smuggling routes to drug markets throughout the United States."

"I'm beginning to reassess my view of whether or not we can win the war on drugs," Mann said.

"Can't think of it that way," Turino said. "Every operation is a battle. You grab up a bad guy and take a kilo of coke off him, that's one less kilo of coke going into your child's nose. Or vein. That's how we do it. One battle at a time. I've devoted my life to it."

"You mentioned Operation Velocity," Dixon said. "What is it, who's running it?"

"It's a DEA op. We've got plans in place for a nationwide sweep that'll involve the Mexican military, FBI, ATF, and ICE. If our recent estimates are anywhere near reality, we think we should be able to take a shitload of drugs out of circulation. A couple thousand pounds of meth, two to three thousand kilos of coke, dozens of pounds of heroin, tens of thousands of pounds of high-potency marijuana. And that doesn't even include the weapons we'll get off the street. If all goes as planned, we figure we'll be able to grab up between two and three thousand traffickers, cartel members, and money launderers."

"Two or three *thousand*?" DeSantos asked.

"A lot of 'em in Mexico, but several hundred here in the States, too. It's one of the most important ops in DEA history, so we gotta make sure all goes as planned. We can't afford any fuckups. Sebastian—Agent Sebastiani de Medina—was playing a key role in opening up avenues to drugs, traffickers, and money launderers we didn't even know existed. It looked like TFO Hernandez was going to get us in close to the part of the operation we hadn't yet penetrated. We've done a quick and dirty assessment, and as far as we can tell, the op hasn't been compromised."

"Speaking of Robby," Vail said, "where do you suggest we start looking for him?"

DeSantos's phone sang a whale song. "Excuse me." He reached down and turned away from the webcam.

Turino sucked on his front teeth a moment, then turned back to the map. He folded tattooed arms across a hairy chest peppered with gray. "I'm not sure there's a good answer to that. We've really got nothing to suggest it'd be any one of a hundred different potential hot spots." He studied the map some more.

"I think we should go to San Diego," DeSantos said, cell phone still in hand. "I just got a call from one of my . . . people. There's been a tremendous amount of cartel activity out of San Ysidro the past year and a half. Assassinations, kidnappings, beheadings. And Carlos Cortez's main residence is in a San Diego suburb. My guy says that's where we should look first. His house."

"Good enough for me," Vail said. She nudged DeSantos in the arm. "Can you get us on the next flight out?"

"We don't have time for that." DeSantos leaned forward, which distorted the features of his face and nearly shifted him off-screen. He lifted Vail's telephone handset, then tucked it between his neck and shoulder. "Let me see if I can scare up a military transport. Or—" he lowered the receiver and said, "Turino. You guys get confiscated shit all the time." He lifted his cell phone and started to press keys. "You've gotta have a jet. I'll give Yardley a call—"

"No need," Turino said. "We picked up a Lear 60XR during a raid last year. A real beauty. Find yourself a pilot and you're good to go. If you fly it right, you'll probably make it without a refueling stop."

"Probably?" Vail asked.

"We've used it a few times for stuff like this," Turino said, passing over her comment. "Very easy on the department's budget."

"Don't need to search too hard for a pilot," DeSantos said. "You're looking at one. If you can give Yardley a shout to alert the ground crew, we'll see you in a few hours."

Vail reached forward and their screen went dark.

Mann logged off the teleconference session.

Turino folded his arms across his chest and rocked back on his heels. "I saw in your file that you've been working with the Napa Special Investigations Bureau on the Crush Killer case."

"Right," Brix said. "NSIB provides support and overflow investigative functions, but their main purpose is narcotics investigation and enforcement. As soon as we were informed about Superior Mobile's operation, I alerted them."

"Before I left the office to come here," Turino said, "we got a call from them. I'd like to have two of you consider staying behind, working with NSIB to monitor the status of César Guevara and Superior Bottling. You'd be our liaisons."

"You sure?" Dixon said. "That leaves us a bit thin."

"With Vail and DeSantos on board, we'll be fine. For a mobile unit, it's easier logistically to get around."

Brix turned to Dixon. "Your call."

Dixon's eyes canted toward the ceiling as she leaned back in her chair. "Redd, you and Burt. Stay here, coordinate with NSIB and DEA."

Brix and Gordon indicated their agreement with her decision.

"Okay then," Turino said. "We've got a lot to do before our colleagues from Quantico arrive. And we've gotta get down south, too." He flipped his folder closed. "Redd, see if you can get us booked on a flight down to San Diego. Everyone else, do you have go packs in your trunk?"

Mann did, the others did not.

"Fine. Pack a bag for three days and meet back here in one hour. No later."

Brix pulled out his cell. "I'll get us some transportation to the airport, too."

Turino lifted the handset of the conference room phone. "See you all in an hour, sharp." He twisted his wrist, stole a look at his watch, and said, "Let's do it."

PART 3

ACCELERATION

A puddle of urine covered one corner of the bare cement floor. Across the room, the captive lay curled in a ball to conserve heat. His thoughts were confused, his brain devoid of the necessary fuel to keep the mind churning out the impulses that fired neurons and formed images. Two days without food or water would do that to you. Especially when coupled with what he had endured during that time.

The duress his body had been subjected to was equal to techniques the CIA had used in the farthest reaches of Afghanistan and Iraq during wartime. He had the scars to prove it—emotional as well as physical.

Roberto Umberto Enrique Hernandez was a man of the law. That's what he kept telling himself. Though he was determined to withstand anything his captors could put forth, the truth was, he had no choice. And he knew it. But accepting the abuse and succumbing to it were two different things. He needed to find a way out, and if there was one thing he had in abundance, other than pain, it was time to ponder potential escape scenarios. Yet nothing of practical value had come to him. And no opportunity had presented itself.

Undercover work was new to him. He knew about it from his everyday work as a detective, but that kind of exposure was like reading how to fire a gun versus actually holding one in your hands, pulling the tension from the trigger, locking your shoulder, and sending the projectile hurtling through the air toward its target. Some things you could learn from a book. Others required the practical experience of trial and error.

Undercover work, he surmised, was like that. But trial and error in this line of work could get you killed.

He was given a private crash course with a retired undercover before leaving for California, but sitting in a room in a briefing is not as efficient as living and learning, experiencing and absorbing over a period of time—a break-in period of sorts.

But he did not have that luxury. He knew the type of people he would be facing: the kind he encountered growing up in a Los Angeles neighborhood that was as far removed from Beverly Hills and Hollywood as is a minnow from a shark on the evolutionary chain.

Robby's drive to succeed, to excel in life and in his career, had brought him to this place. There was no one to blame—not even himself. If presented with the same opportunity tomorrow, he would seize it without reservation.

Unfortunately, at the moment, contemplating his next assignment was problematic. That was getting ahead of himself. At present, he needed to focus on finding a way to survive, of getting out of here alive.

THE RUSTED METAL DOOR cracked a few inches and a bar of light fell across the urine puddle. Robby rolled his eyes upward—not expending the energy to raise his head—and wondered what they had planned for him.

A large man stood at the door—he had earlier told Robby his name was Ernesto "Grunge" Escobar. Robby easily had six inches on the guy, but their weight was roughly the same. While Robby was lithe and muscular, this guy was square and thick. Escobar's job was apparently to make sure no one got the upper hand while in his custody. And in his current state, Robby was not much of a threat to anyone.

Escobar was the one who had inflicted the damage to Robby's body and mind. He had learned his techniques somewhere, Robby surmised. But that knowledge didn't make the pain any less intense, the torture any more humane.

"Hernandez," Escobar said. "Let's go. Up." He folded his broad forearms across his chest and waited for Robby to drag his left leg in toward his body, followed by his right. He then rolled onto his side and summoned his remaining strength to push up his torso.

"Food," Robby said in a low, frail voice. "Water."

Escobar stood there, looking down at his captive. At some point in the next second, he must have brought his leg back—Robby didn't see it—but he sure felt it. Boot to the face. Again. It lifted Robby off the ground and launched him into the adjacent wall. And that's where he lay when the lights went out.

63

Vail and DeSantos had been granted a prime flight path and made excellent time with nary a drop of fuel to spare. DeSantos, chewing hard on a piece of Wrigley's, kept fobbing off her comments about what they had left in the tank, usually with a joke that left Vail more frustrated.

But he seemed at ease, so she finally realized that if it was an issue, he would not only tell her but would be concerned himself. It was only when the low fuel warning sounded that the anxiety rose up in her throat like a bacteria-infested meal. He then explained he had to come in empty because of the maximum landing weight the regional airport required.

"Is that really true?" Vail asked as the wheels screeched against the runway pavement of San Diego's Montgomery Field.

DeSantos guided them toward their slot. "Yes and no. I could've stopped somewhere and put in a couple thousand pounds of fuel, but would you have wanted to waste another hour?"

Of course not. That's not a fair question to ask when Robby's life is at stake.

"Didn't think so," DeSantos said with a wink. "Sometimes you just gotta trust me, Karen."

"I think I just did, with my life."

"Not really. With only us and no payload, I figured we'd be fine. I'm a bright guy. Time you started giving me some credit."

Vail rolled her eyes, then unbuckled her belt.

"Hey, Sammy got us this lead. And you wouldn't have met Sammy if it wasn't for me. Right?"

I think for now I'm going to reserve judgment on just how good this lead is.

They were ushered into the terminal, where Dixon, Turino, and Mann were waiting.

Turino shook hands with his new task force members and they started moving toward the parking lot. He pushed open a door and led them through a hallway. "I got us some wheels from the DEA field division office. Because of who we're dealing with—and since we don't know what to expect—SWAT's been alerted and has been working up a breach plan. They're prepared to rendezvous with us one mile from Cortez's house."

"Any indication he's there?" DeSantos asked.

"SWAT's had 'eyes on' since we first called. No activity."

Mann pushed through a set of doors. "That would've been too easy."

"Let's not give up on it yet," Dixon said. "It's a starting point."

With Turino—the de facto case agent—driving the DEA's black Chevy SUV, they pulled up in front of a house in the tony beach community of La Jolla—one of the most expensive areas in the nation, with homes topping out at $20 million and *averaging* a mere $2 million. Unfathomable—and unreachable—to most Americans.

The white oversize SWAT RDV, or rapid deployment vehicle, and black armored Bearcat were parked and waiting. The mission leader—the tactical commander—was standing by his command car. The large double doors of the RDV, a Ford E-450 Super Duty, were swung wide, revealing the utilitarian steel interior and twenty tactical officers—the equation was two men per room—in full garb.

Turino left the SUV to make contact while the others remained in their seats.

"Been awhile since I went on a raid like this," Mann said. "Hope the asshole's there. Be a pleasure interrogating shit like him."

"You've dealt with people like this," Vail said to DeSantos. "What's your take?"

"Cortez? Long gone. As soon as he got wind Hernandez is a UC, he went into retreat mode. Probably won't be back here for a while, if ever. He knows we're looking for him, so finding him's going to be a challenge. With a huge cache of dough to draw on, I'm sure he's got some secure, off-the-grid places he can go. Homes owned by a shell corporation or in someone else's name. Very, very tough to track shit like that unless we can grab up an associate who can give us something. But finding a guy willing to squeal on one of the most violent cartel families ain't gonna be easy."

"Even though we've issued a BOLO," Mann said, referring to law enforcement's Be On The Lookout alert, "guys like Cortez have ways of getting across the border without going through traditional channels."

Dixon grabbed the seatback and pulled herself forward. "So he could've already fled to Mexico."

DeSantos extracted the package of gum from his pocket. "I'm not sure poking around his house will give us much."

Through the SUV window, Vail took in the stylish beach homes all around her. "To a trained eye, going through his place could tell us a lot. If we know where to look."

DeSantos folded a slice of gum into his mouth. "Such as?"

She twisted her lips. "Don't know yet. I'm a behavioral analyst. I've spent my career studying human behavior. I've never applied it to something like this, but why the hell not? I'll see if something hits me."

Turino came back toward their vehicle. "We're good to go. Eyes on the house haven't seen any movement. They did a covert canvass of the immediate neighbors. No one's seen any activity in days."

"Since they discovered Robby's a UC," Vail said.

Up ahead, several of the SWAT officers hopped onto the Bearcat's steel exterior skids and prepared to make the short ride to the Cortez estate. Hanging off the sides of the vehicle, they would be ready to deploy the second the Bearcat drew to a stop.

Turino yanked the gearshift into drive. As he pulled away from the curb, following the SWAT vehicle, he said, "They'll go in first, clear the house. We'll follow. Anybody got a problem with that?"

"I just hope they don't destroy anything on the way in," Vail said. "I need to see everything as Cortez left it."

"I'll let 'em know. While they're watching out for loaded AK-47s poking around the edges of doors, I'll make sure they wipe their feet so they don't dirty the carpet."

Vail smirked. "I meant we need to preserve—"

"I know what you meant."

Vail felt like cracking Turino across the noggin but thought better of it. Her objective was to find Robby, and at the moment she needed the agent's assistance.

They approached Cortez's home, which was on a hill near a country club overlooking the ocean. Vail craned her neck to peer out the window. Beyond the town of La Jolla, which sported white buildings, red tile roofs, and groupings of palm trees, pristine sky blue–tinted water stretched into infinity, sun glinting off its surface.

She pulled her gaze from the window and her Glock from its holster. The others in the SUV followed suit.

The two SWAT vehicles pulled to a hard stop in front of the Cortez estate. Turino brought their Chevy perpendicular to the wide vehicles. Next came two patrol cars, approaching from opposite ends, to block traffic from entering the street. Turino shoved the shift into park.

The SWAT officers leaped from the Bearcat, then fanned out as they neared the white brick structure, MP-5 submachine guns at the ready. A stone fence wrapped around the home, providing a slight but insignificant impediment as the officers scaled it with aplomb.

The mission leader issued hand signals and his contingent took their positions.

The task force followed SWAT toward the house, pistols gripped in both hands, pointed at a 45 degree angle toward the ground. Over the fence and down the slate steps they went, some remaining out front, others taking up a position at either side of the mansion—but they remained along the perimeter and waited to advance until SWAT gave the all-clear. This was SWAT's show until the structure was secure.

The mission leader checked with his charges. Everyone was in position.

He fisted his hand and rapped on the walnut door. Knock and notice, an "844" in the penal code. Warrant in hand, they didn't need to be nice about it—just efficient. "San Diego Police with a search warrant demanding entry!"

Another officer tossed two flash bangs away from the team, below the side living room windows. They exploded and lit up the area. The intent was shock and awe—to let the occupants get the sense they were overpowered before they could figure out what was playing out on their front lawn.

Normally SWAT would've driven the Bearcat up to the door and used the ram device built into the bumper. But because of the stone wall and uneven terrain of the front yard, they were forced to use a compact battering ram. The mission leader waited a beat, then motioned to the breach specialist, who moved into position, then swung back the weighted device.

Austin Mann's scream came a second too late, as the officer had already brought the heavy cylinder forward, arcing through the air and smashing into the wood door.

Mann's "Stop!" was followed a split second later by the concussive force of a thunderous blast. Windows blew out, wood splintered, and bodies flew backward.

Vail charged forward. "Shit!"

DeSantos and Dixon followed, assisting Vail by grabbing the arms of the fallen SWAT officers and dragging them out behind the Bearcat.

"What the hell happened?" Dixon asked.

"They're alive," Vail said, checking pulses.

"Officers down," Turino shouted, the two-way pressed against his ear. "Medics up!" He looked back toward the house. "Goddamn son of a bitch."

Two Special Trauma and Rescue personnel, kits in hand, hurtled the low wall and immediately began attending to the downed men.

Mann stood there staring at the gaping hole. "I saw it right before they blasted the door open."

"Saw what?" DeSantos asked.

"Countersurveillance camera." He threw out a hand, motioning toward the trees. "I thought, could just be good security. But then I turned back to the door. And I saw it, the trip wire. Hard to see from the breacher's angle, but from where I was, it caught my eye. And in that split second, I thought, shit, the door might be rigged, too. Soon as he busted it open—"

"Sometimes that's the way shit goes down," DeSantos said. "Beating yourself up won't help."

Mann kicked at a tuft of grass that had been dislodged by their trampling on the lawn. It went flying toward the carnage strewn across the front of the house. "I'm the ATF agent here. Should've been first thing on my mind."

Dixon jutted her chin out, indicating the geared-up men. "Why don't you get over there, see if they need your help checking the remaining avenues of entry. We still need to get in there."

Mann grumbled but took her advice, and he started off in their direction.

The thick scent of charred wood mixed with a heavy, gritty sulfur haze made breathing a chore.

Vail brought her elbow up to her mouth and suppressed a cough. *Just what I need.*

"How are they?" Turino asked.

"Unconscious," Dixon said, "but alive. As to head trauma, no idea."

Turino clenched his jaw. "When we catch Cortez, I'm going to take a lot of pleasure in hooking him up."

Vail started toward the house. "I'm going in."

DeSantos took two long strides and caught up with her, grabbed her arm. "Hang on, there. Let them clear the place, then we'll go in. A little extra time isn't going to matter."

Vail wrested her arm free. "Every minute we delay could be one minute too long. We've no idea what's happening to Robby. If he's still alive, they could be pulling the trigger right now." She looked hard into his gaze. "Or *now*." She turned and continued toward the house.

"Jesus Christ, Karen. I'm a cowboy, willing to take all sorts of risks when I'm on a mission. But you're—you're just doing dumb things."

"Really?" she asked, not slowing her stride. "Goddamn it, Hector. What's wrong with you? If Robby was your partner, you wouldn't be so cautious and goddamn slow and—and *apathetic*. Wake the fuck up!"

DESANTOS STOPPED. Vail's comment was like an ice pick in the eye. A few years ago, his partner, Brian Archer, had been killed during an op they were running on domestic soil. The pain was unrelenting, the thirst for payback as ravenous as parched desert soil awaiting rainfall.

DeSantos bit down hard on his bottom lip. He had not been as emotionally invested in Hernandez's kidnapping as Vail had been. Not in the same ballpark, the same state. Hell, not even in the same country. He realized now he had largely been going through the motions, treating this as a mission without consequence. A debt to be repaid, nothing more.

Vail's call to order had done more than she could have envisioned. A comment made in anger roused his memories and rekindled the pilot light that had blown out long ago.

Since Brian's death, he had been sleepwalking through life. His wife, Maggie, had tried telling him numerous times that his life had lost purpose. Lost passion. But he wasn't in a position to listen. To hear her. As her pleas morphed into complaints that he was no longer attentive to her needs, he edged further away. His emotions had calloused over like a farmer's well-worn hands. And it was on the verge of destroying his marriage.

It took an FBI profiler, in a fit of anger, to shake him out of his years-long stupor.

He ran forward, toward the house.

64

Vail stopped at the threshold to the front door, the splintered re-
mains of the frame laid bare. She put her hands on her hips and
stood there, unable to step inside.

DeSantos came up behind her. "What's wrong?"

"My son. That's what's wrong."

"Good decision."

It was Dixon, approaching from the left.

"An impossible decision. But the only one I can make." She stole a
look at her watch. "How long will it take them to clear it?"

DeSantos looked over the expansive structure. "My experience,
three floors, lots of rooms . . . could take awhile."

The SWAT lieutenant, a neatly trimmed Asian whose nametag read
"Kye," came up from behind. He jerked a thumb over his shoulder and
said, "Better if you three waited back there, by the Bearcat."

"How long," Vail said, "until I can get in there?"

"To be on the ultra safe side, a couple hours. We're gonna comb
through every nook and cranny with mirrors and fiber optic—"

"We don't have a couple of hours. Can you do a quick once-over, let
me in, then do the comb-through?"

Kye shook his head. "Standard procedure dictates—"

"We've got an officer who's missing, lieutenant."

"I'm aware of the situation," Kye said firmly. He keyed his mike,
then walked off. "All units, I want . . . "

"You're asking a lot of men to risk their lives by rushing," Dixon
said.

Vail glanced over her shoulder at Lieutenant Kye. "I'm sure they
won't do it if it's not safe, Roxx. They've got their procedures, I get that.
But we're dealing with extenuating circumstances here. Time is a luxury we don't have."

"I'm with Karen on this," DeSantos said. "Moving too fast is a risk, yeah. But so is moving too slow."

Kye returned. "We're going to clear one level at a time. When we've got the ground floor cleared, you can poke around there. When we've got the second floor done, you can check that out. Meet with your approval?"

"Thank you," Vail said. "Appreciate it."

Twenty-five minutes later, the task force was stepping through the littered debris, across the front door threshold and into an opulent mansion. In the background, Vail heard SWAT officers yelling, "Clear."

Vail moved through the rooms, taking in the marble statuettes, museum-grade artwork—including a Renoir, a Chagall, a Matisse—and several gold-leaf framed family photos neatly arranged on a living room coffee table. Apparently the blast blew outward and left much of the interior intact. She took her time going through the formal living room, the dining area, the sitting and family rooms, kitchen, pantry . . . it wasn't often she had the opportunity to see firsthand how the very wealthy lived. But lost in all this beauty was the realization it had all been bought with the proceeds from illegal mind- and life-altering illicit drugs.

Vail was the first of the task force to ascend to the second floor. She had just entered the master bedroom when one of the SWAT officers swung his rifle into the doorway and startled her. "Jesus, lady. I damn near shot you."

"Supervisory Special Agent Karen Vail." She slowly moved her sweater aside, revealing her badge, which was clipped to her belt. "I thought you were done on this floor."

"We are now."

"Anything?"

The man keyed his shoulder-mounted mike and said, "We're good on two. All clear." He listened a second, then said, "Roger that." To Vail, he said, "Team's on three. Doesn't look like anyone's been here for a few days. Mailbox out front stuffed full."

Vail turned away and continued her analysis. Nothing here that would indicate the owner was anything but a wealthy businessman.

She stepped into the spacious walk-in closet and stood there a moment, taking it in. Dark suits lined both sides of the room, the apparel evenly spaced on the bars. Highly polished shoes resting on an angled display stand. Cedar trees pressed inside each pair, keeping the leather age- and crease-free.

As she stood there, she asked herself, *Who is Carlos Cortez?* An organized, intelligent, mildly obsessive compulsive man. *Does that help me? How?*

In the center of the closet, a double rack held more meticulously arranged dress clothing—slacks, sport coats, shirts. Vail riffled through everything, looking for—what? She wasn't sure.

She knelt down and spied the walls. No safes or hidden compartments she could see. Her entire time in the house, she hadn't found one useful tidbit. No lead at all.

Dixon located her and stepped into the closet. "Well?"

"His mind is organized. Either he or his wife is into fine art, and they have good taste. He's intelligent, detail-oriented. He enjoys the wealth he's accumulated and doesn't mind spending it." She thought back to the photos she saw in the living room. "He's got young children, and they're important to him. He appears to have a circle of friends—" She stopped and locked on something. *What is it? Something about the pictures.*

Vail pushed past Dixon and headed downstairs, back into the living room, where Mann was sifting through items in a desk drawer and DeSantos was on his cell phone.

DeSantos covered the handset microphone with a couple of fingers "I've got someone putting together a dossier on Cortez for us. NSA and CIA contacts, I've got them searching for any known cartel hideouts, family members, business associates . . . " He watched her lift the framed photos, examining each one carefully. "Karen? What is it?"

Vail pulled her BlackBerry. She scanned through the call history. *Shit. Not here.* Dialed information. "I need the phone number for the Microsoft corporate campus."

Dixon said, "What do you see?"

Vail handed her the framed photo. "Get the picture out of here. And keep your fingers off the surface."

Dixon took it and flipped it over, then dug a fingernail into the brown paper backing.

"Yes," Vail said, "please connect me." She waited a moment while the phone rang, then said, "This is Karen Vail with the FBI. I need to talk with someone in the Office division; we've worked with a guy who handled security stuff." She turned to Dixon. "The guy Eddie knew, the one who helped identify Mayfield—"

"Tómas," Dixon said.

"His name's Tómas," Vail said into the phone.

"You think they can help us with this photo?" Dixon asked.

"Worth a shot."

"No—no," Vail said into the phone. "I can't wait. Is there anyone else on his team I can talk with? I've got a picture of some violent criminals and I need to see if someone can tell me where it was taken. And I don't have a lot of time." She listened, then said, "Sure, that may work." While on hold, Vail called Mann over.

"What's up?"

Vail rotated the handset away from her mouth. "Those Mayfield photos you sent over to Microsoft. How did Tómas figure out where they were taken?"

"He said he analyzed stuff like textures, lines, vegetation, topography. Then he compared it to some database."

Seconds later, a woman's voice came on the line. "Athena Hu."

Vail nodded at Mann, then turned her attention to the call. "Athena, this is Karen Vail, FBI. A few days ago we worked with a colleague of yours on a case, and I've got another photo here I think will give us some important clues as to where a kidnapped law enforcement officer's being held. Your guy analyzed some photos based on textures, lines, vegetation, that sort of thing. He then compared that to some kind of database."

"Sounds like he used the Flickr GPS-tagged database. Can you email me the photo?"

Vail took the picture from Dixon, who was holding it by the edges. "It's not digital, but I guess I can have it scanned."

"That'll work. Make sure you scan it at a decent resolution." She gave Vail the email address, and Vail gave Athena her contact info.

"As soon as you've got something—a man's life depends on it."

"Do my best."

Vail disconnected the call, then spun around. Facing her were DeSantos and Mann.

"Can they help?" Mann asked.

"We need to get this photo to the DEA field division ASAP." As Vail spoke, Turino walked through the door. "I assume you have a scanner at your office?"

Turino's brow bunched. "We do. But why—"

"I'll explain on the way over."

On the ride back, Vail told Turino that cutting-edge digital photo analysis could determine where in the world a particular picture was taken. It was highly accurate—but a bit of a crapshoot on Vail's part. The photo showed Cortez with two buddies mugging for the camera, Dos

Equis bottles in their hands, shirts off, looking as if they were having a stellar time. But the background was what Vail was interested in. She would also send the image to the FBI for analysis of the other men in the photo in hopes that could generate other leads: known accomplices, people they could track down and interview.

They arrived at the San Diego field division, a modern three-story structure with a solitary American flag flying by its front entrance. Outside, there was no DEA sign proudly displayed, no seal or any indication that it was a building where vital government business was transacted.

Vail and the task force entered and passed through the X-ray scanner. They surrendered photo ID and were cleared to take the elevator up to the third floor. While waiting for the car to arrive, Vail noticed the sign on the wall behind the security guard: they were in the Enrique "Kiki" Camarena building.

Within minutes of entering the field division facility, Vail was in the command center, a cavernous room on the third floor replete with high-tech gadgetry: along the side walls were computer stations, while the front stage was fitted with an outsize rear projection screen, sliding white boards that rode in vertical side tracks, and a Windows PC designed to project PowerPoint presentations and pictures to those in attendance.

Vail set the photo down on the scanner and watched the bright white light pass beneath its surface, turning analog colored ink and paper to digital ones and zeroes. A moment later, the jpeg image was on its way to Athena Hu at Microsoft.

And then Vail was pacing the hall, like a 1950s expectant father waiting for word of his child's birth.

But Vail was hoping for the birth of something far different: a lead they could pursue hard, and fast. Something that would bring her closer to finding Robby.

65

Robby awoke to the sickly sour scent of rotten eggs. Not rotten eggs—sulfur. Why? He didn't know, and in his current state, it did not matter. He had greater concerns. But before he could consider those issues, he drifted off again.

Sometime later, Ernesto Escobar knelt in front of him. A large gleaming silver pistol with a diamond-encrusted handle caught a crack of light and sparkled off the black of Escobar's eyes. His captor made an exaggerated point of displaying the handgun, its power inherent and unspoken, a method of control as effective as a set of handcuffs.

The naps had done Robby good. He glared at Escobar, a newfound defiance etched in the tight set of his jaw.

"You probably don't know it," Escobar said, "but you are a fortunate man. If it were up to me, you'd have been killed days ago. We usually behead traitors like you. Then we cut up your body and cook it in acid. I've done it in the reverse, too. Cook you in acid, then while you're screaming in unbelievable pain, I slice off your head with a machete."

Robby frowned. "I got what you meant when you said you've done it in reverse."

"It's called *levanton*," Escobar said, ignoring Robby's comment. Apparently Escobar felt that using its official name would make it seem more real. He shifted his weight left and pulled a long, thick machete from a scabbard along his right thigh. The silver gleamed except for a red smear that coursed the blade.

Robby kept his face impassive, his gaze riveted to Escobar's, refusing to direct his eyes to the weapon. He was not going to give his captor any ground in this escalating war of nerves.

Escobar leaned back, appraised Robby, and smiled. Then he pressed the knife's edge against Robby's cheek, brought it down swiftly and drew a bead of blood. "I'm looking forward to doing *levanton* on you."

Although the pain was searingly sharp—the nerve endings in his face were already hypersensitive because of the beatings Escobar had inflicted—Robby did not flinch.

Escobar tilted his head, appraising his prisoner's lack of response. His eyes narrowed, no doubt in frustration and anger. If there was one thing Robby was able to draw upon from all that Vail had taught him about psychopathic killers, it was the issue of control. And Robby was not going to accede any to Escobar by giving him the fear he expected and wanted—no, *needed*.

"Because of your attitude," Escobar said, "I will do it in reverse. Cook you first, then cut off your head. What do you think?"

Robby grinned. The broadening of his face opened the cut wider, and the blood trickled across his lips, into his mouth. He licked it, brought his eyes level with Escobar's, and said, "I think, Ernesto, that you are a coward who needs big guns and knives and whips to take me on. Because without all that, I'd wipe the walls with your *pinche* ass." He made a quick move with his head toward Escobar, who recoiled. "So enjoy your advantage, asshole. Because to me, you're just a piece of shit."

Escobar looked down at his knife, tilted it, and examined it as if for the first time. "You think you are a brave man, talking like that. But we will see, won't we? Because in the end, you'll just be a pile of bleeding, burning flesh."

"I may not survive to have my revenge," Robby said. "But I guarantee my friends will hunt you down. And you will pay for whatever happens to me."

Escobar laughed. "Your police buddies? I'm shivering in my boots, *amigo*. If that's the best you've got, I'm disappointed." He rose from his crouch, walked to the door, and knocked. "Coming out."

It swung open and Escobar disappeared into the bright sky. The door slammed shut and Robby was, once again, alone. "Not just police," he said under his breath. "Karen Vail. You know not the wrath you have wrought."

66

The hour passed like honey dripping from a spoon. Outside, the sky was beginning the changeover to dusk. As the clock ticked beyond 6:00 PM, the fading light was yet another reminder that the day was coming to a close. Vail had made a point of perusing the wall displays in the command center, including the photo array and brass bust devoted to the revered and fallen DEA undercover agent, Kiki Camarena, the building's namesake. Farther down was a depiction of the decals and logos of the eighteen state and federal agencies that served on the San Diego County narcotics task force.

As the room lights brightened and the sky shaded a deep steel blue, Vail walked into the next room over, the break room, where she grabbed—and downed—a can of Diet Coke. She then paced the hallway, where she fended off Dixon's attempts to keep her mind focused on other matters. But Vail found it difficult to concentrate on anything other than Robby.

At some point, Mann had ventured downstairs and gotten a status report on the downed SWAT officers. They had suffered moderate concussions and one would likely have a temporary hearing deficit, but otherwise they would fully recover.

DeSantos, after talking with a number of agents and support personnel in the building, now had his sleeves rolled up and was huddled in the corner of the conference room. He seemed deeply committed to working his phone, trying to track down known associates who could provide a lead for them to pursue—some way of narrowing their search in a meaningful manner.

"I've left messages," he told Vail. "We'll see if anything comes of it."

"Yeah, well, jury's still out on the value of Sammy's *lead*."

DeSantos pushed the glasses up his perspiring nose. "You're a tough person to please, Karen, you know that?"

Vail feigned surprise. "No, Hector, I've never been told that before." A moment later, she apologized. Then she resumed pacing.

When Athena's call vibrated her belt, Vail startled, then fumbled the BlackBerry as she attempted to answer it.

"Agent Vail, this is Athena from Microsoft. I've got some good news for you."

"I can use some of that."

"Can't we all?"

Athena, you have no idea what I've been through.

"I've run the photo through that Flickr database," Athena said, "as well as through some new image matching technology called robust hashing that we've developed. And I think I've got a hit for you."

"What's robust hashing?"

"Microsoft Research created it for our digital crimes unit to match up signatures, or hashes, in photos. It's part of our PhotoDNA software, which we developed for the National Center for Missing and Exploited Children to help them catch child pornographers. The idea is to match color grading variations between known and unknown photos using a mathematical algorithm. It codes the colorations across the unknown image to establish a specific signature that can then be matched against the signatures in a known database. I took your photo, applied the robust hashing, then cross-referenced that information with Flickr GPS data. And I've got something."

Vail felt her respiratory rate drop precipitously. She wanted to speak but had to force air up through her lungs, scrape the words from her throat. "So where is he—I mean, where was the photo taken?"

"The picture appears to have been taken in a desolate area near San Diego, east of the Cleveland National Forest. Clover Creek, to be exact."

Vail motioned to Dixon, whose attention had been roused by the phone call. Vail rotated the handset away from her mouth and said, "Clover Creek."

"There are no maps in here."

Vail's eyes searched the room. "The PC," she said. Dixon moved behind the podium and tapped the touchpad. The screen woke, displaying the Windows desktop. "Hang a second, Athena." Vail dropped the Black-Berry from her face and walked into the back room, where the projection and audiovisual equipment was located. A technician stood there stacking digital media. "Can you turn on the projector? We need to find a map on the Internet."

"Sure thing," the woman said. She moved to a stack of electronic equipment, threw some switches, then followed Vail out to the podium. Dixon moved aside and watched as the woman opened Bing maps and pulled up the bird's-eye view of San Diego. Behind her, on the large rear projection screen, the countryside appeared.

"Clover Creek," Vail said to the technician.

The woman typed in the location, then rotated and zoomed, and Clover Creek appeared onscreen.

Vail brought the phone back to her mouth. "Okay, Athena. I see Clover Creek."

"I'm afraid that's all I've got. If you want, I can continue to work on it, see if there's someone else here who can refine that a bit more."

"I'd appreciate that. Anything breaks, call or text me. And thanks for your help." Vail slipped her phone away while eying the map.

Dixon, who was still examining the region identified by Amanda Hu, pointed at the screen. "Look what we've got here."

Vail stepped closer and the bold print nearly hit her like a poke in the eye: three Indian reservations—Mesa Grande, Los Coyotes, and Clover Creek. Given what Turino had told them about some reservations serving as drug trafficking portals, the text didn't need to be highlighted. It jumped from the screen.

"Hey, look at this," Dixon said to Mann and DeSantos, who were huddled against the far wall, looking at a display case of Challenge Cup trophies won by the field division.

Before they could move, the command center door swung open with a whisk of air. A clean-cut mid-forties man rushed in holding a sheaf of papers. "Which one of you is Agent Turino?"

"That'd be me," Turino said from behind the man as he came through the door. "You are?"

"Jack Jordan, NTF. Narcotics task force. I've got something you people might be interested in."

Vail's heart rate ticked up a notch. "Rob—Roberto Hernandez?"

"No," Jordan said. "But some definite activity in the area. It's a bit of a long shot, but Agent DeSantos told us that if we came across something of interest, anything, you people'd want to know."

"We're scrambling for leads," Dixon said. "We'll look at anything you've got."

Jordan slapped the bundle of papers in his hand. "When the economy tanked and the real estate market collapsed, the flood of foreclosures caused some unwanted side effects. Houses were left empty, abandoned by owners skipping out on their mortgage. Renters lost their jobs and moved out. Home builders suddenly had new houses they couldn't sell. Bottom line, there are a lot of vacant homes. In some cases, large sections of communities are vacant or abandoned."

"And an abandoned house anywhere near the border is a haven for illicit drug trafficking," DeSantos said.

"Exactly." Jordan stepped up to the map. "And illegal human trafficking. The illegals are smuggled across the border for a fee, usually around a grand, paid by family members in the U.S. But when the illegal gets here, the price jumps to five grand or more, and their loved one is basically held for ransom. The cartels, looking to expand their business model, got into human smuggling several months ago. It's been a real big problem."

"How do the houses play into this?" Dixon asked. "They hold the relative there while waiting for the ransom to be paid?"

Turino stepped forward, shaking his head vigorously. "They bring dozens of people across and pack them into what we call 'drop houses.' They strip them down to their underwear and beat them, threaten them with pistols. It's all about control."

Vail nodded. *Exactly.*

Jordan said, "They either occupy abandoned homes or they rent 'em out on the cheap from distressed owners who're happy to be getting something, rather than nothing. The owners have no idea how their house is being used. It's been a huge issue in Phoenix, and now we've got it here."

"If you know the location of these vacant houses, why don't you just raid 'em?" Mann asked.

Jordan held up the sheaf of papers, as if that explained everything. "There are literally thousands."

Vail knew no further explanation was needed for those in the room. Law enforcement was stretched to its limits as it was, and committing substantial resources to search thousands of homes was not feasible. Complicating the matter was that they could check a hundred houses, only to have a cartel move into one of the ones they had just cleared.

"There's no way to monitor all the homes that go vacant," Turino said. "And it's too profitable, so the problem isn't going away on its own. Some of the cartels have also taken to storing their drug caches in these houses. We've found entire marijuana grows and processing factories in several of them."

Vail's eyes found the Clover Creek map. A wave of impatience hit her like a blow to the back of her neck. She blurted, "Agent Jordan, you said you had something for us."

"I do," Jordan said. "I do. One somewhat effective way of combating this drop house problem is by using surveillance and phone traps. In some cases, judges have denied us, but we kept at it, and finally got one to sign off on a wiretap warrant."

"You heard something," Dixon said.

"Oh, yeah. They've got a house packed with illegals and one of them is from a family in Carlsbad that's got some money. Once the cartel found out who they had, they went ape-shit. Lots of chatter starting yesterday afternoon. We picked up on it and dispatched a UC to do surveillance, then got a search warrant. This morning, they seemed to be talking about something else, something bigger. 'A major asset.'"

DeSantos poked his glasses with a finger and again pushed them up the bridge of his nose. "How good is your undercover? These cartels, they're wise to that shit."

"No worries. Our guys are good. They're out there doing survey work on the road down the block from the house. So we know which one it is. They've located two of the phone parties, one at the house and one a few miles away."

"If it's illegals, wouldn't ICE be running the show?" Vail asked, referring to Immigration and Customs Enforcement. "Don't you need illicit drugs to be involved?"

"We have reason to believe they're using the garage as a marijuana processing plant," Jordan said. "ICE has been notified, and they'll be going in with us. Along with SWAT, who's been doing their surveillance of the house: they've shot aerial photos, assembled a floor plan, sketched out an entry strategy. They're ready to move. Given the possibility that this 'major asset' could be your TFO, I think we should move now, rather than later this evening, when it was planned."

"I don't know about this," Turino said.

"Did I miss something?" DeSantos asked. "This is good shit. 'A major asset' could be Roberto Hernandez."

"Not likely," Turino said. "I know these cartels. They're not holding Hernandez for ransom, I can guarantee you that much."

"But," DeSantos said, "even if it's not Hernandez, there could be a cartel lieutenant in there who can be squeezed. Right now, we got nothing. If we rattle the bush . . . "

"Fact is, there's no direct evidence Hernandez is being held in that house," Turino said. "I just don't want you getting your hopes up."

DeSantos pulled up a chair and sat down facing Mann, Dixon, and Vail. "Look. These cartels, they're like the terrorists I track every day. They talk in code. There's no way for us to be sure of anything. But this is what the DEA does. In the drug world, there are none better at putting two and two together. And right now Agent Jordan is telling us it's adding up to four. No guarantees, but I think we've got something worth tracking down here."

"I agree," Jordan said.

Vail sat down beside DeSantos. "There's something else. That map," Vail said, indicating the rear projection screen. "We got a hit on a twenty where that photo was taken, the one we took from Cortez's house. I asked Microsoft for help and their analysis located it nearby, about an hour from here. There are three Indian reservations: Mesa Grande, Los Coyotes, and—"

"Clover Creek," Jordan said with a knowing nod. "Makes sense. Lots of rough, desolate terrain. We've seen an uptick in smuggling activity there, especially the past ten, eleven months. We've gone in and raided some meth labs, but the problems there run a lot deeper."

"So," DeSantos said, "we've got two potential leads. Both could lead somewhere and both could lead nowhere. But we need to vet both."

Vail closed her eyes. She couldn't be in two places at once. "All right. We split up. Some go to Clover Creek, some to this drop house." She crooked her head toward Turino. "You okay with that?"

"There's a team ready to move on the drop house, so actually you can all go to Clover Creek."

"No," Vail said. "I'll go with you to the drop house."

Turino held up a hand in protest. "That's not necess—"

"We'll need transportation," Dixon said, eyeing the map.

"Done," Jordan said. "Meet me downstairs in the lobby in five." He grabbed the knob and yanked open the door.

Vail bit down on her lip, then rose quickly from her seat. "Keep me posted, Hector. If you find out anything—proof of life . . . or death—I want to know ASAP."

DeSantos winked at her. "You're already on speed dial."

67

Robby pried open his left eye, then the right. His head—a throbbing mass of pain mounted atop his shoulders—bobbed as he feebly pushed himself upright. He stopped, the pounding worsening as his heart kicked into higher gear to pump against gravity.

Outside the shack—or shed—or wherever he was being held— voices rambled on in Spanish. Anger . . . restrained . . . though now that the headache eased a bit, he realized it was a heated discussion. Not anger, but disagreement.

He rolled slowly onto his knees and crawled closer to the voices. Sat back against the wood wallboard. Listened. His Spanish was fluent— truly a second language—and even in its trampled state, his brain translated on the fly—at least, the parts he could make out.

"Wants him moved—now."

Second voice, which he could now identify in his sleep: Ernesto Escobar. "I'll get him." Jangling of keys, then the metallic click of a tumbler sliding and shifting.

Robby looked up as the door cracked open. A flashlight sliced inward, falling across his face and forcing him to turn away and clamp his eyes closed.

"Up," Escobar said. "Time to go."

"Where?" Robby asked, not making any effort to move.

"You're not in any position to ask questions, *amigo*."

Robby couldn't argue with that. Still, he knew the tenets of safety: when kidnapped, do everything you can to resist at the outset and don't assume your fortunes will improve. When they had taken him and had a pistol shoved against his head back in Napa, he figured they were more likely to kill him than pour him a glass of water. Resisting at that point was not wise.

But at the moment, in the darkness at least, Escobar had no visible weapon—not the sparkly handgun nor the blood-tinged knife. While neither was likely far from his reach, it was perhaps far enough away—tucked in a belt or a shoulder holster—that Robby might have a split second advantage. Escobar likely felt he had weakened Robby to such an extent that he did not have the strength to resist. That was not far from the truth. But when his life depends on it, a determined human being is capable of mustering energy and resources no one knows he has.

So Robby made an effort to appear slow and uncoordinated as he rolled onto his knees, while positioning himself in such a manner that he could launch himself at Escobar. He'd become a human mass that, hopefully, would strike his captor forcefully enough to hyperextend his knees and cause debilitating pain.

"Let's go," Escobar said.

Now on all fours, Robby glanced to his right at Escobar's shoe tops. It was time.

68

A black SUV ferried the task force, minus Vail and Turino, toward Clover Creek. Meanwhile, in the darkness of a low-income suburban neighborhood devoid of the orange hue of sodium vapor streetlights, Vail joined Turino and the geared-up DEA and SWAT teams in the sally port of the San Diego Police Department's Broadway headquarters.

Normally DEA ran its own raids, but given the potential level of violence, SWAT had been called in to run the tactical op. As before, once the area was secured, DEA would assume control of the scene and begin its own drug discovery and evidence collection operation. In this case, due to the presence of the illegal immigrants, Immigration and Customs Enforcement—ICE—was invited to join the raid. However, because of the speed with which the warrant was being executed, ICE would be following a short time after SWAT made entry. The ICE commander was not pleased with the decision to move without their concurrent participation, but understood the urgency.

Vail and Turino, traveling in the SUV they'd picked up at the airport, followed SWAT's Bearcat and rapid deployment vehicle, as well as DEA's tactical truck.

Wheels hugged asphalt as the vehicles swerved in tandem around tight corners and traversed the miles in the shortest distance between two points—though their trip didn't involve a crow and the route it flew.

SWAT pulled to a stop at a predetermined location in a parking garage one mile from the house, not far off the 805, near Palm Avenue. Vail was familiar with the procedure. The team would check in with undercover operatives to determine if they still green-lighted the operation—that no unusual activity had been noted—and to confirm that the cartel members they were targeting were still in the house. If the mission was still a "go," the agents would move in with the speed and thirst of a shark in bloody waters.

Turino sat behind the wheel, his knuckles white, leaning forward in his seat.

"You might want to loosen your grip, Guy, or you'll squeeze right through the vacuum sealed plastic steering wheel."

"There's a lot at stake here. I'm not sure we're doing the right thing."

"Robby could be in there. Your agents have had wiretaps in place. We're moving a few hours early, is all. What's the big deal?"

Turino hesitated a moment before answering. "The potential for collateral damage is very high. These cartels, they couldn't give a shit who gets caught in the crossfire." He craned his head around into the darkness, eyes narrow and face taut. "The *halcones* make it very dangerous."

"*Halcones.* Spanish for . . . "

Turino's eyes kept moving. "Cartels rely on a network of street informants. Taxi drivers, bus drivers, storefront owners. Shit, even teenagers. They're called *halcones*, or falcons. Their job is counterintelligence, to be the lookout for the arrival of law enforcement. Started in Mexico and it's spilled onto U.S. streets where the traffickers are operating. If they see us and know we're headed for their drop house, they'll either jump ship if there's time—or deploy for a firefight. When we circle around back, they could be in a neighbor's yard, waiting to ambush us."

Vail's son Jonathan flashed through her mind. She suddenly wondered if she'd made the wrong choice—going to the reservation would've been vastly safer. And the DEA team certainly could've handled this op without her, as Turino had suggested. *Still, if Robby is being held here . . .*

Turino tapped the wheel. He leaned forward, spied his colleagues in the truck. "C'mon, guys," he whispered. "Make a decision."

A crackle over his radio. "Green. Repeat, green. Ready to execute."

Turino lifted the two-way from his belt. "Roger that." He dropped the radio to the seat between his thighs, threw the SUV into drive, and glanced at Vail. "You ready?"

She pulled her Glock and held the cold metal in both hands, gaining strength and comfort from its stopping power. "You heard the man. Ready to execute."

69

Robby took a deep breath and pushed his left bare foot against the wall of the shed and sprung his body to the right, into Escobar's thigh. But he lacked strength and there wasn't sufficient distance to build enough momentum to do any damage. He glanced off the man's lower leg and fell pathetically behind his captor. Robby was about to reach out and grab, swing, knock—anything rather than be subjected to another boot in the face.

But before he could get hold, the sound of nearby machine gun fire snatched Escobar's attention. He bolted outside, leaving the wood door swinging on its hinges, unlocked.

Unlocked. Robby crawled forward on his elbows, fought to bring himself to his knees and then to all fours. He moved to the door and lifted his head. The glare from a halogen spotlight blasted his eyes and brought an instant headache. Best he could see—his night vision was now virtually destroyed by the intensity of the radiant beam—he was in the backyard of a house. Homes all around him—a development of some sort.

His internal voice told him to get up, get out, get away.

Machine gun fire, mixed with the rapid staccato of automatic pistols, blared in the near vicinity.

He saw Escobar off to the far left, in shadow. In retreat.

And twenty feet away, two men toting heavy metal weapons moved confidently into the yard, firing from their shoulders.

Robby stumbled forward, out of the shed and onto concrete. The unmistakable odor of cordite stung his nose. He slammed his face against the side of the structure, scraping his skin against the rough grain of the wood siding, his fingers crawling along its edge, trying to keep himself steady, his body erect . . . hoping the rounds zipping by would somehow miss him.

Then the gunfire stopped. But Robby kept moving—until four hands grabbed his clothing, his shoulders, and yanked him back, away from the shed.

"No," he said feebly. "No—"

70

S hots fired!" the voice blurted over the radio.

Vail grabbed the two-way off Turino's seat. "Gunfire? From us?"

"Negative," came the filtered, rushed reply.

As they approached the drop house, Vail heard the unmistakable rhythmic drumming of a submachine gun. The SWAT RDV screeched to a stop at the curb. Turino's SUV followed a second later, its headlights splashing across the tactical van's sparse white backside. The doors flung apart and officers leaped out, planted, and pivoted toward the house.

Their deployment was far quicker than their mission plans had outlined. Vail was sure their strategies were now being rewritten on the fly.

She was out of the SUV before it stopped moving. The momentum threw her balance off, and she fell back against the car. She quickly regained her footing, then ran toward the fray.

"Karen!" Turino said.

Vail pulled up to the two-story chocolate brown and cream-trimmed stucco house as the mission leader was running a light over the doorframe, checking for signs of booby traps.

"Clear," he yelled.

Glock in front of her, Vail nudged the man aside and kicked open the door. She was inside before he could stop her.

The interior was nearly dark, but white beady eyes blinked at her from all directions.

"FBI!" she said, her pistol swinging left to right, pointed at the long, drawn faces staring back at her.

An angry mission leader entered, his MP-5 at the ready—in full gear. His tactical light scanned the darkness, showing half-naked men packed shoulder to shoulder, seated on the floor.

Vail shoved her nose into the crook of her elbow to mask the fetid odor of human feces and urine that pervaded what passed as air.

"Jesus Christ," Turino said as he entered. He quickly ducked out the front door. "Get some lights on in there," Vail heard him say to an approaching SWAT officer.

"Dondé está el jefe?" Vail yelled into the darkness.

An overhead stairwell light came on.

A mass of humanity sat packed into the living room to the right, the family room to the left, the hallway ahead of her, the staircase twenty feet away—there was no free space in which to walk.

She tried a different question, in English. "Who's in charge here?"

The faces stared blankly at her. *Too weak to respond? Or too afraid.* Even though Turino had briefed them on the nature of these drop houses, she hadn't been prepared for what lay before her.

"Is there anyone here who can answer some questions?" Vail said. Still no response. "You're not in any trouble. We're here to help you find your loved ones, to take you away from these people. But you need to tell me where they are."

No response.

"Do you know their names? The people holding you."

"Grunge," a woman's voice said.

Vail's eyes frantically scanned the faces, hoping to find the person who had answered. "Grunge," Vail repeated. "Anyone else? Is there only one of them? It's important you tell me. If you want us to help you, I have to know."

"Roger that." Turino came up behind her and tapped her on the shoulder. "Out back," he said by her ear. "You need to see this."

71

Vail stood in the yard staring at the shed, partially illuminated by the spotlight. The structure measured no more than twelve feet square, but her mind was already manufacturing what might lie inside.

She cleared her throat. "Robby?"

"Come see," he said, then grasped her arm and led her forward. Shell casings littered the cement everywhere she stepped.

Off to her right, two bodies lay sprawled across the pavement, expansive red puddles beneath them. Carnage from what was likely a fierce gun battle.

Using the barrel of her pistol, Vail pulled on the wood door and opened it. The stench of rotten eggs, urine, and feces struck her nose like a first-degree assault. "Jesus." She threw her arm up, once again burying her nose in the bend of her elbow. "What is this place?"

Turino handed her a tactical flashlight. "You tell me."

Vail stepped inside, then swept the bright xenon beam around the interior. An object balled up in the corner grabbed her attention. She moved toward it, avoiding the puddles, then knelt down. Droplets of a familiar substance dotted the floor beside it. *Blood. Enough for a wound, but nothing life threatening.*

She leaned forward and examined the crumpled mass in front of her. But suddenly she recoiled, threw herself backwards, and landed against Turino. "No . . . " It would be all she got out—words, that is— because she turned to the left and vomited on the floor. There wasn't much in her stomach, so it was mostly hot, burning acid.

Vail did not speak. Her mind was blank, all thoughts vacuumed away.

She slowly turned her face toward the bundle, then wiped her mouth on her left arm. Stepped closer, reached out and lifted the heavy mass. Ran the light over it. It was what she thought it was.

A leather jacket.

Robby's leather jacket, the one he had bought in Napa. The one he had worn the night they went to Bistro Jeanty. No DNA or fingerprints needed.

Vail shook it a couple times to uncoil it, then slowly searched the pockets. She rooted out a spent matchbook splashed with block letters that spelled "Bistro Jeanty." It was a painful confirmation that these were the matches Robby had used to light the candles on their last night together.

Vail drew in a deep breath. "He was here. This is his." She draped the jacket across her left forearm, then spun on her heels and faced Turino. "The shell casings, the gunfire we heard—" She pushed past him, walked outside the shed, and scooped up a handful of the brass skins. "Still warm."

Turino grabbed his radio. "This is Turino. TFO Hernandez was here, at our twenty. Searching premises. Two DBs discovered. No sign of Hernandez. I want roadblocks in . . . " he closed his eyes, deep in thought. "A five-mile radius. Shut everything down. All arteries. And let me know when ICE gets here."

"Is five miles enough?" Vail asked.

"If they left when we were pulling up, moving through surface streets, five miles should be sufficient."

"I don't think so," Vail said. "Can we expand it?"

"Five's enough," he said firmly.

Vail sighed. "Robby was here. We missed him by a minute?"

"It's possible he's still here."

Vail headed back toward the house. "Doubt it. Whatever happened here was violent and aggressive. Whoever was involved was not interested in staying put. Robby either escaped on his own, or . . . " Vail shook her head.

"Or someone else took him."

"Let's clear that house, do a canvass. We'll need bodies." Turino keyed his radio again. "Request all available personnel to our current twenty to canvass the area. Alert ICE we're on scene and get an ETA. Inform them we've got about three dozen illegals to process." He pointed at a nearby SWAT officer. "Make sure all our vehicles are moved a few blocks east, away from this house. I don't want any obvious police presence out front." He lowered his two-way. "We'll find him, Karen."

Vail drew Robby's jacket against her chest. *He was here. He's alive and I'm gonna find him.* She turned to Turino. "Huh?"

"I said we'll find him."

Vail had moved beyond that. "I don't just want to find him. I want to find him *alive*."

72

Robby's eyes fluttered open. His body bounced and rolled, a disorienting sensation in the near darkness. He tried to lift his head, but he was too weak from lack of food and water. His skin and mouth felt parched, like a sponge left out in the sun too long.

He licked his lips and tried to generate some saliva. As his mind returned to full awareness, he saw that he was in the rear seat of a car. Two men were in front. From this angle, and in this light, he couldn't see either of their faces. His wrists and ankles were bound tightly together. His cop instincts kicked in, and he realized that the best strategy he could take at the moment would be to remain quiet and still. He needed to listen and observe, see if he could ascertain who his captors were.

His chief concern: was he better off now, or as he was before, in the shed? It was hard to imagine his fortunes having shifted for the worse. But until he knew what was going on, it was better to reserve judgment. For all he knew, he was headed to the chopping block and acid bath Escobar had promised.

"If Cortez finds out what we did," the driver said in Spanish, "we're dead men."

"Only you, me, and Mr. Villarreal know it was us. Those two back at the house won't be talking. And I think it goes without saying Mr. Villarreal won't be having dinner with Cortez anytime soon."

The driver squirmed in his seat. "Still."

The passenger pointed to the opposing lanes of traffic. "Look."

Approaching with their lightbars blazing were three San Diego PD cruisers. And coming up behind them, another three.

"Fuck me. What do we do?"

"Keep calm," the passenger said. "Look in your mirror, tell me what they're doing."

He lifted his eyes to the rearview. "Looks like they're slowing all the lanes. Shit, man, they're starting a roadblock. You were right, we shoulda put him in the trunk. If they stop us—"

"Wait a minute. You fucking kidding me? A roadblock—*behind* us?"

The driver cracked a wicked laugh laced with relief. "Are we lucky or what, bro?"

"Maybe we've got some Irish in our Mexican blood."

"Whatever it is, I don't care." He slapped the steering wheel. "We're on our way now. Nothin's gonna stop us."

Robby wanted to sneak a peek at the passenger. Something about the voice sounded familiar. Where had he heard it before? He dared not open his eyes again. He needed to continue listening, and if they thought he was still unconscious, they may say something he could use.

He had already learned that Carlos Cortez no longer had custody of him. Presumably, that was a positive development. But he'd also discovered that his new captors, possibly a rival cartel, had evaded the roadblock. That, certainly, was not a good thing.

Robby had also snatched one other morsel of intel: they were "on their way." Question was, on their way to *where*?

73

Turino knelt down and used a pen to nudge the assault rifle that the dead cartel member was still clutching. "*Cuorno do ohivo*."

Vail crouched beside him. "Come again?"

"Goat horn. Basically, it's their nickname for an AK-47, a favorite weapon of cartel gunmen." He pointed with his pen. "It refers to the magazine's curved shape. See?"

"Yeah, it's curved. So what?"

"They're moving to higher-powered weapons. Stuff like .50-caliber machine guns and 40-millimeter grenade launchers. *Grenade launchers*. Not to mention pistol rounds that can penetrate body armor. They call them *matapolicias*. Cop killers. Nice, huh?" Turino looked around, then put two fingers in his mouth and blew. The on-scene law enforcement personnel, congregated around him at varying distances, stopped their conversations and turned toward him.

"Those of you who've just arrived. Leave everything as is. Don't pick up a shell casing, don't dust for prints. We've taken photos and video, that's it. Right now, the focus is on helping ICE get the immigrants out of here ASAP. They're gonna process them offsite at our staging area, in the parking garage. Any cartel members come by here, we want them to see that mess in the yard. They'll know it was the work of a rival cartel. If they're looking for Hernandez, hopefully they'll think he was snatched up. It's cover for us. We lucked out here big time. Okay, let's move! We've already been here too long."

As the personnel dispersed, Vail corralled Turino. "So you think a rival cartel grabbed him?"

"That's what my gut says. Look at the spray of rounds. It was an aggressive move. Who else would know, or even care, about Hernandez? Gotta be another cartel. Leverage or bragging rights, I'm not sure. But Cortez no longer has Hernandez. I think that's safe to assume."

"And how exactly did we luck out? Whatever happened here, whoever it was, they took Robby."

Turino walked through the kitchen, headed to the front of the house, rubbernecking his head, checking out the progress of his orders. "You're thinking of one person, Karen. I'm thinking about a major op that's been in the works for years, that'll get a ton of drugs off the street and put thousands of major dealers and money launderers behind bars. So if we can cover our tracks by using an intercartel conflict and let them think we weren't even here, and if Velocity stays intact as a result, yeah, we lucked out." He stopped and faced her. "Big time."

"I thought we were on the same side here."

Turino squinted. "You just don't get it, do you? This isn't a war on drugs; it's a series of battles. And the more battles we lose, the more they win. And their wins mean they dig their claws in deeper, degrading our society like a cancer."

"You don't have to lecture me on the dangers of illicit drugs. I get it."

"Do you? I've lived and breathed this every day for the past twenty-eight years. I've seen stuff you don't even want to know about. Ice chests full of severed heads. Burned bodies left on a playground so kids would find them in the morning when they came to play and know, at a young age, that you don't mess around with the cartels. This stuff is making its way from Mexico into *our* communities."

"I've seen bad shit, too," Vail said. "Probably a lot worse than what you've seen. But this isn't a pissing contest, Guy. I just want Robby back alive. He's a federal agent, a member of your team. We owe him."

"DEA is family to me. I get what you're saying. I do."

"Then I don't see any reason why we can't accomplish both goals— protecting Velocity and finding Robby. Do you?"

Turino sighed, then pointed at one of the San Diego police officers. "Pack that shit up and get it out of here. We're running out of time. Five minutes, I wanna be outta here!" He pulled his BlackBerry and, while thumbing the joystick, he said to Vail, "You're right, okay? We're on the same team. We'll do everything we can to get Hernandez back. Now let me do my thing so we don't screw this up."

Vail watched as Turino grabbed a duffel and slung it across his shoulder. She unfolded Robby's leather jacket and slipped it on. It was ridiculously large on her, but she didn't care. She walked outside, rolled up the sleeves, then sat down on the curb and drew the front closed.

74

Hector DeSantos, having run incursions not unlike this one, took the strategic lead. While Mann drove, he pored over the regional map in consultation with his contacts, who knew tribal commissions and the best way to approach them.

His phone rang as they were nearing the turnoff for the reservation. It was Jack Jordan.

"Your team's headed to Clover Creek, right?"

"That's affirmative. We're a few minutes out."

"Got some good news. That photo Agent Vail dropped off earlier. We got a hit on the two guys in it. The one to the right of Carlos Cortez is Ernesto 'Grunge' Escobar and the one to his left is Arturo Figueroa."

"You'll have to help me out, Jack. This is your sandbox, not mine."

"There aren't many guys Cortez lets into his inner circle, but these two made the grade. Escobar is a mean SOB known for torture and brutal murder. Figueroa is a low level confidant of Cortez, someone he trusts enough to oversee some key U.S. drug distribution agreements. Figueroa's the one that caught our attention."

"Go on," DeSantos said as he peered out the window, keeping an eye on where Mann was headed.

"NTF has had a wiretap on his cell and we know he's arranged to pick up a particularly large load of coke, and we think it's going down in the next two days. There's only one problem."

"You have no idea where."

"Exactly."

DeSantos glanced at the GPS, which showed they were headed into vast swaths of undeveloped land. If his calculations were correct, the entrance to Clover Creek wasn't far down the road. "Get to the point, Jack. We're running out of time."

"Right. So here's the thing: Figueroa's last cell signal triangulated somewhere near Escondido an hour ago."

"We're near Escondido."

"That's what I'm saying."

"So you think Figueroa is personally overseeing this pickup and it's possible the handoff is going to happen tonight, on the reservation."

"Combined with that photo you guys gave us, which was supposedly taken on the rez, yeah, we're putting two and two together again. And if you're looking for someone close to Cortez as a bridge to Roberto Hernandez—"

"Got it, Jack. Thanks. I'll keep you posted. If you pick up any further transmissions, let me know. If this thing's going down here, and tonight, we're on-site and ready to act."

"I'm counting on it. We've got a team of agents on their way, just in case."

DeSantos ended the call and informed Dixon and Mann what the narcotics task force had discovered.

"I have a good feeling about this," Dixon said.

"If we can turn good feelings into reliable intel," DeSantos said, "that's the kind of thing that'll get me excited."

They arrived at the Clover Creek reservation moments later. After traversing an ancient paved road that needed a seal coat two decades ago and a repaving some time after that, they arrived at a used brick building with a flag mounted atop a white pole. The whipping material, spot lit from below, depicted the logo of the Clover Creek tribe: a maroon clover leaf with a blue body of water flowing through its center.

They parked and DeSantos entered the structure alone, preferring a low-profile approach. Several federal agents marching into the police station might send the wrong message. DeSantos badged the support personnel and was led to the office of the police chief, whose nameplate read, "H. 'Sky' Thomson."

Thomson was seated behind a bare metal desk, papers pinned to a cork board that covered half the wall to his left. The room was large and vacant save for the chief's furniture and a lone guest chair. DeSantos shook the man's hand and explained that he was working on a DEA task force looking for an officer who had been kidnapped by a cartel they had reason to believe was operating off the reservation.

Thomson nodded silently, his hands perched in a triangle in front of his mouth. He motioned DeSantos to the empty chair. "We've been battling the illicit drug trade for many years. Worse now than I have ever seen it. But I assume you know that."

"I've heard."

"Problem is, we've got 40 percent unemployment. We have a little casino, but there are so many tribes in the area with big, fancy gambling operations that we're small fish. So the tribal commission does what it can with what we have. Which isn't much. Our people need money, and the drug traffickers have plenty of it. Carlos Cortez, his people run a lot of their coke and high-potency marijuana through here. And from their point of view, it makes sense. They transport the contraband across the border, then up here on the 805. They store the drugs in any number of houses on the reservation until one of their lieutenants and a crew come by to pick it up. Then they've got a straight shot up the 5 to LA, the 15 to Las Vegas, or the 40 to points east. In any one of these directions, they're headed to cities where they've set up shop to distribute and sell it."

DeSantos shoved his glasses higher on the bridge of his nose. "Very convenient."

"You know about Cleveland National Forest, I assume."

"Don't assume anything."

Thomson rose from his chair and stepped over to a dog-eared topographical map of the region. He circled an area with his index finger. "They grow marijuana right here, in the middle of the forest. We're not talking a few small plants. One of your colleagues told me DEA seized a million plants last year alone. Just in California. Street value, if I remember right, was something like $5 million."

Thomson sat down heavily in his chair. "Cortez's people typically cut down trees and use toxic chemicals, pesticides, and fertilizers that pollute the watershed, dig ditches, and set up irrigation pipes and dams to divert water from streams and rivers. And the bastards are heavily armed, so you'd better not be backpacking near their farm. Lucky for us, that terrain up there is mountainous and rocky, so they're limited in where and how much they can grow. Problem is that they truck the marijuana *here,* where they process it, package it, and ship it out all over the country."

"Another good reason to have the stash houses in Clover Creek."

"What's that saying? Location, location, location."

They shared a chuckle.

"Do you know which houses on the reservation the cartel uses?"

Thomson's smile disappeared like water droplets in the high desert sun. "The houses, they change constantly. And the drugs are rarely there more than a few hours. We try to keep a watch over areas we know have been used in the past, but looking at the past isn't usually helpful in predicting where they're going to store them in the future."

"Kind of like the stock market," DeSantos said. "Past results aren't a guarantee of future returns."

Thomson looked at him a moment, a blank stare indicating he was not familiar with the reference, then said, "Because we're understaffed, it makes our job harder if not impossible. We pay some informants, but they have to be very careful. Some have been killed. And we can't pay them enough, not compared to the cash Cortez throws around. A year ago, someone I grew up with told me he saw suspicious activity around a particular house. Next day, I found him nailed to the front door of that house. His heart was cut out and shoved into his mouth."

"Sorry to hear about your friend," DeSantos said. "Cortez is among the most ruthless, I know that. Obviously we're trying to prevent that from happening to our officer."

"We do have successes. I don't want you to think we're totally at the mercy of the cartel. But if you're with DEA, you probably know all about the seizures we've made."

DeSantos knew nothing of the sort. Despite the crash course they'd been given, he felt more unprepared for this assignment than any he'd previously taken on—which, at this point, spanned several continents and numbered . . . quite a few. "You know who Arturo Figueroa is?"

"Of course. Why, is he involved?"

"We have reason to believe he is. You aware of any pending activity—tonight, in fact?"

Thomson stood up straight. "Do you have any information—"

"Yes and no. Possibly tonight, but we don't know where."

"That's always the question. Not when, or if, but where. Whenever I hear something, I increase patrols out in those parts. But it's like a needle in a haystack."

"Is there a general area they like to use?"

"Sure, I can tell you which *sector*. But—"

"Even if it comprises a hundred houses, that still might help."

Thomson lifted his eyebrows in a "hey, it's your call" expression, then pushed off the worn arms of his creaky metal chair and limped forward, carrying his overweight torso to the far wall, where an earth-toned map hung. Thomson stabbed a weathered finger at a particular location, then drew a circle. "Twenty square miles. Like I said, not much help."

"You have the GPS coordinates?"

Thomson drew his head back. "I can get 'em, sure."

"Get them." DeSantos pulled his phone, stepped into the hallway, and started dialing.

TURINO AND HIS TEAM had moved their vehicles two blocks away and had extinguished the house's interior lights while they completed their work. The marijuana plants they had expected to find in the garage were photographed while the smuggled Mexicans were transported to the staging area. Most of the officers and agents had left, except for a strategically placed surveillance team.

Vail, sitting curbside down the block from the drop house, tried reaching DeSantos, but his phone went to voice mail. She sent a text to the task force informing them of their close call, as well as their assumption that Robby had been snatched by a rival cartel.

She had questions about the "intercartel conflicts" Turino had mentioned, but she wanted to give him room to do his job as quickly as possible. If what he said was accurate, they didn't want to still be there when any Cortez cartel members arrived.

ONE OF THE PHONE CALLS DeSantos made was to "Benny," his OPSIG tech guru at the Pentagon. DeSantos provided the GPS coordinates he needed to monitor and asked him to angle one of their satellites over that area. When Benny asked what they were looking for, DeSantos's response brought a brief silence to the line.

"That's like a needle in a haystack, Hector. You realize that."

"So I've been told. Just get that satellite over those coordinates and I'll know what I'm looking for when I see it. That's what I'm good at, remember?"

"I've only got one in position."

"There are nine thousand satellites in orbit and we've only got one over that area?"

"Do I really have to answer that, Hector? I'll have a better angle in about nineteen minutes, if you can wait."

"I can't. Give me what you've got."

"Already done. Log in and let me know if it's to your liking."

"Thanks, man. See you when I get back."

DeSantos walked back into Thomson's office. "I need a PC with broadband. Tell me you've got one."

Thomson led the way into their communications room, a six-square-foot space crammed with a two-way radio console, a shortwave set, two computers, monitors, and a variety of electronic equipment that spanned decades. He motioned to the far left PC. "It's yours."

DeSantos texted Mann and Dixon and told them to sit tight, that he hoped to have some info in a matter of minutes. He then opened Internet Explorer, applied the InPrivate Browsing and filtering modes, and navigated to the assigned, covert website. He entered his login information and a moment later was viewing a real-time feed of the reservation land in question. Using onscreen controls, he made a minor adjustment to the zoom, then began scanning in a gridlike pattern.

Ten minutes later, DeSantos leaned forward in his seat. "There." He yelled through the open door, "Chief, come look at this!"

Thomson came running down the hall. "Found something?"

DeSantos pointed at the monitor. "Where is this?" Onscreen, despite an oddly sharp angle, they saw a light duty flat nose truck backed up to what looked like a double wide mobile home, and five men loading what appeared to be rectangular plastic-wrapped bricks into the vehicle. A smaller SUV-size vehicle sat beside it.

Thomson leaned both hands on DeSantos's seatback and squinted at the monitor. "Is that what I think it is?"

"Cocaine, yes. And a big freaking load at that. Where is this?"

Thomson pushed away from the back of DeSantos's chair. "I'll take you there. Too hard to describe if you don't know the terrain. And I want this bust, Mr. DeSantos. They're not getting away on my watch."

THEY RAN OUTSIDE. DeSantos jumped into the task force SUV and Thomson into a battered Ford pickup with Tribal Police black-and-white decals. DeSantos told Mann, who was behind the wheel, to follow Thomson's vehicle, then briefed them all on what he had seen.

"So this is a handoff of coke," Mann said.

The vehicle swung left and they all leaned right. Dixon grabbed the handrail above the door. "So there are drugs. That's great. Any connection to Robby?"

"If Figueroa and several other cartel members are on-site, maybe we can grab one or more and sweat 'em. See what we get."

"But," Mann added, "you said these cartels are like terrorist groups; they operate in cells, where one group doesn't know what the other's doing. So sweating one or more of these guys may not get us anywhere."

"Figueroa's the real prize. He's responsible for some of the cartel's drug distribution agreements. He's the one we really need to grab because he's gonna know more than most."

Mann slammed on the brakes and the SUV slid to a stop on the pot-holed, gravel-strewn road. Ahead, barely caught in the reaches of the headlights, were a group of animals crossing the street.

DeSantos leaned forward in his seat. "Dogs?"

"*Wild* dogs," Mann said as his gaze followed them into the darkness. "Common on reservations." He waited for the last dog to pass, then accelerated to catch up with Thomson.

"Did you get Karen's text?" Dixon asked DeSantos. "She and Turino missed Robby by minutes."

DeSantos checked his phone, trying to navigate the joystick despite the car's rocking and lurching jerks. "What the f—" he muttered beneath his breath. "So Cortez no longer has him."

"Probably not," Mann said.

DeSantos bit his lower lip, then dropped his head back onto the seat cushion.

Ten minutes later, Thomson tapped his brakes and cut his headlights. Mann reached for his controls and likewise went dark. "I think we're getting close."

Everyone sat up tall in their seats and instinctively pulled their pistols.

AFTER LEAVING THE REMAINING two DEA agents on-site to monitor the drop house, Turino and Vail climbed into their SUV and headed back to the DEA field division office.

"You mentioned intercartel conflicts," Vail said. "What were you talking about?"

"There are a lot of turf battles, power struggles between the cartels. You've got traffickers snatching up members of rival cartels and demanding ransom or using hit men to kill enemy lieutenants to settle debts. Messages are being sent—violent ones. Lots of collateral damage to civilians and uninvolved parties. It only used to happen in Mexico, but now it's going on in the U.S."

"How does this tie in to Robby?"

"I think I know what happened back there," Turino said as he navigated a turn.

Vail looked around. She did not recognize the area. "And that was?"

"Cortez is a brazen SOB. He's gotten where he's gotten by being excessively violent and aggressive. He's killed a lot of his competitors. Those who are left are tough in their own right, and either they've agreed to leave each other's turf alone, or for some other reason he's let them be. But there's an unspoken rule—since the Kiki Camarena murder, the cartels don't kill federal agents."

Vail was familiar with the Enrique Camarena incident—all federal agents were. Her memory didn't need refreshing by the field division's wall of remembrance. Back in 1985, a decorated DEA undercover, "Kiki" Camarena, had successfully infiltrated and brought down a number of drug trafficking organizations. But when his cover was blown, he was tortured and then bludgeoned to death. A physician who worked for the cartel repeatedly prolonged his life so the torture could continue. In response, the DEA effectively closed down the border and halted all drug shipments. The cartels realized the price they paid by murdering a federal agent was far too great. They weren't going to make that mistake again.

"So let's say for a minute," Vail said, "that Cortez has decided he lives and dies by his own rules and he has intentions of killing Robby after he extracts information from him. Maybe he's gotten wind of Velocity and he wants to know when it's going to go down. And maybe he thinks Robby knows that answer."

Turino considered that, then slowly nodded. "Cortez has a big ego—they all do—but his is particularly large."

"I've had some experience with narcissists," Vail said. "They think they make their own rules, that the laws of the land don't apply to them. Or it could be his way of saying to everyone else, 'I've got a big set of balls, and I'm going to prove it to you.' If that's what we're dealing with here, it's very possible Cortez gave orders to kill Robby."

"Another problem is that they probably discovered Robby's a state detective. Even though he was given task force officer status, they may not know, or even understand, what that means. Bottom line is, they probably don't consider him a federal agent. So in their mind, killing him—"

"Would have no consequences." Turino turned and a Montgomery Field placard whipped past them. He slowed and brought the SUV to a stop at a light. "If the rival cartel knows he's a TFO, they're well aware of the heat it'll bring if they let Cortez kill Hernandez. They're not willing to give up their business because of Cortez's reckless behavior. So they find out where Hernandez is being held and snatch him up."

"So what is this rival cartel?" Vail asked as her BlackBerry began ringing.

"I can probably narrow it down to a precious few," Turino said. "Soon as we get back to the office, I'll show you what we've got."

75

The stars popped above like white dust blown skyward. Regardless, DeSantos wished he had night vision goggles. In the darkness of this rural land, their SUV running with its lights off, he couldn't see much of anything.

But like a rat sensing a predator, their target picked up their approach. And that's when it all went to hell.

The traffickers ran for the truck cab, then revved the engine. Another got into the adjacent Land Rover and peeled away in a cloud of loose dirt.

Thomson made a neat maneuver with his pickup—cutting off the truck and pinning it against a cinderblock fire wall. Two other cruisers appeared—Thomson must have radioed them while en route—and surrounded the vehicle.

"Go for that Land Rover," DeSantos yelled, pointing at the windshield, as if Mann did not see the fleeing vehicle.

As DeSantos spoke, another police vehicle was approaching, its lightbar flashing and its siren blaring. Mann stole a look in his sideview mirror. "I think they've got the situation back there under control."

"That'll make the police chief happy," Dixon said, watching the scene unfold through the rear window. "Snagging all those drugs, gotta be a feather in his cap, for sure."

"That wasn't a joke," Mann said, "was it?"

The Land Rover's brake lights tapped once, then it hung a sharp left. A fog of dense haze kicked up behind it.

DeSantos leaned forward, squinting through the windshield. "Did he just go off road?"

"Hell yeah," Mann said. "Smart move. He's got a four-wheeler, we got shit."

"We gonna lose him?" Dixon asked.

"Very possible," Mann said as he accelerated and remained on the paved road as long as he could.

DeSantos pulled his phone, hit a key, and waited as it dialed. Vail answered on the first ring. "Where are you?"

"Passing Montgomery Field, about a half mile from the division office. Why?"

"Pull into the airport," DeSantos said. He waited while Vail issued the instructions to Turino.

"On our way in," Vail said. "What's going on?"

"Put me on speaker."

Vail pressed the button on her BlackBerry and said, "Go ahead."

"Turino, does DEA have access to choppers?"

"Of course."

"Get the largest, fastest motherfucker and fly it out to Clover Creek. How soon can you be here?"

"For what?"

"We just intercepted a handoff—kilos of coke. One of the Cortez lieutenants—I'm guessing it's Arturo Figueroa—"

"No shit?" Turino said. "Figueroa?"

"He's in a four-wheeler and we can't off-road. He's a smart shit. If we can corral him, we might be able to sweat him, get info on Hernandez."

"Division has a Super Huey on loan from the Marines, tops out at 185. Best we can do. We can be there in . . . I don't know, about ten to twelve minutes if I push her."

"Push her. Before we lose this guy." DeSantos peered into the darkness, where the dust cloud from Figueroa's four-wheel drive continued to impair his view.

"Coming up on the hangar," Turino said. "But I'm gonna need to get permission—"

"No," Vail said, "You won't." She apparently took the phone off speaker, because her tinny voice was instantly clearer. "See you guys in a few minutes."

TURINO WATCHED as Vail grabbed Robby's leather jacket and got out of the SUV.

"Really," he said, following her. "I need permission. I can't just fly off with a $10 million aircraft."

Vail headed for the Huey, which sat atop a wheeled dolly outside the hangar. "We'll call from the air. But we can't let this guy get away. If he knows something about Robby—"

"It's not likely, Karen."

She spun and faced him. "Hell with 'not likely.' You've been reluctant to take action since you took over the task force, and it's really beginning to piss me off." Vail pulled her Glock but kept it angled at the floor. "Now get in that goddamn helicopter or I'll fly it there myself."

Turino squinted at her, cursed loudly, then trudged ahead toward the Super Huey that sat outside the hangar in quiet repose, on its mark. He climbed inside, got the engines spooled up and the rotor system online, then slipped on the headset. He radioed the tower and requested takeoff clearance for an "emergency departure"—terminology used to signify a life-threatening or urgent tactical situation requiring quick takeoff and traffic priority. With the Huey vibrating and the rotors thrumping, he turned to Vail, who had also placed the bulky radio over her ears.

"Would you have really taken the chopper if I refused?"

Vail looked at him with a clenched jaw, one of those looks that conveyed that she was damn serious. "What the hell do you think?"

They were interrupted by the tower providing clearance. When the helicopter lifted into the air, Vail watched as the lights of San Diego appeared to move away from them.

Turino swung the craft to the left and headed toward Clover Creek. "I think," he said, "that you absolutely would've done it. Anything to find Hernandez. That's why I got in. Ultimately, as task force commander, I'm responsible for the actions you take."

"You're goddamn right," Vail said. "That's exactly what I would've done." *If I knew how to fly a helicopter.*

76

The car pulled abruptly off the freeway. Robby had to force his feet against the door to keep himself from rolling off the backseat. The vehicle's gentle rocking and the drone of the road's white noise, combined with his weakened condition, had dropped him into a light, fitful sleep.

As he woke, he began to key in on the conversation. They were stopping to refuel, and the driver needed to use the bathroom.

The interior dome light popped on and Robby squinted and jerked his head away to shield his eyes. The door slammed shut, rocking the car.

"So, you're awake, my friend."

Robby slowly loosened his squint and turned to face the passenger. He couldn't help himself. In his current state, his defenses were not as sharp. A thought formed in his mind, and he spoke it without a moment's hesitation to process it. "Do I know you from somewhere?"

The man turned away slowly, looked out the side window. After a long moment, he said, "You are a lucky man. If it were not for me, you would probably be dead about now. And if not today, then tomorrow. Or the day after."

"Why would you help me?"

The man shifted his body in the seat but kept his gaze focused on the windshield, occasionally rotating his head or shifting his eyes between the front and side windows. "Does the name Sandiego Ortega mean anything to you?" he finally said.

Robby grinned. "Diego Ortega was my friend, when I was young."

"He was, I know. He thought a lot of you."

"And how would you know that?"

The man reached into his pocket and removed a protein bar. He tore it open and handed it across the seatback to Robby, who struggled to maneuver it in his handcuffed grip. He brought it toward his mouth and hungrily attacked the food.

"Easy, easy. When you haven't eaten in days, you can throw up. And I don't feel like driving the rest of the way with vomit in my car."

"Why are you helping me?" Robby asked again, his voice muffled as he chewed on the food.

"Diego told me you moved, after your uncle was killed. He said he missed you. He was angry at first, because he didn't understand why you would leave him."

"Wasn't my idea. When my uncle was murdered, I didn't have a choice. I went to live with my mother back east." He took another bite of the bar, chewing quickly in case the man changed his mind and yanked it away.

"It changed his life, your leaving. Not for the better."

"Why would anything I did change his life?"

"Your uncle was like a father to him, his house a sanctuary. When Diego was there, he could escape."

"How do you know all this?"

The man reached up and clicked the overhead light, then turned toward Robby. His face was now partially visible, exposed in muted hues with dark shadows exaggerating his features.

Robby stopped chewing and stared.

"Because, Robby, I am Diego."

Robby fought to sit upright, but his efforts failed. "Diego—"

"It is good to see you, Robby. We have much to talk about, but we can't do it with Willie here."

"Willie?"

"Willie Quintero, one of Villarreal's inside guys. He doesn't know our relationship. If he finds out, we will both be killed." Diego turned off the dome light, then craned his neck to look outside. "Finish your bar before he comes back. I've gotta get us some gas." He climbed out and moved around to the pump, sorted it out and shoved the hose into the tank. The front door popped open and Diego stuck his head inside. "I think you know you were being held by the Cortez drug cartel. And I think you know they were going to kill you."

"That was becoming clear, yeah."

"Word of your cover being blown spread. Cortez made no secret that he had a federal agent and that he was going to make an example of you. He said it was time to stop fearing the U.S. *federales,* that he was going to change our thinking. Just like he did in Mexico. He has plans, big plans for the U.S."

"That doesn't explain your involvement."

"I'm with the Villarreal cartel. You asked how your leaving could've changed my life. When you left, I had nowhere to go that was safe. My father . . . I never told you this, but he used to . . . " Diego took a deep breath, his gaze wandering around the interior. "Let's just say I couldn't stay there."

"What did he do to you?"

"Do you really want to know?"

Robby pushed himself up onto his left elbow. "If you feel comfortable telling me."

The pump clicked off. Diego stepped away, handled the gas hose, then got back into the passenger seat and closed the door. "He abused me, Robby. Sexual stuff. That's all I want to say about it."

Robby knew admitting that took a lot of courage on his friend's part, and he let the issue drop. "I'm sorry, man. I didn't know."

"I didn't want you to know. Hard for a boy to admit that shit. I couldn't tell anyone. But that's why staying at your place was so important. It was the only way I could escape that fucker. When you moved, I went to Mexico. Ran away. I had nothing, no clothes, no money. I joined a gang to survive. Eventually I graduated to the cartel. Paid good, gave me a life I could be proud of."

"You're proud of what you do?"

"I was."

"I came back," Robby said. "To LA. I lived in Burbank, joined the LAPD. Because of my uncle."

Diego nodded, thought a moment, then said, "Have you ever told anyone? About your uncle? About what you did?"

Robby looked away.

"I'll take that as a no," Diego said.

"I couldn't. Just like you couldn't tell anyone about your father."

Diego turned to face him. "It's not the same. And the sooner you can admit that, the sooner your soul will be cleansed."

Robby chuckled. "You're telling me about cleansing my soul?"

"I found God, Robby. I'm a changed person."

Robby studied his friend's face. "You're serious."

"The Sandiego Ortega that Willie Quintero and the rest of the cartel members know is no longer. He's dead to me."

"Bullshit. Didn't you just hose those guys in that yard, back at the house?"

"That was Willie. I was shooting, yeah, but I was aiming low and wide."

"Come on, man. How long do you think you can survive in this cartel with your newfound religion?"

"I can't." Diego turned away. "The minute they ask me to blow somebody away, I'm going to have to refuse, and they will then kill me. I won't just be useless to them, I'll be a liability. I know too much. I know a lot."

"Then we've both gotta get out of here." Robby tried again to sit up but couldn't negotiate the maneuver in the small backseat. He held up his cuffed wrists. "Unhook me. Now."

"It's too dangerous. I sold the idea to my boss that you're worth more to him in credits with the DEA. But the real reason is that if I get you out, you have to take me with you. I will confess to one killing. They will probably want to send me to prison, I understand that."

"You'll be killed. The cartel, they'll find you."

Diego leaned close, across the backseat. In a hushed voice, he said, "I'll be in witness protection, *hermano*. I will testify, give them money launderers here in the U.S., tell them how the cartel moves their product. Who helps, what businesses and individuals clean the money. I know a lot of shit about Cortez, too."

"Witness protection or not, I'm sure you realize the danger inv—"

"I can take care of myself, *hermano*, no worries. It's you I'm worried about."

"Me?"

"If we're going to do this, you need to confess, too. Make right with the Lord."

Robby jolted backward, as if burned by a stove. "What are you talking about?"

"You know what I'm talking about." His gaze turned dark and hard. "Don't insult me." He waited and when Robby did not respond, Diego tightened his lips. "If you're going to play games, the deal's off. I'll find my own way into custody. I'm giving you a way out, Robby—for both of us."

Robby ground his molars. He knew what Diego was referring to. Fourteen years ago, Robby's uncle was shaken down by a Los Angeles gang running a protection ring. That his uncle would land on their radar was something Robby never understood. His convenience store made, at best, a modest profit. Regardless, his uncle made the payment for several years, until the store fell on hard times. He then faced a choice: feed his family or cover the monthly protection fee. He chose to buy food.

After a month of warnings, one day after school when Robby was in the store, Gerardo Soto grabbed Robby around the neck and threatened to kill him unless his uncle paid up—with interest. His uncle told Soto he was done, that he didn't have the money—and that no one threatened his family. Soto and his two thugs pulled weapons. Robby broke free and fled, but in the reflection of the Coke refrigeration unit, he saw Soto riddle his uncle's body with hollow point rounds. It was an image Robby had never been able to wipe from his brain.

Robby blinked away tears. "That's no one's business, Diego."

Diego wagged a finger at him. "The Lord is judging you, Robby. Here and now. Do not lie. When you went after Soto, when you hunted him down, and then pulled the trigger, you broke the law. You murdered him. In cold blood."

"C'mon man. I was a kid."

"I'm sure that's what you've told yourself all these years. But you were a teenager. Doesn't matter. Are you saying that excuses it? If you see a teen murder someone now as a cop, do you let him go because he was young, or do you arrest him?"

Robby's hands were fisted knuckle-white. "What do you want me to say, Diego?"

"Say, 'I accept responsibility for what I've done. And I will pay the price and I will ask the Lord's forgiveness.'"

"Soto was scum, you know that. He killed my uncle, and I'm sure he'd killed others. He deserved it."

"Not your decision, was it? That's what you would tell the guys you hook up in handcuffs now, no?"

Robby did not answer. Ahead, out the window, he saw Willie Quintero—Diego's partner—approaching.

"Willie will be back any second. This ain't up for discussion, *hermano*. You're in or you're out. I need to know."

Robby watched Quintero's shuffling gait as he moved closer. Less than fifty feet away. "Get us out of here, man. Now—he's got no way to follow us. Turn around and drive right into the roadblock—"

"Willie doesn't trust anyone, Robby. He took the keys with him. But I got us a plan." Diego covered his mouth, turned, and looked toward the minimart. "He's got a bad prostate, so he has to pee a lot. Next time he pulls over, I'm gonna make a call. You got someone we can trust?"

"Hell yeah. Someone I trust with my life."

"Next stop. I'll call." Diego turned back to Robby. "I need your answer. In or out? Give the word, *hermano*, and we'll be on our way."

Robby's eyes scanned the car's interior, came to rest on the dark gray grease-stained carpet. He had no choice. He had to confront the matter at hand. And that was finding a way to escape. If that meant agreeing to Diego's demand to repent and turn himself in, so be it. But was Diego right? Was that the right thing to do?

Diego craned his neck around and then swung back. "He's coming. Well?"

"I ask the Lord's forgiveness for having sinned." Despite the protein bar, the only thing he had eaten in days, he still felt weak. The stress of his confession did not help. He let his torso lie back on the seat. "I ask forgiveness for taking the life of Gerardo Soto."

"Very good. But make no mistake, *hermano*. If we get away, and you do not confess—if you do not tell them what you did—I will."

Robby nodded slowly. "Okay."

The door flung open and Quintero got in the car. He threw a glance at Robby, then faced Diego. "How is he?"

Diego locked eyes with Robby. "I think he's doing much better now." He swung around in his seat. "Let's get going. We're behind schedule."

77

Mann did an admirable job of keeping the DEA's Chevrolet SUV lined up with the Land Rover, but they were falling dangerously far behind. The road was rough and their vehicle had bottomed out several times. Their heads were slamming into the roof and their shoulders into the doors, despite their seat restraints.

Without night vision equipment to allow him to see in the dark, DeSantos was beginning to think they were going to lose their target into the darkness of a rural, hilly countryside. Then his phone rang. Vail.

"We're approaching your position," she said. "I see you, in a cloud of dust, about a thousand yards ahead."

"Do you see the asshole we're chasing? We're losing visual."

With her headset off, Vail had to strain to hear him. "He's about three quarters of a mile ahead of you."

"You see him?"

"Affirmative," Vail said. "I'm wearing a set of NVGs."

DeSantos looked skyward—and a lurch smashed his forehead against the windshield trim of the roof. He winced, picked up the phone that had dropped in his lap, then said, "I love you, Karen. Go get that sucker. Take him down, hard."

"Will do," Vail said. "Follow us in."

TURINO, ALSO WEARING night vision goggles, banked the Huey and brought them a few hundred yards above the Land Rover.

"You see what I see?" Vail asked.

"That huge body of water up ahead?"

"I don't think he can see where he's going," Vail said. "No headlights, running dark. Unless he knows this rough terrain intimately—"

"We should force him straight into the lake, end this chase sooner rather than later." Turino jutted his head forward, concentrating on the landscape.

"Can you do that?"

"I've landed a Huey at night in a Bolivian jungle. Ended up clipping the rotor tips because the clearing wasn't very clear at all. Thick foliage all around us. But if I can do that, I can do this."

"Yeah," Vail said, "I was thinking the same thing." *Not really. I know nothing about landing in jungles and clipped rotor tips. Gotta admit, though, it sounded damn good.*

"I'm going to drop us down low, take us in alongside him. If you see anything ahead we don't want to hit—trees, wires, poles, whatever— speak up. Anything like that'd seriously fuck us up."

Vail leaned forward and peered out the window, concentrating on the approaching terrain. "How long till he reaches that lake?"

"Approximately half a mile. He's moving about sixty. He'll hit it in about thirty seconds."

"So the plan is to steer him into the water."

"Unless you come up with something better, yeah, that's the plan."

Twenty-five seconds later, the Land Rover braked hard in a dramatic up-churn of dirt, then veered sharply right, executing the maneuver they had anticipated.

Turino dropped lower and lined up the chopper along the right side of the Land Rover, keeping a few dozen yards above the vehicle. He leaned forward and brought his face closer to the windshield. "Just thought of something. Hang on, I think I can pull this off."

Hang on? You think?

Turino glanced over his left shoulder at the vehicle below. He clenched his jaw, then dropped hard and fast. He tightened his grip on the control stick and moved the Huey just ahead of the Land Rover.

Vail didn't know a whole lot about helicopters, but she had seen videos of them catching a skid or rotor blade and jackknifing into the ground in a spectacular and deadly crash.

Jesus Christ. What the hell is he doing?

As Vail opened her mouth to ask that very question, a dense, billowing cloud of dust rose and swirled in front of the SUV.

"This baby's big enough to cause a brownout," Turino said. "Main rotor downwash. Blown up dust and debris, driver can't see where he's going."

The Land Rover slowed. "Okay, this is it!" Turino rapidly swung the Huey alongside the SUV. "Here's the 'hang on' part—"

He shoved the chopper's skids against the roof of the Land Rover, and the SUV swung sharply left, down the graded embankment, skirting the water's edge. With a sudden jolt, its right fender glanced off a boulder, sending the vehicle into the lake.

Turino banked hard right and upward, moving away from the Land Rover as it splashed against the water and stopped abruptly, as if caught in a giant spider web.

"He's down!" Turino said.

Vail phoned DeSantos. "Target's in the water. Repeat. Target is in the water. We're circling back to get a light on him."

Turino and Vail removed their NVGs. Turino switched on the Huey's spotlight and trained it on the Land Rover. Vail moved it around in a sweeping left to right manner, attempting to locate the vehicle's occupant.

"There," Turino said, pointing at a spot below. "Swimming back toward shore."

"Got him." Vail angled the light onto his position. The man was splashing desperately toward the lake's edge. As soon as the area around him became illuminated, he stopped and looked skyward, the downdraft of the rotors flapping his hair and rippling the water's surface.

Vail pulled her BlackBerry back to her face and shoved it beneath the earpiece of her headset. "Your game now. When you've got him in custody, we'll join you on the ground."

DESANTOS WAS FIRST to make it to the lake's edge. He drew down on his target and waited for the man to approach. DeSantos could've jumped in after the suspect, but he didn't have a change of clothes, and he reasoned that due to the temperature of the water, the man had no choice but to return to shore.

And a moment later, that's exactly what happened. A thin man with what appeared to be a gold front tooth slogged onto the rock-strewn edge, then placed his hands behind his head.

DeSantos knew that having him provide answers might be a more difficult task. "Search him," he said to Dixon, who was closest. While DeSantos covered her, Dixon holstered her pistol, then moved to the prisoner and shoved him facedown on the ground. She pulled a long switchblade from his back pocket, a cell phone, and ID that DeSantos was sure would turn out to be bogus.

As Mann stood guard, watching the area behind them, Dixon read the suspect his rights, then placed a set of flex cuffs around his wrists.

Fifty yards to the east, Turino set the Huey down. Vail deplaned and ran toward the knot of task force teammates.

Dixon yanked the prisoner to his feet and DeSantos stepped up to him, remaining far enough away that the man would not be able to land a kick.

"You speak English?" DeSantos asked.

"Yeah," the man said.

"Your name?"

The suspect turned and looked off into the darkness. Vail tried to recall the photo she had taken from Cortez's house, but whether or not it was the stress of the moment—of the past few weeks—she couldn't retrieve the image from the recesses of her memory. She was not sure if this man was Arturo Figueroa.

"Silent treatment ain't gonna work with us," DeSantos said. "Believe me, you don't want to know what I do for a living."

The man lifted his face and turned it toward DeSantos. "And you don't want to know what I do for a living."

"We already know," Vail said, Robby's jacket flapping in the breeze. She walked past DeSantos and stopped a foot from the man's face. "And I'm in no fucking mood to play games. You can either cooperate and answer a few simple questions, or we push you back into that water and hold your head down till your lungs fill up. We cut your cuffs and let you sink. No one would question it. You drove into the water and drowned. And in case you didn't notice, it's pitch black and we're in the middle of fucking nowhere. You see any witnesses? Because I sure don't." Vail tilted her head back and observed. The man tensed his brow and narrowed his eyes.

The wind whipped up, sending a shiver shuddering through her body. She gathered the jacket tighter around her torso. "I get it," she said. "You don't believe me. Federal agents don't kill innocent suspects. Well, you got that right, asshole. But you're not an innocent suspect. And I need the answers *now*. So the rules aren't what you think they are." She stopped and waited for him to process that. "Let's start with your name."

The man did not respond.

"All right, fine. We don't have time for this shit. Drown him," she said, then turned to walk away. Dixon and DeSantos each grabbed an arm and dragged him backward. He fought them, kicking his legs and twisting his torso.

But as they approached the water's edge, he yelled, "Arturo. Arturo Figueroa."

DeSantos and Dixon stopped but maintained their hold on either side.

Vail walked up to him. "Very good. I've got a few other questions, Arturo. Answer, and we may let you go. If you don't answer, I think you know what'll happen." She waited a beat, then said, "We're looking for a federal agent by the name of Hernandez. He was running an undercover op against your cartel. We know his cover was blown and we know you brought him to San Diego."

"Then you know a lot," Figueroa said.

Vail waited, but he offered nothing further. "You're pushing me, Arturo, and I've reached my end. Last chance. Where's Hernandez?"

Figueroa struggled against DeSantos and Dixon. When he apparently realized his efforts were futile, he said, "I don't know. He was being held at a house with smuggled illegals near Palm and the 805. Someone came and busted him out a little while ago."

"Who? Who busted him out?"

Figueroa set his jaw. "I don't know. Information like that isn't shared. We work in groups, so one doesn't know what the other's doing."

"Yeah, but you've got the boss's ear. We know that."

"I'm telling you, I haven't spoken to Carlos. I don't know who took him."

"If you had to guess," Vail said. "Who?"

Figueroa glanced around, shuffled his feet. Licked his lips. Clearly uncomfortable. "We had some discussions with a guy repping Alejandro Villarreal. Know who that is?"

"Yeah," Turino said. For his task force colleagues, he said, "Villarreal runs a rival cartel. Smaller—much, much smaller than Cortez. But they make plenty of noise—and money—in their own right." To Figueroa, Turino said, "What kind of discussions did Villarreal's man have with Cortez?"

"I wasn't there. I only know what my friend told me."

"Who's your friend?" Vail asked.

Figueroa again wind-milled his arms against the grip of DeSantos and Dixon. It was a fruitless effort that nevertheless reminded them to remain attentive.

"Your friend, Arturo. We want a name," Vail said.

"Grunge. Ernesto Escobar."

Turino stepped forward. "Cortez's right-hand man? He's your buddy?"

DeSantos knew what Turino was thinking: Arturo Figueroa was obviously an important catch, but possibly a bigger fish than they had anticipated. If he was close to Cortez's second in command, regardless of their compartmentalized structure, he might hold key information regarding the cartel's inner workings.

With his free hand, DeSantos pulled his phone and typed a short message to Jack Jordan telling him they had Figueroa in custody—and asking him to get Thomson over here with some of his men as soon as possible.

"So what did Escobar tell you about these discussions with Villarreal's rep?" Vail asked.

"That's it," he said, shaking his head. "I don't rat on my friends."

"You haven't ratted on your friends," DeSantos said. "Only on Villarreal. Unless Villarreal is one of your friends."

"I'd like to see Villarreal rot in hell."

"Help us out, and maybe that'll happen."

Figueroa's face contorted into a crooked smile. "We'll take care of it. Our own way. We don't need your help. *El jefe* knows how to deal with it."

"*El jefe*," Vail said. "What do you think of *el jefe*'s plans to kill Hernandez? That doesn't seem like such a good idea to me."

Figueroa tightened his jaw. "Big mistake."

Vail nodded. "So help us find Hernandez before your boss does. No one will know you told us."

Figueroa chewed on that a moment, then shook his head again. "I'm done here. I've told you what I know."

"That's bullshit, and we both know it," DeSantos said. "What did Villarreal want with Hernandez?"

The man looked around into the darkness. He sighed deeply and said, "He wanted us to release him."

"To keep DEA off your backs." Vail nodded slowly. "So Villarreal and his men had something to do with busting Hernandez out. Because if Cortez killed him, they knew it'd bring big time heat, destroy their business."

"Like I was saying," Figueroa replied. "You already knew what I know. So cut me loose."

"Where's Villarreal taking Hernandez?" Vail asked.

Figueroa forced his chin back. "How should I fucking know?"

Vail tilted her head and studied Figueroa. "Because you do. Even if you don't know for sure, you've got an idea."

Figueroa looked down, struggled once more against DeSantos and Dixon.

"You're not hurting yourself here, Arturo. You're helping yourself. And you're helping *el jefe*."

"Las Vegas. They're taking your friend to Las Vegas."

"Vegas?" Dixon asked. "Why Vegas?"

"Villarreal has a place there. Now, can I go?"

DeSantos checked his phone and played with the joystick. Jordan was attempting to pinpoint their position using their cell signals. Thomson was on his way over and would be there shortly. But when DeSantos flipped to the next text, what he saw surprised him. He reread the message to be sure he'd gotten it right.

Turino stepped forward with a set of standard handcuffs. "Dixon, secure our prisoner to the bumper."

"No fucking way!" Figueroa said. "You said you'd let me go if I answered your questions."

Vail shook her head. "First of all, I said we *may* let you go. We decided not to."

Turino tossed Dixon the cuffs, which she caught with her free hand. "Why mo?"

"Because I'm in charge and I don't like what you said back in Napa about my name."

Dixon frowned, then kicked off her shoes and rolled up her pant legs. She pulled and dragged Figueroa to the Land Rover's rear bumper, located the undercarriage tow bracket, and fastened the handcuffs to it. Figueroa continued to resist, but Roxxann "Buff Barbie" Dixon easily controlled the slightly built prisoner. Once the restraint was in place, Dixon backed away and headed toward shore.

VAIL PULLED HER PHONE to call Gifford. She knew he was asleep by now, but she felt he would want to be informed about Robby's whereabouts. He answered immediately, which surprised her.

"Sorry for calling at this hour," Vail said.

"I'm not sleeping. What have you got?"

"A lead on Robby, sir." She explained what they knew, and provided the information they'd gleaned from Figueroa.

"I'm with Agent Sebastiani de Medina and ASAC Yardley, on a plane en route to San Diego. I'll see if Mr. Yardley can make a few calls, get us some info on Alejandro Villarreal. I'll text you anything I find out."

Wind gusted into Vail's face. "You're on your way out here?"

"Mr. Yardley felt it was looking increasingly likely that Robby was somewhere out west, so he invited me to join him on one of DEA's confiscated jets."

"Sounds like they have a whole fleet."

"And semis and even a yacht or two. They come in useful. Maybe we can strike a deal, get a private jet just for the BAU, like on TV. All kidding aside, good work, Karen. No, *stellar* work."

"I'll consider it stellar when I'm holding Robby in my arms. We were so damn close. We literally missed him by seconds."

"You'll find him. I've got confidence in you."

Another blast of wind slammed against Vail's body. She turned her back to block it. "Given our intel, sir, you might want to divert to Vegas."

"Concentrate on finding him. I'll discuss it with Mr. Yardley and determine our course of action. Gifford out."

Vail joined Mann, DeSantos, and Dixon, who was drying off her legs and feet with a rag from the SUV's trunk.

"We've got a problem with Turino," DeSantos said. "I was just told he's—"

"My ears are burning," Turino said with a chuckle, coming up from behind. "Must be talking about me behind my back."

DeSantos drew his Desert Eagle and, in one motion, shoved his pistol into Turino's right ear. The agent's eyes bulged. "What the h—"

DeSantos wrapped his forearm around Turino's neck. "Why don't we start from the top, Agent Turino, and tell us what the fuck you're really up to."

78

W hoa—" Vail said, holding out her hand. "Hector, what the
hell's going on?"
Keeping the Desert Eagle firmly against Turino's head,
DeSantos removed the agent's Glock and shoved it into his own waist-
band. "Seems that Agent Turino has been working against us. Isn't that
right, agent?"

Turino was arching backward against DeSantos's torso. "Lower that
fucking gun. Are you out of your mind?"

"Answer my question."

"I don't know what you're talking about."

DeSantos twisted to face Mann, Vail, and Dixon. "The shit's hitting
the fan on Cortez in two days. Agent Turino here has taken it upon
himself to keep us busy. Specifically, to keep our noses away from
Operation Velocity."

"Why?" Vail asked.

Turino ground his molars. "I told you, Karen. This is bigger than
one person. Going after Hernandez, I understand it. But you're being
selfish. The stakes are much greater. A lot more lives are at stake."

"Son of a bitch," Vail said.

"Look at the big picture."

"We could've done both," Vail said. "I told you that."

"Is that right?" Turino said. "Look what happened when Hernandez
disappeared. You went searching for him, blew his cover, damn near
fucked up an operation that'd been years in the making, and jeopardized several agents we've got undercover. Sometimes you have to work
with the team and not take matters into your own hands."

Vail chewed on her lip. She couldn't argue with Turino—but, damn
it, what was she supposed to do when Robby went missing? Did they
think she'd just go wine tasting and sightseeing?

"Working with the team's exactly the point," DeSantos said. "If we'd known, if you'd shared your concerns with us, we could've worked with you, maybe run a fake op to throw them off, a decoy, so it didn't jeopardize Velocity. There are ways to preserve the overall op but still get things done under the radar."

"I didn't think you'd listen. I did a little research on you people. Karen in particular. Following rules and working for the greater good doesn't seem to be in her DNA."

Vail stepped back. *Jesus. What website did he find* that *on? Even worse, is it true?*

"Now what?" Dixon asked.

"Nothing to worry about," Turino said. "Cortez no longer has Hernandez, so you're no longer a threat to Velocity. Once Villarreal broke him loose, I had no reason to stand in your way anymore." Turino brought a hand to his neck and pried away DeSantos's arm to free up the flow of oxygen. "Look, I want to see Hernandez brought home, no question about that. A LEO in the hands of a cartel burns at me. I lived through Camarena. I knew the guy, worked with him. When we found out what happened to Kiki, it killed me, affected me deeper than I could ever admit. I wanted to track down those fuckers and do to them what they did to him.

"It's what drove me to request assignment on Velocity. I wanna see these bastards taken down. Badly. If there's one thing I have left to accomplish in my career, it's bringing 'em to their knees. Devastate their ability to bring drugs into our country."

"If Camarena affected you so deeply," Mann said, "you'd be busting your ass to find Hernandez."

Turino shook his head. "Not at the expense of blowing a years-long operation that'll save hundreds—shit, *thousands* of lives. And not at the expense of the other UCs whose cover'd be blown if you'd fucked things up. They'd be tortured and killed, too. I couldn't take that risk."

"Is there anything you've kept from us," Vail asked, "that we should know?"

Turino rolled his eyes. "You people've been a goddamn handful. Trying to keep you in check has been damn near impossible. At this point, I think you know everything I know. In the grand scheme of things, I don't think I've slowed you down that much."

"When seconds count, 'that much' may've been *too* much," Vail said, lacing her voice with contempt. "If we'd gotten to that drop house thirty seconds earlier, it might've made the difference."

"That one you can't pin on me."

DeSantos released his hold and pushed Turino away. "Lie down. On your stomach."

Turino twisted around and faced DeSantos, whose Desert Eagle was trained at Turino's center mass. "Why?"

"Because I want to talk with my colleagues and I wanna be sure you're not going to do something stupid."

Turino complied with DeSantos's request. DeSantos patted him down and removed a smaller Glock that was tucked into Turino's ankle holster. He then backed away and huddled with Vail, Dixon, and Mann.

"All due respect to Karen," Mann said, "Turino's not wrong. I wanna get Hernandez back, you know that. But I think we have to take a breath and look at this objectively. One life against hundreds, if not more. A serious blow to Mexico's most violent cartel. Shutting down their money laundering operations. All those drugs and weapons off the streets." He scraped at his forehead with the prosthesis. "I can't fault the guy. In a way, I respect him. It took balls to do what he did."

DeSantos nodded at Dixon. "Roxxann?"

Dixon puffed her cheeks and blew a mouthful of air through her lips. "Tough call. I see your logic, but seems like the guy's been acting on his own. I can't imagine the DEA ordering one of its agents to purposely screw us over."

"They wouldn't," Mann said. "Every DEA agent I've ever worked with is a class act. Professional. Committed. But don't be so quick to judge the man. We got caught up in the Crush Killer case and we cut corners. Lots of 'em. We did shit we shouldn't have done. Right?" He got a nod from Dixon and a conciliatory dip of the chin from Vail. "When you're dealing with a case like that, especially a huge one like Velocity, it's hard not to let emotions get the best of you. We all know that's true."

They turned to Vail. She shoved her hands into the pockets of Robby's leather jacket. "I can't be one to judge him. I'm certainly no angel. The past couple weeks I've . . . crossed the line plenty of times. Too many times."

DeSantos said, "So, what do we do with him?"

"Let's back up a second." Dixon ran her hands through her hair. "What if he's got a broad mandate to run the task force as he sees fit?

Bottom line, we're pissed because he's looking at the big picture and we're focused on getting Robby home safe. Who's right? Who's wrong? Is there a right or wrong here?"

They were silent as they chewed on that.

"So what are our options?" Mann said. "We leave him here or we take him with us."

Vail said, "Trust is everything. Way I see it, question is, Can we trust him?"

"Our goals are no longer conflicting," Dixon said. "It's a moot point."

Vail pulled up the collar on Robby's jacket. "Trust is never a moot point, Roxx."

"Who tipped you off?" Mann asked DeSantos.

He held up his phone. "Text."

"From?"

DeSantos rotated his body, checking out the area. Lowering his voice, he said, "Turino admitted it. Source is irrelevant."

Vail figured it had to be Sammy. But it no longer mattered.

"If it helps any," DeSantos said, "we all understand one another now. And I think we woke him up."

"I'd say grinding your Desert Eagle into his ear definitely got his attention," Dixon said.

Mann cracked a smile. "I kinda liked that. Old-school stuff. Settle it out in the field."

"Fine," Vail said. "We handle this in-house. But I'm done working with him, not until I can be sure we can trust him. If shit goes down and he has to choose between Robby and Velocity . . . " She shrugged. "We can't take that chance. I can't take that chance." She looked around and everyone indicated agreement.

DeSantos checked his watch. "Time to rock and roll."

They released Turino, returned his side arms, and then headed back to the helicopter as the chief pulled up. They handed over custody of Arturo Figueroa and told Thomson to expect a visit from Agent Jordan.

Then, with DeSantos piloting the Huey, they went skids up and disappeared into the black San Diego sky.

PART 4

CRASH AND BURN

2300 Paseo Verde
Henderson, Nevada

Hector DeSantos peered out the window, then made an adjustment with the cyclic and collective controls and guided the helicopter into a gentle descent toward the Las Vegas countryside. He hovered fifty feet above his target, then slowly dropped onto the center of a grassy knoll. The helipad was encircled by a decomposed granite path, bordered by wooden benches and decorative lamps.

The Green Valley Ranch Station Casino was a resort in every sense—but it also served law enforcement as a staging area when the need arose. The helipad, composed of well-tended and close-cropped putting green grass, sat at the far end of the complex's recreation quad.

Upon liftoff from Clover Creek, Vail had explained the task force's decision to Turino. Turino absorbed her comments without reply, but his face conveyed a look she was unable to read—other than that it wasn't full of warm fuzzies.

DeSantos powered down the Huey, then followed Vail, Dixon, Mann, and Turino as they met up with an individual who identified himself as DEA Special Agent Mark Clar. The agent ushered them away from the helipad, briskly walking past a hand-laid rock retaining wall and down a tan gravel path.

After passing the spa building on the right, Vail looked ahead—and all around them in a semicircle, for that matter—and took in the splendor of the Spanish tiled six-story resort, highlighted by strategic and dramatic lighting.

To her left, a security booth was manned by a heavyset guard dressed in a lime green shirt and black pants. He nodded as they passed, then spoke into his handheld radio.

The group ran up the two flights of stairs and entered the hotel. They followed Clar to a generous central hallway with a black and gold lighted sign suspended from the ceiling that directed guests to their desired conference room. They passed El Viento, La Cascada, and La Sirena, then stopped beside a room with a wood-framed sign that read "La Luna." Below the name, an embedded LCD screen displayed images of the room and of the Green Valley Ranch property.

Clar pulled open the right wooden door and motioned them inside.

"Not bad," Dixon said. "Nice job, Clar."

"They take good care of us. Fortunately we don't need to impose too often. But when we do," he let the door close behind him and shrugged, "we get amenities like this."

In the center of the room—which shared the design scheme of the corridors—sat a large rectangular table, a red tablecloth spread across it, with gold ruffled sides that stopped just above the carpet. Burgundy chairs stood lined up alongside, and overturned crystal glasses rested in front of each seat, accompanied by notepads and pens.

Suspended above the table was a candelabra with two dozen lamp-shaded bulbs. Against the far wall of the square room was a retractable ceiling-mounted projection screen. A white board on a wood stand rested off to the side. Various pieces of AV equipment sat nearby, at the ready, like a standing army.

"We don't have a lot of time," Vail said. "Can we get started?"

"The ASAC of the DEA Vegas district office is due any minute," Clar said. "ASACs Yardley and Gifford are en route, as well. I can touch on a few things, but I'd rather wait for—"

Before he could finish his thought, the doors swung open and in walked a dark-suited woman and man.

The woman's eyes raked the room, taking in each member of the task force. "I'm Deborah Ruth, Assistant Special Agent-in-Charge, Vegas district office. I take it you've already met Special Agent Clar," she said with a flick of her head toward the man. "Which one of you is Agent Turino?"

"That'd be me." Turino made introductions to the other individuals. They exchanged nods and stares and half waves.

"Okay," Ruth said. "I have information for you—for all of you. While you were en route, Agent Sebastiani de Medina received a phone call. Sebastiani—" The door swung open again and in walked Sebastian, followed by Thomas Gifford and Peter Yardley. Ruth pursed her lips. "Excellent timing." She made sure Gifford, Yardley, and Sebastian were acquainted with the others.

Sebastian looked healthier and stronger than the last time Vail had seen him. From his demeanor, he seemed fully recovered from his ordeal.

"If I may," Sebastian said to Ruth. He received a nod of approval and said, "About an hour ago, I got a call from a man identifying himself as Sandiego Ortega. Ortega is a lieutenant in the Villarreal cartel. He was talking quickly, said he only had a minute before his partner returned." Sebastian turned to Vail. "He tried calling you, but it went to voice mail."

Vail's hand went to her BlackBerry. "I was in the air." She pulled the phone and saw the missed call. *Shit.* But she realized she now had the man's phone number, so all was not lost.

"Gist was that he had Robby, and that he was safe. He wanted to broker a deal for his return."

"A deal?" Turino asked. "Cartels don't make deals for—"

"He wants witness protection. Says he has valuable information for us on Villarreal and Cortez. If we agree to WITSEC, he'll give us what he's got and testify against his boss. And he'll guarantee Robby's safe return."

"Why the hell would he do that?" Dixon asked. "He's gotta know it's a death sentence."

"I asked the same question," Sebastian said. "He said he's found God and he's no longer able to live the life. They'd kill him anyway if they discovered he wanted out. He also happens to be a childhood friend of Robby's. He was the one who convinced Villarreal to break him free."

"So Villarreal's behind this?"

"Apparently, from what I was able to get from Ortega, Villarreal was concerned about the blowback from Cortez killing a federal agent. Ortega sold him on the idea of grabbing up Robby, then exchanging him for the DEA giving him some passes."

Dixon spread her arms. "So we don't need Ortega. Villarreal will ensure Hernandez's safety."

"If he can be trusted," Sebastian said. "Ortega had his doubts. He said that since no one knew they'd broken out Robby, Cortez would be blamed for his death no matter what happens. And no matter who kills him. Could be that's Villarreal's play: kill Robby, blame it on Cortez. Serious heat comes down on Cortez. When the dust settles and Cortez is arrested, his organization weakened, Villarreal steps in and takes his territory."

"So we're back to having to trust Ortega," Mann said.

"Is this true?" DeSantos asked. "Ortega is a buddy of Robby's?"

"I've never heard him mention a Sandiego Ortega," Vail said. "You?" Sebastian shook his head.

"How do we know we can trust this guy?" Mann asked.

Yardley stepped forward. "We don't. But he's left open his cell signal to let us track him. They're headed here, to Vegas."

"Where in Vegas?"

"Ortega didn't have time to say. But we got an address for Villarreal's place. And we've been monitoring Ortega's call, listening in on the conversation."

"Did you hear Robby?" Vail asked.

Gifford cleared his throat. "No. When we stopped listening a few minutes ago, it'd just been a bunch of nonsense bullshit between two guys on the road. Occasionally they'd mention an awareness of Highway Patrol, keeping to the speed limit, that sort of thing. There's also some muffled talk, but we couldn't make it out. The lab's working on it, but I don't know when, or if, they'll have anything for us."

"Of course," Yardley said, "before we get our hopes up, it's important to point out we've got no idea how long Ortega's battery will last. Right now, until we find we can trust Villarreal, that cell's our lifeline to Hernandez. If we lose it, he'll be on his own unless we can find—" He stopped and looked down at his phone, then pulled a pair of small reading glasses from his suit pocket. "Excuse me a minute."

Ruth, standing beside Yardley, glanced at her colleague, then picked up the discussion. "Agent Clar's a man of many talents. In addition to his fieldwork, he's got a Ph.D. in digital signal processing and did some terrific work redesigning our wire room capabilities. I've asked him to have certain things ready for us." Ruth nodded at Clar. "Are they?"

Clar, who'd been leaning a shoulder against the wall near the AV control panel, straightened up. "Yes ma'am, ready to go." He walked to the wall beside the entry doors and fingered a touchpad LCD. The lights dimmed to half strength and a projector splashed light onto the screen.

"Hang on a minute," Yardley said, his reading glasses perched low on his nose. The glow of his phone reflected off the lenses. "Just got a text from my office. Sandiego Ortega is an American citizen—actually, he's got dual citizenship. Born and raised in Los Angeles. Mexican citizenship granted in '95. No record while in the U.S."

"Robby grew up in LA," Vail said.

Gifford nodded. "So there's potential validity in Ortega's claim. Where in LA did Ortega live?"

Yardley scrolled down the screen on his phone. "Fullerton."

Gifford nodded. "That's where R—Officer Hernandez—lived."

Yardley slipped his phone into a pocket, then motioned to Clar. "Continue."

"Right. This is what we've got." Clar struck a button on his laptop and an aerial image of the Las Vegas strip appeared. He pulled a laser pointer and a brilliant green pinpoint light circled a specific area, in tandem with the agent's hand movements. "The cell signal we've been tracking entered Vegas twenty minutes ago. They were driving here, in a seemingly random pattern, as if taking evasive maneuvers to make sure they weren't being followed. Then they went stationary at a point just off South Las Vegas Boulevard, in an area that appears to be a parking garage. Right here." The green light stopped moving. "The signal keeps cutting in and out, probably because of the steel and concrete in the structure. But it hasn't moved in about five minutes."

Vail was starting to perspire, and realized she probably looked ridiculous wearing Robby's jacket. She pulled it off and said, "They may be waiting for something. Is that garage anywhere near Villarreal's place?"

"Yes," Ruth said. "So here's the plan. The task force will go airborne and assist the search. There's a helicopter tour business at the airport, right off the strip. They do evening tours of the casinos, so you won't raise any red flags. You don't have any identifying markers on that Huey, correct?"

Turino, sitting at the end of the table, a symbolic banishment from the rest of the task force, said, "It's Marine green. Nothing that says DEA. Against the black sky, we'll be fine."

Vail had doubts about the "we'll" in Turino's comment, but she let it pass.

"Very good. From there," Ruth said, "it depends where Hernandez is, where the cartel members are. We can't formulate a viable tactical plan until we're sure of where they're going to be when we move in. We've got a SWAT unit on standby, deployed one mile out. I don't want any cartel spotters catching a glimpse of our rigs hanging around the strip. Even if we move in with their bread truck plastered with fake magnetic plumbing or electrical signs on the side, there's a chance they'll be made. I don't wanna blow this before we have a chance to get close to Hernandez."

"We've got no valid intel whether or not Villarreal truly intends to hand over Hernandez," Gifford said. "So we're treating this as a hostile hostage situation until or unless we find convincing proof otherwise."

"You'll coordinate with SWAT," Ruth continued. "When you've gotten eyes on the layout of the area and have an estimate of how many there are and where they're holed up, take up your positions and turn the show over to SWAT. Set down on that helicopter tour business's landing pad and stay out of the way until the area is secured and Hernandez is safely in custody. Let's do this right."

Vail tried not to squirm in her seat. *She expects me to sit on the sidelines while they go after Robby? Is this woman serious?*

Clar stepped up to the white board. He pulled a cap off the red marker and wrote in abbreviated strokes as he spoke: "First objective. Locate and secure Roberto Hernandez. Second. Identify, locate, and take down members of the Cortez cartel. Now, for those of you who aren't familiar with Vegas, the strip is almost always densely packed with tourists. If we pull our side arms and start blasting away, it'll be near impossible to avoid striking innocents. So third objective. Minimize collateral damage."

"The order of objectives," Ruth said, "depends on logic, not priority. Clearly it's of paramount importance to rescue our man. SWAT has been briefed on Velocity, so they understand our challenges. But I want there to be no confusion: given a choice of securing Hernandez or preserving the success of Velocity, we save the life."

Vail, Dixon, and DeSantos shared a look. They then turned to Turino in unison, who looked away. Vail's gaze was particularly harsh.

"It's our assessment," Clar said, "that Velocity will not be adversely affected by this op. Cortez knows we'd be looking for Hernandez, so any action we initiate will be seen in that light."

Exactly. Vail kept an unforgiving gaze on Turino until he turned back in her direction. After a long second of silent anger between them, he looked away.

Clar capped the marker and tossed it down. "I've brought along an electronic tracking device that'll assist us in triangulating Officer Hernandez's position using Sandiego Ortega's cell signal." He rooted around inside a charcoal gray rucksack and pulled out a black PDA-size unit. Its top consisted of a dark, shiny glass display, with brushed aluminum sides. He held it up and said, "Meet LOWIS."

"Lois, as in Lois Lane?" DeSantos asked.

"As in low output wave imaging sensor. L-O-W-I-S. She's tuned to the quantized discrete-time signal emanating from the ESN—the electronic serial number—of that phone."

"I'm no physics major," Mann said, "but it sounds like a similar kind of technology that allows cell towers to identify particular phones on a network."

"It does utilize that technology, but it takes it a step further. Mobile phones are like two-way radios. They regularly send out bits of data signals, called 'pings,' to the nearest cell tower every two or three minutes. It's a way for the phone and the tower to know where each other is so they can communicate when a call is initiated. The towers forward the location of that phone back to the network. LOWIS uses a smart ping, a unique identifier that we've captured and that she's now tuned for. Which means she's like a hound dog on a scent."

"I've never seen one of those," DeSantos said. "And I tend to come across a lot of fancy technoelectronics the government's got."

"This won't show up in any government agency. Not yet. It's totally experimental. This is the prototype. I built it myself. Well, myself and a buddy of mine in Russia."

"One other thing," Gifford said. "The FBI is in the process of remotely turning off the ringer on Ortega's phone. Once that's done they're going to switch on the microphone. That way, if the phone is powered off, we'll still be able to listen in."

"A roving bug," Dixon said. "Very useful."

"Very. No fancy hardware required. If need be, they can just call the phone and listen in to what's being said by anyone in the vicinity."

Clar held up LOWIS. "Who wants it?"

"I'll take it," Vail said.

"Take care of her," Clar said. "We've grown attached."

Vail took the device. "I think you need to get a life, Clar. But no worries. We'll treat *her* just fine."

Clar ignored Vail's dig. "Keep in mind that even though she did well in our simulations, that's far from being battle-tested. I can't say for sure she'll work like we want her to." He looked hard at Vail and said, "You know how women can be sometimes."

"But," Mann said, "she—it—*LOWIS* has got a lock on that cell, and it's tracking it. Right?"

"Affirmative." Clar flung open a flap on his bag. He dug his hand inside and began pulling out black handhelds. "I've got two-ways for all of you. They're set to channel 9. It's encrypted."

The task force stepped forward and took their radios—Turino included.

"The Huey's still hot," Ruth said. "Another of Agent Clar's many talents is he's a certified pilot. Since he's the only one who knows the intimate workings of LOWIS, he'll be your escort."

Gifford waited a beat, then said, "Okay, let's do it. Let's bring our man home. And round up the bastards who took him."

As Vail huddled with Clar, Mann, and DeSantos, Gifford cleared his throat and caught Vail's attention. She moved over to the huddled suits, who were gathered at the back of the room.

"What's going on?" Gifford asked.

"Sir?"

"Agent Vail, cut the crap. I know you better than your own father." He winced, no doubt realizing the insensitivity of his comment and the reference to Vail's sadistic parent. "Strike that. Point is, I saw the looks you and the task force were exchanging with Agent Turino during the briefing. So I'll ask you again. What's going on?"

Vail scanned the faces of Yardley, Ruth, and Gifford. She hesitated a long moment. She did not want to get into this—certainly not now. And she definitely didn't want Turino leading them on this op. Still, she shook her head and said, "Nothing's going on, sir."

"You're about to embark on a critically important op," Ruth said. "What the hell is the problem?"

"That's not a friendly request," Gifford added. "It's an order."

Vail looked off at the wall. Realizing she was losing valuable time, she acquiesced. "Agent Turino."

"What about him?"

Vail glanced over her shoulder. Sebastian and Turino were huddled in the far corner. Vail turned back and proceeded to outline what she knew. She stressed that they were unfamiliar with DEA policy, and that they were unsure whether or not his actions were above board. When she was done, Gifford, Yardley, and Ruth all wore variations of agitation and disgust.

"DEA policy," Ruth said firmly, "is that a human life is always priority.

Everything we do is based on officer safety. No operation's worth a life—no amount of drugs is worth a life. It's not written in any manual, but it's built into everything we do, every op and takedown we plan." She turned to Yardley.

Yardley threw a strained look across the room at Turino. "Agent Turino."

Turino set his jaw and then walked over, gait confident, shoulders back, chin above level. "Yes sir?"

Yardley said, "We've been made aware of your actions as leader of the task force."

Turino threw a hard, cold stare at Vail. "I'm sure you have."

"Agent Vail was ordered to do so," Gifford said. "And she did so reluctantly."

Turino set both hands on his hips. "Whatever."

Dixon called out from across the room. "Karen, let's go. We're ready to roll."

"The issue," Yardley said, "is *you*. Not her. I'm looking forward to sitting down and listening. You're a decorated, veteran agent and you'll be afforded all due process. And given the benefit of the doubt. But later. We've got a man out there depending on us and some really bad assholes ripe for arrest. That's where our energies need to be focused. There's no time to adequately evaluate this—and I don't even have the authority to put you on administrative leave. But I do have the perfect assignment for you. I want you to rendezvous with SWAT and work out of their command post. I'll radio the tactical commander and clear it."

Through a clenched jaw, Turino said, "Yes sir."

Yardley turned to Vail and said, "Even though this is a DEA task force, I've got no one who's as fully briefed on all aspects of this operation as you are. I'm placing you in charge. Now get the hell out of here and find Hernandez."

"Yes sir." Vail stole a look at Gifford. He was uncommonly quiet. More than concerned, she decided. Worried. Not worried because she was now running the task force, but worried like a father who's dealing with a son who's gotten himself into a heap of trouble. Vail gave him a slight nod of assurance, then led her team back toward the Huey.

80

Willie Quintero drove around the strip, up and down side streets and back again to Las Vegas Boulevard, watching for a tail. They were clean, best he and Sandiego Ortega could determine in the thick traffic and frequent red lights that choked one of the busiest sections of the strip.

Robby asked for the cuffs to be removed, a request that Quintero rejected. "Once we get inside, Mr. Villarreal will tell us how he wants us to handle you. Till then, keep your fucking mouth shut. You've got us to thank for your life, and I wanna hear some grat-titude, *amigo*."

"Thank you," Robby said. "I appreciate what you did for me."

"Damn straight. Now keep your head down until we're ready to get out."

Following another trip through the Vegas streets, Quintero guided the car into an underground garage. There they waited, Robby still scrunched into the rear seat, until Quintero received a phone call. He listened, then said, in Spanish, "Yes, boss." He hung up, then told Diego they were to take Robby up to the condo.

After draping a jacket across his handcuffed wrists, they led Robby through the parking lot, up the stairs, across a larger area, then into an elevator bay. The ride up was long and, according to the LCD readout, fifty-seven stories.

Undernourished—and abused—for several days, Robby felt unsteady and had to lean against the elevator wall to keep from falling over. The car finally drew to a stop and the doors slid apart. Quintero gave him a shove, and Robby tripped forward. Diego tightened his grip on Robby's arm and ushered him into Alejandro Villarreal's ultramodern condo.

"Steady, *hermano*," Diego said in a low voice. "We'll get you some food in a few minutes."

"That'd be good," Robby said, finding it difficult to summon the energy to maintain an erect posture.

Inside, the condo's clean, edgy lines were augmented by Zebrawood cabinets, teak doors, limestone vanities, and white oak flooring. Ahead of them, expansive picture windows dominated the wall. Bright casino and hotel lights sparkled starkly in black repose against the nightscape below.

In front of the window sat a man in a dark, broad-pinstripe suit. Tan and trim, he possessed the constitution of a wealthy individual whose vast amounts of money were well spent. He rose from the soft, cream-colored leather chair and sauntered up to Robby "So this is the man all the fuss is being made over." Villarreal pursed his lips, then nodded. He studied Robby's face, no doubt taking in the abrasions and bruises, in various stages of healing, and the fresh slice inflicted by Ernesto Escobar. "I am Alejandro Villarreal," he said with some flair. "I am responsible for saving your life. You know that, don't you?"

Robby looked down at the man. "I do, sir. Thank you."

He raised a hand and smiled out of the corner of his mouth. "Don't thank me yet, Mr. Hernandez. Don't thank me yet."

A bowl of mixed nuts sat on a coffee table to Diego's right. "May I, sir?" Diego asked, wiggling an index finger at the food.

"Yes, of course. Make our guest at home."

Diego retrieved the dish and held it in front of Robby, who grabbed a fist full of nuts and shoved them into his mouth as a caveman would devour a fresh piece of meat.

Villarreal's phone rang. He pulled a sleek Sanyo from his pocket and flipped it open with a flick of his thumb. "Yes." He listened a moment, then said, "I see. No, no, thank you." Another pause. "I will consider."

Villarreal snapped the lid closed with one hand and looked up at Robby. "You see, Mr. Hernandez, I am a businessman. That is what I do. It so happens my product is cocaine, methamphetamine, marijuana, heroin. A little Fentanyl thrown in to round out the product mix. Demand is strong, so I try to keep the supply flowing." He spread his arms. "And it makes for a very, very comfortable lifestyle. As you can see." He rotated his torso, taking in the décor of the interior.

Robby, more interested in generating needed energy and strength, threw another handful of nuts into his mouth.

"I've been made an offer," Villarreal said. He turned and walked toward the picture windows. Looking at the lights of Las Vegas below, he appeared to be lost in thought.

Robby shared a look with Diego.

"What kind of offer?" Quintero asked.

Villarreal turned slowly. "A very good one, Willie. Snatching Mr. Hernandez has opened up an opportunity I hadn't considered." His eyes narrowed. "That call was from Carlos Cortez. It seems he wants our guest back. And he has made a lucrative offer of exchange. He's sent men over to formalize the agreement."

Formalize the agreement. Robby knew that meant he was going to be returned to Cortez. If Cortez sent lieutenants to retrieve him, how long until they arrived? That depended on when Cortez had first approached Villarreal about striking a deal. Clearly this was not a topic freshly broached in that phone call.

He, or Diego, had to do something—but what? They didn't have much time, he knew that. These were his best odds since he'd been kidnapped. An armed foe to his left, an armed ally to his right. Was Villarreal packing? Probably—though his slim-fitting suit seemed to indicate otherwise.

Diego stepped forward. "With all due respect, sir. We grabbed Hernandez because we know what Cortez is going to do. And the heat his murder would bring would destroy our busin—"

"Yes, yes. But Mr. Cortez is offering us exclusive rights to a rather large territory. And he's proposing a new supply chain for us, through one of his key suppliers in Colombia, which will enable us to increase our kilos moved per month by a third."

Diego rubbed at his forehead. "Sir. None of that matters if the Feds shut us down."

Villarreal turned back to the windows, his face reflected in the dark glass. "For how long can they do that? Seriously, now, Diego. A month? Two months? Three? The cost will be enormous in a down economy, their government deficits at record levels." He shook his head. "I should have thought this through better." He cocked his head. "Then again, it seems to have worked out just fine. Because if we hadn't taken Mr. Hernandez here, this offer wouldn't be on the table right now."

Diego's right hand reached behind his back—no doubt for his pistol. But if Robby saw it, Quintero could see it too, if he was looking. Diego slipped out a Beretta and had cleared his waist band when Robby leaned left and buried his shoulder into Quintero's side, slamming both of them into the adjacent wall.

A gunshot rang out.

Robby scuffled with Quintero but in the periphery of his vision, he saw his friend drop to the floor.

"Diego!"

Quintero yanked his Smith & Wesson free and aimed it at the doorway—his immediate threat—but another blast from that direction took care of any danger Quintero posed.

Robby felt Quintero slump against the wall but did not celebrate. Standing fifteen feet away, holding a hulking chrome .45, was a person Robby never expected to see again—hoped never to see again.

Ernesto "Grunge" Escobar.

Escobar stepped across the threshold. "You are lucky I came when I did," he said to Villarreal. "Looked to me like your own man here was about to shoot you." With his cannon aimed at Robby, he stepped toward Diego and kicked away his Beretta, sending it skittering out of sight. He then walked toward Robby and, with the .45 pointed at his head, bent down and removed the Smith & Wesson from Quintero's stilled hand.

Villarreal squared his jaw. "Sandiego was a fool. I don't know what his problem was. But I have little tolerance for those who cannot follow my wishes." He shook Escobar's hand. "Something like this will not be forgotten."

Robby, still on the floor, peered at Diego. A blood-soaked pulpy exit wound in the center of his friend's forehead stared back at him.

Villarreal took a few steps closer to Robby. "So, Mr. Hernandez. As I said earlier, it was premature to thank me. I am truly sorry for what I must now do."

81

Vail felt the familiar thumping rotor vibration in her chest. She repositioned the headset and pushed her hair away from her ears. As the helicopter approached the strip below, bright lights of all colors splashed across the landscape in a dual line along a central roadway. "Las Vegas Boulevard?" Vail asked over her headset.

"Affirmative," Agent Clar said.

Dixon craned her neck to get a better view. "I haven't been to Vegas in about twenty years. Looks like a totally different place."

Mann chuckled. "Glad I don't have their electric bill."

"Lots of wind," Clar said, shaking his head. "I hope that doesn't give us a problem."

DeSantos motioned out the window. "The wind's not our only problem. If SWAT has to lumber in on the armored rig they've got, it ain't gonna happen." Below, South Las Vegas Boulevard was a tangled mess of vehicles. "I don't know what the deal is, but no way are they getting through."

"I'll let 'em know," Dixon said as she keyed her radio.

Vail studied the packed streets below. DeSantos was right. "Then we're gonna do this differently. Mann, you stay behind with Clar and be our quarterback. The rest of us are going in from the air."

Clar quickly glanced back at Vail. "Our orders were to support SWAT, let them do the heavy lifting."

"We don't know how long Robby has," Vail said. "And you see what the traffic's like. The only way in is by air. Last I checked, we're the only ones airborne. Now—is there a helipad nearby where you can land and drop us off?"

"Just that tour place a mile down. But—"

"No," Vail said. "Something closer."

"A roof would be the closest I can get you. There's no real clearing where I can set down."

"So a roof it is."

Clar reached forward and checked a dial as the Huey was noticeably shoved sideways.

"Karen," DeSantos said, "give me LOWIS. I want to see if I can triangulate on the cell phone. See if we can tell which roof to land on to get us as close as possible to Robby."

Vail handed it to him. DeSantos studied the colored LEDs on the otherwise dark display.

Dixon pointed at a dazzling spray of white shooting toward them from the center of a large body of water. "What the hell is that?"

Mann sat forward in his seat and stretched toward Dixon's window. "That's the Bellagio, their water show. Every fifteen minutes, miles of pipes shoot water hundreds of feet into the air. It's all choreographed to light and music that blasts from loudspeakers around the lake." He watched a moment as they neared, the water spiraling into the night sky beneath the bottom of the craft. "I was stationed here back in '98 when they opened it. Next time you're in town, you'll have to catch it. Nothing like it."

Vail watched as the plume of water danced left, then right, then straight up toward them.

"Approaching CityCenter," Clar said. "Vdara's that flat semicircular high-rise coming up ahead. I'm betting this is where your cell is located. I'm taking us lower. You should see a brown LED on LOWIS."

The chopper descended abruptly, then came to a stop and hovered above the tall, narrow building.

"Yeah," DeSantos said, consulting LOWIS's console. "Vdara's the ticket. Directly below us. How'd you know?"

"This is where Villarreal's condo is," Clar said. "Fifty-seventh floor, number 5711."

"That roof," DeSantos said. "It's so freaking narrow."

"I can't stay this low," Clar said as he struggled with the control stick. "Too much wind. Can't risk hitting the antennas down there. I'm taking us up."

As the Huey rose, Vail looked down at the CityCenter complex and saw a concentration of oddly shaped, stylish buildings, architecturally angled, twisted, and curved, dramatically lit from above and below.

Colors and landscape like nothing she had seen before. "Impressive," she said.

"Actually," Clar said, "the impressive part is gonna come from you people."

"Us?" Vail asked.

"There's no place to set down," DeSantos's voice said in her ears. "Robby's in that building directly below us. But the roof's not large enough for us to land on, and there's no flat ground that can accommodate us, unless we're far off the property."

"No, no. There's no time. Robby's down there," Vail said, thrusting a finger toward the floor. "Get us down there."

"Only way is to drop one of you in," Clar said. "Onto the roof."

Vail looked out the window. Robby was somewhere directly below her. "I'll go."

"Have you ever rappelled before?" Clar asked.

Vail pulled her eyes from the airscape and looked at the pilot. "Rappelled? Yeah, from a training tower, lots of times. From a moving helicopter? Twice. But it's been about six or seven years."

"It's like riding a bicycle," Mann said. "Comes right back to you." He rapped DeSantos on the shoulder with his artificial hand. "I think she should go Aussie."

Vail pressed her headset against her ear. "Aussie?"

"Head first," Mann said. He gave her a thumbs-up. "Big freaking rush."

Dixon grabbed Vail's shoulder. "You sure you want to do this?"

"I'll go," DeSantos said. "I used to be a jump master with SRT. Last time was a couple months ago in the Ukraine."

Vail looked at him. *The Ukraine? Is he serious?* But she knew by now not to ask such questions of Hector DeSantos. "No. I'm the team leader. I'm going." *Did I just say that aloud?*

Clar peered ahead, at the brilliantly lit landscape. "I can drop the rest of you by rope onto the boulevard, about 100, 150 yards from Vdara's entrance."

"Think about this, Karen," DeSantos said.

I don't want to think about this, thank you very much.

DeSantos looked down at Vdara. "Rappelling onto a narrow roof isn't easy. It'd be a first for me, too."

"I can't stay here," Clar said. "Not with this wind. Now or never."

Vail thought of Jonathan, of Robby. She glanced at LOWIS, which was nestled in DeSantos's hand. "All right, let's do it." She reached forward and snatched the electronic device. "And none of that macho Aussie shit. I'm going down feet first."

Dixon looked at Vail and their eyes met. Dixon understood that she needed to do this.

Clar tightened his grip on the control stick as another wind gust slapped the chopper. "Behind the seat you'll find a harness, gloves, and carabiner. Someone help her get that shit on, will you?"

"You got a tactical helmet?" Vail asked.

Dixon located the equipment and held up a black shell. "Affirmative on the helmet."

"Okay," Clar said. "There's a donut in the floor of the Huey." He kept his eyes ahead while he spoke into his headset mike. "Attach that thick wire to the donut ring. Karen, you'll step into the harness and clip the carabiner on the front. The rope goes through the carabiner."

Mann slid open the side door. A rush of air blew into the cabin.

"Got it," DeSantos said as he helped prepare her harness and then rigged the carabiner to the clasp. "You're going back first, butt first."

"Yes, I remember."

"Good. I'm still gonna tell you. I don't want to overlook anything." He wrapped the rope around to her front. "You're gonna lower your feet onto the skids outside the chopper. Form an L-shape with your torso—"

"With my ass hanging out the window, I know."

"Right. And the rope that's wrapped around you—that's your brake."

Vail, still wearing her headset, nodded. With DeSantos guiding her, she moved onto the skids. The downdraft from the rotors rhythmically slapped her back. As she positioned her feet, she caught a glimpse of the buildings and lights below. *I've got the best view in Las Vegas.*

She felt a surge of adrenaline as the wind rippled through her clothing.

"The brake is wrapped around you," DeSantos said. "When you're ready, move your right arm out to the side, a couple inches at a time, and that'll release the brake."

"Got it. Then I kick off, away from the Huey."

"Yes, and then you'll be in freefall. If you do it right, you'll only brake once, about ten feet before you hit the ground. At about ten feet, pull the rope back toward you, into the top of your ass—the small of your back. That'll bring you to a stop."

Vail looked at the rope, at her hand, and then at DeSantos. "Check."

She glanced down again. *Robby's down there. Okay, let's do it. I'm ready.* She nodded.

"Remember, it'll be a pretty fast descent. "We're about seventy-five feet above the high-rise now." He looked her square in the eyes. "You still with me?"

"I'm with you," she said.

"What are you going to do once you're down?" DeSantos asked.

"Unclip the carabiner from the rope."

"Good. Expect some sway from the wind." He set a hand on her shoulder. "Last chance to back out. No one will think any less of you."

Vail narrowed her eyes. "Am I the kind of person who backs out of anything?"

DeSantos smiled. "Hell no. But in case all goes to shit, I had to know I tried." He wiggled his fingers and Vail removed the headset and slipped on the helmet.

The pounding bleat of the rotors was intense without the noise-suppressing effect of the headphones. Vail gave him a thumbs-up. She couldn't hear what he was saying, but she could've sworn his lips mouthed, "Bombs away."

He smiled and gave her a playful thump on the top of her helmet.

Vail took a deep breath, flexed her gloved hands on the rope, then squatted into an L-shape. The downdraft was strong, slamming against the back of her neck like a persistent drumbeat.

With a gloved hand, Vail pushed down on top of the helmet to seat it, shifted her feet on the skids, then kicked away.

She slid down the rope—feeling the burn in her palms, despite the gloves—then moved her right hand back to slow her fall. But the cable swayed more than she'd thought it would, and she was concentrating on the trajectory of the windblown arc.

She started to brake but not fast enough.

The wind blew her past the edge of the roof, and she missed the building's edge. *Fuck!* She yanked her arm behind her and braked, hard, now hanging in midair.

But that wasn't the worst of it. She was now below the top of the tower, which shielded her from the wind. She swung back hard, and the last thing she saw as she hurtled through the air was the thick, black panes of the Vdara's penthouse glass windows.

ROBBY KNELT ON THE FLOOR beside Diego Ortega's body. His friend's cell phone was open, to the left of his ankle. Robby was reaching out to snag it when suddenly something slammed into the living room window.

"What the hell—" Villarreal flinched and hit the floor as the image of a black-jacketed individual scraped across the glass, then disappeared from view.

"Federales!" Escobar said. He turned and headed out the door.

Robby, realizing he might never have another chance, lowered his shoulder and ran forward, ramming into Villarreal's abdomen. Villarreal's hip struck the bottom window sill and his neck snapped back violently, cracking his head against the glass. The expansive pane rattled but did not break.

The black figure again slammed against the window fifteen feet to their left, then disappeared into the darkness.

Villarreal, stunned and disoriented, clumsily threw a punch that connected with air. Robby kneed him hard in the groin then searched the writhing Villareal and the surrounding area for a handgun.

Moans from Villarreal.

Get out now, Robby.

No weapon—but he found Diego's cell phone a few feet away. Robby scooped it up, then scrabbled over to Quintero to search his pockets for a handcuff key. He found one in the man's jacket and, after a quick check of Villarreal—still in pain but fighting to get to his feet—Robby ran out of the condo's open door before another of the man's lieutenants appeared. Two or three mercenaries against an unarmed cop were worse odds than what he had now.

Down the hall, he pressed the elevator button, then went about removing the handcuffs. He had some difficulty, but slowed his efforts and finally freed his wrists.

He tossed the cuffs to the floor as the doors slid apart.

VAIL BOUNCED OFF, then slapped back against the windows, scraping along the surface when suddenly she was pulled up. *Clar must've brought the Huey higher.*

She spun in a dizzying twirl, holding on and hoping she did not slam against the building again. It didn't feel good the first two times, it sure as hell would not feel any better a third.

Vail rose above the rooftop, then swung back over it. That was her cue—before the wind blew her away again. She brought her arm out slowly, lowered her body to the surface, then braked. Unhooked the carabiner and undid the cable. It retracted and the helicopter moved off, presumably to drop Dixon, Mann, and DeSantos onto the grounds somewhere below.

Vail found the roof exit and pulled open the metal door. Clanked down the stairs and came out on the fifty-seventh floor.

Glock in hand, she moved down the hall toward one of the condos, where light splashed out into the corridor. When she arrived, she saw a man of about Robby's age, lying still on the floor. Pooled blood around his head.

She felt a pang in her stomach—but as she approached, she could tell the body type was significantly smaller and slighter. Gunshot wound to the head. No need to check for a pulse.

Vail rapidly cleared the rooms and found them empty. "Robby! You in here?" Listened. Nothing, not a grumble, a moan, a kick against a closet door. She moved back out toward the hallway and pulled LOWIS from her pocket. The signal appeared to be strong, glowing green and yellow.

She pulled her two-way and raised Clar on channel 9. "Mark, LOWIS has two lights: green and yellow. What does that mean?"

"Where are you?"

"Fifty-seventh floor of Vdara. Outside what I'm guessing is Villarreal's condo. There's a DB, GSW to the forehead."

"We'll call it in. Meantime, go down to a lower floor. Here's the key. Green and brown are your friends: they mean you're within fifty yards on the x-axis for green and within fifty yards in the y-axis for brown. Yellow or amber are bad: you're out of range in the y-axis. But blue is the worst. You see blue, you're cold—she's totally lost the signal. They've moved beyond about a hundred yards in all directions."

"Jesus, could you have made it more confusing?" Vail ran toward the staircase. No—the elevator. It was a risk, particularly if they were on a middle floor and she went down too far, she'd pass them by—but walking down dozens of flights would take too long if they were headed out of the building. *How high is a floor in this building? How many yards?*

Vail looked down at LOWIS and stopped. "Wait a minute—the signal. Mark, the display, LOWIS went black!"

"Stand by," Clar said.

Vail stood there, heart pounding, emotion flooding her body, tears forming in her eyes. She stared at LOWIS's blank screen. "C'mon, goddammit, work! What's wrong with you?"

"Okay, okay—" Clar's voice boomed over the radio. "She's fine. She'll come back online. The signal from Ortega's phone cut out. Either it was shut off or the battery came dislodged. But the FBI techs got it back and they're using it as that roving bug we discussed. So here's what you need to do. See that flat button on the right side?"

Vail fumbled with LOWIS and found the slight protrusion. "Yeah, yeah, I got it."

"Push and hold it for five seconds. She'll reboot and then she should pick up the new signal."

"Reboot? I don't have time for that. C'mon, Clar, what kind of piece of shit did you build?"

"Karen, another time I'd take offense to that." His voice was calm and measured. "But I know you're under tremendous stress. Take a breath. She'll be up in a few more seconds."

As Clar promised, the device had begun loading its operating system. "Okay—it's scrolling through some red computer code." She closed her eyes and took a breath. "Sorry about what I said."

"Already forgotten. Now pay attention, she's almost ready. She'll reacquire the signal automatically. Nothing for you to do."

Vail moved forward and pressed the elevator button. "What am I looking for?"

"Green and brown are good, remember? They mean you're within fifty yards on the x- or y-axes. If you see amber or yellow, you're out of the fifty yard range."

The elevator door opened and Vail got in. "What about purple?"

"Oh, right. If she's purple, turn left or right. Don't know which. That'll be in version 2.0. Like all of us, LOWIS has her limitations."

Vail kept her eyes on the glowing green, yellow, and purple lights as the elevator descended rapidly. She pressed the button for 38, and would thereafter stop at 28, then every ten floors—and assess LOWIS's color, because her target would be moving as well.

At 38, the display went blue—and a cold sweat broke out across her forehead. Her gaze flicked over to the numerical floor level display—to hell with the ten-floor plan. She hit *L* and watched LOWIS's screen. As she approached Lobby, the light changed to green.

Bingo.

The doors slid apart and she ran forward, watching the LED display. Brown, amber—and purple. She could only turn left, which led her down the hall, toward the garage and the back of the building. A moment later, she sighed relief: LOWIS sported green and brown lights.

Vail left Vdara and followed the signs into the walkway that led to the Bellagio's Spa Tower, a separate, though connected, high-rise that housed a glass-ceilinged conservatory, convention rooms, and luxury facilities for pampering hotel guests.

According to the placards she had seen, above her was the monorail that ferried guests from CityCenter directly into the Bellagio. She rotated her head left and right, Vegas's unmatched nightscape partially visible through the glass walls. Halfway through the tunnel, she glanced down at the tracking device.

Brown and amber lights stared back at her. They were on the same level as she was, but more than fifty yards away.

Shit! She quickened her pace, then sprinted out of the walkway and into the Spa Tower. Ahead was a large, glass-enclosed storefront, "Newsstand" emblazoned on the sign above the door. She ran past it and continued down the hall. The green LED came on, but the purple light once again flicked to life. She looked ahead, through the throng of passing people, but couldn't see Robby—or anyone else who appeared to be moving at a pretty good clip. But as LOWIS had indicated, about a hundred feet ahead there was a turn in the corridor.

Vail pressed forward, pushing through the masses, weaving in and out, down a slight incline, then past Sensi, a futuristic bar with a water fountain cascading down the wall, its countertop a mirror of black liquid.

LOWIS went dark—then the green and purple LEDs popped on. Vail looked up and swung right, her only choice. Shorter corridor. Dominating the wall to her left—the Jean Philippe Patisserie—the coolest pastry shop she'd ever seen. Multilevel, furrowed blown glass troughs formed what was surely the most unique chocolate fountain ever created.

Vail elevated onto her toes and peered over the heads of the people milling about the wide hallway, but despite Robby's height, she did not see him. She was beginning to think that LOWIS, with her high-tech proximity sensors and smart ping digital signal processing abilities—or whatever the hell Clar had called it—was leading her on an old-fashioned, low-tech wild goose chase.

THE CHOPPER HOVERED over the main artery, South Las Vegas Boulevard, southeast of the Bellagio's main entrance. A tree-studded grass-carpeted knoll stood nearby that separated twin three-lane drives leading up to the property, where the bellmen worked feverishly to unload new arrivals.

Slow-moving traffic came to a stop to watch—and steer clear of—the hovering helicopter. Dixon and DeSantos dropped to the ground, then Clar retracted the rope and took the chopper higher, away from the roadway.

DeSantos slapped Dixon on the arm. "Let's go!"

VAIL FOLLOWED THE CORRIDORS past the conservatory on the left, then ahead into the bright and expansive Bellagio lobby. Decorative molding-edged squares checkerboarded the ceiling. At its center sprouted an oblong bouquet of blown glass flowers bursting with colorful hues, from blood red to lime green.

Her rubber soled shoes gripped the cream-and-brown granite tile as she ran toward the location LOWIS directed her: the front entrance. The LED glowed green and brown, which meant she was close. And headed in the right direction.

Vail exploded through the doors into darkness—her eyes had to adjust from the brilliant lights of the lobby—and she emerged in the carport. Doormen and bellhops were moving about, ferrying new arrivals into the hotel, and departing guests into waiting taxis.

The screen added purple to its array of colors—they had turned. *But which way? If I lose them now, they'll blend into the crowd.* Even with the homing device, there'd be myriad places they could go. It'd be near impossible for her alone to search all the buildings, alleyways, ancillary roads, and casinos. And how long will that cell battery last? What if it wasn't Robby she was pursuing?

Directly in front of her stood a curving roadway that slanted down and away, to the left and to the right, split by a central tree-covered island where people seemed to be gathering to watch something ahead of them.

Vail climbed atop a short cement column—and saw two men running along the roadway to her right.

She jumped down and took off in that direction.

ROBBY BURST THROUGH a crowd in the Bellagio's lobby. Two men, who had engaged him as he exited the Vdara elevator, remained in close pursuit.

He'd knocked down three women a hundred yards or so back, but it couldn't be helped. If those pursuing him pulled a weapon, there'd be a lot of people *permanently* on the floor. And he didn't want that to happen.

Robby pulled Diego's phone and once again pressed various buttons, but in brief glances as he ran, it didn't appear as if the keypad was working. He had already removed and reseated the battery, but it had no effect. He flipped the lid closed and shoved the cell back into his pocket in time to stiff-arm a door with a large brass *B* on the handle.

He exited the hotel and ran through the carport, then angled right onto a walkway beside a dense row of privet hedges. To his left, throngs of people lined a cement retaining wall that bordered a large man-made lake. Loud music began blaring from the speakers. Jets of water spewed forth into the night sky.

Robby chanced a quick glance over his right shoulder and saw the two men paralleling him on the other side of the tall, wide row of hedges. If he could get to the end of the road before they did, he'd be on the main strip, where, despite his height, it'd be easier for him to get lost in the throng of milling tourists—or find a circulating Vegas police cruiser.

He pushed forward and began picking his way through the crowd.

VAIL RAN TOWARD the cement walkway that snaked along the periphery of the manmade lake she had seen from the Huey.

There—bobbing up and down, the unmistakable form of the head and shoulders of a six-foot-seven man as he twisted and bumped his way through the dense mass of humanity.

Vail felt a swell of excitement—Robby was alive, and he was only a few dozen yards away.

But off to the right, two large Hispanic men ran alongside the hedges, one slightly behind Robby and the other considerably ahead.

As Vail opened her mouth to scream his name, the roar of bass-booming music blared from the large, camouflaged speakers, followed almost immediately by the spurting of high-powered water jets. As if vacuumed away, her shout was swallowed by the noise.

Vail pushed forward, forcing her way through the crowd, twisting sideways and using her shoulder to part the masses.

Robby's only fifty yards away.

And an armed hit squad was in pursuit.

Either Robby or one of the two men pursuing him was carrying the cell phone she'd been tracking. As long as she could maintain eye contact with Robby, it didn't matter. The dense wall of privets was, for the moment, preventing the men from reaching him. But in the distance, the hedge—and the path—came to an end.

She had to get to the pursuing assassins before they could get to Robby—or risk firing off a few rounds into the lake. The gunshots would hopefully cause a stir and be reported to Vegas Metro Police, which she figured maintained a respectable presence on the strip. Problem was, she didn't see any cops where and when she needed them: here. And now.

The water jets blasted and the music boomed, sounding like a twenty-one-gun salute.

And up ahead, a glimpse of Robby's head. So close—and yet unreachable.

She yelled—knowing he couldn't hear her—but she didn't know what else to do. She grabbed her radio. "This is Vail. Anyone on Las Vegas Boulevard, near the Bellagio entrance?"

She brought the radio to her ear, uncertain she would be able to even hear the response above the noise.

"Negative." DeSantos's voice? Clar's? Mann's? Vail couldn't tell.

"I've got eyes on Robby," Vail said. "Being pursued through the crowd by two armed mercenaries. Need assistance."

"In pursuit—"

Dixon's voice. But she couldn't make out the rest of her transmission.

Vail looked skyward. *Where the hell's the Huey?*

As Robby approached the boulevard—amid the intense glare of Planet Hollywood's turquoise lights and Paris's neon-striped hot air balloon—she saw Robby's head and shoulders stop abruptly.

He turned back in her direction, took a step, stopped again, then looked around.

Other armed men must've appeared ahead of him, blocking his way. Shit—

Robby was now moving. Climbing. Standing on something.

Facing the expansive lake, his body was silhouetted against the pluming, brightly lit white wall of water.

She pushed forward. "No!"

But her voice was swallowed by the spouting jets, the booming horns, and masses of people in front of her.

Vail figured she was the only one who saw the two men raise handguns. Not even she heard them fire their suppressed rounds. But the buck of the barrel was unmistakable.

AS ROBBY NEARED the strip ahead, the high-def billboards and neon glow of Las Vegas excess reflecting off glass everywhere, his mind sifted through various scenarios. A substantial obstacle remained: the two men assigned to kill him, held at bay by a natural barrier of hedges.

And coming up ahead, from the boulevard, another two *sicarios*, fighting their way toward him.

He turned and looked in the direction from which he had just come. Go back? He took a step, then stopped. No—even if he could fight his way through the crowd, the men on the other side of the hedges would arrive ahead of him.

He had mere seconds to figure a way out.

There was only one unblocked path: the water. He pushed a man and two women aside, then hoisted himself to the top of the cement wall— and felt the hot sting of a bullet slam into his left arm.

With no further thought required, he jumped.

It was a ten foot drop, and he hit the lake's surface sharply, feet first. That wasn't the problem—it was the cold water and the spray of the jets raining down on him as the show built in intensity. He no longer felt the sting of the gunshot wound. The chilled water had numbed it, and his urgent need to avoid any more lead spinning through his flesh pushed him to move forward.

He paddled his right arm and legs through the water, slamming into something rock hard and immobile. Pipes. When he'd jumped, he had apparently come dangerously close to landing on a portion of the extensive network of plumbing that spidered off into the distance, as far as he could see.

He hadn't appreciated how expansive this body of water was until he was in it, enveloped in its cold grasp, no reachable land in sight. Swimming ahead would only take him into the middle of the lake, and make him an easy target for another gunshot—one that might find center mass. He pulled his body around and faced a series of arched aqueducts, which appeared to lead under the roadway he'd just traversed.

Wherever they led didn't matter—it meant he would be out of the line of sight of the hunters who were determined to notch him onto their bloody cartel belts. He thrust his legs and right arm outward and pushed on, beneath the nearest stone archway, into the pitch darkness.

VAIL SHOVED AND PUSHED her way to the edge of the lake's retaining wall. The rockets' red glare was booming from the speakers. The nozzles were blowing tight streams of water fifteen stories into the air, and smaller walls of synchronized spray cascaded across her field of sight. And—

what the hell?—a fog began spreading rapidly across the lake. *You've gotta be kidding me. Fog?*

She stood there, looking for Robby—for any sign of life.

She saw nothing. No blood. No floating body. No flailing arms. And the dense cloud enveloping the lake was making it nearly impossible to see.

What to do. How—where—

Along the lower end of the right side wall of the lake, arched aqueducts. The water flowed into them. But where did they lead? Had Robby swum through one of them?

Vail pulled out the tracking device, hoping it was Robby who'd been carrying the phone. A black screen stared back at her. If Robby had the cell, it would be underwater now, shorted out, no longer transmitting a digital or electronic signal.

It was clear the device would bring her no closer to locating him. She shoved LOWIS into her pocket and headed back the way she had come, into the hotel.

ROXXANN DIXON STOOD on the pedestrian overpass that connected the Via Bellagio shops to the walkway that led to Caesars Palace. On a lower level directly ahead, a permanent tented structure arced over a plaza that housed tables catering to the adjacent Serendipity3 eatery.

As she descended the steps, off to her left, her eye caught a flash of movement and the glimpse of a man who looked familiar.

César Guevara.

Looming over the immediate vicinity was one of the towering rectangular Roman-themed buildings sporting a red neon Caesars Palace sign at its upper periphery. Keeping her focus on Guevara's last known location, she ran through the well-lit tented area, then along a narrow passageway that led to the hotel.

Tall, slender evergreens rose to her right, which bordered the intensely lit main entrance to the Caesars complex. Limousines and luxury sedans were parked beneath the long and broad overhang, where bellmen awaited the next approaching vehicle ferrying a tip-bearing arrival.

There! Beneath the bright lights of the hotel's brick plaza.

Dixon took off in Guevara's direction, pulling her Glock with her right hand and fumbling for her badge with the left. It did not say "federal task force officer," and would thus carry no jurisdiction in Nevada. But it would have the intended effect. Those in the vicinity would know she had a legitimate reason for brandishing a pistol and running through the crowds.

Yet no one seemed to notice. Some glanced in her direction, but the density of people provided adequate cover.

Seconds later, Dixon burst through the crowd. Guevara was nowhere nearby. She turned in a circle, looking, hoping—and then saw him behind the dark glass of the main entry doors. She scaled the steps and shoulder-slammed her way into the lobby. She almost froze, taken by the grandeur before her: dramatic ceiling lighting and frescoes, rose quartz columns, blown glass chandeliers, black and ivory marble everywhere—and a central fountain that spouted water into a basin below three scantily clad limestone women.

Images of lavish, elegant opulence plowed through her brain, but she didn't have time to process any of it because the lobby was more expansive than the eye could immediately comprehend. César Guevara was not stopping to take in the surroundings, nor was he evaluating its magnificence. He was moving at a rapid pace into the casino. And now, so was Dixon.

A violet, gold, black, and burgundy carpet extended throughout semiprivate and public gambling areas.

"Can I help you?" a security guard asked, eyeing first her badge, then the Glock.

"I'm following a suspect. Outta my way," Dixon said as she edged around him.

"Hey—hold on a second—"

Dixon held up her badge. "Get the fuck out of my way!"

"You got a warrant? You can't just walk in here with a gun—" he said, then maneuvered himself in front of her.

"I'm a federal agent," she said, moving her head to see around him in hopes of catching a visual of Guevara. "Move!"

"That's not what your badge says," he said, then grabbed her arm. She was about to do something nasty to his closely held male *compadres* when she broke free, then shoved him hard into a crowd of youths passing by. He tripped backward and sprawled to the floor.

But as she moved on, she heard him key his two-way. Reinforcements would be en route—very shortly, she surmised.

Dixon moved deeper into the gambling areas, thick with people and the pungent smell of perfume and cigarette smoke. Guevara had to be around here somewhere. As her eyes roamed the large room, beeps and whirls sounding in her head off in the distance, she felt a creeping sense of anxiety. Had he gotten away?

Had she blown it?

VAIL PUSHED HER WAY through the crowd, then sprinted across the carport and into the Bellagio's lobby. People of all ages milled about in seemingly haphazard activity. She needed to find someone who knew about the hotel.

To her left, a suited man with a brass nametag.

She dug out her creds and held them as she ran left, toward the bellman's station, an ivory and gold counter that stood in front of a wall-size floral mural. "The fountains, the water—" She stopped, collected herself. *Be coherent.* "The water outside—the lake. There are arches, aqueducts that go under the roadway. Where do they lead?"

The bellman leaned back slightly and swung his head toward the front of the building. Apparently the answers weren't there, because he turned back to Vail and shrugged. "I—I don't know. I've never been asked that question. People usually want to know how often the fountains go off, how many stories into the air the water reaches—"

Vail swung her head around the lobby. "Anyone who might know?"

"You can ask at registration. They might be able to call a manager—"

With five long strides, Vail covered the distance to the nearby desk, which stretched across the cavernous room as far as she could see into the distance. She slapped a hand on the tan granite countertop in front of a woman who was checking in a guest, shoved her badge forward, and said, "The goddamn fountain—I need someone who can tell me where the water goes."

The guest gave her a dirty look for being so rude—but the eyes of the hotel service worker were wide with shock and glued to Vail's credentials case. She seemed to be reading every word.

Vail flicked it closed and snagged her attention. "A manager. Call a goddamn manager."

The woman stumbled over some words, then reached for a phone and dialed. She spoke into the handset, then lowered it and said, "He'll be up in a few minutes."

"I don't have a few minutes." Vail pulled her radio. "Vail to Mann. Over."

A second later, her two-way crackled. "Mann."

"Where the hell are you?"

"We swung around to assist SWAT, why?"

"Those fountains at the Bellagio. Where do they lead? I mean, there's gotta be pipes, right? Some kind of plumbing, machinery and computers or something that plays and synchronizes the jets to the music. Right?"

"Affirmative. One of the designers once showed me around. He took me down to 'the back of the house,' which runs underneath the entire property. Catering tunnels, a massive kitchen, the pump rooms and maintenance shop for the fountain, all sorts of shit like that."

"Okay, listen to me. Robby jumped into the lake. He may've been shot but I don't know. There are arches, aqueducts that look like they go under the roadway that leads up to the hotel."

"Affirmative. Bellagio Drive, south area of the lake. But those aqueducts are fake. They don't lead anywhere. Do you see him on the lake?"

"I'm in the lobby. There's some kind of fog hanging over the water. I couldn't see shit."

"Part of the show. It'll lift in a few minutes."

"There were assholes shooting at him. If I'm Robby, I'm swimming like Michael Phelps trying to get away. The drop from the roadway is about a dozen feet; I don't think there's a way to climb up out of the water. Is there any outlet into the hotel? Any way in?"

"North side of the lake," Mann said. "There's an opening in the fake rock that leads into the maintenance shop for the fountain. I think they called it the Bat Cave. From what I remember, there's a boat launching ramp that leads into the cave. It's the only place he can go. Find that and you'll find Robby."

"How do I get there?"

"Ask how to get down to 'the back of the house.' The corridor will lead to the north end of the complex."

"Got it. Over." Vail shoved the radio in her back pocket and pivoted in a circle. Signs for everything except "the back of the house."

She stopped herself from thinking like a woman looking for a hotel room and thought like a cop. She was in a casino, a place filled with surveillance cameras. *And security guards.* Security guards would know more about the layout of the hotel's underbelly and hidden locations than a bellman.

She reached into her holster and pulled out her Glock, held it up in one hand and her creds in the other. Then she started yelling. "FBI! Everyone down!"

Screams. Movement. People hitting the floor. *Now that's more like it.*

Security should be here any second. Damn, I should've thought of this sooner.

Sure enough, two guards dressed in red blazers and black pants approached on the run, from the direction of the casino that fed into the lobby.

They were yelling at her, but that was a game Vail always won.

"FBI! Federal agent!" She made sure they saw her badge and credentials—because she had no idea if casino security guards were armed and she couldn't afford any misunderstandings.

As they neared, Vail saw they were not packing. One was chattering on his radio and the other appeared to be unsure of what to do. She couldn't blame him. This probably wasn't something they'd ever encountered.

"I need one of you to take me to the Bat Cave. And I need someone to lock the place down. Tight."

They looked at one another.

"Now!" She advanced on them.

That got them moving. The man to her left stepped forward and said, "Did you say the Bat Cave?" He asked it as if she had lost touch with reality.

"Yes, the Bat Cave. The back of the house. The maintenance area for the fountains."

"Yeah—okay. The Shop. I can show you where it is."

Vail swiveled to the other guard. "No one out, any exit. Only federal agents in. Got it?"

"Yeah, but—"

"Tell your boss we've got an emergency."

The guard keyed up his radio.

Vail and the other man moved off, toward the lower reaches of the complex.

THE ARCHED AQUEDUCTS turned out to be dead ends. The lake was too far below ground level to even attempt to climb out, so Robby moved off into the framework of piping and water jets. He swam as best he could with one arm, following the plumbing as it led toward the other end, into a blue-tinted darkness.

Pipes meant a water supply—and that hopefully translated into some kind of apparatus that he might be able to use to climb out of the lake.

He was not sure where or how he had summoned the energy to go on, but thinking about seeing Karen again, holding her, caressing her, kept his arms and feet moving through the chilled waters.

At least the *sicarios* were not shooting at him. The fog that had provided him cover had evaporated from the lake's surface. Was he out of range? Were they moving to a better perch? He couldn't worry about any of that—he had to get out of the cold water. Not only was he feeling the effects, but he did not want to still be in the lake when the immensely powerful fountain jets rumbled to life again.

How long did he have?

Ahead, he saw something reflecting off the rock wall—no, not a reflection, and not off the rock's surface; off an *opening* in the rock. A way out? He swam toward it—and about twenty yards later, he was able to confirm it was, indeed, something resembling a cavity of some sort in the stone wall. And the water appeared to be flowing in.

As he approached, a rumbling vibration built inside the pipe to his right.

The fountains.

But before they exploded into the air, the slap of water behind him snatched his attention. Movement. A body. He yanked his head around but never saw it. A blow to the face caught him off guard, like a truck broadsiding a car at an intersection.

Dark—

Dizzy—

Music roaring, water raining down around him.

Head shoved underwater—can't breathe—

Blow to the back—

He reached and grabbed—at anything—something to make it stop—

And found purchase on a shirt—

Yanked, twisted, elbowed his arm up and under the hand holding down his head and—

Leveraged himself free.

Robby forced his face up through the water's surface and sucked in air—saw a large dark head, body in front of him—

And threw up his left arm in time to block another punch. The blow landed instead just beneath the gunshot wound, causing a stab of ice-pick intense pain.

Enough of this shit. Robby swung his right hand out of the water and snatched a grip around the man's ear. He nearly slipped off the appendage, but he closed his hand as tight as he could, with whatever strength he had left, and pulled.

The ear is a sensitive part of the anatomy, and the innate desire not to have it separated from one's body provided the survival mechanism Robby needed: his attacker instinctively refocused his attention and bent his neck to reduce the angle of Robby's pull.

But Robby did not release his grip. The *sicario* switched tactics and grabbed Robby's arm, but couldn't pry it free. Robby squeezed harder— the man's mouth opened—and if the music and fountains hadn't been so damn loud, his yelp would've reached impressive decibels.

Robby yelled as well, infusing himself with the will to win . . . *the will to live*.

But the man extracted a knife from somewhere on his body. Light glinted off the chrome blade, seizing Robby's attention. He yanked the man's head toward him, then slammed his forehead into his attacker's skull. It hurt like hell—but not as much as the pain inflicted on the asshole who'd tried to drown him.

The *sicario's* eyes rolled up in submission. His head slumped to the side, and Robby grabbed him by his neck and plunged him down, beneath the surface.

The knife floated from the man's open hand, then sunk impotently toward the lake's bottom. An arm burst through the surface, reached up and clawed at Robby's chest, grabbed for his wrist, his face—anything to make Robby release his grip.

But as the seconds ticked by, the man stopped struggling and went limp. Robby realized he was breathing rapidly—too rapidly—and was in danger of hyperventilating. He calmed himself, told himself this was not over.

He felt around, trying to move the man's dead weight in the water, rolled him face up, and found a wallet. Shoved it into his back pocket, then searched for a handgun. Pancake holster—empty.

Robby's body began quivering. The fight had depleted his adrenaline. He released his grip on the corpse and maneuvered himself toward the wall's maw and—hopefully—land.

HECTOR DESANTOS had identified the men he was pursuing: Ernesto "Grunge" Escobar and Alejandro Villarreal. He had first engaged Villarreal, who then—fortunately for DeSantos—had met up with Escobar as they exited CityCenter. He followed both fugitives as they fled through the Via Bellagio shops, then spilled out onto the boulevard.

Dodging traffic and tourists, they headed south past the raucous Margaritaville bar and restaurant across the street on the right and Caesars Palace directly to his left. They then coursed along the winding sidewalk and plazas of the Forum Shops.

A two-decker bus painted bumper to bumper with Blue Man Group advertising slowed to a stop. DeSantos kept an eye on Villarreal and Escobar in case one or both hopped onboard. Splitting up—with only DeSantos in pursuit—would ensure one of them a successful escape.

As if they had a direct line to his thoughts, Villarreal cut left and Escobar right, onto the bus, as the rear doors folded closed. With the vehicle accelerating away, Escobar pressed his face against the window and glared at DeSantos, a slow smile broadening his face.

DeSantos couldn't stop the bus—the recipe of a confined space packed with tourists and a cornered, armed killer was not a stew he wanted to stir up. It would've been bloody, with unacceptable collateral damage.

Instead, he pulled his Desert Eagle and cut a path forward, darting between, around, and over lovers holding hands, drunken fraternity youths on a weekend junket, friends in town for a bachelor party . . . DeSantos wasn't discriminating. If they were in his way, they went down.

He yanked the two-way from his back pocket and keyed it. "Suspect Escobar headed north on Vegas metro bus, got on in front of Mirage. In foot pursuit same twenty suspect Villarreal. Over." Someone else would have to follow up.

People were gathered along a railing just past the Mirage main entrance, staring at a darkened outcropping of artificial mountain rock. He picked his way through the crowd, attempting to keep track of Villarreal, who was still moving south—when a blast of flame and volcanic fire rose high into the night sky, then exploded to his left. The crowd roared. DeSantos flinched—nearly sending a .44-caliber round into an unwitting vacationer—then realized the pyrotechnics were merely more Vegas-style theater.

He felt the heat from the dancing fire warm his skin as Villarreal darted right, across the street. The traffic light had changed, and there was a break in the flow of cars.

"Freeze!" DeSantos said. "Federal agent!"

Villarreal didn't respond but DeSantos did. He dropped to a knee, squared up low, and brought Villarreal into his Trijicon night sights. He knew he'd be violating protocol—but it was akin to a white lie. Roughly stated, if you pull your gun, you're planning to use it, and if you're planning to use it, you're planning to kill—that is, aim at center mass to take down the target.

DeSantos was many things, but model soldier was not one of them. He was an exceptionally good shot with a sniper rifle and nearly as good with the less accurate handgun. But he didn't need pinpoint accuracy. He just needed to bring down the fleeing suspect without hitting innocent bystanders.

And at this very moment, Villarreal was in the clear—that is, by Vegas standards. No innocents within twenty feet, no cars in the immediate vicinity. And a low trajectory shot.

One more warning. "Freeze!" Then he fired. Villarreal grabbed his right thigh, tried hopping forward a couple steps, then crumpled to the pavement, draping himself across the curb.

DeSantos ignored a screaming bystander as he approached his writhing prey, Desert Eagle out in front of him, not taking any chances that Villarreal could bring his own weapon to bear.

"Where do you think you're going?" DeSantos said, now standing five feet away, his pistol aimed squarely at Villarreal's face. "I mean, really? Do you want me to put a .44 in your head? Or are you gonna interlock your fingers behind your neck and make nice?"

"It's not what you're thinking," Villarreal said between clenched teeth.

"Since you don't know what I'm thinking, there's a good chance you're wrong."

"You think I had something to do with kidnapping your agent. But I didn't. I was trying to help, I was trying to get him back to you."

DeSantos pursed his lips. "What do you know? You were right about what I was thinking. But I'm in a good goddamn mood right now, so I'm gonna give you the benefit of the doubt. Thing is, you still need to get your hands behind your neck. Otherwise, my gun might go off and you'd never get the chance to prove you're telling the truth." DeSantos cocked his head toward his right shoulder. "Fair enough?"

Villarreal did not reply but slowly interlocked his bloody fingers behind his neck. DeSantos approached and rested his knee in Villarreal's back as he cuffed the man's wrists, then patted him down.

"By the way, I really like your suit," DeSantos said. "Sorry about the hole I made." He pulled his two-way and keyed it. "DeSantos to Mann. You there?"

A moment's hesitation, then, "Affirmative."

"Suspect Villarreal in custody. Needs a bus. GSW to the leg." As he was speaking, a young Vegas Metro PD officer pulled up on a white motorcycle. The man got off the bike and quickly squared up.

"Let me see your hands!"

"What's happening?" Mann asked.

"Ah, shit. Nothing. Stand by." DeSantos lifted his hands and said, "I'm a federal agent. ID's in my back pocket. I'm gonna take it out, okay?"

"Slowly," the cop said.

"I wouldn't think of doing it any other way." He removed his creds and tossed them at the cop's feet. The man bent at the knees, keeping his weapon trained on DeSantos, inspected the ID, and then nodded.

DeSantos keyed his mike. "Mann. I'm turning over custody of Alejandro Villarreal to VPD." DeSantos retrieved his credentials from the officer. Stole a look at his tag, then said into the two-way, "Suspect now in custody of Officer David Rambo." DeSantos shoved the radio back in his pocket. "Serious? Rambo?"

"Was Rambowski. Rambo's cooler. I shortened it."

DeSantos nodded thoughtfully. "I probably would've done the same thing." He pointed a finger at Villarreal. "Look after this scumbag. Very dangerous felon. Make sure you get a photo with him in cuffs. Never know, it could make your career." He gave the officer a wink.

DeSantos walked off, back toward the Bellagio. Into the radio, he said, "Mann, you got a status on Vail and Dixon?"

"Vail is headed to the basement of the Bellagio," Mann replied. "Hernandez may be shot. Last seen in the lake, possibly heading toward the fountain's maintenance facility. Dixon's in Caesar's. Due for a SIT REP. Clar and I are headed to the Bellagio to drop off SWAT."

"Roger that. On my way to Vail's twenty. Over."

DeSantos shoved the radio into his pocket and took off, sprinting back the way he came.

ROBBY SWAM THROUGH the opening in the wall of rock, which led to what appeared to be a launch ramp for boats. Off to the right, a secured dingy bobbed alongside a barge—necessary equipment, he figured, for repair and/or maintenance of the fountain.

As the canted concrete floor rose, the lake's depth gradually decreased from four feet to a few inches. Robby followed the ramp as it doglegged left, then right. There he stopped moving and lay facedown, the water lapping against his cheeks.

Two ducks started quacking and flapping their wings. They went airborne and flew past his head. Had he had more energy, he would have flinched.

When he had gathered sufficient strength, he struggled to his knees, but even lifting his soaked pant legs required effort. He crawled forward onto the cement floor and lay down again. He'd lost blood, he was sure of that.

He gathered the wet shirt sleeve in his right hand and yanked. The cotton fibers gave in and tore, slowly, along the shoulder seam. He twisted the cloth into a thin band, then tied it above the wound, tightening it as best he could.

He'd made it this far, through beatings and drug dealers and hired killers. He wasn't about to let a piece of lead kill him.

VAIL FOLLOWED THE GUARD, whose name tag read "Pryor," through the hotel's ground floor to the room service elevator.

"Aren't there stairs?"

Pryor, who sported a belly that had likely played host to many a six-pack evening, sighed audibly. "You didn't say you wanted to walk it. What are you, some exercise nut?"

"No, I'm a federal agent in a goddamn hurry."

"Faster to take the elevator," Pryor said as he reached out and poked the button again with a stubby finger. "By the time we'd gotten to the staircase over by the retail shops, elevator would've been here twice over."

Vail keyed her radio. "This is Vail. En route to the lower level of the Bellagio. Waiting for the elevator."

Mann's voice boomed over the two-way. "You kidding me? Take the fucking stairs!"

Vail brought the radio to her mouth and faced Pryor as she spoke. "Now there's a brilliant idea. Why didn't I think of that?"

Pryor looked up at the ceiling and rocked back on his heels. Not a worry in the world.

Vail thought of Robby and grabbed her temples. *I can't believe this.*

The elevator doors slid open and she practically leaped inside.

ROXXANN DIXON HAD LOCATED César Guevara attempting to circle back and exit Caesars Palace through its front entrance. She was determined not to lose him again, but he appeared to be moving urgently—and he had a cell phone to his ear. If he had spotted her, bodyguards would not be far off. Armed bodyguards.

"This is Dixon," she said into her radio. "In foot pursuit of suspect Guevara. Leaving Caesars' main entrance. Request available backup."

Dixon followed him as he ran across the pedestrian overpass that arced above South Las Vegas Boulevard at Flamingo Way. To her left, building-size pictures of Donnie and Marie Osmond smiled back at her.

Ahead, amid people moving in both directions across the bridge, César Guevara was thirty feet from the down escalator and staircase.

"Hold it right there," Dixon yelled. "Agents are coming right at you, there's nowhere to go." Not true, but what the hell.

The tourists who saw her SIG veered away, but those who were oblivious bumped her from behind or weaved around her. Guevara slowed and glanced through the clear Lexan walls, no doubt attempting to verify Dixon's claims of nearby reinforcements.

But Guevara apparently felt that if there were federal agents approaching, he would be no worse off than if he were to surrender. And he surely knew she wouldn't discharge her weapon with innocents in such close proximity.

Down the stairs they both went. Dixon keyed her radio.

Guevara negotiated a sharp left at the bottom of the staircase, passing Bill's Gambling Hall and Saloon and moving toward the Flamingo Hotel.

"Guevara headed north at the intersection of Las Vegas Boulevard and Flamingo Way," Dixon said into her two-way.

Guevara sidestepped the open casino entrance, where two scantily clad women were dancing atop a raised pedestal. Dixon struggled to stay in visual contact with Guevara, as the crowd was now considerably thicker than it had been on the bridge.

Guevara fended off Latino workers shoving porn trading cards into the hands of passersby. He looked right, at the raucous college students pulling on neon green drinks in Margaritaville, then glanced left at the thick, slowly moving traffic.

Dixon made up ground and was only thirty feet behind him when Guevara stopped suddenly, shoved a man aside, drew his handgun, and—

Before Dixon could reach him, his weapon bucked, followed by his body.

He'd been hit—but by whom?

As Guevara slumped back into the trunk of a streetside palm tree—he'd taken a round but was not incapacitated—Hector DeSantos stepped off the planted median in the center of the boulevard, his gold Desert Eagle out in front of him, approaching Guevara with caution.

Cars stopped, drivers gawking at the man in front of them advancing across the roadway with a handgun—and making no attempt to hide it.

"Don't make me shoot you again," DeSantos said. "Drop the gun or you'll be joining all your dead cartel brothers."

Guevara, his face contorted in pain, did not acquiesce.

But Dixon came up behind him and pressed her SIG against the man's temple. "Does this make the decision easier?"

Guevara dropped the handgun. He was bleeding from the abdomen—a notoriously painful wound—but Dixon showed him no mercy as she grabbed his hands and yanked them behind him, then fastened her set of cuffs to his wrists.

"That's for Eddie," Dixon said of her deceased ex-boyfriend.

Guevara winced. "Don't know who that is."

"John Mayfield killed him."

"Don't know who that is, either."

"Lying pisses me off, César. And that's not something you want to do."

"I don't know—"

Dixon slapped him on the head. "Just shut up, asshole." She turned to DeSantos. "Robby?"

"Haven't heard anything," DeSantos said as he holstered his weapon. "Call this in. I'll go see if Karen needs help."

ROBBY TRIED TO GET TO HIS FEET, to right himself. But he was still dizzy from the punches he took and the head butt he meted out. After all he'd endured lately, his tank was running dry.

He sat back down on the cold floor, water dripping from his face. His clothing was thick and heavy, and his arm throbbed.

And he couldn't shake the image of holding the man's head down as his lungs filled with water. He had killed him. But it was different from the time as a teen when he had murdered the man who had done the same to his uncle. Here it was a matter of survival. Before . . . it was as Diego had said: revenge. Raw, inexcusable, premeditated revenge.

He'd repressed those memories, those thoughts and feelings, for so long that he'd gotten skilled at it. Too skilled. He now realized he had been cheating. He had broken the law and never paid the price.

But was the price too expensive now, given that he had dedicated his life to catching those who would harm others? Did that balance out the scales of justice? Did it tip them in his favor?

Robby shivered. He had to get to his feet, find help, dry clothing, some food, and medical attention for his gunshot wound.

He rolled left and pushed himself up.

VAIL FELT THE ELEVATOR bottom out, then leaned forward as the doors slid apart. She side-slithered through, Glock in her hands, and swept into the hallway.

"Which way?" she called back to Pryor.

He remained behind her and silently pointed ahead, no doubt realizing that, with the handgun clenched in both hands, out in front of her, Vail's frenzied demeanor wasn't an act. He was probably beginning to wonder what he'd gotten himself into.

Pryor directed her through the seemingly endless, curving corridor.

"How much farther?"

Pryor slowed, then looked back over his shoulder. "I don't know. The back of the house isn't my patrol area. I've only been down here once." He pursed his lips, stopped walking, then again glanced behind him. "There's no elevator at the north end of the property. I'm pretty sure the room service elevator was the best way to get there."

"But you're not really sure where 'there' is."

"I think if we keep going, we'll eventually get to the maintenance shop."

Vail tightened her grip on the Glock. *Great. Robby could be in trouble—if he's still alive—and I get the tour guide with no sense of direction.*

"Don't *think*," Vail said. "Use your radio, find out, and get me there. Fast."

82

After struggling with the soaked, clinging material, Robby stripped off his shirt. There was a gentle flow of oil-scented air swirling through the dimly lit area, which helped evaporate the dampness from his skin.

The breeze made him shiver. His shoes sloshed with each step. And his waterlogged pants rubbed against his thighs.

But none of it mattered. Because he was free—no one with high-powered ammunition or bloodstained machetes was threatening, beating, or chasing him. In a few minutes, he'd reach safety. Dry clothing. Medical attention. And, hopefully, Karen.

But before he'd gone twenty feet, something struck him in the head. Hard. And he went down.

Two arms pulled him upright and a dark figure approached.

A few steps more and the glow of a nearby incandescent bulb shadowed across the hard features of Antonio Sebastiani de Medina.

"Sebastian—"

"You had to fuck everything up, Robby. Everything came together the way it was supposed to. I just needed a few more days, *a few more goddamn days.*" Sebastian shook his head. "A $3 million payoff. And everyone would've won. DEA, me, you, all of us would've gotten what we wanted."

"Is that right?" Robby asked weakly.

Sebastian's men struggled to force Robby erect. One of them yanked up on his injured arm, eliciting a cringe. But Robby was still dazed and had difficulty keeping himself steady.

Sebastian sighed and stepped closer. "DEA would get Guevara, and if we were lucky, maybe even Cortez. You get your special agent creds. And me—I get my cut. A million big ones and a shot at a comfortable retirement when the time comes."

"I always thought you were a smart guy, Sebastian. Until this. Then you got really stupid. And greedy. But greed can be so intoxicating it can blind you to what's going on." Robby tried to bring his shoulders back, to give him some sense of authority. "You never saw it coming."

Sebastian's face stiffened. "What the fuck are you talking about?"

"Yardley. He suspected something wasn't right. That's really why he agreed to bring me on. When your partner got into that accident, it turned out to be a dream come true for you. Too good a dream."

"You're the one who's dreaming, buddy."

Robby shifted his weight to lessen the strain on his shoulder. "You figured you could convince Yardley to bring me onboard because of my street cred. And you knew I'd drool over the chance—and that Gifford would do what he could to help get me signed on."

"Nice story, but—"

"Best part is you thought you'd be able to control me better than a veteran agent who'd adhere to procedure and would be all over anything that smelled like shit. And to a seasoned nose, you were reeking. That's what got your partner killed, isn't it?"

"I don't need to listen to this crap."

"Worst part is that I was your friend, so you knew I'd give you the benefit of the doubt."

Sebastian laughed weakly. "You think you've got it all figured out."

"You'd work the op and help bring down the cartel, but at the same time you were angling to score a last big payoff. Skimmed off that huge black tar heroin shipment coming in. You'd then collar Guevara, maybe Cortez, too, and no one would know about the missing money." Robby cricked his head to the side. "Does that sound about right?"

Sebastian reached back into the darkness and thrust a fist into Robby's abdomen. He doubled over and dropped to his knees.

Robby sucked in his breath, then tried to sooth the abdominal spasm that prevented him from speaking. He lifted his head, anger spilling forth like the saliva that dripped from the corner of his mouth. "You're a fucking disgrace to the badge, Sebastian. You've shit on all the honest DEA agents who put their lives on the line every fucking day."

"Like *I* did for nine years. Years of deep cover." He spit in Robby's face. "No fucking way to live."

"That's the life you chose. And now . . . you're living on the wrong side of the law. You're a huge disappointment. As a federal agent. And as a friend."

Sebastian looked at him—and for a second, Robby thought he saw sorrow. An apology? For all the fun times they'd had. For a friendship that was now forever tainted. Dead with no hope of resuscitation.

But maybe Robby was projecting what he'd like to see . . . an admission that what Sebastian had done was wrong.

"We don't have a lotta time," Sebastian said to his two lieutenants. "Take care of him, then meet me where we discussed." Sebastian slipped past them out of the light's reach, his footfalls going suddenly silent as he disappeared.

Robby heard the slide of a semiautomatic pistol, dangerously close to his left ear.

"I'll make this quick," the man said.

Robby threw up a hand. "No. Wait—"

The gunshot echoed loudly.

83

When Pryor radioed his supervisor for the exact location of the maintenance shop, he was told they had another hundred feet to go, around the bend—but he was informed that SWAT and Vegas Metro PD were on their way. They were to stop and await their arrival.

"Bullshit," Vail said to Pryor as he reholstered his two-way. "I'm not waiting."

Pryor pulled a ring from a clip on his uniform and sifted through the various keys before making his choice. "The engineers are all gone for the night."

Vail took the key and said, "Stay here. No one goes past unless they're law enforcement. Got it?"

"Got it."

Vail jogged down the curving corridor until she reached a gray metal door that bore a red and black sign:

FOUNTAIN MAINTENANCE SHOP
AUTHORIZED PERSONNEL ONLY

Vail slid the key into the lock and entered the room. She quietly shut the heavy door and proceeded forward. A network of pipes extended the length of the ceiling—as best she could see in the room's low light. Machinery lined both walls: what looked like a welding apparatus, a band saw, a large pipe cutter, a circular saw.

Because it was dimly lit, she had to move slowly to make sure she didn't trip on a spike or fastener bolted into the ground.

Vail pointed her BlackBerry's lit display at the floor and used it as a flashlight. She followed the machinery until she heard voices nearby.

Workers? Pryor said they'd all gone home for the night. She stopped and listened. *I know that voice. Where've I heard it before?*

" . . . skimmed off that huge black tar heroin shipment coming in. You'd then collar Guevara, maybe Cortez, too, and no one would know about the missing money. Does that sound about right?"

That *voice she knew. Robby. Who's he talking to?* Vail edged forward another few steps.

"You're a fucking disgrace to the badge, Sebastian . . . "

Sebastian? What the hell's going on?

She turned her head left, then right, trying to triangulate on the echoing voices.

"We don't have a lotta time. Take care of him, then meet me where we discussed."

Vail advanced forward, Glock out in front of her. To her left, the room opened up into a larger space. Two men were standing by Robby.

And one of them had a pistol pointed at his head.

Robby, no!

The gunshot was deafening. And it was followed by a second, equally as loud—but Vail's hearing was blown from the close-quarters echo of the first, so she more or less felt, rather than heard, the latter round.

The dead man to Robby's left hung in the air, but the one to his right was heavier—and he hit the ground with a thud, that sickening hollow *thrump* when a skull strikes cement with significant force. His colleague followed a split second later, dropping to his knees before falling forward onto his face.

Robby's eyes caught Vail's and she merely stood there, emotion welling in her chest, threatening to erupt. She found herself unable to move, her feet still planted in a Weaver stance, both hands squeezing the Glock. The smell of cordite stinging her nose.

Robby, on his knees, was crying—she could see that much in the dim light from the overhead bulb. Tears streaked his cheeks.

She dropped her arms to her sides, took a tentative step forward, then ran. Ran into his arms, and joined him on the floor. Hugged him tight.

Neither said a word.

Outside in the carport, an ambulance sat idling in front of the Terrazza di Sogno—the Terrace of Dreams—an Italian balcony overlooking the Bellagio fountains. Peter Yardley and Thomas Gifford had just arrived from the Green Valley Ranch Resort and were jogging toward them, accompanied by three men in black windbreakers with light gray DEA block letters on the back, chest, and arms. Two men in suits, presumably FBI, took up the rear.

Robby lay on a gurney, his torso elevated and an IV snaking from his arm. Roxxann Dixon and Hector DeSantos stood at his side, shoulder to shoulder with Vail, who had her phone pressed to her ear.

"How's he doing?" Gifford asked the medic.

"I'm doing fine," Robby said.

The medic frowned in annoyance. "Vitals are stable. It was a through and through. The constricting effects of the cold water helped. Some blood loss, but I've stopped the bleeding. Motor and sensation are intact. We'll transport and give him a good look-see in the ER."

"That really necessary?" Robby asked.

Vail, having ended her call with Jonathan—she'd woken him, but needed to hear his voice and couldn't wait till morning—said, "Yeah, Robby, it's really necessary. Not up for discussion."

"For once," Gifford said, "I agree with you." He looked at Robby. "Anything we can get you? Something to eat?"

"Someone already brought me a fancy chili burger—"

"Yeah, that'd be me," Dixon said, playfully raising her hand.

Vail chuckled. "Which he downed in two bites."

"You earned it," Gifford said. "That and a whole lot more." He nodded at DeSantos. "Status."

"Escobar's in the wind. BOLO's been issued and checkpoints have

been set up. Lots of places in Vegas to get lost, so I'm not overly confident we're gonna find him."

"Villarreal and Guevara are in custody and being treated for GSWs,"
Vail added.

A black Chevy SUV pulled up beside them, drawing their attention.
Turino stepped out and faced Yardley. "I've got something for you, sir."
He pulled open the rear door, where Sebastian sat restrained in silver
handcuffs and leg irons.

Sebastian and Robby locked eyes, then Turino slammed the door
closed. "Apparently someone placed a tracking device in his phone."

Yardley grinned. "How rude. I wonder who'd do something like that.
And those blanks in his gun. Definitely not standard issue."

"My pleasure to bring him in, sir," Turino said.

"I thought you'd appreciate it." Yardley's face turned serious. "We're
due for a chat. Half hour, back at the office?"

Turino pulled open his door. "Yes sir. Looking forward to it."

As Turino drove off, Yardley took a deep, relieved breath, then said,
"Fine work, agent."

"Thank you, sir," Vail and DeSantos answered in unison.

"No offense." Yardley motioned to Robby. "I was talking to *my*
agent."

Vail couldn't suppress her smile. Robby had earned that. She glanced
at Gifford, who seemed to be sporting a proud, though subtle grin.

"Given Agent Turino's concern over Velocity," Yardley said, "I
thought you'd like to know that DEA moved up its timetable. We figured
that with Cortez and Villarreal busy sparring over Robby, the distraction
would make our jobs easier. We launched Velocity—" he consulted his
watch—"sixty-five minutes ago. Early reports are very encouraging. Ar-
rests in five states. More to come through the night."

"Cortez?" Robby asked.

"Nothing yet. So far he's slipped the net. But if not tonight, we'll get
him some other time. Our job's not done till guys like him are out of
business."

Gifford extended a hand toward DeSantos. "Hector, you've been a
godsend. Next time I see Detective Bledsoe, I'll have to thank him for
bringing you into the fold."

"Yeah." Vail gave DeSantos's shoulder a playful shove. "Thank you."

He looked at her a long moment, then said, "This case ended up
meaning more to me than you could know. If my wife were here, she'd

thank you, too."

Vail tilted her head in confusion but let it go. DeSantos gave her a quick hug, then motioned to Dixon.

"We'll let you rest," Dixon said to Robby. "We're gonna grab something to eat."

Gifford caught Vail's attention with a jerk of his head. "Can I have a word with you?"

"Sure—I just need a moment. Roxx," she called after Dixon. "Hang on a sec."

Vail walked with Dixon back toward the Bellagio entrance, away from the knot of personnel.

They stopped beside a large conical planter at the edge of the carport. Vail stood there looking at Dixon, not speaking, unsure of what to say.

Finally Dixon broke the silence. "It's been incredibly . . . exciting. You make things interesting, Karen."

Vail hiked her eyebrows. "So I've been told. Look, I—I can't tell you what you've meant to me these past couple weeks. It sounds trite, but I don't know what I would've done without you." She leaned forward and gave her partner a warm embrace.

A moment later, they pushed away from each other, both wiping tears from their eyes.

"So let's not let this be good-bye," Dixon said. "Okay? Email, phone. Facebook?"

Vail chuckled. "Jonathan'll have to show me how to set up an account. But, yeah. Of course. And when you make it out to D.C.—"

"Lunch, dinner, whatever. And a tour of the academy."

Vail's face broadened into a grin. "It's a date. And—do me a favor. Thank everyone for me. Brix, Mann, Gordon . . . except, well, Matt Aaron."

Dixon laughed. "I'm going to miss you, Karen."

They hugged again, and then Vail walked off to join her boss.

VAIL'S TIRED, SORE LEGS felt heavy as she ascended the gentle incline of the Tarrazza balcony. Gifford was silent until she reached the railing. The police were in the process of clearing the vicinity, though onlookers lined the boulevard along the periphery, outside the barricades.

Gifford leaned both forearms on the concrete balustrade and looked out at the lake. "Karen, nice job with all of this. I—well . . . thank you."

Vail extended her arms beside him and took in the view of the lake. "Don't take this the wrong way, sir, but I didn't do it for you." She grinned and noticed he had cracked a smile, too.

They stood there another silent moment. Then Gifford said, "You were right. About Robby being my son."

"I know."

He turned to Vail. "But I need you to keep that between us."

Her eyes widened. "Sir, that's your personal matter. But to ask me to keep it from him, to lie—"

"I'm not asking you to lie. I'm asking you to give me a chance to tell him. I want to do it the right way. It's not an easy thing to admit to your son you've been absent from his life."

"But you *will* tell him," she said.

He looked back out over the water, then nodded. "Yes."

YARDLEY WAVED A FINGER at Robby's bandaged shoulder. "When you're healthy, I'll make a few calls, get you enrolled at the academy." He paused, then said, "That is, if you still want to be an elite agent with the Drug Enforcement Administration."

"I do, sir. Very much."

Yardley nodded slowly. "Good. We need people like you." He gave Robby's uninjured shoulder a pat, then walked off with his entourage.

As Robby watched him leave, he noticed Vail standing beside Gifford thirty yards away, near the edge of the lake.

His discussion with Diego played back in his thoughts. He had killed a man—and he'd done it for revenge. That was something he would have to come to terms with. Was it the right thing to do? No. He could answer that without deep thought. But now, given who he was and what he did for a living—and what he was about to do—who would be served by his paying the price for his past transgressions?

But what gave him the right to serve as judge and jury? How many rehabilitated criminals could say they were devoting their life to catching other violent criminals?

Am I a criminal?

He looked over at the clear IV bag hanging near his head. Too much to consider for now. As Yardley said, he had to get healthy.

"Hey."

He turned and saw Vail and Gifford heading for him. *Will she read my face? My mind?* She and Robby often had an idea about what the other was thinking. *She'll know something is bothering me. Can I keep it from her? Lie to her, again?*

As they approached, music started blaring from the speakers, followed by the fountain's jets shooting skyward. He recognized the song: Andrea Bocelli's "Con Te Partiro."

Time to say good-bye.

86

Gifford stood a little behind Vail, as if he didn't want to intrude. "Do you—you have any plans for lunch tomorrow?" Gifford said above the din of the fountain show.

Robby laughed. "I think it's safe to say my calendar's pretty clear."

"Good. Assuming you're up to it, want to grab a bite with me? Before I head back home?"

"With *you*, sir? And Karen?"

"No. Just us."

Robby pursed his lips, glanced at Vail, then said, "Yeah, sure."

Gifford nodded and then walked off.

Robby extended his bent elbow and Vail took it. She maneuvered the gurney toward the lake so they could watch the rest of the show.

"What was that about? Gifford asking me to lunch."

Vail kept her gaze on the fountain. "You'll have to ask him."

The paramedic called to them from the open rig. "You ready? Gotta transport—"

"Give us a minute," Vail said. "Till the end of the song." She turned to Robby and studied his face, then leaned in close. "What's wrong?"

He did not look at her. He was staring ahead, not following the arcing path of the fountain's surging jets as they rapidly spread from left to right, across the expanse of the lake.

After a long moment, he said, "Just mentally and physically drained." He lay there. Music blasted. Water sprayed. But none of it registered, not really.

Vail's eyes narrowed. "But something's on your mind."

Here it was . . . the choice Robby had been dreading. What did it say about a man who can't be honest with the woman he loves? What kind of relationship would that be?

But this is . . . different. *I murdered my uncle's killer. I hunted him down and shot him.* Once that simple sentence left his lips, his life would change forever. *Would she be able to overlook the admission? Would I lose her? Would she turn me in?*

He bit his upper lip. *Don't say anything. But I have to. Can I face her if I don't?* "I'm sorry," he started. "I guess I owe you an explanation."

The music stopped playing and the fountain's water jets went dry. Vail pulled back her arm and rested both hands on the side of the gurney. "Trust is important to me, Robby. Coming off my failed marriage with Deacon, trust is all I've got."

How could she know? How? Had Diego told her somehow?

Robby rubbed the back of his neck. He didn't know what to say. "I know. I'd say I'm sorry, but that wouldn't really mean much. It doesn't even come close, does it? What's done is done."

"But are you sorry?"

He didn't answer for a long moment.

"Look," she said, "I realize it's not a black-and-white thing. I understand it's complicated. But if you love me, like you've said you do, then we have to be able to tell each other things like that. We can't keep secrets."

Robby rubbed his face with his free hand.

"I'll make this easy," she said. "You apologize for not telling me about your undercover op, and I'll apologize for blowing your cover. I showed your picture to Guevara, I leaned on him. He made the connection, and . . . well, I just plain blew it."

Robby's head snapped so quickly toward her his neck popped. "Apologize for—" *She doesn't know.* He sighed relief—then had to think fast before she read him. "Look," he said, reaching out and taking her hand. "You don't need to apologize. I disappeared. I—with a serial killer on the loose, threatening Jonathan, you must've assumed the worst. I'm the one who needs to apologize. So yes, I am sorry. Very sorry. I thought I was doing the right thing, but . . . I now know it—I should've just told you the truth."

She looked at him, into his eyes, deeply. What was she thinking? He couldn't tell. He was tired—no, exhausted.

"Will you accept my apology?" she said.

"For what?"

Vail appeared irritated she had to repeat her transgression. "For endangering your life, for nearly getting you killed."

Normally she had a sense of what he was thinking. But right now, she apparently wasn't getting a clear read.

"Tell you what," he finally said. "Let's forgive each other. Start with a clean slate."

VAIL STUDIED HIS FACE. She loved this man. Was the trust issue something she could overlook? For now, yes. He apologized—and it seemed like he genuinely meant it. That was all she needed, to be able to relax her defenses and know there were no secrets between them. At least, that would be the case after Robby's lunch tomorrow with Gifford.

Vail gently leaned her head against his. The emotional release of having Robby back, of touching him again, was like a river overrunning its banks. Tears spontaneously flooded her eyes and flowed down her cheeks. Whatever issues they still had to deal with were unimportant; they would work themselves out.

Robby wiped at her cheek with a thumb. "There's something I have to tell you."

But he fell silent, and as the seconds passed and he failed to elaborate, Vail pulled back and looked into his eyes. "What is it?"

"I . . . I . . . " He looked down, hesitated, then brought his eyes up to hers and said, "I killed a man."

She jutted her chin back. "The guy in the lake? C'mon, we've both killed people in the course of—"

"This wasn't in the course of work. It happened a long time ago. When I was a teenager."

Vail looked at him a long moment, searching his face. *This is a confession.* Certainly not something she was expecting. She cleared her throat and said, "Why?"

"Because he was a murderer, a gang banger, and a drug dealer." Robby bit his bottom lip, teared up, and then looked down. "And because he killed my uncle."

Vail chewed on that, looked off into the darkness, then brought her eyes back to Robby's. She took his hand and squeezed.

"I didn't know what to do. I didn't want to lose you, I didn't know what you'd think of me, I didn't—"

Vail placed a finger on his mouth. "You already know what I think of you."

"Yeah, but—"

"No buts. I study human behavior for a living, remember?" She moved her hand to his chest, over his heart. It beat fast and hard. "I know what's in *here*, and that's what matters."

Robby took a deep breath, then wiped a tear from his eye.

"Truth is," Vail said, "when I thought Mayfield was in Virginia, going after Jonathan . . . " She stopped. *What would I have done if he'd harmed my son?* "Robby, if he'd—if Jonathan . . . I honestly don't think I could've let the bastard live. Even spending the rest of his days in a prison cell, that'd have been too good for him."

"What does that make us?"

She didn't take long to answer. Given all she knew and had observed about behavior, this was a question that went back to the beginning of time. "It makes us human."

"Human." He seemed to ponder that a moment.

Vail stroked his forearm. "Now . . . soon as you're released from the ER, we'll get a room. I think we're long overdue for a vacation."

He looked up at her. "You've used up all your vacation time."

Vail took his face in her hands. "I won't tell anyone if you won't."

Robby leaned forward and gently touched his lips to hers. "You know what they say. What happens in Vegas stays in Vegas."

AUTHOR'S NOTE

THIS WAS MY FIRST EXPERIENCE working with the Drug Enforcement Administration, and it was a tremendously positive one. My research opened my eyes to the enormity of the illicit drug trade and its pervasive role in our society, our neighborhoods, and our schools. Much of the profit from the drugs sold in the United States goes directly into funding terrorist activities at home and abroad.

Surprisingly, mainstream media and the political establishment haven't kept the illicit drug problem at the forefront of our consciousness. Or perhaps it's the other way around: we need to let our elected officials know that we're aware of the damage drug trafficking causes, and we want them to use their powers to hamstring it. Unfortunately, the long-running nature of the "war on drugs" allows apathy to set in, forcing it to the background in the face of pressing economic, job, and security issues that demand our attention.

But there's one group that does not shrug these issues aside. Ask any DEA agent, whose job it is to catch those involved in the illicit drug trade, and you'll learn that these agents see their role as crusaders, tackling one battle at a time. We owe them a debt of gratitude for the dangerous work they perform, on our behalf, on a daily basis.

ACKNOWLEDGMENTS

I RELY ON PROFESSIONALS in the real world for their knowledge base, perspective, and expertise that give my stories depth and credibility. For *Velocity*, I'd like to thank the following individuals:

At the Drug Enforcement Administration, I've had the good fortune to work with the following professionals: **Paul Knierim,** Supervisory Special Agent, whose real-world and undercover experience and explanations of the illicit drug trade, cartels, and DEA procedures were integral to my telling of the story. Agent Knierim's review of the manuscript helped immensely in ensuring I had all my DEA i's dotted and t's crossed.

Steve Parinello, Special Agent, for his overview of the world of illicit drug trafficking, border enforcement, and DTOs; **Rusty Payne**, acting section chief of DEA Public Affairs Office, and **Mary Irene Cooper**, chief of Congressional and Public Affairs, for working with me to obtain DEA access; **Meghan McCalla**, public affairs, for facilitating my resource list; **Amy Roderick**, Special Agent, San Diego field division office, for San Diego area illicit drug information and a tour of the field division facility.

Dr. Sandra Rodriguez-Cruz, DEA senior forensic chemist, for information on the chemistry behind illicit drug trafficking and covert smuggling; for helping me understand the facts and realities that formed the underpinning of my ideas involving Superior Mobile Bottling; and for her thorough tour of the Southwest Laboratory. **Scott R. Oulton**, DEA laboratory director, Southwest Laboratory, for helping me obtain the information I needed and for the time he spent with me at the lab. **Fracia Martinez,** DEA forensic chemist, for making the initial introductions and setting me on the right path.

Greg Brenholdt, DEA Special Agent Pilot, for sharing his helicopter experiences and flying expertise with me, for his creative input, and for providing an easy-to-comprehend primer on piloting a helicopter.

John France, U.S. Border Patrol assistant chief patrol agent, former jump master for BORTAC (the Border Patrol's special response team), who counseled me in the finer points of jumping from a helicopter. If Karen Vail knew John was responsible for that, she'd hunt him down and . . . well, it wouldn't be pretty.

Jean Donaldson, captain, Napa County Sheriff's Department, for once again serving as my Sheriff's Department "knowledge base," for expeditiously answering my technical questions, and for granting access to all areas of the department.

Mark Safarik, senior FBI profiler and Supervisory Special Agent (ret). I never tire of thanking Mark for his contributions to my novels. Mark's attention to detail ensures that Vail's behavioral analysis, FBI and law enforcement procedure, and terminology are correct. I treasure not only his nearly two decades of BAU tutelage but his special friendship.

Joe Ramos, lieutenant, San Diego Police Department, SWAT unit, for acquainting me with the SWAT training facility and tactical vehicles, and for reviewing SWAT procedure in detail with me. Thanks to **Monica Munoz,** PIO, for obtaining clearance for me. As with the DEA, I was extremely impressed with the tactical unit's professionalism, dedication, and level of training. These officers do a very tough job, very well.

Carl Caulk, deputy assistant director, U.S. Marshals Service, Judicial Security Division, for his assistance with the WITSEC program.

Micheal Weinhaus, Special Agent, Immigration and Customs Enforcement, for information on warrants and proper search procedures (Karen Vail could learn a thing or two from Mike).

Jeffrey Jacobson. Yes, *Velocity* is dedicated to him, but he deserves to be acknowledged here, too. As the associate general counsel for the Federal Law Enforcement Officers Association and a former assistant U.S. attorney, he's eminently qualified to answer questions about Border Patrol, ports of entry, canine handling, and search and seizure issues. One might say Jeff is "a jack of all federal law enforcement trades." (I wouldn't say that, but *someone* might.)

Keely Dodd, senior probation officer, Napa County Probation, for her assistance with selecting certain settings and locations in downtown Napa.

Gary Hyde, associate director, process engineering, at Mannkind Corporation, for his explanation of, and assistance with, the drug delivery method described in *Velocity*. Though BetaSomnol was fictitious, the concept behind it was not. Gary was a senior process engineer at a major pharmaceutical company that produced such (legal) "transdermals."

At the Bellagio Hotel, **Keith Fels,** show control engineer in fountain control, was enormously helpful in walking me through the intricacies of the exquisite Bellagio fountains, the pump room, and fountain operation and maintenance; **Mary Cabral** and **Kristen Lacer** assisted me in attempting to gain access to restricted areas; **Jason Harrison**, Bellagio executive chef, and **Mark Szczepanski**, general manager of Jasmine Restaurant, for their descriptions and explanations regarding the "back of the house" and associated areas.

At CityCenter, I was assisted by **Mariksa Quintana** and **Carolyn Leveque**, who acquainted me with all aspects of the complex, its features, amenities, access roads, and connections.

David Pearson, CEO of Opus One, for assistance with establishing the legal timeline of wineries relative to Herndon Vineyards.

Ariana Peju of Peju Vineyards for information regarding TTB and California's Alcohol and Beverage Control's application process for starting a winery. I can't say enough about the fine people (and fine wine) at Peju. In particular, a special acknowledgment goes to Herta and Tony Peju, Peter Verdin, Katie Vandermause, Alan Arnopole, Caroline King, Scott Neumann, and Robert Sherman for their assistance.

Tómas Palmer, software security consultant, for his technical musings and information pertaining to the workings of the LOWIS device.

Samantha McManus, communications manager, Microsoft Digital Crime Unit, for information on COFEE and PhotoDNA (yes, both are real).

Maury Gloster, M.D., for his medical counsel on the injuries sustained by John Mayfield, James Cannon, and Robby, including associated terminology and treatment outcomes.

Lisa Black, fellow author, who also happens to be a forensic scientist, for her assistance with Sandiego Ortega's gunshot wound.

My old friend **Steve Kitnick** (okay, so he's not *that* old), for shuttling me to/from, through and around the Green Valley Ranch Resort, and serving as my personal Las Vegas sidekick. **Jeff Ayers**, friend and author, for once again going way beyond the call of duty while ferrying me around Seattle.

The exceptional people at Vanguard Press: **Roger Cooper**, publisher, **Georgina Levitt**, associate publisher, and **Amanda Ferber**, publishing manager. It's a pleasure to work with three very professional and talented individuals; **Peter Costanzo**, and the entire **Vanguard sales force and production staff**, whose tireless efforts behind the scenes are responsible for getting my novels into the hands of my readers; **Jennifer Ballot**, my publicist, who worked her tail off to make my *Crush* tour a success—no small effort in today's bookselling climate.

Kevin Smith, my editor. Working with Kevin is like applying a coat of Meguiar's premium wax to a Bentley: when you're done, the car sparkles and looks damn fine. Michael Connelly said "Alan Jacobson is my kind of writer"; Kevin Smith is Alan Jacobson's kind of editor.

Chrisona Schmidt, my copy editor. Having a skilled copy editor is invaluable, and Chrisona is one of the best I've ever worked with. **Cisca Schreefel** and **Renee Caputo**, my project editors. Cisca and Renee made sure all parts of the production puzzle came together in an orderly fashion. It's a huge undertaking, and I appreciate all their efforts.

C. J. Snow, for his thorough review of the manuscript. Although it's not his profession, C. J. is a skilled copy editor with an exceptional eye. His markup is first-rate and much appreciated.

My agents, **Joel Gotler** and **Frank Curtis**, Esq. There is no substitute for their decades of experience. Their guidance, opinions, and input mean a great deal to me.

My wife, **Jill**, who also serves as my sounding board, first-line editor, and brutally honest critic. Jill is an avid reader of the genre, but because she approaches characters and situations differently than I do, she gives me a perspective I may not always see. Writing aside, she means the world to me.

Thanks, as well, to those who went above and beyond to help sell my books:

Jane Willoughby and **Ingram Losner** for their extraordinary work in San Diego, and **Wayne** and **Julia Rudnick** for their Herculean efforts in Arizona. **Samantha McManus** and **James Patton** at Microsoft for all their efforts in helping me launch *Crush*.

Len Rudnick, my uncle, for ushering me to and around Phoenix like no other media escort could. Between the tours for *The 7th Victim, Crush,* and *Velocity*, we've amassed some great memories. I'll always cherish the time we spent together. **Melodie Hilton**, director of marketing and public relations, Napa Valley Wine Train, for making the Wine Train available to us for filming, and for arranging our Wine Train book signing event. **K. R. Rombauer** for his hospitality and for allowing us to film in **Rhombauer**'s extensive wine cave.

Gretchen Pahia, Larry Comacho, Bill Thompson; Tom Hedtke, Beth O'Connor, Vicky Lorini; Colleen Holcombe; Douglas Thompson; Russell Ilg; John Hutchinson, Virginia Lenneville; Jean Coggan, Kristine Williams; Alex Telander; Jeff Bobby; Donna Powers, Pamela Ervin; Covahgin Van Dyk; J. Paul Deason, Betsy Ostrow; Marlee Soulard; Chris Acevedo (and Sophie), Daniel Piel; Maryelizabeth Hart, Terry Louchheim Gilman, Patrick Heffernan, Lori Burns, Linda Tonnesen; Barbara Peters, Lorri Amsden, Patrick Millikin; Bobby McCue, Linda Brown, Pam Woods, Kirk Pasich; J. B. Dickey, Fran Fuller; Joan Hansen; April Lilley, Christine Hilferty; Marc Hernandez and Ronny Peskin; Kara Schneider, Dena Roy, Valerie Burnside; Greg Hill; Lisa Haynes; Teresa McClatchy; Laura Sylvia, Marisa Ferche; Jessie Portlock; Joe Wilder; Mandi Holstrom; Tracy Puhl; Marsha Toy Engstrom and her "Hoodies"; Michael Troyan; Deborah Lee; Keith Kilby, John Keese, Nathan Spradlin; Marc Stiles; Patrick Malloy.

Marvin Kamras; John Hartman; Andrea Ragan; Russell and Marion Weis; Corey Jacobson; Mikel London, Andrew Gulli; Lindsay Preston, Brendan Twardy, Geof Pelaia, Stephen Mlinarcik, Virginia Matri, and the College of Art and Design in Cleveland, Ohio.

To **my readers . . .** As always, thanks for your support, for spreading the word about Alan Jacobson's novels to friends, family members, neighbors, colleagues, book clubs, and bloggers. I promise to always try my best to entertain you with unique characters and interesting stories. Come out and see me sometime at one of my signings, or check out my Web site and Facebook fan page. I'm here for you.

As always, I conducted exhaustive research in an attempt to ensure accuracy. If I've blown some fact, it's my responsibility, not that of the individuals mentioned above. Likewise, if I've accidentally omitted someone, please forgive me (and let me know, so I can correct it).

Due to its sensitive nature, certain aspects of SWAT procedure may or may not have been altered to protect those in the field. Likewise, certain DEA operational procedures and capabilities or locations may have been modified to protect those who are risking their lives to keep us safe. However, all other information, including that regarding drug-related statistics, methods of transportation and subterfuge used by the cartels, the pervasiveness of illicit drugs, and other such information included in *Velocity* are accurate to my knowledge at the time of this writing.

In a few instances of hotel/casino layout, I've taken some minor literary license for both security and dramatic reasons.

About **Margot**, Roxxann Dixon's white standard poodle . . . My wife and I are proud owners of two standards, one of which came from a local rescue organization and one from a breeder in North Carolina. The latter's mother, Margot, recently passed away unexpectedly. She was not just a champion on the show circuit, but a special dog with tremendous intellect and personality, which she passed on to our big guy. Margot has been, and will be, missed. Dixon's fictitious poodle is named in the real Margot's honor.